Disney

CHILLS

BE CAREFUL

what you WISH FUR

Disney CHILLS

BE CAREFUL
what you WISH FUR

by

Vera Strange

Disney PRESS

Los Angeles · New York

Based on the book THE HUNDRED AND ONE DALMATIANS
by Dodie Smith. Published by Viking Press.

Printed in the United States of America
First Paperback Edition, April 2021
3 5 7 9 10 8 6 4 2
FAC-025438-21162

Library of Congress Cataloging-in-Publication Data

Names: Strange, Vera, author.
Title: Be careful what you wish fur / by Vera Strange.
Description: Los Angeles : Disney Press, 2021. • Series: Disney chills ; #4 •
Audience: Ages 8–12. • Audience: Grades 4–6. • Summary:
Thirteen-year-old Delia's obsession with being fashionable and popular
at her elite private school turns scary when she acquires a cursed coat
from the fashion house of Cruella De Vil.
Identifiers: LCCN 2020030918 (print) • LCCN 2020030919 (ebook) •
ISBN 9781368065412 (paperback) • ISBN 9781368065429 (ebk)
Subjects: CYAC: Popularity — Fiction. • Blessing and cursing — Fiction. •
Characters in literature — Fiction. • Horror stories.
Classification: LCC PZ7.1.S768 Be 2021 (print) • LCC PZ7.1.S768 (ebook) •
DDC [Fic] — dc23
LC record available at https://lccn.loc.gov/2020030918
LC ebook record available at https://lccn.loc.gov/2020030919

For more Disney Press fun, visit www.DisneyBooks.com

SUSTAINABLE
FORESTRY
INITIATIVE
Certified Chain of Custody
Promoting Sustainable Forestry
www.sfiprogram.org
SFI-01054
The SFI label applies to the text stock

The dreams that you
FEAR will come true.

1
#SELFIE

Click.

Delia studied the selfie on her phone, displayed in the PicPerfect app. Her face stared back at her from the screen—familiar, yet almost like a stranger. Hazel eyes, freckled cheeks, wavy brown hair, heart-shaped lips. Her eyes were the one thing that she liked about her appearance. Emerald flecked with cinnamon and even a little gold. It was a rare eye color, and she'd gotten it from both her parents. Mom had the emerald-green eyes, while her father had cinnamon brown—or so she'd been told. She'd never actually met him, nor did her mother keep pictures of him around.

Still, Delia frowned at her picture. She could spot every flaw in her skin, especially the monster pimple threatening to explode on the tip of her nose. Why did it always choose that spot? She approached the standing mirror, crammed into the corner of her little attic bedroom of their Chicago brownstone, and peered at her skin up close. She picked at the zit, but that just made it worse. Red and angry and swollen.

"Why today of all days?" she muttered. "Why not yesterday, or even tomorrow?" It was like the zit *knew* that it was her first day at her new middle school.

It was an evil zombie zit. It had a life of its own.

A rush of anxiety crashed through her. There was no way to hide this thing. And she needed to look perfect for her first day. Her mother had always drummed that idea into her head.

You only get one chance to make a first impression.

Almost as if reading her thoughts, a prompt pinged from her phone.

Ready to post to PicPerfect?
Don't let your ranking slide!

#SELFIE

Delia's heart stopped—*No, I'm not ready!*

Couldn't the app detect the zombie zit on her nose?

Apparently not. But the app so needed to add that feature. She quickly hit DISMISS, even though she did need to keep posting fresh content to her profile to keep her ranking high. At her old school, she and her two best friends in the world, Aaliyah and Zoe, had the highest rankings in their class. That also meant they were the most popular kids.

Pretty much every kid her age had the PicPerfect app and monitored it closely, the way adults watched the weather or the stock market, tracking the slightest shifts and changes. If you didn't keep posting selfies and getting comments, then your ranking would plummet.

But there was a catch.

You couldn't post just any old pic.

Posting bad selfies was *worse* than not posting at all. The goal was to collect the pink heart emojis, and avoid the dreaded red devil faces. Users clicked one if they liked your selfie and the other if they didn't. The more hearts, the more views you got, and the more popular your account became.

That was the goal. Grow your followers. The more hearts, the better.

But one devil could make your account ranking plummet.

And fast.

Delia didn't want to post a bad selfie and lose her high ranking. Plus, there was even more pressure today. From experience, she knew that the first thing the kids at her new school would do after they met her was search out her PicPerfect profile and check out her ranking and feed. At the top of it would be her selfie from that morning. First impressions mattered.

That meant it had to be even more perfect than usual.

Zombie zits were not allowed.

Delia studied the selfie, still displayed on her phone screen, waiting for her to post it. It just didn't look . . . perfect.

Delia tried dabbing on a little pale cream concealer, but the zit was still visible like a volcano about to erupt and spew gunk. She swiped on some mascara and pale lip gloss, the only makeup her mother allowed. Mom had lots of strict rules, which annoyed Delia, but she found ways around them. Mrs. Smith, their landlady, let her do chores around the house for a modest payment, which Delia used to buy forbidden makeup, like pink blush and eye shadow, at the drug store.

Delia stashed the contraband in a makeup bag and tucked it into her backpack to apply later at school, where her mom wouldn't bust her. That was her normal routine, and usually Zoe and Aaliyah were there to help. But today, she'd be on her own, and it was especially important that she look her best. She needed every bit of help she could get, even if it came from a lipstick tube or blush palette.

Her eyes flicked back to her face in the selfie. She frowned and hit RETAKE.

The camera screen loaded up again in PicPerfect. The "PP" icon stared back at her, daring her to try again. She changed her shirt, slipping into a purple top. She aimed the phone at her face but then grimaced.

Ugh, why did I ever think I look good in purple?

Delia tossed the purple shirt aside, where it landed in

a heap on the floor, and swapped it for an off-the-shoulder, loosely woven turquoise sweater. She peered back into the camera, angling it high and down at her face. Still, she wasn't satisfied. While the sweater had looked great in the store, the turquoise now seemed to make her skin look pallid and greenish.

She switched to a black turtleneck, hoping a neutral color would help. But it just made the zit on her nose more visible. Worse yet, with every wardrobe change, her hair was getting more disheveled and frizzier.

Finally Delia gave up on trying new tops and instead tried changing the angle of the selfie, posing by the window in natural light, despite the chilly winter day outside, then casually leaning on her bed with its colorful bedspread, which she'd had since childhood, then full-on model-glamming it up in front of her mirror.

Click. Click. Click.

She snapped away.

But each picture . . . wasn't *PicPerfect* perfect.

She sighed. No matter what she tried, something always seemed to be . . . wrong. Suddenly she missed her friends like a stab to her heart. They'd always take selfies together — on the way to school, or in the bathroom between classes, or after class let out in the afternoons, when they'd gather at one of their houses to work on their homework. Aaliyah and Zoe would have been able to help her troubleshoot her morning selfie woes, fixing what was wrong. They'd know if it was the wrong top, or makeup, or simply the pose or angle of the shot. They always did everything together.

But that was over now.

Her friends were still attending her old public school, and Delia would be starting at Gilded Crest Academy, the fancy private school uptown. All alone.

Missing her friends terribly, she flopped down on her bed and scrolled over to their profiles, feeling worse with each selfie that she flipped through. Their pics were so perfect. Pink hearts clustered under each image. Not a devil face in sight. But that wasn't what made her feel bad. Of course she wanted her friends to get all the hearts and have tons of loyal followers.

What made her feel bad was the post from that morning.

Her eyes studied the pic at the top of their profiles.

Aaliyah and Zoe posed together on the "El" train. The caption read, *First day of second semester!* with a cluster of trendy hashtags trailing after it. Her friends looked so happy . . . even though Delia wasn't there.

They didn't look sad, or like they missed her at all.

In the past, it would have been the three of them riding the train to school together, snaking through the tops of the city's redbrick buildings with the *clackety-clack* of the tracks beneath them. The more Delia studied the pic of her friends, the more it felt like she had been photoshopped out of it—almost like she had been erased from their lives.

Worse yet, they looked like they were having so much fun without her. Their faces grinned into the camera—Aaliyah with her dark skin and tightly curled black hair cropped short like a runway model, and Zoe with her blond bangs and shoulder-length bob, cut perfectly straight, almost like an antique porcelain doll. They both wore puffy coats and stylish, vintage-inspired clothes.

"You don't even miss me," Delia whispered to the selfie, feeling sorry for herself.

For the thousandth time, she wished that her mother wasn't making her switch schools, especially in the middle of the school year. Her stomach twisted.

But then—

Ring. Ring. Ring.

A vid-chat call was coming in on the app.

Delia's heart leapt with joy, recognizing the caller. She hit ANSWER.

"We miss you!"

Aaliyah's voice echoed out of her phone. Her face lit up, and she squealed into the phone when she saw Delia. Then another voice cut her off—

"Hey, stop hogging her! Gimme some screen time. . . ."

That was Zoe.

And it was so very . . . *Zoe.*

She pushed Aaliyah out of the shot in a playful way, flashing a big grin and waving manically at the screen. Zoe was super high-energy and played almost every sport imaginable—softball, swimming, tennis, volleyball, even Ping-Pong.

Delia smiled at the memory of them piled on pillows on the floor of Zoe's basement to watch the summer Olympics, a once-in-every-four-years event. Her favorite event was the high dive. She loved how graceful the divers looked arcing through the air before plunging into the deep end.

Meanwhile, Aaliyah's favorite sport was virtual. And it wasn't played at the Olympics . . . yet. She was a big gamer, loving RPGs the most. *Battlestar Asteroid* was her specialty. She even had followers online and streamed her game play live for them to watch. She was sort of a legend, if you were into that sort of thing. Delia wasn't into games. But she loved how different she and her friends were, and how despite those differences, they could still be the very best of friends.

"We saw you lurking on our profile," Aaliyah said with a mock-accusing look. "And posting hearts to all our selfies."

"So we decided to call you," Zoe chimed in. "And have, like, a convo—"

"IRL," Aaliyah finished.

Delia laughed. Zoe and Aaliyah had been friends for

so long, they could basically finish each other's thoughts. The two of them had met in day care, though technically, neither of them could remember that, while Delia met them her first day of second grade, when her mom had moved them from Philadelphia to Chicago. Sometimes the closeness of Aaliyah and Zoe's bond brought out Delia's insecurities, but her friends had a way of making her feel like she belonged with them, no matter what was happening.

Just like today.

"So are you super excited for your first day at your posh new school?" Zoe asked.

Both their faces crammed into the shot. They peered at her eagerly.

"I don't know. You have no idea how much I miss you."

"We miss you, too!" Aaliyah said. "But something else is wrong."

"Yeah. Spill it," Zoe added. "I know that tone in your voice."

"No secrets, remember?" Aaliyah added with an arched eyebrow. "We're best friends *forever*. Going to different schools doesn't change that. Forever means forever."

"Okay, okay," Delia said, feeling her nerves flare up. "I guess . . . I'm nervous about the new school. It's different than Shady Grove. It's a private school with all these traditions and new people and—"

"And they're lucky to have you!" Zoe said. "You're the best! And you're the smartest person I know. You're the only reason I passed math last year. They're gonna love you."

Aaliyah nodded. "Yeah, you'll have zero problems making new friends."

"But how do you know?" Delia said, her insecurity so deep, it felt like the undertow in a big wave threatening to suck her under. "What if they already have their friend groups and no one wants to, like, sit with me or talk to me or whatever?"

"You made friends with us, and we were already a 'friend group,'" Aaliyah said pointedly, exchanging a look with Zoe.

"And we're awesome," Zoe agreed. "Just look at our PicPerfect ranking!"

Delia's eyes flashed to the number in the corner of

the vid-chat screen. It was true. They had the highest rankings in their school. That made Delia feel better. Her friends knew her better than anyone. Their faith in her ability to make new friends boosted her confidence.

She felt her nerves about her first day and her FOMO about not being with her besties ebb a bit. Their selfie on PicPerfect was just one picture. And deep down, despite their perfect appearances and worry-free smiles, her friends really did miss her. She had to remember that pictures didn't always tell the whole story. In fact, sometimes they even lied.

"Thanks. You're the best," Delia started, feeling gratitude thrumming in her chest. "I really mean it. I don't know what I'd do without you—"

"Oh, sorry," Aaliyah cut her off. "Gotta go. We're at our stop."

"Yeah, one more tardy," Zoe said with a panicked expression, "and I swear, my folks are gonna disown me. And make me quit Ping-Pong. They said it's stretching me too thin."

"And no more *Battlestar Asteroid* for me," Aaliyah

said. "Screen-time grounding is, like, worse than regular grounding. I'm happy to stay home, just don't take away my Wi-Fi."

"Bye, Delia! Good luck!" they chorused.

With that, the screen went dead, dissolving back into the PicPerfect home screen. Delia wished they had more time to chat—or better yet, that they still attended the same school so they could spend the whole day together.

Virtual friendship is better than nothing, she told herself.

Delia posed one last time and raised her phone to try again. *Click.* She snapped the selfie, forcing a brave smile. And this time, for some magical reason, when she checked the photo on her screen she actually liked the picture. While the zombie zit was still there, it looked less monstrous somehow. Her frizzy hair also looked less . . . *frizzy.*

It was the magic of friendship, she decided. It had boosted her confidence.

She wrote a quick caption. *To the two best friends in the whole world . . . I miss you!* Then she tagged Aaliyah's and Zoe's accounts. Perfect.

At that moment, an impatient voice reverberated through the town house, making her jump and hit POST before she could properly hashtag it.

"Delia, you're gonna be late for school!"

2
LITTLE DEVILS

"**D**on't make me come up there and get you!"

Her mother's voice reached her bedroom clear as day, somehow echoing up all those winding stairs to the attic without losing an ounce of strength.

Delia and her mom lived in a town house in the Old Town neighborhood of Chicago, which they shared with their elderly landlady, Mrs. Smith. It had been in Mrs. Smith's family for generations, and its age showed in the worn wooden floorboards, rickety windows that stuck when you tried to open them, and creaky bathroom fixtures that went *drip, drip, drip.*

In all truth, it could use some serious updates. But it stayed warm in the winter and cool in the blistering Midwest summers, and Delia and her mom were lucky to have a nice place to live in a safe neighborhood. Delia had her own room there, even if it was in the attic. In their last apartment, which was technically public housing, they'd had only one bedroom to share.

Delia's father had taken off when she was just a baby, and her mother almost never talked about him. Delia didn't know a lot about him or why he left, just that he wasn't ready for a kid. She wished her mom would say more, but recognized it was a source of pain. It represented a visible way that she'd failed her daughter, or so her mother thought, even if it wasn't true.

If it was anyone's fault, it was Delia's for showing up in this world. That was why her father left, wasn't it? But she knew better than to voice that opinion out loud.

Often, Delia found herself at a loss for words when her friends talked about their fathers, even if they were complaining. She *wished* she had a dad to complain about.

Despite her mother's busy schedule with work and

night school, and her strict rules like her makeup ban, Delia respected how hard her mom worked to give them a better life. They'd been able to move in with Mrs. Smith when her mom landed her new job working at a law firm.

"It's your first day, remember?" her mom called up the stairs now. "You know what I always say: First impressions matter. . . ."

Delia mouthed along to that last part because she'd heard it so many times. Two of her mother's other favorite sayings were *Always make the best of a bad situation* and *Never look down, only up.*

It was true, though, Delia supposed. First impressions did matter, especially on first days at new schools. Especially one called Gilded Crest Academy. Even the name sounded super fancy.

Delia had just turned thirteen and was entering the second half of seventh grade. With high school just a year and a half away, everything seemed to matter more. She had to do well at this new school to get placed in honors classes in high school, and she needed to ace those honors classes to get into a good college, and college was her ticket to a better life. Her mother had drummed that into her head since Delia was a little kid.

That was why her mother had pulled major strings through Mr. Jefferson, her boss at the law firm, to help get Delia accepted at the elite private school. Her mom had also spent what felt like countless weekend hours filling out scholarship applications, for which Delia had been required to write multiple essays, to help pay the steep tuition bill. Even with all that work, from what Delia could gather, the school was still costing her mom a good chunk of her income. Delia was grateful for the opportunity, and for how hard her mom had worked to make it happen, but that didn't change the fact that she was going to miss her friends and her old school. It felt like being pulled in two directions at once—between her old life, the one that she knew and felt comfortable in, and a new life that was exciting and full of opportunity, but also unknown and scary.

Delia glanced back at her phone, grimacing at her improperly tagged post. But there was nothing she could do about it now. Hearts were already racking up in the comments, boosted by Aaliyah's and Zoe's likes. *They're gonna love you.* Zoe's words echoed through her head again, followed by Aaliyah's voice right after. *Yeah, you'll have zero problems making new friends.*

Her friends meant well, but they didn't know what her new school was going to be like. Even Delia herself didn't know. What if the kids there didn't like her? And even if she made new friends, Zoe and Aaliyah weren't replaceable. She didn't want *new* best friends. She wanted her old friends.

With a pang of sadness, she flipped back to their profiles, her gaze lingering on their morning selfie again. Delia was about to turn off her phone and finish getting ready for school, when an ad popped up for a pair of fur-lined boots. According to the ad, they were the top-trending fashion item on PicPerfect. Selfies flashed across the screen of fashionable teen influencers wearing them. Curiosity tugged at Delia, and she clicked on the ad.

House of De Vil Faux-Fur-Lined Boots

The Must-Have Winter Fashion Item!

LITTLE DEVILS

The boots were black and white with zebra stripes running across them. Tufts of soft black-and-white faux fur poked out of the tops. They were simply gorgeous—the most beautiful boots Delia had ever seen. They'd be perfect for snapping winter selfies for PicPerfect, not to mention, they could help her fit in at her new school. Delia was sure that girls at a place called Gilded Crest would be on the cutting edge of fashion. She flipped through the images, each more tantalizing than the last, and her pulse began to race. She wanted those boots. No, scratch that.

She *needed* them.

But then she saw the price tag, and her heart sank. The boots were $250.

Way too expensive.

Delia glanced at the window. Frost blossomed on the panes, and outside a few snowflakes drifted down. Winter was in full force and would continue mercilessly until spring suddenly appeared out of nowhere, far later than it did in the rest of the country. Chicago tended to do that—snap from one season to the next without warning. But winter was the longest one by far.

With a deep sigh, Delia pulled her beat-up snow boots out of her closet. They were ratty and fraying around the edges, made of cheap plastic material that was flimsy and didn't hold up long.

Even worse, they made her feet sweat. Like, soak-through-her-socks sweat. She was constantly worried that they'd start smelling and somebody would notice, which would be a fate almost worse than death in middle school.

"Delia, I'm counting to ten," her mom yelled once more, her voice snapping Delia to attention. "This is your final warning. Get your butt down here! *One, two, three . . .*"

Her mother was taking night classes at a law school, so she wasn't a lawyer yet, but she sure sounded scary like one sometimes.

"Coming!" Delia yelled back, sliding on the old boots and cringing at the smell.

But she didn't have time to do anything about it, not with her mom's last warning. Quickly, she shut her phone and bounded downstairs for breakfast, her feet in their smelly boots thumping on the old steps and making them creak.

Flap. Flap. Flap.

She glanced down at her ratty old boots. The sole on the left boot was worn thin and starting to peel off, making that flapping noise, while the right one wasn't faring much better. This was the last thing she needed for her first day at Gilded Crest.

She so wished she had those House of De Vil boots. Envy gripped her heart and squeezed—envy for every girl she'd seen wearing them in her feed. She'd never wanted something so much in all her life. And her old boots definitely needed to be replaced. Maybe, just maybe, she could beg her way into a pair of new boots.

She rehearsed the line of argument in her head as she tromped down the remaining two flights of stairs. She'd have to make a compelling case. Delia knew from thirteen years of experience that her mother wouldn't be easily persuaded.

But her mom did always say that first impressions

mattered. And what better way to make a good first impression at her new private school than with a trendy pair of boots?

She was going to do it. She was going to ask her mother for the boots. Her mom had to understand that this was practically a matter of life or death. Well, social life or death.

But what was the difference?

It was worth a shot, right?

* * *

Yap, yap, yap!

When Delia entered the kitchen, she was greeted by the sound of dogs whining and barking. The room smelled of dog and hot cocoa, a wonderful combination, in Delia's opinion.

For the first time all morning, she smiled for real.

"How're the little devils?" she asked, rushing over to the playpen in the corner of the kitchen, which was layered with torn newspaper, old blankets, ratty towels, and chew toys. Wriggling around in the middle of the mess were fifteen plump Dalmatian puppies.

"It's a bit much, I must confess," Mrs. Smith said. She looked up from her cup of tea. The cup was chipped, but it was fine bone china. Like many things in her house, including her, it spoke to quality that had diminished over time from the grind of aging. She wore a pink cashmere sweater that was pilling and worn in places, paired with a wide skirt. Her skin was weathered, papery thin even, but her brown eyes shone young and bright.

Her town house was decorated with framed pictures of her posing with different dogs that she'd rescued and fostered over the years. Goofy golden retrievers; regal poodles with their fancy haircuts and poufy heads; wrinkly pugs that resembled old men, or maybe aliens; hyperactive Scottish terriers with wild eyes and stumpy legs. The dogs were all different breeds and ages, but the common denominator was Mrs. Smith.

"But the rescue needed a foster mom to take them in," Mrs. Smith went on, her gaze falling affectionately on the puppies squirming around. "I simply couldn't refuse."

Mrs. Smith had a habit of taking in unwanted things, including Delia and her mother. But they were lucky she had a soft spot for helping those in need. Her mother had answered a housing ad online for a landlady taking in new tenants, thinking nothing would ever come of it, but Mrs. Smith had called them back the next day and now Delia couldn't imagine their lives without her—or her puppy-filled home.

"Fifteen puppies," her mother sighed over her coffee mug, which wasn't fine or china and sported a baseball logo. "Can you believe it?"

Delia's mother wore a simple navy pantsuit, impeccably clean and pressed—her usual uniform for work at the law firm. Her mother always looked put together and spent a lot of time and effort maintaining her black hair in a sleek, stylish bob and nails in a pale French manicure. She may not have been rolling in money, but no one would ever know it. Unlike Mrs. Smith, who sported wild, unkempt graying hair and short, stubby nails chewed to the quick.

"They're little angels," Mrs. Smith said, gazing at the dogs lovingly, clearly blind to their poor puppy manners and desire to chew up or pee on everything.

"I feel bad for their mother. Having one was hard enough," her mother added, shooting Delia a wry smile.

Delia giggled, reaching into the pen to scoop up a puppy. She snagged Radar, the runt of the litter and her favorite pup. Their eyes had only started to open last week, and their black spots were just starting to come in, too.

"I'm not that bad," Delia said with a mock pout. She petted Radar's soft fur, peering into his crystal-blue eyes. He let out his distinctive bark—higher pitched because of his small size, yet strong and defiant. "At least I've never gnawed on any of your shoes."

"Yes, but you are a teenager," her mother shot back without missing a beat. "That's almost worse."

Delia rolled her eyes. "I'm barely a teenager. I just turned thirteen."

"It counts," her mother said. "Trust me, it definitely counts."

Mrs. Smith nodded. "Kids grow up so much faster now. What with all that social media and phones."

Delia glanced at Mrs. Smith's old rotary telephone affixed to the wall, next to the ancient, pale-yellow stove that still worked surprisingly well for its age.

"How else do you expect me to keep in touch with

my friends?" Delia said with a little edge creeping into her voice. More often than not, adults just didn't seem to understand how the world worked these days. "Especially since you're sending me to a brand-new school in the middle of the year."

"Delia, we've been over this already," her mother said in a stern voice. "This new school is your ticket to—"

"A good college," Delia finished her mother's sentence. "I know."

"Then act like it," Mom said. "Not everyone gets these opportunities. You know I didn't. I'm doing this for you."

Delia felt the sting of those words, followed by a surge of guilt. She knew how hard her mom had worked to get her into Gilded Crest. The problem was her mother never asked her if she actually wanted to go. What if she liked her old school? She'd been at the top of her class there, after all. And what if she wanted to stay with her friends and go to the local high school?

Wasn't thirteen old enough for her to make her own decisions?

But she knew that arguing with her mother was a bad

idea. There was a reason her mom was doing so well in law school—she *lived* to win arguments. It was pointless to disagree.

Delia could only lose. And not just the argument—but her phone privileges, too. Her bestie Aaliyah was right. Screen-time grounding was worse than regular grounding.

Delia stared down at Radar, but he gnawed on her hand with his sharp puppy teeth, making her wince. She plopped him back down in the pen. He squirmed over to chew on his sister's ear, rolling onto his back. He might be a handful—but he was an adorable one.

"Time to change the newspaper," Mrs. Smith said in a cheery voice, inspecting the pen. She turned to Delia. "Wanna help out? I can toss in a little extra since there are fifteen of them."

Delia scrunched up her nose. But while changing gross, pee-soaked newspaper wasn't exactly her favorite pastime, this was how Delia afforded to buy contraband makeup. She suspected Mrs. Smith *knew* that was what she did with the extra cash, but the landlady never busted Delia to her mother. Right now, she was saving up for the glitter nail polish that was the big trend on PicPerfect.

"Ugh, you spoil her," Mom groused from over her nearly empty cup of coffee. "You shouldn't have to pay her to help around the house. Delia should do it for free."

Delia's mouth dropped open in horror.

Clean up pee for free? Was her mom crazy?

But before she could argue—and risk getting in trouble again—Mrs. Smith signaled for her to zip her lips. Then she turned to Delia's mother.

"Oh, come on, Megan. A few extra bucks won't hurt," Mrs. Smith said in a voice as sugary-sweet as her hot cocoa. "Plus, doesn't doing chores for money build character and teach kids their hard work will be rewarded?"

Even her mom couldn't argue with that. Her mother might be a future lawyer, but Mrs. Smith had a special way of getting what she wanted. They were a funny pair, almost like the good cop/bad cop in Delia's life. But they balanced each other out. She needed both of them.

"Fine, you two win. But let's be quick. We don't want to be late."

With that settled, Delia busied herself with caring for the puppies. While Mrs. Smith took the dogs outside to the small, grassy backyard, Delia stripped out the soiled paper and replaced it with freshly torn pages. Sometimes Mrs. Smith complained about the puppies being so much work, but Delia understood why she loved being their caretaker so much. There was something rewarding about taking care of tiny, vulnerable souls who needed your help.

This wasn't the first litter that Mrs. Smith had fostered—even if it was certainly the biggest—and it wouldn't be the last. Since Delia and her mom had lived there, many puppies had come, grown bigger, and then gotten adopted and left their home, and Mrs. Smith cried big, sloppy tears every time. They were tears of sadness, but also of joy that they'd found their forever homes. She wondered if she would cry those tears when Delia went away to college, but that was still years away. It seemed like a lifetime.

After she finished her chores, Delia helped herself to some eggs from the cast-iron skillet on the stove, taking a seat at the breakfast table. She spooned them into her mouth, trying to muster up the courage to ask the question that had been plaguing her all morning.

Well, all morning since she saw that ad on PicPerfect and all those selfies.

"Uh, Mom . . ." she ventured between chewing. "You know, it's getting colder. Soon, there'll be a big snowstorm. I kind of need some new boots."

Delia pointed to her ratty old ones with the loose sole. She pried it away for extra drama. Mom looked over. She clenched her teeth—*tension*. Her mother was stressed. Never a good sign.

"You're right. That does not look good." Mom sighed. "I'm a terrible mother. I've just been so busy, I haven't even thought about new snow boots."

"That's okay!" Delia said brightly. "I already found the perfect ones. Wanna see? I was hoping maybe we could order them before they run out of my size."

She unlocked her phone and flipped to the House of De Vil shopping page, pulling up the trending faux-fur boots. Her mom looked over, her eyes lighting up when she saw them.

"Oh, those are very cute," she started. "They look warm, too."

Delia felt a surge of hope. Maybe she had been worried for nothing. But then her mother balked when her eyes hit the bottom of the page and landed on the price.

"*Two hundred and fifty dollars?*" her mother said in shock. "I've never owned a pair of shoes that cost that much."

"Yes, but these are so trendy!" Delia said, pointing to the pics. "It's what all the kids are wearing now. Also, look how nice they are. I bet they'll last forever. Unlike these boots," she added, flapping the loose sole again for good measure.

"Honey, you know even if I wanted to buy them for you, we can't afford those," Mom said, casting her gaze down. "Especially with the tuition costs for your new school."

The school I don't even want to go to, Delia thought. She felt a stab of irritation. She'd much rather have the boots and go back to her old school.

"But, Mom, look . . . everyone else has them," she said in a pleading voice, flipping to the trending selfies of girls wearing the boots. They flashed across the screen. Each picture made Delia feel even more like she *needed* the boots.

"We're not everyone," her mother said. "You know that. Plus, it's a waste of money. I can find a perfectly good pair at Replay Vintage. You won't know the difference."

Replay Vintage was the local thrift store. Nothing trendy or fashionable was ever going to come from that store. And everything was "gently used" and smelled like moth balls—or worse.

Why didn't her mother understand that it wasn't the same thing?

"Ugh, just this once I'd like to get something new!" Delia said, hating how bratty she sounded but unable to help it.

Her mother frowned. "Teenagers," she muttered under her breath. "Lord give me the strength to survive this."

Delia felt her anger escalating. It burned hot and fiery in her chest. It made her want to yell and scream, even though she knew she was acting like a spoiled brat.

"You never ask me what I want!" Delia cried. "Or

what school I want to go to! You just decide for me. Well, I *want* those boots."

"You're being shortsighted," her mother shot back. "Trust me, this school is your ticket to a better life. And one day, you won't care what kind of boots you wore. You'll thank me later."

Angry tears pricked Delia's eyes. Her chest felt like it was constricting. She hated her life—and right then, in that heated moment, she hated her mother. She was *never* not going to care what boots she wore. Appearances mattered, especially when you were starting a new school. Kids her age did notice these things. It was why they were trending on PicPerfect.

She knew her mother was trying, but why didn't she understand?

Her mother saw her tears. "Look, I know it's a lot changing schools like this," she said in a softer voice. "I should have considered that. It's just so hard to get these scholarship slots."

"I miss my friends," Delia said, her voice thick with tears. And there it was—the thing that was really bothering her. She looked down at her ratty boots, feeling hot tears drip down her cheeks. "It won't be the same without Aaliyah and Zoe."

Her mother followed her gaze.

"Look, no promises," Mom said. "But I'll see what I can do."

3
NEW SCHOOL BLUES

"**D**elia Ward, welcome to Gilded Crest Academy," Headmaster Dudley said, folding her hands in front of her. She sat behind an ornate mahogany desk—or Delia thought *perhaps* it was mahogany, not that she knew what that was exactly. Just that it was something rich-people furniture was made of.

In fact, everything in the office, and in the entire school, looked upscale. Even the way the headmaster pronounced Delia's name made it sound more special, rolling off her tongue with just the right emphasis and enunciation.

The carpet in the office was a plush burgundy shade

with gold crests bordering the edges that matched the school's colors. Framed college and graduate degrees from elite schools hung on the wall behind her, along with paintings that looked like they'd been borrowed from a museum. Not posters—actual paintings.

At her last school, Principal Riggins had a battered metal desk that had seen more years than he had, which was saying a lot judging by his head of white hair and his grizzled face. And the only things hanging on his walls were wilted, curling posters of 1970s basketball teams. Nothing about that place had been fancy.

"Uh, thanks, Headmaster Dudley," Delia said, fidgeting with the peeled-back sole of her shoe. Even the word *headmaster* felt clunky and unnatural on her tongue. "I'm happy to be here . . . at Golden . . . I mean *Gilded* Crest . . . um . . . school. . . ."

She trailed off, stumbling over her words and feeling out of place. Mom shot her a look and mouthed, *Sit up straight*.

Oh, right. Proper posture was another thing her mother cared about. Delia thought she was sitting up straight, but she lengthened her spine until it ached, trying to appear taller. Thank goodness she was starting classes during a shortened week. Because of the way the new year had fallen, the school's first day back was a Wednesday. She only had to live through three days of straight posture before the weekend.

"Yes, like my daughter said," Mom jumped in to cover for her, "we're thrilled to have her enrolled here for the remainder of her school year . . . at Gilded Crest *Academy.*"

Right, not school . . . academy, Delia thought, feeling like a doofus. She'd only been staring at the glossy school catalog for a month.

"And beyond, let's hope," Headmaster Dudley said, smiling warmly. But then she turned sterner. "Let me be clear, however, that Gilded Crest has different standards from your last school—"

"Like what?" Delia blurted before she could stop herself.

"Well, it's important for our students to uphold the Gilded Crest name, both inside and outside the class-room." With that, she slid a thick book across the desk toward Delia.

Delia felt a ripple of anxiety. Her eyes flashed over the title printed on the cover—*Gilded Crest Academy*

Student Code of Conduct. It was both boldfaced and italicized.

Code of conduct? The Gilded Crest name?

What did all of that mean?

"As you can see, we enforce a strict code of conduct for student behavior," Headmaster Dudley said, nodding at the thick book. "I expect that it was different at your last school. I assume they take a more relaxed approach to decorum, shall we say."

Her eyes tracked up and down Delia's clothes. Suddenly her "gently worn" jeans, pretty-but-inexpensive blue blouse, and ratty boots didn't seem up to Gilded Crest standards. Delia shrank back.

But her mother didn't seem to notice. She sat up straighter and smiled.

"Of course, we understand," Delia's mom said quickly. "Delia is a model student and very capable. Her public school had such big classes, it was easy for her to get lost, even with her incredible grades."

"I assure you that won't happen at Gilded Crest," Headmaster Dudley said. "We maintain optimal teacher-to-student ratios to meet every learner's complex needs. Your daughter will get the specialized attention she craves at our academy."

"Good. That's what I like to hear," Mom said with a curt nod. "I know this is the path to the best colleges and universities in the country."

"Indeed, let's hope she measures up. Mr. Jefferson's family has been attending this school for generations and he's one of our biggest donors. His recommendation holds a lot of weight, and it's why we decided to take a chance with Delia. Don't let us down, young lady."

Her eyes bored into Delia. So did her mom's. They both were waiting for her to speak. Suddenly her mouth felt dry and her tongue thick.

"I won't, Headmaster Dudley," she managed to get out. She tried to make her voice sound steady and brave, but inside she was shriveling up. She had never felt smaller or less up to a challenge.

And she'd never missed her old school more.

* * *

"Delia, have a great first day," Delia's mother said as they stood in the reception office after their meeting with the headmaster. She looked Delia in the eyes. "Make me proud. I know you can do this."

She hugged Delia fiercely, then left her clutching her class schedule and the thick student handbook.

"Hey, Mom, wait," Delia started, not ready for her to leave yet. "Don't you want to see the classrooms?"

She half wished her mother would walk her to class like she had in elementary school, even though Delia knew she was too old for that. But her mom had her phone to her ear and was already halfway out the door.

"Sorry, Mr. Jefferson," Delia heard her mother say. "The meeting with Headmaster Dudley went longer than I expected. . . ."

In that moment, Delia felt a surge of guilt for not appreciating everything her mother did for her. The fight they had that morning came back to her in a rush, making her stomach churn. Her mother worked so hard for every little thing that they had—even this school. Maybe

Delia still didn't want to be here, but she knew her mother was doing it for her. Well, for both of them.

They were a team of two.

Delia and Mom.

That's how it had always been. Delia had never known any differently.

Well, they were a team of two that sometimes included other substitute players who tended to pass in and out of their lives, much like the litter of foster puppies. Her father was the most notable member who had disappeared, while Mrs. Smith was the newest addition to their team, but Delia hoped that she would become a permanent member of their roster.

They might be a small team, but they were strong and resilient, more than capable of winning.

Besides, her mother was right. Delia had found it hard to concentrate at her last school. The classes were too big, often thirty-five kids in a class. And there were behavior issues that sucked up her teachers' valuable time. Maybe this new school was what she needed after all, even if it meant that she couldn't have those trendy boots or afford fashionable new clothes or other nice things like the highest-ranked accounts on PicPerfect.

Buoyed by that thought, Delia glanced at her schedule, then headed for the door. Mom was right.

She could do this.

As soon as she stepped into the hall, Delia heard the stampede of feet. Students marched in orderly packs, bound for class before the bell. These halls didn't have the kinetic, chaotic rush of her last school. Gilded Crest had a much smaller student population and was therefore less crowded. Students didn't have to push and shove to get to class, which made it feel more civilized.

Or they're all just following this code of conduct, Delia thought, clutching the thick student handbook closer to her chest.

These students walked like they had it all under control. Like they belonged here. Like they'd one day be the ones to rule the world. And most likely they would. But that wasn't what caught Delia's attention.

Her eyes tracked over the students and landed on their feet.

Clomp. Clomp. Clomp.

Practically every girl in the hall was wearing them—the House of De Vil Faux-Fur-Lined Boots. The ones that had been trending on PicPerfect that morning. The ones that cost $250.

The boots looked even more stunning in real life, with their signature black-and-white faux-fur lining. Not only were almost all the girls wearing *the boots*, but they all looked so fashionable. Even the boys looked like they'd just stepped out of magazine ads.

If I looked like them, Delia thought, *I'd have a higher ranking on PicPerfect for sure.*

They probably had no trouble taking effortless selfies, unlike Delia. She bet none of these kids had ever agonized for hours before posting something. She glanced down at her ratty old boots, and her stomach clenched.

I don't belong here.

Ducking her head, she bolted for her locker, wrestling to punch in her new combination while juggling her nerves and the student handbook. She finally got the locker open. A mirror was affixed to the inside of the door.

Nervously, she checked her appearance. She felt like she'd looked good when she posted her selfie this morning, but now her hair looked frizzier than ever. Her clothes looked dumpy and old. That pimple had bloomed into a full-blown whitehead right on the tip of her nose.

She tried to smooth her hair and tuck in her shirt, but it didn't help. At least at her old school, not everyone looked like a PicPerfect model. Here, she stuck out like a sore thumb. Worse yet, because the school was so much smaller, it was harder to hide. Delia felt exposed.

Her eyes tracked over and landed on a group of three girls across the hall, standing by their lockers. They were all wearing the House of De Vil boots. But beyond that, they looked like the kind of girls that Delia would want to be friends with. Fashionable and hip and smart. She needed to make friends at her new school. For a moment, she felt unworthy with her ratty boots and frizzy hair, but then she remembered what her friends had said that morning.

They're gonna love you.

Yeah, you'll have zero problems making new friends.

At her last school, she and Zoe and Aaliyah had tons of friends and tons of pink hearts on their profiles. There was no reason why Delia couldn't make friends here. She took a deep breath, then walked up to the girls across the hall, focusing on the one at the center—a tall redheaded girl with long, wavy hair.

"Hey, it's my first day here," Delia said. "So I thought I'd say hello. Uh, so like . . . *hello*." Instantly she hated how clunky the words sounded, but she smiled through it.

The redhead gave Delia a hard up-and-down stare, then she and her two friends burst into giggles. Delia's cheeks burned, but she tried to forge ahead anyway.

"My name is Delia. I'm in seventh."

"Right, I'm Harper," the redhead replied. "That's Charlotte and Ella." She pointed to her friends. Charlotte was Asian with long black hair, while Ella was dark-skinned with curly hair that looked effortlessly hip. They all wore expensive clothes paired with the trendy boots.

Finally Delia felt like she was getting somewhere. "Nice to meet you," she said. "By the way, I just *love* your boots. I'm planning to get some—"

"As if," Harper cut her off. "Pretty sure they're out of your budget."

"Wait, what do you mean?" Delia stammered.

"Yeah, aren't you that new scholarship kid?" Charlotte chimed in, twirling her long, shiny dark hair around her finger. Her eyes bored into Delia, staring down at her ratty boots.

"That's right. We heard you were transferring from the public school," Ella added with a snort. "What makes you think you can be friends with us?"

They all stared at her. As if they really expected her to answer that question.

Mortified, Delia retreated across the hall and shut her locker. She could still hear them snickering behind her and their catty whispers. Harper's voice cut through the hall noise.

"Did you see her *boots*?" Harper hissed to Charlotte and Ella. "I wouldn't be caught dead in those. And like she could ever get a pair of House of De Vil boots. Yeah, right."

Keeping her head down, Delia bolted to class. She could hear the *clomp, clomp, clomp* of her ratty boots with each humiliating footstep. She ducked into the classroom and made a beeline for the back, sliding into an empty desk. After her encounter with Harper and her friends in the hall, she just prayed that nobody would notice her. Gilded Crest was nothing like her old school.

And these girls weren't like her friends.

The teacher approached the board and scrawled *Picture Day on Monday!*

Ugh, more pictures. Ones that would be printed in an actual yearbook. At Gilded Crest, no less. That was the last thing Delia needed to worry about right now.

A boy took a seat at the desk next to hers. Delia risked a sideways glance at him. He looked different from the other kids she'd seen in the hall. For starters, half his hair was dyed purple, with long bangs cut just above his very blue eyes, and he wore a black leather jacket. He looked edgier and more alternative than the other kids, and he had earbuds in, bopping his head along to the beat.

Suddenly he caught her eye. Delia tore her gaze away and opened her code of conduct, pretending to be engrossed by the zillions of rules, but it was too late. He slid his earbuds out.

"You're that new scholarship kid, aren't you?" he said with a smirk.

Delia slowly closed the book, feeling even worse.

"Ugh, is it that obvious?" she said, bracing herself. "Are you going to make fun of me, too? Like Harper and her friends?"

"Are you kidding? Takes one to know one," he said instead. "Guess you already met our official welcoming committee. They're super annoying, if you ask me. Don't pay attention to them."

Delia looked over in surprise. "Wait, what do you mean?" she said. "You're on scholarship, too?"

"Art scholarship," he said, lifting one shoulder like it was no big deal. "Well, technically music. But they lump it all together. Guess it's easier that way. I'm Grant."

"Delia. And, uh . . . just *normal* scholarship here," Delia said. "No hidden talents."

"Nah, that means you're smart," Grant said, giving her a nod of respect. "Wanna hear my new beats?"

Delia felt a bit taken aback. He was the first person who was actually being nice to her at this school. Well, aside from the headmaster, but that didn't count. She felt herself letting her guard down. That wasn't something she did easily.

"Yeah, sure," she said, accepting the earbuds. She slid them into her ears. The tune was catchy with deep, thumping bass tones and a cool, upbeat piano riff. "Wow, you wrote this? It's sweet."

"*Sweet* just happens to be my middle name," he said smoothly.

She blushed. "Do you post your music on PicPerfect? I bet you get tons of hearts and followers. What's your account? I'll totally follow you and heart your stuff."

"PicPerfect?" he said with a frown. "What's that? Never heard of it."

Delia's jaw dropped. "You're kidding."

He just shrugged.

"PicPerfect is the hot new social media app," she said. "Like everyone—*and I mean everyone*—has an account. Do you live in a cave without Wi-Fi?"

"Well, I guess I'm not everyone," he replied. "Call me old-school, but I'm not on social media. I prefer to exist entirely in the real world."

Delia laughed. "Are you, like, from Mars or something?"

"Yup, I'm a Martian," he said, smirking. "You caught me. Wait . . . actually, that might be a cool idea for a song."

He pulled out a battered notebook and started scribbling the idea down.

"Like, I'm really this cool alien checking out Earth," he continued. "And shunning social media apps. And maybe I do live in a cave deep underground. That would be amaze, right?"

"Super amaze." Delia giggled in spite of herself. "Hey, I want songwriting credit," she joked. But then she turned more serious. "But don't you want to share your music so other people can hear it?"

"Nah, I make it for myself," Grant said, still scribbling. "And for my *real* friends. I love writing and creating it. I don't care if random strangers like it."

"Random strangers?" Delia said, still puzzled. She pulled out her phone to show him PicPerfect. "But once you friend them on social media, they're your friends. You like each other's posts. You stay in touch."

Grant eyed her phone dubiously.

"I mean, come on. Your stuff is great," Delia continued. "It could get really popular. You could even become an *influencer.*"

She was sure he understood *that.* He had to. In her mind, being a PicPerfect influencer was pretty much the greatest thing you could possibly become. It was one thing to have a high ranking at your school, like she and her friends did. But being an influencer meant having a top-ranked account in the whole world.

Grant just frowned at her phone, clearly noticing the devil icons marring some of the posts, pushing them down the rankings.

"But are they really your friends?" he said, sounding equally confused. "To me, it still sounds like a bunch of strangers judging your stuff. Why should I care what they think?"

"Maybe you're right," she hedged, clicking her phone off, even though she didn't fully agree.

Sure, she didn't know some of the people in her PicPerfect friend list in the real world, but some *were* her actual friends from her old school. And it did matter what they thought, didn't it?

"Like I said, I don't care what random people think about my music," Grant said, tapping his notebook. His eyes locked onto hers—they were very, very blue.

"But I do care what *you* think," he added.

"Uh, you do?" she stammered, feeling suddenly unworthy. Harper and her friends' snickers echoed through her head. What if he was just mocking her? Playing some kind of long-game prank?

But then he smiled and melted her fears.

"Yeah, because we're going to be friends in real life," he told her.

"We . . . we are?" Delia managed to say. An actual friend at this school? The idea sounded amazing.

"Yes, we are. I can feel it. Wanna make it official?"

Grant stuck out his hand and Delia shook it, feeling silly. She'd never shaken hands with someone her own age.

"Now you can't back out," he said. "We're friends."

"Real ones," Delia affirmed.

"Yup, real ones," he agreed.

Just then Harper and her friends filed into the classroom, clomping along in their House of De Vil boots. They passed by Delia's row on the way to their desks, forcing her to release Grant's hand.

He glanced at them, then rolled his eyes. "Harper and her Glam Posse," he said in a low voice. "I'm sorry she was mean, but don't let her get to you. She acts all important around here, but she's actually pretty basic. All she cares about is her appearance."

"Thanks for the warning," Delia said as he slid his earbuds back in.

Harper shot Delia a withering look as she settled into her own desk. "Looks like the charity case made friends with the artsy weirdo," she snickered to Ella and Charlotte.

"Yeah, they, like, totally belong together," Ella added.

"Takes one weirdo to know one," Charlotte giggled.

Shame exploded in Delia's chest like an atomic bomb. Even worse, her new friend was witnessing her complete and utter humiliation. She glanced over at

Grant, expecting a pitying look in return, but thankfully, he was preoccupied, scribbling lyrics in his journal and listening to his earbuds. He seemed completely oblivious.

Who cares what strangers think? she told herself, remembering his advice. Plus, she had her other friends. Aaliyah and Zoe were still her besties, even if they went to different schools. Delia tried to follow Grant's example and ignore the girls, but they continued to whisper and snicker from the other side of the classroom, casting side-eyed glances her way.

Delia caught bits and pieces.

"*Scholarship kid . . . look at her clothes . . . did she find them in a dumpster . . .*"

Delia started to feel short of breath. Her heart pounded in her chest. Their whispers sounded like the volume had been turned up, drowning everything else out. It was all she could hear.

Before Delia knew what she was doing, she jumped up from her desk and ran past the girls in their House of De Vil boots, bolting for the door. She grabbed the bathroom pass on her way out, their snickers echoing in her ears.

NEW SCHOOL BLUES

One thought shot through her head as her hideous, tattered boots flapped against the polished linoleum floors.

I don't belong here.

4
#TRENDING

Delia bolted into the bathroom, struggling to breathe. Her heart thudded faster. She knew that it was probably a panic attack—not deadly, but it *felt* like she was dying, suffocating, about to black out. She'd had them before, but not since she was a kid, back when they lived in tight quarters in public housing and everything felt stressful.

I wouldn't be caught dead in those.

I wouldn't be caught dead in those.

I wouldn't be caught dead in those.

Harper's cruel words echoed through her head on repeat. Delia could still hear Harper and her friends laughing and whispering like they were right behind her, even though they were back in the classroom. The taunts felt real and immediate and very, very cruel.

Delia tried to steady her breathing by splashing cold water on her face. She peered at her reflection in the mirror. Her hair looked like a puff ball, and her skin was splotchy and red from the panic attack. Not to mention the zombie zit. She looked horrid.

She couldn't go back to class like this. Not with Harper and her Glam Posse just waiting to pounce. She couldn't give them that much ammunition. She pulled out her contraband makeup, trying to touch up her face and cover it up. She brushed on pink blush and some cream eye shadow, then dabbed concealer over her zit and pulled her hair back into a low ponytail. When she was finished and felt calmer, she took a step back to survey her efforts.

Her jaw dropped. Somehow she'd made everything worse. Her already flushed cheeks just looked rosier, the eyeshadow was too much, and the concealer couldn't conceal the monstrous zit. It practically had a life of its own at this point.

It refused to die.

She turned on the hot water, splashing it on her face

to wash the makeup off so she could start again. When she looked up, steam from the hot water had fogged up the mirror, distorting her face. With the smudged and running makeup, she looked like some kind of evil clown.

She leaned in closer, transfixed, a sense of cold dread sweeping through her.

Ping.

An alert from her phone made her jump.

Ready to post to PicPerfect?
Don't let your ranking slide!

Delia felt a vague sense of panic when she saw the alert. But then her eyes flicked back to her reflection. As if she could post looking like . . . *this.*

She clicked open the app to dismiss the alert. The home screen with the top trends loaded onto her phone. Sure enough, #HouseofDeVil was number one. Without thinking, she clicked on the hashtag and images splashed onto her screen.

Her mouth dropped open. The top trending pic was of . . .

Harper.

There was no mistaking her face or that stunning red hair. In her selfie, she wore an oversize Gilded Crest sweatshirt, skinny jeans, and the boots. She was posed with her head thrown back, like the camera had captured her in a casual, effortless moment. Her loose red waves cascaded across her shoulders. Her skin looked flawless. Delia was sure that Harper was wearing makeup and used filters, but it looked so . . . *natural*. Her besties, Charlotte and Ella, flanked her, also posing in their trending House of De Vil boots.

In fact, all three girls looked like models in a teen magazine for top influencers.

Delia would give anything to take one picture—just one selfie—that looked half as perfect as Harper's post.

Anything.

Heart emojis filled Harper's comments, too many to count. Every second, more hearts popped up. Delia scrolled through the comments feed, knowing it was bad to hope to find a negative comment but wanting to find one all the same. She kept scrolling.

And scrolling.

And scrolling.

And scrolling.

Hundreds and hundreds of comments. But there wasn't a single red devil in sight. Those hearts had boosted Harper into the top slot on PicPerfect at their school, followed closely by Charlotte and Ella. The Glam Posse had the highest-ranked accounts at Gilded Crest.

Of course they do, Delia thought with a sigh. She studied the pic, envy pooling in her heart. It was a bitter brew but also somehow surprisingly tasty.

Delia tapped on Harper's friend list. Sure enough, all her friends followed House of De Vil. It seemed like they all had the boots. They all shopped at the fancy stores on Michigan Avenue. They all looked impossibly perfect in their profile pics and had way more followers than Delia.

If she thought her old friends looked perfect and fashionable in their PicPerfect posts, the Glam Posse at her new school took it to a whole new level. They weren't just popular and gorgeous and flawless—they were almost like influencers.

They were the definition of PicPerfect perfect.

They were everything Delia wanted to be, but wasn't.

She glanced back at her reflection, grimacing at her disheveled, clownish appearance. Then she looked down at her ratty old boots. Harper was right—they were awful.

Delia felt her shame grow exponentially, just like Harper's friend list was growing every second because of the trending House of De Vil boots. Delia clicked on the House of De Vil official profile page. The fashion line's profile pic was a photo of a woman taken from behind. This was Cruella De Vil, the icon who was rumored to have started the fashion line back in the day. Though you couldn't see her face, her hair was half white and half black, parted dramatically in the middle, and her signature one-of-a-kind black-and-white faux-fur coat was draped luxuriously over her shoulders.

The Cruella Coat.

Delia had always thought it was weird that there were never any pictures that showed Cruella's face. Some people didn't believe that Cruella had ever existed. They thought she was an urban legend, or perhaps just a character invented to market the brand and give it cachet. But Delia wasn't sure what to believe.

She zoomed in on the pic, trying to find more clues about the mysterious designer. Suddenly a chill worked its way up her spine. The bathroom felt colder, and she shivered despite the hot steam wafting out of the sink, where the tap was still running full force.

Delia scrolled down to the House of De Vil boots on their page. The boots stared back at her. *I need those boots to fit in*, she thought. Even more, she needed them to post to PicPerfect and boost her ranking at Gilded Crest so she could win the respect of Harper and her Glam Posse—and somehow survive the rest of the school year without dying from extreme humiliation.

The boots would fix everything.

Delia had to find a way to get them. She knew that with such certainty that it made her mouth water. She shut off the tap and wiped the fog from the mirror. Her makeup was still running. She couldn't take a selfie in this state, but she had another idea.

She took a screenshot of the House of De Vil boots

and tagged it—#wishlist #HouseofDeVil #fauxfurboots #fairygodmother.

Then she hit POST. After all, what did she have to lose?

Ping.

Suddenly her phone chimed as a direct-message alert popped up. Someone was DM'ing her. That was weird. It was from a strange account she didn't recognize.

She clicked on the DM. The profile pic showed a mannequin's expressionless face. The smooth plastic features were blank and unnerving. The name on the account was "Fashion Addict."

Delia scrolled through the feed, viewing the posts. Each image in the account showed a creepy-looking mannequin posed in different House of De Vil outfits, like something out of a storefront window. They were all black-and-white, the fashion line's iconic color palette.

Under the mannequin's profile pic, there was a short bio posted:

My friend wanted to be perfect.
#HouseofDeVil #RememberHer

BE CAREFUL WHAT YOU WISH FUR

Weird, Delia thought.

She flipped over to read the DM in her private messages. It was only one sentence—and it made her heart race.

Be careful what you wish for.

Delia read it, then reread it. Why would someone send this to her?

She quickly tapped out a response—

What do you mean?

The ticker blinked, indicating the other user was typing out a response. Delia's heart thudded in exact rhythm with the ticker, waiting for the next message to pop up.

Beware of the Devil Woman.
This is what she did to my best friend.

Red devil icons followed, one after the other, filling the DM page and making her phone *ping* nonstop. Delia's hands shook so hard she almost dropped her phone. It was probably just some fake robot account trying to scare kids. Delia knew they were common on social media apps. Her mom had warned her to be careful. Even so, she didn't hit BLOCK . . . yet.

The DMs ran through her head, making her feel even more unsettled. *Be careful what you wish for . . . Beware of the Devil Woman . . . This is what she did to my best friend.* The messages must have been triggered by her last post tagged with #HouseofDeVil.

But what did it mean?

With a shudder, Delia shut the PicPerfect app and clicked over to her texts. She wasn't going to let some online bully account or urban legend scare her off.

She pulled up her mother's number and tapped out a text message.

Mommy, pretty please?

Then she attached a link to the House of De Vil boots and hit SEND. She looked back at her reflection. It stared at her mournfully, so she forced a smile. She hadn't gotten this far in her life by giving up so easily. Harper and her friends may have teased her, but she remembered Grant with his goofy grin and thumping beats. Not everyone was like the Glam Posse.

She could still make friends here, right?

Plus, she had Aaliyah and Zoe in her corner, even if they didn't go to the same school anymore. They could still vid chat like they did that morning and trade comments on each other's PicPerfect posts. And they could chill on the weekends in Zoe's basement, or hit the skate park. That thought made Delia feel better. Who needed the Glam Posse anyway?

She took a deep breath and went to work fixing up her appearance so she could return to class. She couldn't believe she'd missed so much of her first period already but hoped the teacher would excuse her absence as first-day nerves. She retied her ponytail, then reapplied her makeup. This time, she looked . . . *better*. Not perfect, but better. That would have to do for now.

But then her eyes tracked down to her ratty boots.

Delia's face fell. The boots could not be fixed with

makeup and concealer, or hidden behind a flattering filter. Despite her best efforts, she was never going to fit in here.

She had only one hope.

She needed those boots.

5
KNOCKOFF

"**H**ow was your first day at your new school?" Mrs. Smith trilled as soon as Delia trudged through the front door.

Delia had taken the train home—the "El," as it was called in Chicago. It was an elevated train, which meant that, unlike in other cities, which had mostly underground subway stops, the platforms where you waited were above the street; you were completely exposed to Chicago's punishing recipe of wind, rain, sleet, and snow, depending on the day.

On this day the sky had pelted her with a wintry mix of rain and ice, while the wind tore through her old coat— she was going to need a new one of those, too. By the time she got home, she was shivering and miserable. The perfect end to her very *not* perfect day.

"Horrifying," Delia groaned, slamming her backpack down for emphasis. "No, *worse* than that. Horrendous. Horrible. Hideous. Got any more?"

"You forgot . . . *horrific*," Mrs. Smith said, unable to contain a chuckle.

"Perfect," Delia said, plopping down on the sofa in a funk. "And it's not funny. My new school is awful. I miss my old school. And I miss my old friends. It's not the same without Zoe and Aaliyah."

"Well, I've got something that will make it all better," Mrs. Smith said, then lowered her voice. "Just don't tell your mother. We both know she doesn't approve of sweets before dinner."

"Where is she, anyway?" Delia asked, glancing around the town house for any sign of her mom, even though she suspected that she already knew the answer.

No purse and overcoat piled on the kitchen table. No neutral pumps cast off by the front door. No smell of her sweet, baby-powder-scented perfume wafting through the house.

She wasn't here.

Her mother always worked long hours with her new law-firm job—the one that had enabled them to move in with Mrs. Smith in the nicer part of town. She often missed dinner altogether, or rushed home just in time, bursting through the door in a blast of cold, wintery air, breathless and clutching steaming takeout containers, only to gobble down food like it was her first meal of the day and then vanish into her bedroom to take night classes online. The steady *clack-clack-clack* of her keyboard would echo out. It was the signal to not interrupt her.

Of course, Delia loved her mother and appreciated how hard she worked, especially as a single mother who had to support their little family on her own. But often, Delia found herself wishing she had the kind of mother who could stay home and bake chocolate chip cookies and greet her when she got back from school in the afternoons, like some of her friends had. Not that baking cookies was her mother's strong suit, even if she did have more time. It was her father's fault, in a way. Delia understood that. But blaming him was like blaming some invisible force—or just thin air. She had no real concept of him, or what he was even like as a person. All she knew was that her mom believed they were better off without him.

But were they really? Delia didn't always know.

She glanced at the clock, guessing her mom would be home late. *Again*.

"She's still at work," Mrs. Smith said, following Delia's gaze. The clock ticked away the afternoon, which was quickly transforming into evening. In winter, the sun set extra early. "But she's picking up pizzas on her way home. And then she has classes online tonight."

With that, almost as an apology, Mrs. Smith handed Delia a steaming mug of hot chocolate. Tiny, pillowy marshmallows floated on the top of the rich, frothy concoction.

"Thanks, Mrs. Smith," Delia said morosely.

So she wouldn't have much time tonight to beg her mother for the boots. All the horrible things that had happened at school flashed through her mind again. Harper and her friends teasing her and laughing at her clothes. She felt so naïve for thinking she could just waltz into

Gilded Crest looking like that and make friends with the most popular girls at the school. If her mom was right and first impressions mattered that much, then she'd sealed her fate today.

But she didn't want to give up. If she could somehow get a pair of the House of De Vil boots, then maybe she could change their minds about her and make friends. Or at the very least, fit in better and not get teased so much. Just thinking about their jeering taunts made her heart sink.

Still, as soon as she took a whiff of the hot cocoa, her mood lightened the tiniest bit. Mrs. Smith always had a way of cheering her up, even when it felt impossible.

"Anyway, I simply don't agree about the sweets rule," Mrs. Smith said with an approving smile. "Your mother means well, of course. But chocolate is practically its own food group. And it's appropriate any time of the day—or night, if you ask me."

Delia laughed in spite of her terrible mood. "Don't worry, my lips are sealed." The mug warmed her hands. "It'll be our little secret."

She sipped the hot chocolate and closed her eyes. It

was rich and heavenly. The warm liquid ran down her throat, coating her tongue and heating her from the inside out. She sighed with relief. Mrs. Smith was the perfect counterbalance to her mother's strict rules. Delia often felt annoyed at them. Well, more like, *all the time*. But she knew that her mom was just trying to be a good parent, even if she went overboard at times, and probably in some way, to make up for her father not sticking around.

"There now, my dear," Mrs. Smith said, nodding as Delia inhaled the hot cocoa like it was medicine. "Chocolate has a way of making everything better, doesn't it?"

It sure does, Delia thought. She wandered over to the litter of puppies, who seemed to have sprouted more black spots while she was at school. They also seemed to have grown an inch each.

"Look, they're growing up so fast," Delia said, pointing to the new spots. The dogs were clearly thriving here, but that meant they'd be leaving sooner rather than later for their adoptive homes.

Delia put down her mug and snagged Radar by his neck, then cradled him in her arms, already missing him. As if reading her mind, Radar licked her face, then nibbled on her nose. She smelled his sweet puppy breath and smiled. Puppies liked you no matter what boots you wore, or how frizzy your hair was, or how many likes you got on PicPerfect that day.

Suddenly the phone rang in the kitchen. The old rotary one. It sounded like a fire alarm.

"Coming! Hold your horses," Mrs. Smith called out.

She snagged the phone, holding it to her ear. "Hello?"

She listened, then said, "How did you get this number? I'm sorry, we're not interested. Don't call here again!" Then she slammed the receiver down angrily.

"Who was that?" Delia asked, looking over in alarm. "What did they want?"

Mrs. Smith rarely raised her voice, so her reaction to the call was surprising.

"Can you believe it?" Mrs. Smith said. "Somebody was trying to buy the puppies!"

"But how did they even know about them?" Delia asked.

"I guess the rescue listed them as available for adoption," Mrs. Smith said. "But they're sorely mistaken. We don't *sell* puppies. We adopt them out to loving homes.

Only after a rigorous application and thorough house inspection."

"Well, did you tell them to apply to adopt a puppy?" Delia asked.

"No, you don't understand," Mrs. Smith said, wringing her hands. "They didn't just want one puppy—they wanted to buy all of them!"

"Somebody wants to buy the whole litter?" Delia said in shock. She glanced over at the pen. They were cute now, sure. But they'd only get bigger and bigger and transform into rambunctious, full-grown dogs. "But why would they want that many puppies?"

"No idea," Mrs. Smith said. "But they belong in a loving, adopted home. We're not in the puppy-sales business. That's just wrong. It goes against everything we stand for!"

Delia felt a surge of affection for her landlady. "That's right, you belong with us," she whispered to Radar, petting his head. Then she set him back in the pen. "Don't worry, we're not gonna sell you. We'll find a good adoptive home for you. And your brothers and sisters."

Just then the front door flew open, and Delia's mom

rushed through, carrying pizzas—and a wrapped box. The bitter wind whipped through the town house until she slammed the door.

"Sorry I'm late," Mom said, out of breath. Her cheeks were red and flushed from the cold. "But I do have a special surprise."

"Really, what is it?" Delia said.

"Oh, I simply love surprises," Mrs. Smith added, clutching at her skirt.

Mom plopped the pizzas on the counter, then thrust the wrapped gift at Delia. The box was big enough to hold . . . a pair of boots. Delia's heart started to race.

Could it actually be the House of De Vil Boots?

"Mom, what is it?" Delia asked, hardly daring to hope. She turned the box over in her hands. Her excitement was so strong and pure, she could actually taste it on her tongue.

"A special gift for my special student," Mom said. "I got your text."

"Oh, no way! Really?" Delia squealed, clutching the box.

"I know our budget has been tight lately," Mom went

on. "But I wanted to do something nice for you, since it was your first day at a new school. Plus, you do need them. Those are getting old."

Delia's old boots sat by the door, looking worn and soggy.

"Well, what are you waiting for?" Mom said, clasping her hands together eagerly. "Go ahead, open it up."

Delia tore off the wrapping paper. She lifted the lid and her eyes landed on a pair of black-and-white boots lined with tufts of faux fur. She couldn't believe it. Her heart soared. This was the answer to all her problems.

"Mom! This is incredible! Where did you get them?"

Delia's mother beamed. "Well, I couldn't believe it, but I found them at Replay Vintage! According to the shopkeeper, I got really lucky. They're super popular right now."

"Oh, thank you so much," Delia said, unable to believe her change of luck.

She lifted the boots out of the box and immediately noticed the label.

Haus of De Veel.

No. No, no, no!

BE CAREFUL WHAT YOU WISH FUR

This couldn't be happening. They were knock-off boots. A cheap imitation, not the real thing. Worse yet, they were clearly used. The fur inside was crushed down, while the soles were worn and scuffed up. And they had a smell, like somebody else's feet had been inside them.

"Well, aren't they great?" Mom said, oblivious. She peered at Delia excitedly. "Go ahead, try them on and model them for us."

"Mom, they're the wrong brand!" Delia said, feeling dismayed.

Her mother looked confused. She glanced at Mrs. Smith for help.

"But they're Haus of De Veel," she said, pointing to the logo on the box. "That's what you wanted. They look exactly like that picture you texted me."

No, they don't, Delia thought, making a mental list of all the imperfections. The cheap plastic soles. The leaching color of the faux fur.

"I asked for House of De Vil," Delia said, enunciating carefully. "These are . . . a knockoff."

Mom sighed in exasperation. "What's the difference?

Nobody will be able to tell. They look exactly the same."

"No, they don't," Delia said. "It's obvious they're a cheap copy. Everyone at school will know we can't afford the real thing. There's no way I can wear these out of the house!"

The smile finally fell off her mother's face. "That's enough, young lady," she snapped. "You sound like a spoiled little brat. I raised you better than this."

Even Mrs. Smith shook her head at Delia's tantrum. But they didn't understand. Why couldn't they see that these boots weren't the real thing? And worse yet, would probably get her teased at school even more mercilessly than she already had been! She simply couldn't wear them. She would rather die. Harper was right. They couldn't afford the real thing. It was hopeless. She was never going to fit in at Gilded Crest.

"You're wearing them to school tomorrow," Mom said. "And that's final. They're perfectly good boots. I spent hard-earned money on them."

Delia threw the box down in anger. "But, Mom—"

"But nothing," Mom snapped back. "Now pick that

box up. There's a gift card in it for the thrift shop, so you can pick out a new winter coat after school tomorrow, too. Your coat is getting old, and there's a blizzard forecast to hit this week."

"A new coat?" Delia said, feeling tears prick her eyes. "Everything in that stupid store is old and used. For once, I wish I could get something that's actually new."

"New things are a waste of money when you can get perfectly good clothing at half the price," Mom said in a stern voice. "One day, when you have to work to pay for things, you'll understand."

No, I won't. I'll never understand, Delia thought, pouting.

"And I want you to get something warm and practical," her mother railed on. "It's going to be a long, bitter winter, according to the weather forecasts."

Practical meant one thing. . . . *ugly*.

Could it get any worse? A hideous coat to go with her knockoff boots?

But Delia knew better than to argue more. That would only get her grounded, and worse yet, she'd lose her phone, the one good thing left in her life. It was the only way she could stay on PicPerfect—and connected to her old friends. In short, it was her lifeline.

"Fine," she said quietly.

"All right, good. Now that that's settled . . . want some pizza?" Mom said, trying to break the tension. "I got veggie, your favorite."

"No thanks," Delia said in a mopey voice. "I'm not hungry."

Her mother exchanged a look with Mrs. Smith, but they both knew better than to push the issue. "Okay, have it your way," Mom replied with a frown. "It'll be in the fridge if you get hungry later."

Delia retreated to her room with the boots and gift card, feeling utterly defeated, and slammed her door. At least she could message her old friends about how unfair her mother was being. Aaliyah and Zoe would totally understand. They'd get that her mom was the one who was acting totally crazy and unreasonable—not the other way around.

Everyone her age knew that knockoffs weren't the same thing. So why couldn't her mother understand?

Delia flopped on her bed and opened PicPerfect to

a flood of alerts. Her heart raced excitedly when she saw them.

I got comments on my post!

But then she opened the app, her eyes falling on a slew of red devil faces in the comments under her pic wishing for the House of De Vil boots, pushing her profile further down the ranks. But it got worse when her eyes fell on which users had left the devils on her post.

It was Harper, Charlotte, and Ella.

The Glam Posse.

Their bullying wasn't confined to the school halls. It had moved online, too. The other comments came from kids at Gilded Crest who she didn't even know, but who must have noticed Harper and her friends leaving devil comments on Delia's post.

Delia scrolled down her feed in horror. The devil faces left by her classmates seemed to laugh at her, taunting her—*You're not PicPerfect*, they seemed to say. Delia felt more tears prick her eyes, then fall down her cheeks and plop on her phone screen, blurring the images.

Meanwhile, Harper's #HouseofDeVil selfie continued to trend at number one for her school.

This was undoubtedly the worst day of her life, from feeling completely out of place at her new school, to getting teased by Harper and her friends, to her mom buying her knockoff boots, to the devil comments on her PicPerfect post.

And it wasn't over yet.

I have to wear those horrible boots tomorrow, she thought before she fell into a restless, hungry sleep.

* * *

Delia ran through the school hallways as voices chased after her. The halls in this place were like a maze. She had to get to class, but she couldn't find the way.

"You're going to be marked tardy, young lady!"

The headmaster's voice echoed around her. Something heavy landed at her feet—it was the *Gilded Crest Academy Student Code of Conduct*. The book flipped open on its own, the pages fluttering. It landed on the chapter marked "Grounds for Student Expulsion."

Delia backed away in horror, then bolted for the front

door. At least, she thought she was heading for the front door. Everything looked the same. The lockers around her flew open, their metal doors crashing, and hands reached out to grab her—their fingernails manicured, trendy jewelry dripping from their wrists.

Charity case!

We wouldn't be caught dead in those boots!

Loser! Loser!

Cackling laughter surrounded her, making her sweat and bringing tears to her eyes.

Delia bolted into the bathroom and dove into a stall, shutting the door and latching it. Her breath burst out in ragged gasps. She reached down to tug off her horrible boots, pulling hard—

But they wouldn't come off.

The boots stayed stuck to her feet as if superglued to her soles.

She pulled harder, but no matter what she did, they wouldn't come off.

Bang!

Delia jumped back. Someone had pounded on the

stall door. But she hadn't heard anyone come into the bathroom.

"Wh-who-who's there?" she stammered, pulling at the boots.

Bang bang bang bang bang!

Could there be more than one person out there? Why were they all chasing her? What had she done wrong?

"Please! Leave me alone!" Delia pleaded, tears running down her cheeks.

She pushed down at the boots from the top, she tried to pry them off from underneath, she even tried to rip off the already torn sole, but it wouldn't budge.

Suddenly a tall, shadowy figure rose up behind her, cackling. Delia whipped around in terror. The figure had short, spiky hair that flew wildly in all directions.

"You're not fashionable enough to fit in here!"

6
CHARITY CASE

Delia woke from her nightmare and whipped back the covers.

Her heart thudded like a drum in her chest. She expected the boots to be there, still stuck to her feet, but her feet were bare. She could still hear the jeering laughter echoing in her ears. It took a moment for her breathing to normalize. She wiggled her toes, just to make sure everything was as it should be. The dream had felt so real.

It was just a nightmare, she told herself. *It didn't really happen.*

Still feeling jittery, Delia forced herself out of bed to get ready for school. She took a deep breath, surveying her shoe options. She had one pair of sneakers, one pair of flip-flops, and her "new" boots. The ratty old ones had been tossed in the back of her closet, but they weren't really an option. Not only did they not keep her feet warm, but also, she had no doubt that Harper and her friends would tease her relentlessly if she showed up in them again.

She stared at the box containing the knockoff boots, feeling sick to her stomach. The *Haus of De Veel* logo seemed to glare back at her. She didn't have a choice, though, did she? She dropped to her knees, pulled the box to her, and removed the lid. Her nose wrinkled. The boots even smelled secondhand.

Maybe they won't notice, she told herself, glancing down at the boots.

But she knew it was just wishful thinking, because she had no choice but to wear them. Her mom had insisted on it. Plus, Delia felt a little bad about last night's tantrum. Her mom did work hard and had tried to get her something nice. She clearly did not understand that these knockoff boots weren't the same as the real thing.

Steeling herself, Delia pulled on the boots. At least

they weren't uncomfortable. She clomped downstairs, keeping her eyes on the shoes. Actually, they didn't look so bad when she wasn't staring right at them up close. Maybe, if she was really lucky, Harper wouldn't notice.

She entered the kitchen, avoiding looking at her mom or Mrs. Smith directly.

"Uh, I'm sorry about last night," she said to her feet, to the boots, and to her mother, who sat at the table sipping her coffee. The air felt thick with tension. Mrs. Smith watched silently.

"Apology accepted," her mother said, rising and sweeping her up into a tight hug. "I love you. You know that. Even when you act like . . ."

"A teenager?" Delia finished with a snort. "Yeah, sorry about that."

"Yup, that," Mom agreed. "Plus, I think the boots look super cute on you."

"Me too," Mrs. Smith agreed. "Not that anyone's asked me for fashion advice in ages. Though, back in the day, you should know, I had quite a few gentlemen suitors."

"Wait, you did?" Delia giggled. "What happened?"

Mrs. Smith glanced at the puppies. "Honestly, none of them loved me as much as my doggies. Well, except Mr. Smith, of course. But after he died, I didn't want to settle down with anyone else. And I was happy living here on my own."

"Honestly, Mrs. Smith, I think you get wiser every day," Delia's mom commented with a wry smile. She turned to Delia. "Today after school, you can go use the gift card to pick out a coat to go with them. Just don't forget to donate your old one. What you don't want . . ."

"Somebody else's family might need," Delia finished her mom's sentence. She had heard that line a thousand times. But it was true. Delia knew because they'd been one of those families.

She glanced down at her feet, feeling cheered. Her mom was right. Maybe she could find a cute coat at the thrift store, even if it was used. She fingered the gift card in her pocket.

At least these boots were nicer than her old ones, right?

* * *

BE CAREFUL WHAT YOU WISH FUR

Delia rode the subway across the city, climbed down from the station, and headed for school. The sky was the kind of slate gray that promised bitter, cold weather and lots of snow.

She was grateful for her new, warmer boots. She passed under the ornate seal that marked the entrance to Gilded Crest Academy, inhaling the hallway smell—this school even smelled clean and sterile, unlike her old school, which reeked like the boys' locker room. She liked that about her new school. Plus, not having to push and shove just to make it to class on time was a welcome relief. Maybe Gilded Crest wasn't all bad; maybe there were good things, too.

But as soon as she stepped inside, Harper spotted her from the other side of the hall, where she was clustered around her locker with the Glam Posse. Just like yesterday, they looked like they'd stepped off an influencer's feed—their makeup perfect, their hair effortless, and their clothes flawless. They had their phones out and were showing each other PicPerfect posts.

Each of them wore the House of De Vil boots—the real ones.

Delia froze the second Harper locked eyes on her. She watched as Harper's eyes tracked down her body . . . and landed on her rip-off boots.

O-M-G, Harper mouthed, elbowing the other girls in the posse. Charlotte and Ella followed her gaze. It really did seem like these girls always moved in a pack.

Three sets of eyes fixed on her boots. Three sets of glossed lips broke into cruel snickers.

"Look at her *faux* boots," Harper cackled, pointing at her boots and laughing. She aimed her phone at Delia.

"Nice try, charity case," Charlotte mocked her.

"How could she wear those?" Ella sniffed.

Hot humiliation shot through Delia's entire body into her cheeks, and her stomach clenched. Everyone in the hall—every single kid in her new school—turned to watch the commotion. She had hoped they wouldn't notice. She'd even convinced herself that the boots weren't that terrible. That her obsession with the brand was misplaced, like her mother had said.

But soon, more kids started laughing and pointing at her boots. It was just like her horrible nightmare. Even

Grant noticed her this time, pausing as he walked by. He pulled out his earbuds, eyeing her with concern.

"You okay, D?" he asked.

But Delia couldn't find her voice. She couldn't take it. It was her nightmare coming true. She ducked her head and ran for the nearest bathroom.

"Delia, where are you going?" Grant called out.

But she ignored him.

The last thing she needed was for him to pity her. That was the last thing she wanted from any of her friends. Pity wasn't kind—it was the opposite. It was embarrassing. Worse than that—it was cruel.

Delia flung herself into the bathroom, shutting the door behind her. The jeering laughter faded away, but it wasn't good enough. She ducked into the last stall and locked the door, feeling worse than she ever had her whole life.

That was when she noticed her phone was pinging nonstop. She pulled it out and checked the screen. A bunch of PicPerfect alerts popped up.

Delia's heart all but stopped.

She opened the app and clicked on the alerts.

Apparently, somebody had tagged her in a post—and not just anybody. It was Harper, who had the top account trending at their school.

Oh no, Delia thought in alarm. *She wouldn't. She couldn't!*

Delia clicked on the post—and almost dropped her phone.

Harper had posted a pic of Delia. In it, Delia was running away from her, hair flying, ugly boots on full display. Harper had even circled her cheap boots with a virtual red marker. The caption read:

#PHONY #KNOCKOFF #FAUXBOOTS #CHARITYCASE
#GOBACK #PUBLICSCHOOL

Delia felt like fire was consuming her body. Under the post, hearts poured into the comments. All the kids in her new school were liking it, pushing the humiliating picture up the rankings for their school. Delia couldn't believe it.

Then familiar names began posting hearts as well—Delia's friends and classmates from her old school. When

Aaliyah's and Zoe's names popped up, Delia almost threw the phone at the wall. How could they? Her best friends! She had never felt more betrayed. It was one thing for Harper and her posse to make fun of her. But it was a whole other level of terrible for her real friends to like the post.

Or the people she *thought* were her real friends.

Now Delia felt like the whole world was laughing at her. Her chest was tight. She had to get out of here. She couldn't face another day at this school. Just then another DM popped up from the mannequin account. Delia scanned the message.

Keep your faux boots. Trust me.

What did that mean?

Delia frowned at the message. Why would she want to keep the faux boots? They were ruining her life.

The plastic mannequin face stared back at her, offering no clue. Delia felt a shudder. Why was this stranger stalking her account like this? And sending her all these weird messages?

She quickly hit BLOCK and shut the app, feeling exposed.

Delia thought about ditching school, but she'd never done that in her life. She wouldn't even know how to do it, and she definitely didn't want to face her mom when she found out. No. She was just going to have to suck it up and get through the day.

She waited until the bell was about to ring, watching the seconds tick down on her phone, before slipping into class at the very last second, making sure not to make eye contact with a single living soul.

* * *

After school let out—the worst day of her life—Delia headed for the shopping district off Michigan Avenue. The wide, tree-lined street had the most luxurious designer stores. Town cars dropped off shoppers clad in designer clothes looking to add to their wardrobes, while other fancy cars squealed into parking garages or metered parking spots.

Delia trudged down the street from the train, trying to stay warm despite the punishing wind whipping off the lake, for which the street was named. Her eyes roamed over the stores, each fancier than the last one, with mannequins posed in their front windows and lit by glamorous spotlights. Not that she could afford to shop at any of them.

She was bound for Replay Vintage, which occupied a little storefront in a narrow side alley. It was off the beaten path for a reason.

As she walked in her faux boots, each footstep reminding her of the horrible day at school, she window-gazed. While not everything had gone terribly that day—at least she'd done well on her math quiz—nothing, not even good grades, could make up for the mocking laughter in the halls and Harper's post to PicPerfect. Delia distracted herself by studying the windows she passed. Mannequins in various glamour poses and adorned in designer garb stared back at her, while shoppers swarmed into the shops off the sidewalk, only to emerge with hefty shopping bags. Envy sparked in Delia's heart, cold and fiery at the same time.

She skidded to a halt in front of her dream store— House of De Vil's flagship shop. It was bustling with patrons browsing the racks and trying on clothes and shoes. Inside, girls her age snapped selfies — probably posting them to PicPerfect.

Delia watched them, her envy intensifying. What she wouldn't give to be able to shop there, too. She glanced down at her faux boots. The salespeople would probably peg her as a poseur the second she stepped through the door, just like Harper and her friends had. Or an alarm would go off to inform the whole shop that she didn't belong there.

She reached down and felt the hard outline of the gift card in her pocket. The thrift store was her only option. Still, she couldn't quite tear herself away. Not just yet.

The mannequins in House of De Vil's windows posed in black-and-white faux-fur coats, and each one of them wore the infamous boots. Knowing how expensive the boots were, Delia couldn't even imagine how much those coats cost.

She peered up at one mannequin wearing a striped coat, trying to imagine herself twirling in front of the mirror wearing it. The mannequin's eyes stared right back at her from its expressionless plastic face. A chill shuddered through Delia. The eyes seemed to be boring into her.

Feeling unsettled, Delia turned her attention to the next mannequin—this one in a plaid coat—and her heart jumped. This mannequin was looking at her, too, but she could have sworn that a minute ago it had been facing in the other direction. She moved down the sidewalk a bit and looked back again.

Wait . . . How . . . ?

Now *all* the mannequins were looking at her, their heads turned in her exact direction. Delia tasted fear on her tongue. She blinked purposefully, and when she opened her eyes again, all the mannequins were looking away, their heads tilted in the opposite direction. What was going on? Delia's pulse began to pound. The mannequins were moving on their own. She was sure of it.

Or was she?

Mannequins weren't alive. They couldn't turn their heads on their own. And it wasn't as if they were actually *watching* her. She was just anxious and overtired. That was the only explanation. She should just get this ugly coat-buying situation over with and get home to do homework. Get this awful day over with already.

Resolutely, Delia turned away from the display window and headed down the street. As she was passing by the glass doors to House of De Vil, they whipped open, caught by the biting wind, and a pack of girls emerged. And not just any girls—

Harper and her posse.

No, Delia thought, freezing in place. *This cannot be happening.*

"Look, it's the charity case!" Harper sneered. "Did you like my PicPerfect post?"

The Glam Posse snickered at her. They all clutched black-and-white House of De Vil shopping bags stuffed with pricey merchandise.

"I see you're still wearing the faux boots," Harper scoffed. "What're you doing here anyway?"

"Yeah, you can't afford the real thing," Charlotte added with a sneer.

"That's right." Ella snickered. "You don't belong here."

The Glam Posse stared at her. Delia looked down, feeling humiliated.

"Wh-what's the big deal?" she stammered, her cheeks burning. "My mom just made a mistake. She just got the wrong brand. They were out of my size and she—"

"Yeah, right," Harper said. "Prove it. Show up to school tomorrow in anything House of De Vil and I'll take that PicPerfect post down."

Delia couldn't breathe. Harper had called her bluff. She knew Delia couldn't afford anything in that store. Not even a pair of socks or a keychain. But she couldn't show weakness. Girls like them preyed on weakness.

It was what they lived for.

"Fine, I'll see you tomorrow," Delia said with as much confidence as she could muster, given the situation, even though she had no idea how she could follow through on her promise.

Then she turned and fled down the street, angry tears prickling her eyes. She didn't belong at Gilded Crest. Why did her mom think it was a good idea to send her to that stupid school? And now, thanks to Harper's trending PicPerfect post, she couldn't go back to public school either. She'd be the laughingstock of the whole campus. Even Zoe and Aaliyah thought she was a loser now.

She thought about messaging her friends, or even vid chatting to see if it was just one big misunderstanding. But how could that be a mistake? They knew what they were doing and they had to know that she would see all their hearts and comments.

She needed Harper to take that post down, but there was only one way. Show up tomorrow in anything House of De Vil. The dare from Harper echoed through her head. But that was impossible. Harper was right. Faux boots were all her family could afford. She was doomed to be a charity case forever. She couldn't show her face at Gilded Crest ever again.

Her vision blurred by tears and shame, Delia ran down the alley toward the thrift store, and she ran head-first into someone. Her feet slipped, and she fell backward. She heard a familiar voice.

"Hey, slow down! Are you okay?"

7
OL' BLUE EYES

An arm reached out to steady Delia, keeping her from falling flat onto her butt. It yanked her back to her feet. She looked up, and her eyes locked onto—

Grant.

"Uh, careful there," he said. "Training for the track team?" he added with a chuckle.

He'd dropped the paper sack of records that he'd been holding on impact, and colorful squares featuring musicians' faces and vintage artwork had slipped out across the ground. Luckily they looked unharmed. The snow had cushioned the fall.

Tears ran down Delia's cheeks. She tried to brush

them away, but they kept coming, making her feel even worse.

"Y-you probably don't wanna . . . be seen with me . . ." she blubbered.

"Uh, why's that?" he said with a puzzled expression. He crouched down to pick up the records, dusting the snow off them. She started helping him. She'd never actually touched a record before. They were bigger and heavier than she'd imagined, their cases almost as large as pizza boxes, though a lot slimmer.

"Because I'm a charity case," she said in a shaky voice. Her eyes fell to her boots. "Haven't you heard? I'm going viral on PicPerfect. And not in a good way."

"Uh, I don't have social media, remember?" Grant said with a grin. His eyes shone with amusement.

"Oh, right," Delia said, again amazed at how different he was from every other kid she knew. She hesitated, unsure if she should tell the truth. But something in his eyes, in his demeanor, made her trust him. "Harper posted a pic of my new boots, calling them knockoffs. And now everyone at school is liking it and making fun of me."

She pulled out her phone and showed him Harper's post. It had registered hundreds of hearts, pushing it up the ranks to the top of PicPerfect. Now even strangers were liking the most humiliating pic of her life.

"Why do they care what boots you're wearing?" Grant asked, sounding even more puzzled. He squinted at the post, then glanced down at her feet. "Actually, I think they're pretty cool."

"Pretty cool?" Delia exclaimed in horror. "How could you say that?"

"Well, if I was on that app, I'd give you a *like* for wearing them," he added. "Or a thumbs-up. Or a heart thingy. Or whatever you're supposed to do."

Delia just stared at him. "First of all, if you *heart* this post, then it means you like that Harper's making fun of me. You have to use a devil emoji. . . ."

"Sounds complicated," he said with a shake of his head. His purple-and-black hair flopped into his eyes. "See, this is why I hate social media. Sometimes it seems like it exists only to make people feel bad."

"You're missing the point," Delia went on with a frustrated sigh. "They *are* knockoffs. You know, cheap imitations of a designer brand," she added, hoping he'd finally get it. "It's pathetic to not have the real thing."

"I dunno, they seem like nice boots to me," he said with a shrug. "You nearly plowed me over. Good traction for winter, right? And they look warm, too."

"Well, everyone else in school disagrees," Delia said with a sigh, shutting her phone. "I appreciate you trying to make me feel better and all that. But, like, everyone's making fun of me on PicPerfect. Maybe she'll take it down, but only if I show up in the real thing."

"So let me get this straight—you need another pair of new boots?" Grant repeated, scratching his head. "Even though those seem perfectly fine? Just to impress Harper and her Glam Posse? And all the strangers on PicPerfect?"

"Yes, that's right!" Delia said, feeling like she was finally getting somewhere with him. "Only, I can't afford the real thing. Which is why I'm totally stuck!"

She stared at him expectantly. But Grant just shrugged again.

"That stuff on Michigan Avenue is all way overpriced anyway," he said. "You're just paying for the brand name. It's got nothing to do with the quality."

She stared at him. Now he sounded like her mom.

Who didn't care about the brand? That was crazy talk. She glanced down at her boots. But all of a sudden— if she forgot about the brand—they did look pretty cute.

And her feet did feel warm.

But that didn't matter.

"Well, most kids feel the opposite," she said, remembering what happened at school that morning. "Just ask Harper and her friends."

"Why would I care about her?" Grant said. "I've always thought she was pretty basic and superficial."

Delia's jaw dropped. Was he kidding?

"Well, she's got the top account on PicPerfect at our school," Delia said. "And she's the most popular girl."

"Well, I stand by what I said earlier," he said. "Plus, you're pretty awesome, if you ask me. You're so smart, people are willing to pay for you to go to their school."

His eyes locked onto hers, holding her gaze. Despite her humiliation, Delia started to feel slightly cheered up. Maybe she didn't need Harper and her friends to like her.

"Uh, thanks," she said, blushing.

She glanced at the storefront next to them. They

were standing in front of Replay Vintage. The dusty display window featured mannequins wearing vintage clothes that looked like they came from another era—because they did. None of it was remotely hip or trendy. It all looked slightly worn and frayed around the edges, too.

Delia caught sight of her tearstained face reflected in the dusty glass. Her hair was a frizzy mess. And that zit on her nose seemed to have doubled in size in the last hour. It looked angry and red.

"Ugh, I look hideous," Delia exclaimed, shrinking back from her own reflection. She tried to smooth down her hair.

Grant gave her a curious smile. "Actually, I think you look great right now," he said with a shake of his head. "Better than Harper and her plastic friends, in my opinion."

"Are you blind?" Delia said. "Can't you see all my imperfections? I'd give anything for a filter in real life."

"It's because you look like . . . you," he said simply. "The *real* you. And I happen to like you."

His words hung in the air, making Delia feel awkward.

She appreciated his support, but had a hard time believing it was true. Couldn't he see her?

"What're you doing here anyway?" she asked.

"Oh, this is the best place to buy used vinyl," he explained, fanning out his collection of newly purchased records.

All Delia's music was digital, streamed directly into her phone. She'd never even noticed a record section inside the store. "But don't you have MusicList? The streaming app? Why would you want to buy records anymore?"

"Vinyl still sounds the best," Grant explained. "Warmer and richer and more human. New and trendy doesn't always mean better, ya know. These albums are like sonic gold."

He flipped through the stack of records. Delia fixed her gaze on one, not recognizing the singer in the black-and-white photograph. He was older with white hair and kind, clear eyes.

"Who's that old guy?" she asked.

"Oh, I should introduce you. Delia, meet Frank Sinatra," Grant said. "One of my all-time faves."

"Frank *who*?" Delia said. "Is he related to Frank Ocean?"

Grant chuckled. "Uh . . . you could say Sinatra influenced him. So, in a sense, they're *musically* related. Hey, you should come over sometime and listen to Ol' Blue Eyes."

"'Ol' Blue Eyes'?" she repeated with a frown.

"Yup, I'll fire up my turntable for you."

"'Turntable'?" she repeated, feeling like a parrot.

"Right—it's another term for a record player," Grant said with a chuckle. "You've got every social media app, but you've never listened to an actual record or heard of Sinatra?"

"Guess not . . . but sounds like fun," she added, even though she wasn't sure that it actually did.

Grant glanced at his watch. "Hey, I gotta go to jazz band practice. But slow down, okay? I might not be here next time to cushion your fall with my vinyl."

She watched him back down the alley with his collection of used records and a shy smile on his lips. He waved once, then vanished around the corner.

Delia smiled to herself. She'd never met anyone like

Grant before. He was different from all her friends. Every kid she knew was obsessed with PicPerfect and social media, not to mention brands and fashion. She wasn't sure what it meant—or what to make of it. Only that she kind of liked it.

8
REPLAY VINTAGE

The bell jangled as Delia pushed open the doors to Replay Vintage. Her eyes swept over the store, making her cringe. Dust swirled in the air, catching the light. She inhaled the stench of mothballs, mildew, and decay—and probably other things she didn't want to imagine.

The shopkeeper looked up from the register, one of those antique ones with real buttons. She had short white hair dyed with hot-pink streaks, making her look both old and young at the same time. She also wore vintage clothes and sported a pair of thick black-rimmed glasses that made her look super hip in an alternative sort of way.

When she saw Delia, she broke into a warm smile.

"Well, dear, hello there," she said. "Let me know if you need any help."

"Uh, I'm looking for the coats," Delia said, feeling self-conscious. This was the *last* place where she wanted to be shopping.

"Oh yes, it's getting colder," the shopkeeper said with a warm smile. "Back-left corner. We've got quite a fine collection. They'll keep ya warm."

Delia headed for the back corner, passing by the used kitchenware, vintage glasses, and bins of dog-eared books turning brown from age. The store was packed floor-to-ceiling with shelves and racks stuffed with unwanted things. All this junk that somebody got rid of.

She imagined their owners selling it here for a little extra cash, or simply depositing it in the donation bins out front, happy to be rid of it.

Whose lives had these objects been discarded from? What was their story?

It was sort of fascinating, but also . . . gross. Delia wanted *new* things, not used ones. She started flipping through the coats crammed onto the racks, searching for something that might pass as fashionable. Or at least, not hideous. The tiniest part of her held out hope that she might even stumble upon a rare designer find. Something Harper couldn't tease her about.

Her mission was futile.

Every coat was puffy and ugly—in short, practical, like her mom wanted her to buy. Was it her imagination, or was each coat uglier than the one that came before it? Nothing even remotely designer appeared on these racks, like the coats that the mannequins modeled in the glam storefronts on Michigan Avenue, let alone something from House of De Vil.

Of course not, Delia thought. Nobody who owned that stuff wanted to get rid of it. These were things that nobody wanted, left here so some poor girl like her could find them.

If being taunted for her faux boots wasn't bad enough, wait until she showed up at school in one of these monstrosities. *I wouldn't be caught dead in that coat,* she imagined Harper saying, making her wince and con-template what illnesses she could fake to get out of school tomorrow.

Measles. Mumps. Malaria.

BE CAREFUL WHAT YOU WISH FUR

All the scary *M*-ones flashed through her head, though she wasn't sure of the exact symptoms of any of them. But her mom would never fall for it. She had incredible fake-sickness radar. She was basically a human lie detector. Delia felt sorry for any witnesses that would have to be interrogated by her mother on the witness stand one day, once she graduated and became an attorney. They didn't stand a chance.

Delia pulled a puffy coat off the rack, checking the tag. It was used, but at least it had a decent name brand from an outdoor company—not that it qualified as high fashion. And the price came in just under her gift card amount.

She turned to head toward the register, when suddenly she bumped into a mannequin shoved in the back of the store. The expressionless plastic face glared at her with empty eyes.

Delia jumped back in alarm.

But it was just a mannequin. It wasn't alive. It couldn't hurt her.

"I'd like to buy this coat," Delia said, sliding the coat onto the counter, along with the gift card from her mother. "And I'd like to donate my old one." Her mother had reminded her before school to do so.

The shopkeeper scooped the "new" coat up, feeling how soft it was. "Oh, what a beautiful coat," she said in admiration. "Hard to believe somebody didn't want it. But I guess their loss is your gain."

Delia felt a rush of humiliation. The coat was ugly. It wasn't what she wanted. She remembered all the glamorous displays on Michigan Avenue, desperately wishing she could afford something from House of De Vil. Or basically any other store on the street.

But that was impossible.

"Wow, and just under your gift card amount," the shopkeeper said obliviously, beaming at Delia. She rang it up. "Guess it must be your lucky day."

"Yes, I'm so lucky," Delia grumbled.

"Are you friends with that boy Grant?" the shopkeeper asked. "Saw you out front with him. He's in here 'bout every week asking if any new vinyl came in. He practically keeps my little shop in business, I swear."

"Uh, yeah . . . he's pretty cool," Delia managed. "We go to school together."

"He's a good guy. I'm glad you're friends with him," the shopkeeper said. "He's been shopping here since he was a kid."

She slid the coat along with a receipt into a Replay Vintage paper bag, then handed Delia a handful of loose change.

"There's the difference," the shopkeeper said. "Stay warm out there. Gonna be a tough winter, I hear. Forecasts are calling for a blizzard later this week."

"Thank you. I will."

Delia accepted the bag, then walked out of the store, feeling defeated. If her boots had gotten her teased, this ugly puffy coat wasn't going to help matters. In fact, it would probably make them worse. Harper's dare to show up in House of De Vil was still fresh in her mind. The walk to the door seemed to take forever, even though it was only a few seconds. Delia put her hand on the doorknob, then glanced back into the store, toward the mannequin she'd bumped into. The mannequin's eyes seemed to lock onto her. Its blank stare sent a shudder up her spine.

Delia ducked out into the cold. The sun was setting fast, casting the alley into darkness. Her breath puffed out, freezing in the air. She pulled on her new coat and immediately felt warmer, but then she frowned when she caught her reflection in the window. It looked hideous, shaping her body into a fluffy blob. She turned toward the street, but then hesitated. The last thing she wanted was to run into Harper and her friends again on the way back, carrying the Replay Vintage bag and wearing this ugly thing.

Instead of tramping down Michigan Avenue, Delia cut through the back alleys that wound behind the designer shops. She passed behind the House of De Vil store, marked by a small sign above the delivery door out back. Then she saw something out of the corner of her eye that made her freeze. She skidded to a halt, kicking up gravel.

Her eyes widened.

It couldn't be.

Hanging on a lone mannequin in the alley right next to the dumpster was a coat. And not just any coat—it looked like the House of De Vil black-and-white color block faux-fur coat. The famous, iconic one worn by the mysterious designer who had founded the fashion line.

But that was impossible. According to the lore that she'd read on their profile page, only one coat was ever made, making it priceless beyond all measure. The color block coat in the window out front was longer and cut differently from the iconic one. But this . . . this looked just like the original.

It had to be a fake. Maybe they were starting to produce copies of the iconic coat?

Delia glanced around to make sure nobody was watching. But the alley was strangely deserted. She approached the mannequin and peeled the coat back from the neck. As soon as her hand brushed the collar, she felt how incredibly soft it was, like nothing she'd ever felt before. Her heart pounded as she checked the label by the neckline.

HOUSE OF DE VIL
CRUELLA COAT

The words stared back at her. The label was even stitched from fine golden thread, making everything about the coat scream elegance and glamour and high fashion.

This was *the* #CruellaCoat.

How could something this rare and precious have ended up in the alley? Were they planning to throw it out? Why was it here next to the dumpster?

With her heart racing, and even though she knew it was wrong, Delia peeled the coat all the way off the mannequin, stripping it from the stiff plastic arms. She just wanted to feel what it was like to wear something like this for once. That was all.

I'll put it right back, she promised herself.

She slipped out of the puffer coat and draped it over the mannequin. Then she slid her arms through the Cruella Coat's sleeves, pulling it over her shoulders. The coat seemed to settle in place, gripping her body like it belonged to her already.

It's like it was made for me, Delia thought, in awe that it fit her so perfectly.

She spun around in the alley. As the coat swirled around her body, she found herself falling in love with it. She knew she should put it back. Someone could walk out of the back door of the store or down the alley and catch her at any moment.

But she simply couldn't do it.

It was too perfect. It was like everything she'd ever dreamed of.

But there was more to it. Harper's dare to show up at school tomorrow in House of De Vil echoed through her head. Well, now she could show them all. This was exactly what she needed to impress Harper and fit in at her new school. Not to mention, it was perfect for picture day, which was only a few days away. She could always return it later, right?

Plus, they left it out here by the dumpster. It was practically like it had been abandoned. Even like they were going to throw it out. At least, that's what she told herself. She was good at putting together convincing arguments, a useful skill she had learned from her mother. She slid the puffer coat—the one that she'd purchased from Replay Vintage—over the mannequin's arms. She was just swapping the coats out. If one of these two coats was being thrown away, it should be that one.

Her heart thudded in her chest. She knew it was wrong to take the coat without paying for it, even if they left it out in the alley like trash. Technically, she was stealing from them.

But she *needed* this coat.

It's not like she was doing it for a bad reason, right? Surely, they'd understand. Despite her sound reasoning, guilt sloshed in her gut. Quickly, before she could change her mind, she started down the alley away from the store. It was getting darker and hard to see. Mrs. Smith would worry if she didn't turn up at home soon.

A cackling laugh rang out behind her. Delia froze.

Slowly, she turned around toward the back of the store. It was almost closing time, and all the shops were shutting down for the day. The alley was deserted, except for the mannequin wearing the puffer coat over by the dumpster. She was just convincing herself she'd imagined it, when the laugh sounded again, louder this time, making Delia flinch. It seemed to be emanating from the mannequin's plastic face, even though the lips remained frozen. The mannequin's blank eyes seemed to bore into her as it laughed and laughed and laughed.

Without thinking, Delia turned and fled down the

alley, clutching the Cruella Coat close to her chest. The soft coat encased her body. She knew that taking the garment was wrong—terribly wrong. That was probably why she'd imagined that eerie laughter. Not to mention, it was getting dark and harder to see. Her eyes were probably playing tricks on her. But even so, guilt mixed with fear churned in her gut. She should go back and return it. She had to.

But instead, she clutched the coat even tighter, melting away her guilt. As she ran down the alley heading for the train station, she was certain of one thing:

She needed this coat.

9
SPOTTED

"**H**ow could you?" **Delia's** mother exclaimed the second Delia stepped through the front door wearing the stolen coat. "That coat isn't made for snow! It's completely useless. A waste of money!"

"You said get a coat," Delia sniped in her best teen voice. "So I got a coat."

She sashayed into the living room, brushing past her mother. Delia felt like a totally new person in the Cruella Coat. She even walked differently—like she was strutting down a runway. On the way home on the train, Delia had snapped a few selfies and they'd come out perfect.

Her skin looked flawless, her hair tamed, cascading

in loose waves. And she hadn't done a single thing to fix herself up. All she'd done was shed her old coat like shedding an old skin—and slip into the Cruella Coat.

It was like the garment had magic powers. But of course, that was impossible.

Delia tried to ignore her mother's rant. The coat was everything she needed to make everything right tomorrow at school, not to mention boost her PicPerfect ranking. She ran her fingers over one sleeve, then the other, feeling the fine, downy faux fur. It really was softer than anything she'd ever touched. Well, anything other than the little puppies crawling in their pen.

Her mother glared at her. "I said a practical coat. That is not practical. I'm disappointed in you. You're returning it tomorrow! You know how tight our budget is!"

"You sound like you're stuck on repeat!" Delia shot back. "It's no wonder Dad left."

They stood facing each other, angry tears glistening in their eyes. "Delia!" her mother breathed.

"Mom, I'm so sorry," Delia started, seeing how much she'd hurt her mother. She knew how much her mom hated talking about her dad. Why had she even said that? "I didn't mean—"

But her mom stormed off, slamming her bedroom door. The house nearly vibrated from the force of it. Delia felt shocked. She was usually the one who threw the tantrums and slammed doors—not the other way around. Her mother was her rock. She always kept it together, no matter what. What was she doing storming off like that?

"Even adults have hard days sometimes," Mrs. Smith said, slipping up behind her. "Your mother means well, she's just under a lot of stress. Her boss is too demanding and hard on her."

Mrs. Smith handed Delia a mug of hot cocoa. She accepted it, feeling guilty. She sat down on the sofa, being careful not to drip onto her new coat, the magic of which seemed to have dissipated. Even the hot chocolate didn't make her feel better.

"It's because of that stupid job that she got me into this snooty school," Delia said, her voice thick. "And I hate it there. All the girls are mean to me. They call me . . . charity case."

Tears coursed down her cheeks. She couldn't help it. Mrs. Smith stiffened up. She went over to the pen, lowering her hand into it so the puppies could lick her fingers. Delia did the same thing.

"There's nothing wrong with accepting charity," Mrs. Smith said with a warm smile. "It means people care for you. That's a wonderful thing in my book. Don't let those mean girls tell you otherwise. You got into that school because you're smart. And one day, you'll see that you're better than them."

"I guess you're right," Delia said, even though she didn't fully believe it.

She pulled Radar into her lap. He snuggled into her arms, sleepy. The puppies had been abandoned shortly after birth, just like Delia and her mom had been abandoned by her dad. They had that in common. Yet, the puppies were thriving, getting more spots every day.

Why couldn't she thrive, too?

"That little one almost didn't make it," Mrs. Smith said. "The rescue told me. He's the runt. They had to bottle-feed him to get him through. He's lucky, though. So many pets get abandoned."

"Not everyone finds a fairy godmother like you," Delia said, giving the old woman a warm smile.

She was talking about the puppies—but she was also talking about her and her mom. She tried to console herself by petting Radar, but then she noticed something peculiar.

His fur was so soft, just like her new coat.

Delia felt a chill but pushed it out of her mind. It was just a coincidence.

After Radar fell asleep in her lap, she settled him back in the pen with his siblings, then escaped to her room. She still felt unsettled after the fight with her mom, and a bit guilty for taking the coat, even though it had been abandoned in the alley. *I can still return it in a few days*, she promised herself. *After I prove Harper wrong and get through picture day.*

Besides, they had, like, a zillion coats inside the store. They probably wouldn't even notice this one was missing.

As she lay on her bed, rubbing her hands through the thick faux fur, a deep sense of belonging settled over her, like nothing she'd ever known before. She felt warm and safe. She rose from the bed, almost in a trance, and snapped a few quick selfies. She just seemed to know how to pose now with the coat gripping her limbs.

Click. Click. Click.

She checked her phone. In each pic, she looked amazing.

No, better than amazing. She looked . . . perfect.

Her skin glowed. Her hair was shiny and healthy-looking. And the coat draped over her body effortlessly, making her look glamorous. It was like a stylist had appeared out of thin air and done her up, then a filter had been layered over her, even though she'd done nothing to the selfies.

Still, she waited to post anything. She wanted the coat to be a surprise for Harper and her friends tomorrow. She'd wait to post until the morning, when they could see her wearing it in real life and verify it was true. Then Harper would *have* to take down that horrible post. She dragged her fingers through the soft faux fur, feeling sleep tug at her. An effortless, dreamy beauty sleep. This coat would make up for everything bad that had happened to her that day. No, scratch that.

Everything bad that had happened to her in her whole life.

* * *

Yap! Yap! Yap!

Delia woke to a terrible sound—the sound of puppies crying and shrieking. They sounded like screaming children. She bolted out of bed and ran for the kitchen, sprinting down the stairs.

But the pen was empty.

No puppies.

Something creaked behind her. Delia turned, and a mannequin lurched toward her from the shadows.

Delia screamed, cowering away from the creepy figure.

"No, don't hurt me!" Delia cried, scrambling backward. She glanced around in a panic. "What did you do with Radar and the other puppies?"

The mannequin's expressionless face rotated on its plastic neck, turning slowly, then locked onto Delia, peering at her with an empty, eerie gaze.

"Give the coat back, thief!" the mannequin said in a

robotic voice, even though its mouth remained frozen. *"You stole it! It doesn't belong to you!"*

"No, I'm sorry," Delia pleaded, backing away. "I'll give it back tomorrow. I didn't know it was your coat. I thought somebody was throwing it out. I promise, I'll return it—"

The mannequin lunged at her.

Delia struggled, trying to get away. But the plastic hands moved robotically and grabbed her by the shoulders. The mannequin stared down at her with its blank, empty eye sockets.

The lips didn't move, but a cackle emanated from the frozen plastic face.

Delia fought harder, wrenching her body back and forth and trying to break the mannequin's grip. But it was hopeless—she couldn't escape.

Suddenly a dark shadow rose up behind the mannequin, growing taller and taller and looming over her. The sounds of puppies barking grew frenzied.

Another voice with a lilting accent cut through the kitchen.

"Darling, don't you know that coat belongs to me?"

It came from the shadowy figure leering down at

her. The mannequin's grip tightened as she spoke, as if the voice was controlling the mannequin. Delia panicked, flailing about, trying to escape, but the mannequin wouldn't let go. The plastic hands squeezed and squeezed, the sharp fingers cutting into her shoulders. Delia saw stars dancing in her vision from the pain. She gasped for breath, but none would come. She was too panicked. Her lungs started to convulse.

The last thing she saw was a cruel, wicked smile.

Then everything went black.

10
VIRAL

"No, don't hurt the puppies!"

Delia woke from her nightmare with a scream. Her neck burned from trying to breathe. She could still feel the mannequin's plastic fingers locked around her shoulders. She remembered the puppies screaming, and finding their pen empty.

She bolted out of bed and down the stairs, taking them two at a time, and rushed into the kitchen in a panic.

"Radar . . ." she said, skidding across the room. "Are you okay?"

But the pen was empty.

The puppies were gone.

Someone took them! Delia thought.

Panicked, she was about to yell out for help, when her eyes landed on the bay window in the living room.

It was a rare, clear, sunny winter day that made it feel warmer than it actually was. Mrs. Smith was outside in the small, grassy backyard with the puppies. They were crawling around on the narrow strip of dead grass, which was dotted with puddles from the melting snow. The puppies played with each other, biting ears, noses, tails—basically whatever came within reach of their needle-sharp puppy teeth.

Mrs. Smith saw Delia in the kitchen and waved. A bright smile broke over her face as she beamed down at her miniature charges. She was in her happy place. Sunlight. Puppies. Helping needy souls. What more could she want?

Delia almost fainted with relief. *The puppies are okay.* Even little Radar was wrestling one of his bigger brothers, flopping around in an adorable way.

It was just a nightmare.

What had gotten into her?

But then everything came flooding back. She remembered how, in her dream, the mannequin leapt out of the shadows at her and called her a thief.

And that was exactly what she was.

A surge of guilt welled up inside her, making her throat constrict. That's probably what had triggered the nightmare—her guilt over taking the coat. She climbed out of bed, realizing that she'd fallen asleep wearing the thing. She rubbed the sleep from her eyes and peered at the coat in the mirror. Instantly, a deep feeling of possessiveness washed through her.

Compared to her appearance over the previous two days—with the zombie zit on her nose and frizzy hair—she looked flawless this morning. The monster zit had magically vanished and her skin was perfection. It looked like a filter had been layered over her reflection, but that was impossible.

This was real life.

It had to be the coat, she realized with a start. Maybe there really was something magical about it. And if that were the case, how could she ever give it up?

But then she remembered her fight with her mom

the night before and the nightmare she'd just suffered through. How could she *not* take the coat back?

Delia stared into her own eyes in the mirror. A day or two. That was all she needed. Then she could return it to the store.

In the meantime, she needed to show up at school and prove Harper and her friends wrong. She had to show them that she could wear House of De Vil and pull it off. All she needed was for Harper to take down the horrible post about her. Then, maybe, she'd even change her mind about Delia and want to be friends.

Buoyed by that thought, Delia stripped the coat off to change her clothes and get ready for school, draping it carefully across her bed. She hated not having the coat on for even a few short minutes. She kept glancing at it to make sure it was real and still there on the bed.

That it wasn't something she'd imagined.

Ping.

Ready to post to PicPerfect?
Don't let your ranking slide!

This time, Delia was actually excited by the alert on her phone. She slipped back into the Cruella Coat and spun around. Stretching her arm overhead, she snapped a few quick selfies in different poses, her head thrust back, her hair falling over her shoulders.

Click. Click. Click.

Then she flipped through the pics on her phone. The Cruella Coat made her look more glamorous with its color block pattern and beautiful tailoring. It hugged her body in all the right places, looking both warm and sumptuous, yet sleek and fashionable at the same time.

But it was more than the coat.

Every selfie she took came out flawless, even without using any filters or doing any corrections. She compared them to her prior selfies, all posted in her feed, from before she'd discovered the coat. She couldn't believe how different she looked in the new ones. She almost didn't recognize herself. But it was her—just a more perfect version of her.

Usually, Delia hated every single selfie she snapped. They never seemed to come out right. She could always pick out flaws in her appearance. But not today. It was true. The coat had some sort of magical powers.

This was what she had always dreamed about. This coat was the answer to all her prayers. She quickly posted a collage of selfies to PicPerfect without filters and tagged them.

#HouseofDeVil #nofilter #selfie

The second she hit POST, she felt a secret thrill, imagining what people would say. She clutched her phone as she waited for her PicPerfect post to go live, but before she could see it, her mom yelled at her to get ready for school.

"Coming!" Delia called out in a cheerful voice. For the first time all week, Delia was actually excited to go to her new school. She couldn't wait for Harper to see her wearing the Cruella Coat—to prove her and the Glam Posse wrong. Not to mention Aaliyah and Zoe. They would so regret hearting Harper's awful, embarrassing post.

Delia sashayed into the kitchen wearing the coat. She could feel a smile stretching her lips. She was even . . .

humming. This was very unlike her, but she couldn't hide her good mood.

Her mother looked up from her coffee in surprise.

"Well, someone's in a good mood today," she said, looking Delia up and down. Delia stood there in the coat. She cringed for a second, expecting another fight. Or for her mother to demand that she return it again, which was the last thing Delia wanted to do at that moment.

"Listen, Mom, I'm sorry about last night . . ." Delia started.

But then to her surprise, her mom gave her an approving nod.

"I have to admit, that coat suits you," Mom said. "Maybe I was wrong about it. It does look awfully warm and stylish. Maybe I should get one, too."

Delia's mouth dropped open in shock. Her mother almost *never* admitted when she was wrong, even when it was obvious. Another reason she would probably make a great attorney.

"I completely agree," Mrs. Smith said from the sofa in the living room. She caught Delia's eye and winked conspiratorially. Clearly, she'd been working on her mother to change her mind about the coat.

Delia grinned, pulling the coat tighter around her and stroking the soft faux fur. She glanced at the puppies in their pen and realized she was growing up and getting her own metaphorical spots now, too. This coat was changing everything. It was making her life better in ways that were more than just purely fashion-related. She couldn't fully explain it.

All she knew was this was going to be the best day ever.

* * *

The second Delia stepped into Gilded Crest Academy wearing her new coat, students flocked over to her like she was famous. She strutted down the hallway, the coat swishing luxuriously around her ankles. She felt like a celeb. Or an influencer.

Yeah, there was no way she was returning this coat. At least, not yet. Harper met Delia's eyes, then approached with Charlotte and Ella on her heels. They all wore their

House of De Vil boots as they clomped toward her down the hall. The hallway grew hushed, but Delia stood her ground. She placed her hands on her hips, feeling the soft faux fur of the coat. It gave her the confidence to face them.

Harper came to a halt right in front of her. Delia braced herself as the mean girl gave her a sharp up-and-down look, then cocked her eyebrow.

"Did you check your PicPerfect account recently?" Harper said.

"Uh, why? Did you see my morning post?" Delia said, twirling her hair around her finger and trying to sound nonchalant.

"Did I see it?" Harper said. "Uh, like, the whole world saw it."

"Wait, what do you mean?" Delia said in surprise. In the rush to get to school, she hadn't checked her phone since she got off the train. Sure, her morning selfie had been racking up plenty of hearts from some Gilded Crest kids. Even Aaliyah and Zoe had sent her hearts. Maybe she would forgive them for liking Harper's post yesterday. Maybe.

"Your post, like, totally went viral," Harper said. "And everyone is majorly hearting it!"

"Yeah, just a few minutes ago," Charlotte added with an excited squeal. "A bunch of people started sharing it and it was trending and then . . . *boom*. It's everywhere suddenly."

"You're practically like an influencer now!" Ella chimed in.

The Glam Posse nodded excitedly, looking at her like she was a superstar.

"It did . . . what?" Delia said, unable to believe it. She pulled out her phone and checked the comments on her post. Sure enough, hearts spilled down the feed, pushing her post to the top of the ranks. Not even one devil face appeared. The only accounts ranked higher at her school were . . . the Glam Posse. She couldn't believe her eyes. All her wishes were coming true.

Harper studied Delia's coat in awe.

"Gotta admit it, I didn't think you'd really pull it off," Harper said. "After your post, I had to see it for myself. I thought it would be another fake. But look at that coat!"

"I . . . Yeah . . . I know, right?" Delia stammered, still reeling from the shock.

"Like I almost died of FOMO when I saw your post," Charlotte added, her long, dark hair swishing around her shoulders. She pursed her lips approvingly.

"And it looks like an actual Cruella Coat!" Ella chirped up, studying the distinctive black-and-white pattern. "They're super rare and, like, impossible to get."

"Like, *super* rare," Harper added. "I heard there was only *one* made."

"Well, I don't know about that," Delia said, trying to sound chill. "But I know I'm super lucky to have this one."

"Look, I'm sorry I doubted you," Harper said, looking genuinely apologetic. "I guess you were just trying to play it cool your first couple of days here."

"Uh, thanks," Delia said. "And yeah, that's exactly right."

Harper looped her arm through Delia's, leading her down the hall. Charlotte and Ella trailed behind them. Other students stopped to stare as they passed by. They'd all seen her post by now. She could hear them whispering.

"Wow, look, it's her!"

"That coat is gorgeous!"

"So where did you get it?" Harper asked, pulling Delia close and whispering in her ear. Her fingers stroked the faux-fur sleeve. "You've gotta hook me up. I've been on the House of De Vil waiting list for a coat forever. And you got the *color block* one. You can't even order that one!"

The Glam Posse stared at her excitedly. Harper met her gaze and lowered her voice.

"You gotta tell me your little secret . . . how did you find it?" she cooed.

"Uh . . . I promised I wouldn't tell," Delia said. Her throat went dry. She couldn't confess to Harper she stole it. Or, well, lifted it from the garbage. Sort of.

An irritated look crossed Harper's face, but it was gone as fast as it appeared.

"Okay, well stick with us," Harper said with a smile. "You belong in the Glam Posse."

A thrill went through Delia's chest. *The most popular girls in school want to be my friends.* She knew it was superficial to care about things like PicPerfect rankings and popularity, but she couldn't help it. Plus, she needed to make friends at her new school, right? Might as well be the Glam Posse.

They continued down the hall, as all the students parted to let them pass. Delia had to admit, being popular again felt great. And this was even better than her old school. They strutted to class, she and Harper arm in arm, with Charlotte and Ella close behind. Her phone kept pinging as more and more hearts poured onto her post. The selfie kept getting more popular.

Everything was going better than ever. "Wait, let's take a selfie," Harper squealed. "Like, together, okay?"

"Really, you want to take one with me?" Delia said, stunned.

"Of course, you doof," Harper said with a wink. "And if we tag each other, it will boost both our PicPerfect rankings. It's, like, a win-win scenario."

Before Delia could object, Harper whipped out her phone and cocked her head, posing with Delia.

Click. Click. Click.

She snapped a bunch of selfies. Delia posed, feeling glamorous with her new, trendy friend and high-fashion coat. Every selfie came out perfect.

She couldn't believe how different today was from the day before. She had popular friends. She had a viral PicPerfect selfie. She was fitting in at her new school. Even her mother seemed to like her new coat now, and wasn't mad at her anymore. Could her life be any more perfect?

But then she locked eyes with Grant, who was standing across the hallway. He just shook his head in dismay and turned away.

"Hey, wait," Delia called, rushing over to him. But he didn't stop.

"I thought you were different," he said with a frown when she caught up to him. "But I barely recognize you. You're just like them."

"No, it's just nice to have friends again," she said. "You don't know what it's like changing schools. I'm the same person you met that first day."

"Actually, I do know what that's like. You think Harper's your real friend?" he replied, glancing over at the girls. "Good luck with that. She's just using you. They all are."

"What do you mean?" Delia said.

But he didn't respond. He just slid his earbuds back in,

turned up his beats, and headed for class. Delia's stomach flipped, but then Harper whispered to her.

"Who cares about that loser?" she said, glaring at Grant's back. "He's a scholarship kid. Did you know that?"

Delia swallowed hard against the bad feeling in her stomach.

"Oh, right," she agreed. "He's a . . . loser. Who needs him, right?"

But what she was really thinking was *I'm a scholarship kid, too.* Had Harper forgotten?

Suddenly her phone pinged, making Harper shriek in excitement. "OMG, look at all the hearts on our selfie."

"Wow, we're the two top-ranked accounts at Gilded Crest," Delia said.

She couldn't believe her eyes. Thanks to her new coat and selfie with Harper, her account had soared to the number-one slot. She was even ranked higher than Harper. All the hearts and new followers pouring into her phone made her whole body tingle with excitement.

"Look, we're almost PicPerfect famous!" Harper said. "Which is, like, better than normal famous. We're basically celebs at our school now."

"You mean like influencers?" Delia said, meeting Harper's gaze.

"Exactly," Harper said, eyes wide. "Stick with me, and we can stay at the top. How does that sound?"

"It sounds . . . amazing," Delia said as Harper led her to class.

Without a doubt, this was already shaping up to be the best day of her life. She stroked the soft sleeve of her Cruella Coat, butterflies dancing in her stomach.

She would do whatever it took to stay at the top with Harper.

* * *

Sitting still and not checking her phone in class was . . . impossible.

Delia squirmed in her seat, twitching to check her PicPerfect ranking and how many hearts her posts were getting. She couldn't pay attention to the teacher, or focus on any of the lessons.

Finally she bolted out of her seat and grabbed the bathroom pass. She waited until she got into the bathroom to check her phone, which felt like an eternity.

BE CAREFUL WHAT YOU WISH FUR

With sweaty palms and a racing heart, she unlocked her phone and opened PicPerfect. Then she gasped in excitement at what she saw.

More and more hearts had continued coming in, keeping her ranking at the top for their school. And all because of a coat. Delia admired her reflection in the mirror, stroking the soft fur. This was all thanks to the House of De Vil. Their mysterious designer—if she was even a real person—was clearly some kind of genius.

Her phone pinged again, a new alert flashing on it. She checked the message.

PicPerfect Tip:
Keep posting new selfies to keep your
ranking high!

Oh no, she thought. She needed to snap a new selfie right away. She couldn't risk her ranking slipping, not now that she had the top slot at Gilded Crest. Just look at how fast her account had risen in the rankings. The truth was, it could fall just as fast, if not faster.

She aimed her phone at her face, tilting her neck, putting her hand on her hip.

Click.

She snapped a selfie. But then out of the corner of her eye, she saw something dart past the mirror. As if it were *inside* the mirror itself.

Delia paused. Her heart gave a little thump of warning.

She glanced around the bathroom, but she was the only one in there. She must have been seeing things. She was about to hit POST and upload her selfie when she saw it again.

Her eyes tilted up to the mirror—and met her own reflection. Then the strangest thing happened.

Her reflection grinned at her.

Delia gasped. Because *she* was not smiling. She was sure of it. Her face was rigid.

Fear shot through her like an electric current. Slowly, she backed away from the mirror. But her reflection didn't move in sync with her. It stayed right where it was.

"What? This isn't . . ."

The mouth of her reflection didn't move as she spoke.

It glared at her; then, as Delia stood frozen in silent terror, her reflection's lips did move. They mouthed one word:

Thief.

Delia fled from the bathroom, almost dropping her phone. Sweat beaded on her forehead.

Once she was back in the hallway, she felt a bit calmer. She was seeing things. That was the only possible explanation. Her guilt over taking the coat was probably making her see things that weren't there. Her reflection couldn't move on its own.

Maybe she should return the coat after all. She'd promised herself she'd take it back.

But then she reached out and stroked the coat, feeling that weird possessiveness again. The soft faux fur caressed her fingers. She needed the coat to fit in at school and keep her new friends and PicPerfect ranking. She had to take at least a few more selfies in it.

Plus, school picture day was on Monday. Another few days wouldn't make a difference, would it?

She caught sight of herself in the glass of a framed award of some kind, and something came over her.

"Forget it," she whispered to herself, almost fiercely.

She wasn't sure where that feeling came from, but she kind of liked it. "I'm keeping the coat. It's mine and I deserve it."

She couldn't let anything ruin the best day of her life, right?

11
SCHOOL
PICTURE DAY

Over the weekend, Delia slept with the coat draped over her like a second skin, not wanting to let it out of her sight. She woke up on Monday morning before her alarm, excited to get out of bed for school.

It's school picture day, she thought, unable to believe that realization made her happy. Usually, she dreaded picture day and agonized over how to do her hair and what outfit to wear.

But she knew that as long as she wore the Cruella Coat, all her pictures would come out perfect.

When she climbed out of bed, though, it was hard to lift the coat off of her. And her limbs felt tingly and stiff, almost like they didn't want to bend. She flexed her arms a few times and did some squats, and the sensation wore off.

That's strange.

Maybe she'd just slept weird. She slipped the coat on and peered in the mirror, twirling around and feeling the soft faux fur. She snapped a few selfies and posted them to PicPerfect, needing to keep her feed fresh with new content for her friends at school and her top ranking.

Click. Click. Click.

POST. POST. POST.

#MORNINGLOOK #RISEANDSHINE #NATURALLOOK
#HouseofDeVil #CruellaCoat

She watched as the hearts poured in—not a single red devil face in sight.

Harper hearted it, then Charlotte and Ella followed suit, and also her friends from her old school. Aaliyah and Zoe sent hearts. She still hadn't talked to them since they'd liked Harper's bullying post, even though she knew it didn't make sense not to forgive them. She'd forgiven Harper, and they'd become friends.

But that was part of it, too. Now that she had new friends at her new school—*glamorous* friends—she didn't need Zoe and Aaliyah so much anymore. When she switched schools, every other thought had been about how much she missed her old friends. Now it was more of an occasional afterthought, when their DMs pinged her phone. She hadn't returned the last few messages. She was just busy with her new school, she told herself. But she knew it was something else. Something deeper.

She scanned their latest messages, feeling a stab of guilt.

> **AALIYAH: Rad coat! You look so glam.**
> **How's that fancy prep school?**

> **ZOE: Wassup, D! We MISS you so much.**
> **School isn't the same without u**

Her mind flashed to Harper, and how they'd been inseparable at school yesterday, walking to class and lunch together arm in arm, snapping selfies all day. She'd also started to like Charlotte and Ella. All three girls had attended Gilded Crest since kindergarten. Occasionally, their inside jokes made Delia feel left out. And their life-styles sounded so exotic, with family vacations to places like Bali and the Maldives. But it was expected when switching schools that you'd have to adjust to different things. At least, that's what her mother had told her. She tried to hide it and play along, act like she totally belonged. Of course, she didn't mention that her little family didn't actually take vacations. Mom was always too busy with work and law school, not to mention their tight budget.

Ping. Ping. Ping.

Suddenly her phone rang with an incoming vid chat. It was from Aaliyah and Zoe, probably on their way to school. Her finger hovered over the ANSWER button.

But then a DM came in from Harper.

HARPER: OMG, school pic day!
R u wearing the coat?

Delia ignored the vid chat, hurrying to write Harper back. She didn't want to keep her waiting. Delia did feel slightly guilty, so she shot Aaliyah and Zoe back a quick DM.

> **DELIA: Busy with school pic day today!**
> **Chat later!**

I have new friends now.

She didn't have time to worry about her old ones. She had to get ready for school. She didn't want to be late, or miss her slot for getting her picture taken. It was going to be her best school picture yet.

* * *

Delia lined up with Harper and the Glam Posse in the auditorium to get their pictures taken for the yearbook, excitement welling in her chest.

"We're gonna look so cute," Harper said, fluffing her hair, teasing out the waves. She applied a layer of pink lip gloss, then passed it over to Delia.

Delia followed her example, layering it on. It tasted sweet, like roses. She handed it back to Harper, but then she caught Grant's eye. He was standing in the back of the line of students, with his hoodie over his shaggy hair and his earbuds in, bopping his head to the beat.

Their eyes met. He shot her a little lopsided smile. But then his eyes flicked over to Harper, and he looked away quickly. Wincing, she remembered what he said yesterday.

You think Harper's your real friend? . . . She's just using you. They all are.

She wanted to deny it, but then she remembered something else. Harper said taking selfies together would boost their rankings. But Delia already had claimed the top spot, thanks to her coat. What Harper and her friends really meant was it would boost *their* rankings.

But she decided not to think of it that way. Best friends always took selfies together. They did everything together, in fact. That's how it had been with Aaliyah and Zoe. They posted group selfies to PicPerfect all the time.

What did Grant know about having friends? He wasn't even on social media. He didn't care about brands or fashion. He listened to old records. Maybe Harper was right about him.

But then why did she feel so sad that he seemed upset with her now?

Delia reached the front of the line. But instead of her usual attack of nerves, she felt confident and glamorous. She adjusted the Cruella Coat, feeling the soft swish of velvet-lined faux fur around her hips. Then she strode forward, walking with a poised grace to her gait.

"Good luck," Harper squealed. "Knock 'em dead, diva."

Delia took her place in front of the backdrop, jutting her hip out and posing like the girls in the magazines. The photographer suddenly perked up when he saw her and aimed the camera.

"Nice coat," he said in a British accent. "Now give me a smile."

Flash. Flash. Flash.

He snapped several rapid-fire pictures of her. When he was done, he checked his camera and frowned. He called his assistant over and they talked heatedly, gesturing at the camera.

"Uh, what's wrong?" Delia asked, suddenly self-conscious.

All the kids in line were staring at her, including Harper and Charlotte and Ella. They looked confused, whispering among their little posse. Even Grant slid out his earbuds, watching her with concern etched on his face. They were all thinking the same thing.

What was taking so long?

Most of the kids were in and out of there in less than a minute. Delia started to sweat a little. For the first time, she felt how heavy the coat weighed on her shoulders. Somehow, despite the fact that it was a faux-fur coat, she'd never noticed its heft before.

"Hang on, just technical difficulties," the photographer said. "We're rebooting it. Let's try that again."

Then he snapped several more pics of her, the flash strobing at her. Delia tried several different poses this time, moving in rhythm with the camera. She wasn't sure how she knew to do that. It was almost like the coat took over and made her strike those poses.

Wow, I could get used to this, she thought, pursing her lips and smiling at the camera. But then the photographer lowered the lens and stared at the display in dismay.

"Uh, what's wrong?" Delia asked.

"I don't know," he said. "It's so strange. This has never happened before."

He approached Delia and showed her the pictures that he'd just snapped of her, flipping through them. She stared at them on the camera's display, then flinched back in alarm.

"What the—?" she exclaimed.

In every picture, her face looked blank and expressionless, even though she was sure that she had been smiling. Her lips still tingled from holding them in a wide smile for that long.

"Let's try one more time," he said, sounding a bit shaken. "Now *smile!*"

This time, Delia made sure to smile big and wide, until her lips ached and her cheeks hurt. She could feel sweat dripping down her neck. These *had* to work.

Flash. Flash. Flash.

But again, when they viewed the pictures, Delia's face looked vacant and lifeless. Her lips were frozen. Her eyes empty. She almost looked like . . . a plastic doll.

"Your camera . . . it must be broken . . ." she said, backing away in alarm.

"All the other pictures came out fine," said the

photographer, showing her the other portraits he'd snapped that day of her classmates. Each student smiled cheerfully, full of expression. Face after face. Smile after smile. Then—

Delia's blank, creepy stare in picture after picture.

All the kids were still gawking at her, wondering what the holdup was. She could hear their heated whispers.

What's wrong? Grant mouthed, catching her eye. *You okay?*

Delia wasn't okay. She was totally freaked out, but she didn't want Harper and her friends to know how hideous her school pictures were.

She needed them to like her, and that meant she had to look perfect.

"Want to try again?" the photographer said, sounding exasperated. He gestured to his assistant, then raised his camera. "Can you try to actually smile this time?"

But Delia knew that she *had* been smiling the whole time, just for some reason the camera didn't register it.

Suddenly she felt like crying. This wasn't how school picture day was supposed to go. Her heart started to race, and cold sweat broke out on her forehead. Harper was watching her closely with a frown on her face. She whispered to Charlotte and Ella, who giggled.

The photographer raised his camera, but Delia couldn't stand to take another terrible picture where her face looked frozen, like a deer in the headlights.

Or worse, some kind of plastic doll.

"Sorry . . ." she said, turning and bolting out of the auditorium.

She ran down the empty halls, but the coat felt like it was choking her. It squeezed her body like a tourniquet and made running harder. Her limbs fought to move inside its iron grip. She struggled against it and burst outside into the school parking lot.

Even though it was cold, the midday sun glared down at her, making her sweat even more in the heavy coat. Her breath came in short gasps. The coat clung to her, but instead of making her feel good, it felt heavy.

She struggled to understand what had happened back there. Why did her face come out blank, even though she was sure she was smiling in every pic?

Vrooooom.

Suddenly a bloodred antique car raced through the

school parking lot straight for her. The headlights were on full blast, making it impossible to see the driver's face. But she heard a strange cackling laugh, like the one from her nightmare. Or, if she was being honest with herself, the one from the alley on the day she'd taken the coat.

"Darling, you're not worthy of my couture!" a voice with a lilting accent yelled at her from the driver's-side window.

Delia tried to move out of the way, but the coat tightened and held her in place, almost like it wanted her to get run over. She couldn't move. The car accelerated even faster, the tires squealing on the asphalt and kicking up dust. Delia smelled the acrid burn of exhaust.

But she was frozen.

"No! Noooooo—"

She screamed as the car barreled right for her.

12
ROADKILL

The car raced toward Delia.

She stood frozen in place. The headlights blinded her. Her body wouldn't move. The coat held her tight, restricting her movement. The driver revved the engine, accelerating.

"Nooooo!" Delia screamed, unable to even raise her hands to protect her face—they were locked at her sides, encased in the coat and stuck in place. What was happening? *How* was it happening?

She braced herself for the impact, fully expecting that it would kill her, when suddenly someone slammed into her, pushing her out of the way. It was Grant. She was processing the fact that he'd saved her as they crashed to the pavement together, a tangle of arms and legs. The car sped past, nearly clipping Delia's boots. It left Delia and Grant lying there in a cloud of dust and debris.

The driver honked maniacally, then zoomed out of the parking lot, vanishing down the road with a squeal of rubber. Delia spotted the name of the car model on the back of the trunk: *Panther DeVille*.

She locked eyes with Grant. He was breathing hard and clutching his elbow. There was a hole in his hoodie and a scrape on his arm, but he looked okay otherwise.

"Wow, that was close," he said in a shaky voice.

"Um, yeah. You literally just saved my life."

"I guess," he said modestly. "Anyone would do the same." He shook his arm out and stood up, brushing himself off. Delia scrambled to her feet as well, noticing his hands were skinned and caked with gravel.

"Are you kidding? That was total superhero stuff! Thank you!"

Grant blushed. "It was pretty cool, wasn't it?"

Delia gave him a wan smile, feeling queasy suddenly.

"Hey, are you okay?" Grant asked.

"Ummm . . . I don't know." Her limbs were tingly from

being held in place, but they'd finally become unstuck. She didn't understand what had just happened. Had she frozen up in fear, or was it something more? It had felt as if the coat was holding her prisoner, keeping her from jumping out of the way.

But that was impossible.

"Maybe you should sit." Grant gestured at the curb along the sidewalk, and Delia sat down heavily. "Jeez, talk about major road rage," he said, looking in the direction the car had driven off. "We should report the driver. Did you see the plates?"

Delia shook her head, following his gaze.

"I couldn't see the driver either," she told him. "The headlights blinded me. But I did see the name of the car. It was a Panther DeVille. And it was red and looked kind of antique, too."

"Well, you should at least tell the school," he said. "You could've been killed."

"I have no idea why she wanted to run me over . . ." Delia started, but then she remembered the cackling laughter and what the driver had yelled at her.

"I thought you didn't see the driver."

"I didn't."

"So how do you know it was a she?" he asked.

Darling, you're not worthy of my couture!

Because she'd heard that voice. Could that really be why? Was whoever behind the wheel after her coat? But nobody knew that she'd taken the coat from the alley. She'd been completely alone when she'd done it. And even if someone somehow did see her, how would they know that she would be in the school parking lot at this specific time? Even Delia hadn't known that she would be out here.

Delia shuddered, despite the warmth of the coat. The driver had said it was "my couture." If this was actually the famous Cruella Coat, that meant it had once belonged to the mysterious designer herself. But nobody knew if she had even been a real person. Plus, even if she *was* a real person, she would be long dead.

None of this made any sense.

"Uh, what were you doing out here anyway?" Delia asked, choosing to ignore his last question.

"Well, you looked pretty upset after getting your picture taken," Grant said. "I saw you run out of the auditorium. So I decided to check on you. I didn't think it would be a superhero moment."

"Thank you," she said. "If you hadn't come after me, I'd be . . ." She trailed off.

Their eyes met, but then she looked away. This day had started out strange and just gotten stranger. First the numbness when she'd woken up, then her face looking blank and plastic in all her school photos, then the near accident and the fact that the coat had seemed to *want* her to get run over.

And had she *really* heard that voice shouting about her couture?

What if someone was really after her because of the coat? She could have been killed—and gotten Grant killed, too. She started to back away from him, feeling panicked. She didn't want to drag him further into this mess, not when it was her fault. She was the one who'd taken the coat. She would have to figure out what was happening on her own.

I don't want anyone else to get hurt.

"Look . . . Thanks for saving me . . ." Delia stammered. "But I've really gotta go."

It was the middle of the day, and she was technically skipping school, but she didn't care. She couldn't face Harper and her friends being excited about how great their pictures had come out, or having to explain what went wrong or why she'd run from the school. She had to get out of there.

She turned and fled down the road, running for the train station.

* * *

The train sped by the rooftops, zipping through the cityscape. Lulled by the *clickety-clack*, Delia watched the buildings pass by the window in a rush, as familiar to her as the backs of her hands. But something was still bugging her.

Climbing the stairs to the elevated platform had been harder than usual. Her muscles had felt heavy and her joints almost numb, and it wasn't from the cold wind hitting the platform. She'd felt something similar when she'd woken up that morning, but that had cleared up quickly. Was something wrong with her, though? Did she need to see a doctor?

Or was it . . . somehow . . . the coat?

Delia glanced down at her hands, nestled against the soft faux fur of the coat. They appeared smoother than normal. She curled and flexed her fingers, and they tingled ominously. Feeling a twinge of worry, she held both hands up to her face and peered closer.

Was it her imagination—or did her fingers look kind of . . . *plastic*?

Suddenly her phone pinged, startling her.

It was an alert from PicPerfect. Delia hadn't checked her profile since . . . when? Since before the car incident. She hadn't gone that long without clicking on PicPerfect in ages. She unlocked her phone.

Keep up your streak—post a selfie.

The alert message flashed at her. She felt panicked as she clicked on her profile. Had her ranking dropped?

Relief rushed through her when she saw that her top ranking at Gilded Crest was still intact. But it wouldn't stay that way if she didn't keep posting. Users had to keep posting selfies and giving their followers fresh content to stay on top. That was the number-one rule on PicPerfect.

Well, that and post #perfect selfies.

Automatically, without even thinking, she held her phone out and aimed the camera lens at her face, tilting her neck and smiling. Her arms felt a bit tingly, but nothing alarming. At least she could move them.

Click.

The selfie came out perfect. She was even smiling in it. Delia's heart instantly felt lighter. Clearly, the situation with the school pictures was just a crazy fluke—probably a technical glitch with the photographer's camera. Nothing more.

Delia layered in hashtags—#ElTrain #TrainSelfie #HouseofDeVil #NaturalLook—and hit POST. She watched as the selfie went live on the app. Heart emojis started to flood into the comments, and Delia felt a thrill each time a new one popped up.

But then something shifted. The selfie began to change, right in front of her eyes. White hair began to sprout out of one side of her head, while black hair sprouted out of the other.

Heart pounding, Delia refreshed the feed.

The hair was still there, just a bit longer. *Refresh.*

Her part moved to the center of her forehead, dividing the hair perfectly in half—one side black, one side white. *Refresh*. Her lips turned bright red.

"What the—?"

She hit REFRESH one more time. She couldn't seem to stop herself. This time her eyes looked odd. They looked almost as if they were swirling with strange yellow light.

Delia almost dropped her phone.

Suddenly little red devil emojis started to flood the comments and fill the screen, pushing her post down in the rankings. There were fewer and fewer hearts and more and more devils.

"No! *No!*" Delia cried aloud.

She tried to block the accounts that were posting the devils, but she couldn't stop them fast enough. For each account she unfriended, five more devils popped into the comments. She had too many followers, many from her viral post. The little red devil faces seemed to grin at her from her screen, as if mocking her hideous appearance.

And how could they not? She looked like some kind of horror-movie clown. Who was doing this to her picture? Had somebody hacked her account?

Suddenly her phone pinged with a new DM.

With shaky fingers, Delia clicked on the private message, hoping that it might provide some answers. But her stomach flipped when she saw the user's name on the account.

It was from—

The Devil Woman

The profile pic showed a red devil face. Delia gasped when she saw it. Quickly, she scanned the message. The words jumped out, making her heart thump against her chest.

Having fun with my coat, darling?

Suddenly a cackling laugh echoed through the train.

Heart in her throat, Delia glanced around the train car—but it was empty, aside from a few commuters with their heads buried in their phones. None of them were cackling at her. It was as if they hadn't even heard the laughter.

Where did it come from?

Her eyes darted back to her phone, and that red devil face staring back at her from the profile pic. How did this random user know about her coat?

A horrible mixture of guilt and terror crashed through Delia like a blast of bitter wind. Somebody who worked for the House of De Vil store must have seen her take it. Delia hadn't noticed any security cameras back there, but what if they were just hidden really well? Someone definitely could have caught her transgression on video and might now be using their knowledge of what she'd done to mess with her. She glanced down at the luxurious black-and-white coat draped over her body. Suddenly it didn't feel so great to be wearing it.

Delia had wanted the House of De Vil coat more than anything, but now she wished she could just get rid of it. All she wanted was for everything to go back to normal, even if it meant not being as popular on PicPerfect anymore. She remembered how she'd initially promised herself that she would return the coat after a few days. But then everything had been going so great, she had decided to keep it.

Clearly that had been a big mistake. Delia swallowed hard against the lump in her throat.

At the next stop, Delia sprang up from her seat and hopped off the train. She was close to the shopping district now. She would return the coat to House of De Vil and end this mess once and for all. Harper would probably never speak to her again, but she would just have to deal.

It was time to make this right.

Delia bounded down Michigan Avenue, passing the crowded House of De Vil flagship store on her way to the alley behind it. The store was, of course, packed with shoppers. She paused in front of the windows, suddenly getting the spine-tingling feeling that someone was watching her. She glanced across the street.

Idling at a metered spot was the red Panther DeVille.

Delia's blood went cold. Had the car followed her here? Was the driver stalking her?

Terrified, Delia cut around the corner to the back alley where she had first discovered the coat. She had to get rid of it, and now. A row of mannequins was lined up by the dumpster. They were each posed in glam House of De Vil clothes and boots. Clearly this was where they staged the mannequins, dressing them for the display booths and windows. Maybe that was why the coat had been out in the alley—because they were getting it ready for the store's display.

Delia gulped. It was official. The coat wasn't abandoned. She had stolen it.

Delia glanced around, but there was no one in sight. The alley was deserted. She approached the last mannequin in the row. This one hadn't been dressed yet. Its naked plastic body looked creepy next to the fully dressed ones.

Delia hesitated for a moment, feeling strangely possessive of the coat, and ran her fingers through the soft faux fur. Almost like it had a mind of its own, the coat gripped her limbs tighter, like it didn't want her to get rid of it. Her arms started to feel tingly again. Suddenly she remembered what had brought her back here.

I have to return it, she told herself forcefully. *It's the right thing to do.*

And if it made all these creepy things stop happening to her, all the better. Before she could second-guess herself, Delia stripped off the coat, struggling to peel it from her limbs. The coat clung to her like a second skin.

It didn't want to let her go.

Finally, with a desperate grunt of effort, she tore off the coat, panting for breath. She stared at the garment in horror. Why was it so hard to take it off? Then she dug through her bag for paper and a pen and scribbled out a quick apology note:

Sorry I took the coat.

She stuck the note in the pocket of the coat and carefully draped it over the mannequin.

"Good riddance," Delia whispered, and turned away.

Instantly, she felt better—lighter and freer—without the heavy coat weighing her down and restricting her movements. Delia flexed her arms, bending her elbows. They no longer felt tingly. She could move freely again. Also, that strange plastic sheen on her skin was gone.

A cold wind hit her, whipping off the lake. Delia shivered. She wrapped her arms around herself and walked briskly up the alley, needing to get home before she froze to death. The sun would set soon, making it worse.

Vroom.

Delia glanced around, feeling a stab of fear. But there were no cars in the alley. That was weird. She kept walking, picking up her pace —

Vroom.

Delia froze. Two headlights snapped on in front of her, almost blinding her. She narrowed her eyes, trying to make out the car, even though she was sure she knew what she would see. And she was right. It was the red Panther DeVille.

Delia squinted over the glare of the headlights. She could just make out the silhouette of a woman with red lipstick and spiky hair.

Suddenly a cackling laugh emanated from the car. It echoed down the alley.

How had the car gotten back here? Had it followed her down the alley?

Delia backed away in terror. "I'm sorry. . . . I gave your coat back," she shouted to the driver, struggling to be heard over the engine's roar. "Please! Please leave me alone—"

Vroom. Vroom. Vroom.

The woman was revving the engine again and again, taunting her, purposely drowning out her voice.

Delia had to run. But there was nowhere to go. The alley was just wide enough for one vehicle to get through at a time. If the driver floored the gas, Delia was toast.

Then the driver clicked on the brights. Delia's eyes stung horribly and she squeezed them shut, bending at the waist against the pain. The car was about to come at her. She could feel it. There was nothing she could do. Even without the coat weighing her down, she was frozen in fear.

But then, suddenly, silence. Carefully, Delia opened her eyes. The car was gone.

The alley was dark.

She was the only person in sight.

But no. That was impossible. Cars couldn't just disappear like that.

Another blast of cold wind hit Delia square in the

chest, knocking the air out of her lungs and snapping her to attention. Delia couldn't explain what had just happened, but she was not wasting another second. She turned and bolted down Michigan Avenue, dodging the shoppers laden with hefty designer bags, and careened down the sidewalk toward the train.

I gave the coat back, she thought in desperation as she climbed the steps to the El. *Just please leave me alone.*

The only answer was the cold wind hitting the elevated platform with a mournful *whoosh*. Standing there, shivering as she waited for the train, Delia was scared and lost and unsure. When she'd found the coat, it had made her feel like she was beautiful and popular. Tomorrow, everything would be different. But how?

Without the coat, who was she?

13
FASHIONISTA

Delia arrived at her stop, still relieved to be rid of the coat despite the deep chill that had set into her limbs from the subzero wind blasting the elevated train platform.

But strangely, as she wound her way through her tree-lined Old Town neighborhood filled with brownstones, cutting home from the Brown Line stop, she found herself feeling emptier and emptier. The loss of the coat started to haunt her. It almost felt like she'd lost a limb. She couldn't believe how much she could miss something that wasn't even alive—and that she'd very much wanted to be free of.

What would happen to her PicPerfect ranking? And

what about her new friends at Gilded Crest when she showed up without the coat? Would Harper and the Glam Posse still like her? Would they even talk to her?

Not to mention, she'd also have to come up with some story for her mother to explain how she had lost her brand-new coat. She braced herself for a lecture about *taking better care of her things* and how *money doesn't grow on trees.*

Suddenly she wanted to go back for the coat.

But that was crazy.

That coat almost got me killed, she reminded herself with a shudder.

Looking fashionable was not worth dying for, no matter how many followers and likes she got on PicPerfect. So why did she feel so anxious? Why was she so convinced she *needed* to turn around and go back?

* * *

Delia finally arrived at her doorstep, but the door was flung open wide before she could even grab the knob.

A very irate Mrs. Smith greeted her. "What were you thinking running out in this weather without a coat? You're gonna catch a cold."

"Uh, how did you know I didn't have my coat?" Delia asked.

Mrs. Smith didn't answer. She just thrust a coat at her: *the House of De Vil coat*—the one Delia had just draped over a mannequin outside the store. Delia gasped and backed away in shock.

"Wh-where did you get that?" Delia said.

This could not be happening. How had the coat gotten back to her house? All the way from Michigan Avenue? And into Mrs. Smith's arms?

"I decided to let the pups run around the house a bit," Mrs. Smith said with a roll of her eyes. "Too cold to let the wee little ones outside. Little Radar ran into your room— and when I burst in, the coat was on your bed!"

"That coat . . . was on my bed?" Delia repeated, numb from shock.

"Young lady, what were you thinking?" Mrs. Smith said. "Look, I won't tell your mother—it'll be our little secret. But don't go running off without a coat, not this time of year. The last thing you need is to get sick and miss school, especially when you just started at Gilded Crest. You don't want to fall behind, do you?"

"Uh, right . . . I'm so sorry," Delia said, struggling to understand what was happening. It was like she couldn't get rid of the stupid coat. Like it was . . . haunting her.

Oblivious, Mrs. Smith shoved the coat at Delia, who struggled to grab hold of it. Then her landlady sashayed into the kitchen, where the puppies were yipping for their supper and climbing around in their pen.

"You're just lucky I caught little Radar," Mrs. Smith said. "He was squatting on the coat to . . . *you know what*. Last time I let them have free rein of my house." Mrs. Smith pulled the milk from the fridge. "You must be frozen, dear. Want some hot cocoa to warm you up?"

Delia forced a smile. "Yes, that would be great."

While Mrs. Smith busied herself making the cocoa, and the house filled with the warm, sweet, rich, buttery aroma of chocolate, Delia snuck out the back door with the coat.

The wind hit her full blast, but she didn't care. She stared at the coat in disgust.

"I'm done with you," she muttered to it. "Don't you dare come back again!"

With that, she stuffed it into their garbage bin, pushing it down and shutting the lid. *Thud.* Then she snuck back inside. Mrs. Smith soon reappeared from the kitchen, handing her a steaming mug of hot cocoa. Delia accepted it gratefully. It was already warming her up.

"Thanks so much! I'm gonna go do my homework," she said, grabbing her backpack and heading upstairs. "Busy day at school!"

It was just an excuse. She was simply exhausted from everything she'd been through that day. But when she returned to her room, thrusting open the door—

The coat was on her bed.

Delia gasped, tears instantly prickling her eyes. "No. That's impossible. . . ." But there was no denying it. The coat was somehow following her.

But how? Was she losing her mind?

Nobody else was home, besides her and Mrs. Smith

and the puppies. And she was pretty sure Radar hadn't dragged the coat out of the trash and up to her bed.

Why couldn't she get rid of it? Why did it keep coming back?

Her reflection caught her eye in the mirror. She turned, shocked at what she saw. Her face looked . . . plastic.

Delia tried to smile, straining to make her lips move and stretch her cheeks. But her expression remained . . . expressionless. Her lips wouldn't move. Her eyes looked dead.

Her reflection looked like a mannequin.

What was happening to her?

That's when it hit her. The strange account she had blocked on PicPerfect. The one with the mannequin profile picture. Delia whipped out her phone, not even bothering to check her ranking for once, and flipped through the blocked accounts. She zeroed in on the mannequin profile—"Fashion Addict." The creepy plastic face in the pic stared back at her.

With a deep breath, she clicked UNBLOCK.

A warning message flashed on her screen.

Are you sure you want to unblock this user?

It glared at her.

Delia didn't feel sure. But she clicked OKAY anyway.

The message exchange popped back up. She scanned the messages, reading the last one that the user sent to her before she blocked their account.

From Fashion Addict:
Beware of the Devil Woman.

Delia's heart beat faster as she stared at it. A cold sweat broke out over her body. But she forced herself to type a message back.

Who is she? And what do you mean?
What happened to your friend?

She hit RETURN, sending the DM, then collapsed into bed, keeping her eyes on the screen for a reply. But none came.

Before long, Delia's eyes grew heavy. This day had

been too much. She was so exhausted. Maybe if she just closed her eyes for a little while, she could face her homework—and whatever was going on with the coat.

Without even changing her clothes, Delia fell asleep. It was a restless sleep, filled with violent nightmares about mannequins and speeding cars and a cackling woman with horrible hair. Delia tossed and turned until a sound broke through.

Yip! Yip! Yip!

She bolted awake. It was the puppies.

Delia blinked at her dark room. The hot cocoa by her bedside remained untouched—it had turned to thick sludge. She was lying on top of the coat, fully clothed.

Yip! Yip! Yip!

The puppies were screaming for help. She jumped out of bed and stumbled into the hall, still foggy from sleep. The house was dark. It was late, but the night-light shone bright. Her legs felt tingly and a bit numb, but she didn't have time to worry about that right now.

The puppies sounded like they were in trouble.

Muddy paw prints marred the kitchen floorboards, and when she peered into the pen, the puppies were gone.

The pen was empty. Mud was splashed all over the kitchen. She could make out footprints from what looked like two large men's boots along with the tiny paw prints.

Suddenly a dark shadow rose up behind her. The hands with their long, sharp nails reached out and grabbed her. The razor-sharp claws dug into her flesh.

Delia thrashed about, trying to free herself from the hands. But it was no use. They squeezed tighter. The shadow's eyes lit up with crazy, swirling yellow light. They stared down at Delia.

A cackle cut through the house. Then a voice rang out.

"You let those filthy mongrels crawl all over *my* coat! How dare you?!"

14
PLASTIC GIRL

Delia woke up with a start, feeling like she was being strangled.

She tried to scream, but nothing came out. She clawed at her neck, gasping for breath, but her arms were heavy and creaky and she could barely move them. The coat was wrapped around her throat, suffocating her in her sleep.

"No, get off me!" she gasped, and finally tore the coat off her neck. She flung it to the ground, where it landed in a pile of faux fur. Her arms flopped down and hung limp in her lap.

Delia stared at the coat in horror. It was like she

couldn't get away from it, no matter how hard she tried. Not even in her sleep. How had it wound up wrapped around her neck?

It took a minute for her to catch her breath. Light was streaming in through her window. It was morning. Time for school. Snowflakes drifted down, powdering the streets. Her eyes darted to the coat. She'd have to wear it. It was the only coat she had. She'd donated her old coat to the thrift store and left the puffer coat that she bought with her gift card on the mannequin at House of De Vil.

If she left it at home, Mrs. Smith would find it and be angry. Or worse, it would just follow her to school. She shuddered, not wanting to put the coat on again, but feeling trapped.

Delia flipped her phone on. After yesterday's disastrous post, her PicPerfect ranking was way down.

Suddenly her phone buzzed with a new DM . . . from Fashion Addict. The mannequin account. The one that she'd unblocked yesterday before bed.

Her heart thudded harder as she clicked OPEN. Her eyes scanned the message.

BE CAREFUL WHAT YOU WISH FUR

From Fashion Addict:

Once upon a time, my best friend just wanted to be fashionable and popular. All she wanted in the world was a House of De Vil coat. I still don't know how my friend got the Cruella Coat. She would never tell me. She said it was a big secret.

At first, it was great. She loved the coat and almost never took it off. She even slept in it. Her skin started to look perfect. All her selfies came out flawless. Her ranking on PicPerfect soared . . . but then the coat started to change her.

Her skin looked plastic. Her limbs would barely move. They became stiff and rigid, so it was hard for her to walk. It got to the point where I could barely recognize my friend anymore. Eventually, she couldn't even leave her house.

Then one day she vanished—along with the coat. The police searched for her, but all they found were muddy boot prints leading through her front door.

I started messaging PicPerfect accounts that follow House of De Vil to warn them! Stay away from the Devil Woman! Her fashion line is cursed!

Delia stared at the message in shock, then quickly shut her phone. Her heart was hammering. Sweat broke out on her forehead. It was probably a hoax. Somebody playing a trick on her. Like an urban legend. Those were all over the internet.

She remembered Grant talking about how her friends on PicPerfect were really just strangers. You didn't know who they were in real life, nor could you trust them.

Delia hit BLOCK again, shunning the account so no more messages could come through. She struggled to steady her racing heart, but some details from the story were impossible to ignore.

She glanced down at her hands with their plastic sheen. She bent her elbows, but they felt tingly and stiff.

Above all, the detail about the muddy boot prints was super spooky. In her nightmare about the stolen puppies, she had seen muddy boot prints in her kitchen.

Was that some kind of sign?

"Delia! It's getting late! Are you ready for school?" her mother called up the stairs.

"Almost," Delia called back in a croaking voice. She had no choice. She quickly changed her clothes and slipped on the coat, feeling like it weighed a hundred pounds. She'd have to figure out a way to get rid of the coat for real this time. But how?

* * *

Delia arrived at Gilded Crest and scanned the hall for Harper and her Glam Posse. They were clustered by Harper's locker, twirling their hair and wearing their House of De Vil boots.

"Hey, Harper," Delia said, making a beeline for her, grateful for some normalcy. Talking to her friends would cheer her up. Maybe they could even help her figure out what to do about the coat.

"Uh, like, do we know you?" Harper said, giving her a strange look, like she didn't recognize her. She exchanged glances with Charlotte and Ella, who also squinted at Delia.

"Yeah, who are you again?" Ella said with a frown.

"Right, we don't talk to strangers," Charlotte added, whipping her hair around.

With a jolt, Delia remembered the story about the girl's friend and how the coat changed her appearance. *It got to the point where I could barely recognize my friend anymore.*

Was that what was happening to her?

"Hey, wait up!" Delia said, waving at the girls as they passed her by. "It's me . . . Delia? Don't you recognize me? We're friends! We even posted selfies on PicPerfect together?"

Harper's eyes struggled to focus on her, then they widened.

"Delia?" Harper said uncertainly. "Oh my gosh. You look so . . . different."

Delia breathed a sigh of relief. "Oh, thank you! Yes, it's me! It's this coat! It must be cursed or something.

It's somehow changing my appearance. I have to get rid of it—"

Harper frowned. "Get rid of it? What do you mean?"

"Yeah, what are you even talking about?" Ella said, stifling a snicker. "Why would you want to get rid of a House of De Vil original? I'd give anything to get my hands on a Cruella Coat!"

"Exactly! Why are you acting so bonkers?" Charlotte added with a smirk.

The Glam Posse burst out laughing.

"She thinks the coat is *cursed*. That's hilarious." Harper snickered. Her eyes fixed on Delia, then narrowed. "Maybe you're just not cool enough to pull off House of De Vil."

Delia felt her cheeks flame red hot. She had thought these were her friends. But now when she needed help, they were laughing at her. Suddenly she realized just how right Grant was about these girls. He said they were just using her for her PicPerfect ranking, and now that was abundantly clear.

Suddenly a wonderful, wicked idea struck Delia. She needed to get rid of the coat, didn't she?

"Maybe you're right, Harper. Maybe I'm not cool enough. But you clearly are. And if you want it so much, then you can have it!"

"Wait, what do you mean?" Harper said. "You're giving that coat away?"

"Yup." Delia nodded. "That's exactly what I'm doing."

She felt slightly off-kilter. Just a few days ago, Delia would have done anything to get a House of De Vil coat. Now all she wanted was to get rid of it. She was certain that the coat was cursed . . . but Harper was so awful. If anyone deserved a cursed coat, it was her.

"Great. Then hand it over," Harper said, calling her bluff.

She held out her arms. Relief washed over Delia. She was sure this would work. If she gave the coat to someone else, then it would stick to the new owner, and she'd be rid of it for sure. Delia gripped the sleeves, trying to shrug them off her shoulders, but the coat clung to her. It tightened around her body like a vise. The more she struggled, the tighter it cinched.

It didn't want to let her go.

Delia struggled with the coat, doing everything

she could think of to try to wrench it off her body, but it wouldn't release her. She ended up red-faced, out of breath, looking ridiculous . . . and still unable to take it off.

Harper and her friends watched the pitiful performance with wide, shocked eyes. Then they burst out laughing again.

"Wow, she really is bonkers!" Harper said. "Come on, girls. Let's get out of here!"

They marched off, leaving Delia sweating in her coat.

This was not good. Delia bolted for the bathroom, but her joints felt even more tingly and stiff now. She ended up half running and half hobbling. She burst into the bathroom and staggered up to the sinks, staring at her reflection in the mirror.

Her gasp filled the small room.

Her face didn't look like her face at all—it looked like a plastic doll face. Her skin was smooth and varnished. Her eyes looked wide and blank. Her lips were frozen in a pout.

No, not a plastic doll.

She looked like a mannequin.

Like the ones displayed in the fancy storefronts on Michigan Avenue. The coat hugged her body, mocking her. No wonder Harper and her friends hadn't recognized her at first.

She backed away from her reflection in a panic.

"You did this to me . . ." Delia whispered, tearing at the coat in horror.

But it clung to her. It still wouldn't come off. Her heart hammered against her rib cage. Her mind raced, trying to think of anyone who could help her.

Only one person leapt to mind.

Grant.

Delia rushed from the bathroom and scanned the hall. She spotted him by his locker. He had his old hoodie pulled up over his hair and was nodding to some beat that only he could hear.

She hurried up to him. "Grant . . . I'm so sorry . . . but I need your help," she stammered, having to force her stiff lips to even form the words. They came out raspy and thick.

He slid out his earbuds and frowned at her face.

"Uh, hello?" he said, blinking at her in confusion.

He didn't recognize her.

"It's me. . . . It's Delia. . . . Please say you know me!" she rasped in desperation, trying to force expression into her features. "Listen, I need your help. I don't know who else to turn to. . . ."

He studied her face, almost like he was struggling to see beneath her plastic skin. He tilted his head and peered deep into her eyes, then startled.

"Delia . . . what happened to you?" he exclaimed.

"Oh, thank you!" she gasped, hugging him before she could stop herself, her stiff limbs barely able to grip him. "You recognize me!"

"Yeah, but what happened?" he said in alarm. "You look kind of . . ."

She pulled back and met his eyes, feeling ashamed. She forced the word out.

"Plastic?"

15
CRUELLA DE VIL

Grant led Delia into his apartment after school, waving to his mom on the way in. She brightened when she saw him—and especially when her eyes landed on Delia. "Well, hello there!"

"Hey, Mom, this is Delia," Grant said. "My new friend from school."

"Very nice to meet you," Grant's mother said, wiping her hands on a dish towel as she stepped out of the kitchen. Something was burbling on the stove, and the delicious scent of it made Delia's stomach grumble. "He calls me Mom, of course. But you can call me Claudia."

"Nice to meet you, too!" Delia said, but then Claudia's

brow knit and Grant grabbed Delia's arm. It felt stiff and plastic in his grasp as he turned her away from his mother. Delia's heart caught as she realized he didn't want his mom to get too close a look at her. It must have been getting worse. She was turning more and more plastic by the second.

"Do you two want some snacks?" Claudia offered.

"Actually, we've got a lot of homework," Grant said. "We should probably just get started."

"Of course. I'll bring you something to eat in a bit. It'll help you focus," his mom said with a knowing smile. Her eyes landed on Delia's heavy faux-fur coat. "Do you want me to hang that up for you?" she asked.

Delia hesitated. As if sensing that she might try to remove it, the coat tightened around her torso, squeezing her. After the whole mortifying hallway struggle at school, she knew that she couldn't take it off, and didn't want his mother to witness her struggling with it.

"Uh, no thanks," she said quickly.

"She's always cold," Grant added with a forced chuckle. "We'll be in my room."

Grant quickly led Delia down the carpeted hall. His family lived in a modest but homey apartment in Old Town. It was one floor, unlike Delia's town house, and newer construction. But sunlight streamed through the many windows, giving it a cheery vibe.

Delia plopped down in Grant's desk chair and relaxed slightly. Something about Grant made her feel better. Maybe it was just having a friend. A *real* friend who didn't make fun of her on PicPerfect or drop her at the first sign of trouble.

Her eyes swept over his room. Vinyl-record covers were affixed to the walls. A fluorescent green lava lamp sat next to the bed on a little table. A laptop sat on the desk, with an old record player next to it. Stacked against the wall were crates and crates of vinyl. Two vintage speakers bookended the wooden desk, which looked like it came from Replay Vintage. In fact, a lot of the furniture in their apartment looked that way.

But Delia didn't mind. Somehow, it made the place feel cozy—like everything had a history, but one where people had cared for the items, then passed them on when it was time.

"Your room is really cool," Delia commented. None of her friends had rooms that looked anything like this. "And look how many records you have!"

"Wanna hear one?" he asked, clearly excited to play them for her.

She nodded eagerly. Her neck felt stiff and tingly, but she tried to ignore it. He leaned past her and hit a button on the record player. The black vinyl started spinning. Then he dropped the needle. A sultry voice echoed out of the speakers over melodic jazz music.

"Music always makes me feel better," he said, sitting down on the edge of his bed.

Delia listened to the music, letting it carry her mind away on a symphonic ride. It was so different from anything she'd ever heard. It warmed her ears and her brain. Even her body felt less stiff.

It was the most human she'd felt in days.

"I love this song," she told him.

"Really?" Grant said, looking thrilled. "This is jazz, my favorite style of music. But it's usually a bit of an acquired taste. Not a lot of kids our age listen to it anymore."

"Is this him?" Delia asked. "Ol' Blue Eyes? The one you told me about?"

"Sure is . . . What do you think?"

Grant waited for her answer while she searched for the proper words to describe the indescribable way the music made her feel. He seemed nervous almost—like he cared.

"His voice sounds like . . ." she started, closing her eyes to listen. "Butter."

Grant snorted a laugh and then his eyes widened. "You're a genius. It does!"

"I love it," Delia said. "I've never heard anything like it."

Delia sat forward and automatically tried to remove her coat, but it tightened around her and, just like that, the bubble of contentment around her burst. Grant spotted the look on her face and turned more serious.

"What's going on?" he said. "Start from the beginning. Tell me everything."

She looked down and chewed her lip, feeling a surge of doubt. "You're not gonna believe me. Honestly, I wouldn't believe me."

"Go ahead," he said. "Try me."

Delia took a deep breath, and it all spilled out. The more she talked about it, the less stiff her mouth felt, as if confessing helped her get better.

She told him everything. About finding the coat in the alley outside the House of De Vil store and taking it, even though she knew it was wrong. How it was great at first—her physical transformation. Her skin clearing up. Her hair looking sleek and healthy. Every selfie coming out perfect. How Harper and her friends actually liked her, and her PicPerfect ranking soared.

Then how it all started to backfire. The horrible nightmares. The car trying to run her over and stalking her. How her limbs got tingly and stiff. She held out her hands for him to see.

"I think it's turning me into a . . . mannequin."

"No way," he said, studying her plastic-y skin. "But how is that possible?"

Delia shook her head. "I don't know, but look at this." She showed him the DMs from the Fashion Addict account on PicPerfect. "I can't explain it, but I think the coat is cursed."

He frowned at the messages. "That does sound . . . impossible."

She turned away. "Ugh, I knew you wouldn't believe me—"

"You didn't let me finish," he cut her off. "But that doesn't mean I don't believe you. I can see how you're changing. Not to mention, I did save you from that out-of-control driver."

"Also, there's more," she went on, wanting to cry—trying to, even—but her eyes felt frozen. They couldn't form tears. Delia stood up in a panic, but it took longer than it should have for her to rise out of her chair. "Oh no. Oh *no*!"

"What . . . what is it?" Grant asked in a worried voice.

She turned to the mirror on the back of his bedroom door and stared at her face. She looked like one of the old-fashioned dolls she used to play with when she was little.

"It's getting worse," she said, pulling at the corner of her eyes, trying to make them move. "I can't even cry anymore. What is happening to me?"

Grant looked over the coat. "You really think it's this coat that's doing this somehow?"

Delia nodded, then tugged at it to demonstrate how she couldn't take it off. "No matter how hard I try, I can't take it off, or get rid of it. And trust me . . . I've tried."

She told him about trying to leave it back at the House of De Vil, and how it was back home when she returned. Then throwing it in the trash, only to find it back on her bed waiting for her. How she always woke up with it covering her and now couldn't take it off.

How it kept getting *heavier* and *tighter*, like it was literally strangling her.

"Ugh, I wish I'd listened to you," she said mournfully. "About Harper and social media. And that I'd never heard of House of De Vil."

Grant made a strange face. "What did you say?"

"House of De Vil," Delia repeated. "It's the big fashion brand."

Grant bolted up and grabbed a pen and paper. "How do you spell it?"

Delia gave him a strange look, but then jotted the name of the brand onto the pad. Grant took it from her and circled "De Vil." Then he wrote something else underneath it:

D-E-V-I-L

"OMG, you're right," Delia said. A chill ripped through her stiff body. How had she never realized that before? "It can't be a coincidence, can it?"

Grant hopped up and logged onto his computer. He googled "House of De Vil" and pulled up articles on the fashion line. He clicked on the first one. The headline read:

HOUSE OF DE VIL DISAPPEARANCES

He scanned it, then looked at Delia. "It says here that back in the day, they had to discontinue a line of famed coats because it seemed as if everyone who purchased one mysteriously disappeared."

Delia looked down at her coat.

"Dis . . . disappeared . . . ?"

Grant was suddenly so pale he looked sick. "That's what this article is saying."

Delia shivered. She wanted to rip the coat from her body, but she knew it was useless. The coat clung to her tighter, as if sensing her intentions.

Grant continued reading. "'Only ninety-five of the one hundred and one limited-edition coats were sold before the House of De Vil was forced to recall the remaining garments amidst accusations of foul play. Although no malice was ever proven, the remaining House of De Vil factories were shut down, seemingly for good. But then, a few years ago, the factories mysteriously opened back up and House of De Vil reappeared on the fashion scene as if it had never gone.'"

"It's so weird. I feel like the brand has been around forever. I've been following their social media since . . . since I had social media," Delia said.

Grant's eyes scanned the rest of the article. "This says nobody knows for sure who reopened the factories, or who's behind the new fashion line and stores," he told her, looking up from his computer and meeting her gaze. "Even the iconic Cruella De Vil might not be a real person. Nobody knows if she ever really existed."

"So it's all a mystery?" Delia asked, her throat going dry.

"Yup, a mystery that makes their famous black-and-white coats and fashion accessories even more coveted," he said with a frown. "It's kinda genius when you think about it."

"Or totally manipulative and creepy," Delia suggested.

Grant shrugged and hit a few keys on the keyboard. "Apparently, the coat you're wearing with the color block design is the famed Cruella Coat."

Delia would have rolled her eyes if she could have. Everyone knew about the Cruella Coat.

"It says they destroyed the unsold coats, but the designer herself is always pictured wearing one," Grant said after scanning the rest of the article. "But only from the back. Nobody's ever seen her face or knows what she looks like." He pointed to a picture of Cruella De Vil from the back wearing the coat. "So weird."

It was the same as the one in House of De Vil's profile picture on PicPerfect. Delia looked down at the coat. "So you're saying this coat . . . might've belonged to her?"

"Yes, it's possible," Grant said. "If she ever really existed. Who knows?"

"None of this explains why this is happening to me, though," Delia said desperately, focusing to get the words past her plastic lips. "If this coat is cursed and slowly turning me into a . . . you know what . . . then what am I gonna do?"

Grant frowned. "I don't know yet, but I'm going to do more research. There must be a way to make it stop. I won't let this happen to you."

Delia couldn't explain it, but she believed him. She clung to that hope, even as her body grew stiffer and her face refused to smile. She glanced at the picture of Cruella De Vil with her half-black, half-white head of spiky hair and her faux-fur coat, then met Grant's determined eyes.

His friendship made all the scary things she was facing feel somehow *less* scary. It was better medicine than even hot chocolate or jazz, and that was saying a lot.

"We're going to fix it," Grant promised. "If it's the last thing I do."

"Together," Delia said.

16
DOGNAPPING

When Delia arrived home on stiff legs, a locksmith was tinkering with the front door. The window next to it was smashed, and glass was sprinkled all over the doorstep and *Welcome Home* mat like confetti. She scanned the wreckage.

"What happened?" Delia asked, her lips barely moving.

"Oh, thank heavens, you're safe!" Mrs. Smith exclaimed the moment she saw Delia. She wrapped her up in a shaky hug.

At least her landlady still recognized her. Delia was just starting to feel relieved by that when she noticed the muddy boot prints marring the doorstep.

Delia gasped. It was just like in her nightmare—the one where the puppies were missing. And just like Fashion Addict's warning. When her friend had vanished along with the coat, the only thing the police found was . . . muddy boot prints.

"Did . . . did someone break in?" Delia stammered.

Mrs. Smith released her from the hug. She was a blubbering mess, wringing her hands. "When I told them . . . I wouldn't sell the puppies . . . they kept on calling and calling . . . but I didn't think . . . they'd actually *steal* them. . . ."

"Wait . . . what do you mean?" Delia said with a start. She rushed inside as fast as her plastic-y limbs would allow, feeling her heart thumping. "Is Radar okay?"

In the kitchen, her eyes fell on the pen. It was empty. The puppies were gone. Someone really had stolen them.

"No," Delia wailed. She backed away from the pen in horror.

"Oh yes, it's terrible . . . just awful," Mrs. Smith said, coming up behind her. "I called the police, but they won't do anything about it because they're not . . . human."

"Well, they're human to me," Delia said, wanting to cry, but her plastic eyes refused.

"My dear, I know," Mrs. Smith said. "They are to me, too. But I'm afraid no one will help us."

"Who do you think did it?" Delia asked, feeling cold from the inside out.

Her eyes darted to the smashed window. It felt so violating that someone had broken into their house and stolen their puppies. The kitchen was also ransacked and the muddy boot prints were everywhere, splashed across the floor and carpet, leading up to the puppy's empty pen.

"Well, the Rescue says there have been a series of dognappings all over the state, focused on Dalmatian puppies," Mrs. Smith said. "But they don't know who's behind it."

"But who would do such a thing?" Delia said, pulse thrumming. "Stealing puppies? That's beyond terrible."

"*Monsters*, that's who," Mrs. Smith said tearfully. Her face hardened, and her upper lip stiffened. She broke down in sobs next to the empty pen. The house sounded so quiet without the puppies. It felt empty, terribly empty.

"Yes, monsters," Delia repeated, rubbing Mrs. Smith's back. She wished she could cry. She felt like an emotionless doll. It was horrible.

She looked down at the coat. At the faux fur. And remembered the day she had noticed that the faux fur was as soft as the puppies' fur.

Her heart lurched.

Cruella De Vil.

Not a monster, Delia thought. *A devil.*

Was it possible that Cruella De Vil was sending her some kind of message?

But she had to be long dead, if she had ever existed. Too many things didn't add up.

Ping.

The sound of Delia's phone alert startled her. While Mrs. Smith returned to deal with the locksmith and the window repairman, Delia walked as fast as she could to her bedroom.

With trembling hands, she unlocked her phone. A new DM popped up in her PicPerfect account. It was from *the Devil Woman.*

DOGNAPPING

Those filthy mongrels belong to me!

Delia stared at the message in horror. Her heart plummeted through her chest. She wrote back, her hands so stiff that it was hard to type. It seemed that the curse kept getting worse the longer she wore the coat, especially now that she could no longer even take it off.

Why would you steal them?
Who are you?
Please, you have to give them back!

The response came through instantaneously. *Ping.* Text bubbles popped up from the Devil Woman. *Ping.* The terrible words cascaded over the screen.

Why would I give you back what you claim is yours?
Why, when you've stolen what is mine?

Suddenly a cackle echoed out of her phone, even though that was impossible. Then images of plastic mannequins wearing the Cruella Coat flooded the screen. The mannequins stared at Delia with their plastic, frozen eyes and dead smiles, draped in faux-fur coats.

Delia dropped her phone, but it kept loading more mannequin pictures. They swirled around the screen, glaring at her with frozen eyes and blank, expressionless faces.

Then another sound echoed out of the phone, one that made Delia's blood run cold.

Yip! Yip! Yip!

It was the sound of the puppies barking. And not just any puppies—it was *their* puppies. She could feel it. Then a dark silhouette appeared on the screen—a woman with spiky hair wearing a fur coat.

You have one chance to save them!
Bring my coat in exchange for the puppies.
You have 24 hours.

Delia tried to type back, but then an error message flashed across the screen:

DOGNAPPING

Profile Deleted.

The messages wouldn't go through. The account had vanished.

The Devil Woman was gone.

17
THE DEVIL WOMAN

Sleep that night was impossible.

For one thing, Delia kept expecting her phone to come alive again with cackles and puppies crying. And for another thing, she couldn't take the coat off anymore, no matter how hard she tried. She had to sleep with it strangling her body. She also kept thinking about the break-in and the muddy boot prints on the doorstep. And worst of all . . .

The puppies. Where were they? Were they scared? Was this Cruella person—or Cruella imposter—being mean to them? And how *could* it be Cruella? If Cruella had existed, she would have to have been dead by now. Which would mean . . .

No.

She could barely even think it.

But it would mean she was being haunted by Cruella De Vil's ghost.

But ghosts didn't exist. They *didn't*.

Delia glanced down at the coat. A few days ago, she would've thought cursed coats that could transform a person into a plastic mannequin didn't exist either.

At this point, anything was possible.

Delia didn't sleep at all. She kept listening for another break-in, even though Mrs. Smith had the locks changed and the window fixed, along with steel bars placed over it to protect their town house. It just didn't feel safe anymore. Not even with her mom and Mrs. Smith asleep downstairs.

The sight of the empty pen and the messages from the Devil Woman haunted her all night. She had to figure out a way to rescue the puppies.

And fast.

* * *

When Delia arrived at school, hobbling on her stiff limbs, she found Grant right away by his locker. He took one look at her and his jaw dropped.

"Oh no, it's getting worse," he said.

"I know. I feel like I don't have much time," she said, trying to be brave.

She had noticed it right away that morning—the curse was getting stronger. Not only could she barely bend her arms and legs, but she looked almost nothing like herself when she looked in the mirror.

"What does that mean?" Grant looked completely spooked. "You're not—"

He stopped talking as Harper and her friends waltzed past in their House of De Vil boots. Harper glanced at Delia—then her gaze passed right over her, as if she didn't even recognize Delia anymore. But for the first time, Delia didn't even care. She knew they weren't her real friends, and she had much more important things to deal with.

She turned back to Grant and blurted out the whole story about the puppies and the messages from the Devil Woman on PicPerfect.

"Wait, you think they stole your puppies?" Grant said in shock. "House of De Vil?"

"Yes, exactly," Delia said. "Maybe. I don't know! There's a lot I still can't explain. If Cruella was even real, then she'd be long dead. But House of De Vil *is* real and making new clothes, so somebody is behind it. *Somebody* wanted me to find the coat. *Somebody* stole the puppies. *Somebody* sent me all those horrible messages. It's all connected."

"You think it's . . . Cruella? Like, her ghost or something?"

Delia bit her lip. "Look, I don't know. But the messages said I had twenty-four hours to bring the coat back to get the puppies. But I don't know where! The account was deleted."

Grant ran his hands over his hair and held it back from his face. "I can't believe they'd actually steal your puppies."

All around them students rushed to get to class, calling out to each other, laughing, sharing thoughts on the homework. These snippets of normal life all seemed so foreign now. Even Aaliyah and Zoe. Even her PicPerfect ranking. None of it mattered. Delia was turning into a mannequin, and their precious foster puppies had been stolen.

All because of her.

Delia wanted to cry. She wanted to scream and freak out. She pressed her fingertips into her cheeks, feeling how stiff they had become. Even her lips struggled to form words now.

Her face felt so . . . plastic.

"Well, I've been doing some research. Remember that article about the limited-edition coats?" Grant said. "And the people who disappeared?"

"Yes, of course," Delia said, forcing the words out through her stiff lips. They came out a little muffled.

"Listen," Grant said, glancing around. He pulled her aside and lowered his voice. "After you went home, I did some digging. It took some time, but I found House of De Vil's original address. It's an abandoned factory on the outskirts of town."

"An abandoned factory?" Delia said, feeling a stab of hope. "Maybe that's where she took the puppies?"

"Right," he agreed. "What if we go there and give her

back the coat? Maybe she'll stop haunting you and reverse the curse. And give the puppies back."

"Do you really think it'll work?" Delia said hopefully, though she couldn't smile or raise her eyebrows at the thought. She wanted to show emotion again. Feel her expression change. She was desperate for it.

"Well, I admit it's a long shot," Grant said, meeting her gaze. He reached out and squeezed her stiff hand. "But what other choice do we have? We have to try."

That was when it hit Delia. She was dragging him into this all over again.

"No. *I* have to try," she said. "I'm the one they're after. It could be dangerous. They broke into our house and stole our puppies. Who knows what else they could do?"

Grant shook his head. "No way; I'm not letting you do this by yourself."

Delia met his eyes, forcing her gaze to turn even though it was hard. "I should've listened to you . . . about all of it. . . . I was so wrong. . . ."

"Delia, it's not your fault," Grant said forcefully. "She's the Devil Woman. This shouldn't be happening to you. It should never happen to anyone! Look, I know we don't have much time left. The message said twenty-four hours. When do you want to go to the factory? We can take the train out there."

"After school?" she said, feeling the urgency like a kick to her stomach. "You're right. Also, I don't have much time left. My symptoms are getting worse all the time."

She held up her hands for him to see how plastic they had become. Her fingers were stiff and no longer bent fully.

"Yes, after school," he agreed. "We can meet outside and take the train to the factory. The end of the line stops not far from where it is."

Delia tried to smile. Her lips fought her, but she forced out the barest hint of one.

She was so thankful that she wasn't in this alone. She thought about all her PicPerfect friends. Or *so-called* friends. Even Aaliyah and Zoe, but especially Harper and the Glam Posse. The ones who professed to adore her, then sent her devil icons and abandoned her as soon as she wasn't trending in the rankings anymore.

She was grateful for a *real* friend.

She met Grant's eyes. He held her gaze. "Don't worry, we're gonna fix this and get your puppies back," he said, and in some deep way, she knew he meant it. "Delia, I promise."

He was her real friend. And that meant everything.

* * *

Getting through the rest of school was a nightmare. The curse seemed to be worsening with every passing moment. The coat felt heavier and tighter than ever. Delia didn't want to look like a plastic doll—she wanted to be herself. She was sorry she ever wanted to look different or change her appearance. She'd made a huge mistake. And she wasn't the only one paying for it now. She couldn't stop thinking about the puppies and how alone and scared they must be.

One thought shot through her head as the final bell rang and she hurried outside with Grant to catch the train. She didn't know what awaited them at the factory, but she knew this:

Radar, I'm gonna save you if it's the last thing I do.

18
HOUSE OF DE VIL

Delia and Grant took the train to the outskirts of the city, the buildings growing more dilapidated and run-down with each mile as they entered an area filled with old factories.

The passengers around them thinned out, each getting off at their stops, until they were the last ones left on the train. Finally it slowed with a squeal of the brakes. "Last stop," the conductor announced over the speakers.

"Last stop . . . House of De Vil," Grant said, clutching Delia's hand tighter. Their eyes met. She felt a shiver. "It's the end of the line."

"I hope the puppies are here," Delia said, guilt still churning in her gut. She clutched the soft coat tighter around her, even though it was what got her into this mess in the first place. If it wasn't for the coat, the puppies would be home safe, and she'd be normal.

Not turning into some plastic doll.

Delia followed Grant off the train, hobbling down the stairs from the station.

"It's getting worse, isn't it?" he said, shooting her a concerned look as she stumbled on the steps. He caught her arm, steadying her.

Delia nodded, feeling her neck strain to move at her command. "My legs feel like they don't wanna bend."

"Then we don't have much time left," Grant said in an urgent voice. "Let's hurry."

"Easier said than done," Delia responded, her legs fighting her. But she forced them to move and keep up with Grant.

A cold wind tore at them as they tramped away from the commuter station. The skies had turned slate gray. Delia could smell snow in the air. She could taste it on her tongue, cold and pure and crisp. It felt like a big winter storm was bearing down on the city.

Delia peered ahead, her eyes falling on an old,

crumbling factory perched atop a hill. It was surrounded by an iron fence and looked completely abandoned. Even the fence drooped.

She gasped and grabbed Grant's arm when she saw the golden crest emblazoned on the front gate.

"House of De Vil," she whispered, recognizing the signature seal.

Grant set his jaw, his eyes fixed on the factory. Tall smokestacks jutted out of the concrete building. It was a large, sprawling facility, but collapsing and dilapidated. This was where they'd manufactured the original House of De Vil line before they shut down.

It was eerily silent and deserted.

"It's a little late to say this now," Grant said in a low voice. "But I have a bad feeling."

"Me too," Delia said.

The factory was abandoned—not a soul in sight. She'd expected that. But it also felt so ominous, so eerie—as if the empty, broken windows were staring down at her.

It felt . . . haunted.

Delia took a deep breath. "Look, we don't have a choice. We have to save those puppies. Or, well . . . *I* do."

"Wait, what do you mean?" he said, skidding to a halt.

"I mean you can still back out," Delia said, feeling a rush of fear sweep through her stiff body. "It's not too late. This isn't your fault. It's my fault. I don't have a choice—I have to do this. Plus, if I don't . . . I'm gonna turn plastic. But I'd hate to put you in danger. . . ."

"Stop it," Grant said, shaking his head vehemently. "You're my friend. This is what friends do—they help each other when they're in trouble. They don't run away because it gets hard."

Delia's heart lurched. Why did she never understand that before? Why did she want to be popular with strangers online who turned on her the second she wasn't perfect enough anymore? Harper and Charlotte and Ella had dropped her the second things turned even slightly *weird*, let alone hard. Even Aaliyah and Zoe seemed to have completely forgotten her.

If she'd just understood what real friendship was, then she wouldn't be in this mess. But she couldn't change what happened. All she could do was try to make things better now.

Grant helped Delia climb up the hill toward the front

gate. It towered over them. He reached out and touched it. . . .

Creak.

It swung open by itself.

"Uh, yeah. That's not creepy at all," Grant said, meeting her eyes. "Totally normal."

"Right, it's almost like . . ." Delia started, but then he finished her thought.

"They're waiting for us," he said, meeting her eyes. "Whoever *they* are."

Snow started falling from the sky, while the wind picked up. "Hurry, let's get inside before it gets worse," he said, pulling her through the gate and toward the factory. The front door gaped open, lopsided on its hinges.

If the outside looked bad, the interior was even worse. Dim light swirled with dust. Industrial tables stacked with sewing machines and other hulking equipment, like huge vats for dyeing and manufacturing clothes, filled the cavernous space. But everything was shut down and covered with a thick layer of dust. It looked like it hadn't been in operation for a very long time. So who was making the House of De Vil clothes now? And where?

"Radar . . . can you hear me?" Delia called, her voice coming out raspy and stilted through her plastic lips. "Here, boy . . . Are you here?"

Silence.

Delia braced herself and tried a new tack. "Hey, Devil Woman! Look! I brought your coat back! Just like you asked!"

The factory was silent.

The sun was starting to set, casting the interior into shadow.

She tried again. "Radar . . . come on, boy . . . bark for me!"

But still . . . nothing.

Delia swallowed hard. She glanced at Grant, who looked crestfallen. She had gotten her hopes up that the puppies would be here and they'd find them. That there was still a chance to save them from the terrible, evil dognappers.

"I'm so sorry—" Grant started, but then Delia shushed him. She heard something. It was faint . . . but could it be?

Yip, yip, yip.

"Radar, boy!" Delia called out, her raspy voice echoing

through the factory and reverberating back. "Come on, bark for me! I know you can hear me!"

Her voice echoed and died out. But her ears must have been playing tricks on her. She turned to Grant. "It was a good try, but let's go home—"

Then, suddenly, she heard it again. For sure this time. *Yip! Yip! Yip!*

"That's Radar!" Delia exclaimed.

She'd know his bark anywhere. It was unique—higher pitched because of his small size, but defiant and strong. He was the runt of the litter, not even supposed to survive. But he had. He was a fighter. She grabbed Grant's hand and hobbled on stiff legs toward the barking.

They burst into a back room, and Delia gasped at what she saw. This was the design workshop for House of De Vil—sketches for the original line were pinned to the walls. Even the famous Cruella Coat with the color block pattern. The design sketches sent a chill down her spine.

But then she noticed something even worse. There were pictures—black-and-white printouts curling at the edges—of women wearing the Cruella Coat. At first glance, nothing was odd about them. But Delia noticed that each was stamped with a red date and the word "Disappeared."

"Oh my . . . She kept track!" Delia exclaimed.

Grant followed her gaze and approached the wall of photographs, touching a few of them, running his hands over the dates.

"She kept track of the women who bought the coat and disappeared. And when." Delia felt sick to her stomach.

"I can't believe this," Grant said quietly, still studying the photos. "She was a monster."

"A devil," Delia corrected.

Yip! Yip! Yip!

Delia startled, and then hope cascaded through her. There was still a chance to rescue the puppies. They rushed from the design room as fast as Delia could go, and moved toward the barking. All around them now were huge conveyor belts, mountains of moldering fabric, and giant sewing machines. Grant was about to shove open another door when a new sound reverberated through the factory.

It was so loud that it shook the floor.

Clank. Clank. Clank.

All the machines started up out of nowhere.

"But how . . . ? Who's doing this?" Delia rasped. "The factory's deserted."

A cruel laugh cut through the air. Delia and Grant locked eyes, then slowly turned as one. Right in front of them, a huge shadow rose up from the ground, towering over them. Its hair was spiked and its skinny fingers were like claws.

"Darling, you're here! And you brought my coat."

19
YOU BELONG TO ME

The shadow vanished as fast as it had appeared.

"Here . . . you can have your stupid coat back!" Delia said, struggling to wriggle out of it, but it still constricted her body like a tourniquet. It made no sense. If the Devil Woman wanted it back, then why was the coat still sticking to her? She scanned the dark factory for another glimpse. "I don't even want it anymore. Just give the puppies back! They don't belong to you—"

"As my coat does not belong to you!" the voice screeched from the shadows. "Take it off now!"

But no matter how hard Delia tried, the coat wouldn't release her. She started to feel desperate. "I'm trying . . . but it won't come off. I swear!"

"Stupid girl!" the voice cackled. "Then I shall take my coat off your plastic, stiff body myself!"

Suddenly the machines grew louder and began moving faster. They churned and whirred, filling the factory with awful industrial noise.

"No, please!" Delia yelled to be heard over the machines. "You have to let the puppies go! I don't even want the stupid, ugly coat."

Everything stopped. The machines, the noise. Everything. Delia's heart caught. She looked at Grant, his breath coming shallow, making clouds in the cold air.

"What is happening?" Delia whimpered.

Then she felt a coldness slip across her shoulders, followed by an even colder breath in her ear.

"How dare you call my coat ugly?" the voice whispered. It was *right* next to her. "You're such a vain little girl. So vain you had to steal my couture. And now you've fallen right into my little trap."

The machines clanged to life again. Grant grabbed Delia's hand.

"Run!"

Delia tried. She tried to keep up as Grant dragged her

forward, feeling the voice—the ghost—whatever it was— behind her the entire time. The cackling grew louder and closer and closer and louder. But then—

Yip! Yip! Yip!

Radar was still barking for them. Delia and Grant burst into another room and staggered to a halt. The puppies!

Radar saw them and scrambled to the edge of the pen where the puppies were being kept, jumping manically. His distinctive bark rang out.

Yip! Yip! Yip!

"Yes! Let's get them and get out of here!" Grant cried. They ran toward the pen, but Grant tripped over a wire and fell, twisting his ankle. He tried to stand, but his leg buckled. He couldn't run.

Delia looked around in desperation. Cruella was coming for them.

"Leave me," Grant gasped from the floor. "Just save the puppies—"

"No way, I won't leave you," Delia said, helping him up despite her stiff body. "We're friends, remember? We don't leave each other at the first sign of trouble."

Suddenly the doors burst open and Cruella's shadow loomed. "Stay away from them! Those mongrels are mine!"

The shadow stretched across the room, filling the cavernous space. Little Radar and the puppies snarled and barked.

"I will have the puppies *and* I will have my coat!" the voice screeched.

But Delia had a plan. She motioned Grant toward the pen, then turned to confront the Devil Woman. Out of the corner of her eye, she saw Grant crawling toward the puppies in their pen.

"What do you want with my puppies?" Delia rasped at Cruella's ghost. She could feel her body turning more plastic, but she didn't care anymore. She only cared about one thing. She had to save Radar and the other puppies—even if it was the last thing she did.

The room filled with an evil cackle. "Get rid of them. Get rid of all of them," Cruella said. "And I will, unless you hand over my coat."

"Look, I already told you," Delia said, still struggling with the coat. Her body felt stiffer and more plastic than ever. "I don't want it anymore. I don't care how fashionable or popular it made me. I just want to be me again. Like . . . the *real* me. Your fashion line is cursed!"

"It's too late for you, darling," the voice drawled. "You and your puppies all belong to me."

Delia gulped. "What . . . what do you mean I belong to you?"

But before the voice could answer, the puppies swarmed Delia's ankles.

Grant had released them from their pen while Delia was distracting Cruella. They stampeded through the factory, heading for the exit.

"Nooooooo!" Suddenly the shadow coalesced again into the size of a woman and lunged for Grant. "They're my puppies! You can't have them!"

Pandemonium broke out. The puppies leaped at the front doors, barking and growling. Grant hobbled after them on his twisted ankle, pushing the doors open to release them from the factory. His eyes flashed back to Delia, who could feel herself transforming even more quickly now. Her body stiffened completely; she couldn't walk anymore. She could barely move.

"Just promise . . . you'll save them . . ." she croaked. "It's too late for me. . . . I know that it's too late. . . . I made too many mistakes. . . . Just save them!"

She tried to turn toward him, but it was no use. Her joints locked into place, stiffening as they turned fully plastic. Grant took one last look at her, clearly torn about what to do. But then Radar bit at his ankles, trying to herd him outside.

"I'll get help!" Grant shouted. "I'll come back for you!"

Then he turned to lead the puppies to safety. But Delia knew it was too late for her. The Devil Woman was right. Delia belonged to her now.

The last thing she remembered seeing before her eyes froze completely into place was the shadow towering over her, fingers curled overhead like claws.

"You're going to pay for this!"

20
#CRUELLACOAT

The House of De Vil flagship store was busier than ever, packed with high-end shoppers flashing their credit cards and leaving with fancy tote bags stuffed with boots, coats, and other accessories. It was spring fashion season, coming on the heels of the worst winter in Chicago's history.

The Glam Posse from Delia's school browsed the aisles, pulling items and holding them up for inspection.

"OMG, look! The Cruella Coat!" Harper shrieked, rushing over to the special display case in the center of the store. Inside, a mannequin posed in the iconic black-and-white coat.

Harper modeled in front of the display, snapping

selfies for PicPerfect. She moved her face, choosing the perfect angles, positioning her arm to snap them.

Click. Click. Click.

She tagged them #CruellaCoat and hit POST. Her account still trended at the top.

"Ugh, I *wish* I could get my hands on that coat," Harper sighed enviously, taking in the mannequin with her arm on her hip. "But there's only one. And it's not for sale."

"Hey, remember that girl who had the coat?" Charlotte asked.

Harper sneered. "Not really. . . . Who knows? I bet it wasn't even the *real* thing. It was probably a knockoff like her boots. She was a scholarship kid, remember?"

"Whatever happened to her?" Ella asked, studying the mannequin. "She kind of disappeared. Just stopped coming to school one day."

"Bet she went back to public school," Harper said. "Where she belongs. I bet we never see her again."

The girls all snickered, then moved on from the display as Harper's phone chimed from all the hearts piling up on her PicPerfect post about the Cruella Coat.

Maybe they wouldn't see Delia again, but she could see them. As they traipsed toward the counter with their chosen items and their parents' credit cards, she watched. Delia would always be watching, trapped in the display case, wearing the Cruella Coat.

Forever.

THE END

ACKNOWLEDGMENTS

Dah-lings, I hope you enjoyed the nightmares! Penning these *unhappily-ever-after* endings is my favorite part. Can't wait to hear what you think of this one. Don't worry, I've got something especially wicked cooked up for book five. You won't want to miss it. As I type this, I'm in the middle of the draft.

I can't believe I'm already writing the gratitude section for the fourth book in my Disney Chills series. For a long time, these books were just spooky little stories that I had in my head. Getting to write these characters is a dream come true. Or maybe . . . a nightmare (ha).

I have to thank my amazing team at Disney Books, including my fabulous editor, Kieran Viola, my design team, and my publicity team for working to get the word out to readers, even in this roller coaster of a year. Also, thanks to my book agent, Deborah Schneider, and the rest of my rep team at ICM, Gersh, Archetype, and Curtis Brown. Disney Chills and my other books and writing take a whole dream team, and I am grateful for your efforts on my behalf.

I also want to thank everyone behind the classic Disney film, which is one of my all-time favorites, and pay special homage to Dodie Smith, who wrote the original book, *The Hundred and One Dalmatians*, and cowrote the script of the film. Cruella De Vil truly is one of the greatest villains ever. Adding to her story is extra special. I'm so thankful I got the chance to tackle her—and bring her to life with as much wit, cunning, charm, and style as she deserves. *Dah-ling, you're simply fabulous!*

Finally, extra-huge thanks to my readers for embracing this new series. The enthusiastic response to the first book has kept me inspired and writing, even during one of the hardest years in recent memory, maybe in my lifetime. Dear sweet readers, you're the reason I do this. And don't stress—we've got more villains coming soon for you!

Can't wait for you to find out what's next for Disney Chills.

Happy nightmares!

—Jennifer Brody (aka Vera Strange)

"I want you . . ."

Though he wasn't looking at her, Zane felt her inch closer; he was aware of her all along his length, in his every pore, even in the air he breathed. The ladder had him several feet above her, which placed her face—her mouth—parallel with his lap. *Damn damn damn.* He tensed, waiting, and more images drifted into his mind.

"I want you," she repeated, a little louder but still low enough that no one seemed to notice.

He hadn't imagined it.

Anger erupting, Zane glared down at her, this time catching and holding her dark, mystical gaze. Her long, coal-black lashes fluttered, but she didn't look away from him. Staring into her eyes, he felt her, her thoughts and emotions invading his mind. Her nervousness touched him bone deep, the way she forced herself to remain still. And that, too, affected him.

How the hell did she manage to toy with him so easily?

Also by Lori Foster

THE WINSTON BROTHERS

Wild

Lori Foster

JOVE BOOKS, NEW YORK

WILD

A Jove Book / published by arrangement with
the author

PRINTING HISTORY
Jove edition / January 2002

Visit our website at
www.penguin.com

ISBN: 0-515-13229-2

A JOVE BOOK®
Jove Books are published by The Berkley Publishing Group,
a division of Penguin Group (USA) Inc.,
375 Hudson Street, New York, New York 10014.
JOVE and the "J" design
are trademarks belonging to Penguin Group (USA) Inc.

PRINTED IN THE UNITED STATES OF AMERICA

19 18 17 16 15 14 13 12 11 10

One

"*I want you.*"

The suggestive, husky whisper stroked over Zane Winston with the effect of a soft, warm kiss to his spine. It devastated his senses.

He froze, then clenched hard in reaction, his muscles tightening, his pulse speeding up. He nearly fell off the stepladder.

The motherboards balanced precariously in his arms started to drop, but Zane managed to juggle them safely at the last second.

He didn't want to look, didn't want to acknowledge that soft whisper. He knew without looking who had spoken to him. Still, as was generally the case where *she* was concerned, he couldn't *not* look.

His gaze sought her out, and found her standing a mere two feet away, her eyes downcast, her waist-length, black hair partially hiding her face like a thick, ebony curtain.

People shuffled through the small computer store, taking advantage of the sale he was running, grabbing at clearance items, storing up on disks. Yet no one bumped into her, no one touched her. Alone in the crowd, she stood to the side of his ladder, and Zane could feel her intense awareness of him. It sparked his own awareness until his breathing deepened, his skin warmed.

Damn it, that always happened when he was around her—which was one reason why he tried to avoid her.

She didn't say anything else, didn't even bother to look at him, so Zane went back to restocking the shelf. Perhaps he'd misunderstood. Perhaps he'd even imagined it all. He hadn't been sleeping well lately—or rather, he'd been sleeping too hard, dead to the world and caught up in lifelike, erotic dreams that left him drained throughout the day. He felt like a walking zombie—a *horny* walking zombie—because the dreams were based on scorching carnal activities.

With *her.*

Zane's computer business had done remarkably well the past year, and it required a lot of his attention. The location in the small strip mall was ideal. Her antiquated two-story building stood right next door, only a narrow alley away, and the scent of the sultry incense she burned often drifted in through the open door of his shop. Worse than that, the pulse-thrumming music she played could be heard everywhere, and it made his heart beat too fast. With all these distractions, concentrating on software and modems wasn't always easy, no matter his level of resolve. And now with the damn dreams plaguing him, his iron control was fractured.

His brothers had taken to heckling him, tauntingly accusing him of too much carousing. Zane didn't bother to correct them. No way would he tell them the truth behind his recent distraction—that his carousing had only been in his dreams, and his distraction was a little Gypsy he didn't even find appealing.

Especially since he was determined to deny any such distraction.

The last thing he needed was a face-to-face visit with her.

Though he wasn't looking at her, Zane felt her inch

closer; he was aware of her all along his length, in his every pore, even in the air he breathed. The ladder had him several feet above her, which placed her face—her mouth—on a level with his lap. *Damn damn damn.* He tensed, waiting, and more images drifted into his mind.

"I want you," she repeated, a little louder but still low enough that no one seemed to notice.

He hadn't imagined it.

Anger erupting, Zane glared down at her, this time catching and holding her dark, mystical gaze. Her long, coal-black lashes fluttered, but she didn't look away from him. Staring into her eyes, he felt her thoughts and emotions invading his mind. Her nervousness touched him bone deep; the way she forced herself to remain still affected him, too.

How the hell did she manage to toy with him so easily? It outraged Zane, left him edgy and hot and resentful. Despite what some of his female associates might think, he was always the pursuer, not the pursued. He subtly controlled every intimate relationship, took only what he needed, gave only as much as he wanted, and no more.

Zane realized he was breathing too hard, reacting to her on an innate level. Deliberately he jammed the boxes of motherboards onto the shelf before climbing down the ladder.

Facing her, his arms folded over his chest, he did his best to intimidate her while hiding his discomfort. He needed her to leave. He needed to stop thinking about her.

He was nearly certain his needs didn't matter to her in the least.

"What do you want?" He sounded rude to his own ears, obnoxious and curt. But this was a battle for the upper hand, and he intended to do his best to win.

Her full lips, painted a shiny dark red, were treated to a soft, sensual lick of uncertainty. Filled with tenacity, her gaze wavered, then returned to his. Her chin lifted. "As I said, I want . . . you."

God, she'd said it again. This time straight out, to his

face. Zane braced himself against the lure of her brazenness and her bold request. She looked like walking sex, like a male fantasy—*his fantasy*—come to life. He would *not* let her suck him in with obvious ploys.

"For what?" *There*, he thought, *deal with that, Miss Gypsy*. And she *was* a Gypsy, no doubt about it. He almost believed the signs, painted in the front window of her shop, that claimed she could read palms and predict the future. The signs, backlit by the eerie glow of a red lamp and dozens of flickering candles inside, also said she could cast spells and enlighten your life.

It was the spell-casting part that made Zane most uncertain. After all, he was familiar with curses firsthand. And he didn't like them worth a damn. At least, not when applied to himself. For his brothers it had worked out just fine. Better than fine. *For his brothers.*

Agitated, she shifted her feet, and the tinkling of tiny bells rose above the noise of the crowd. Zane found himself staring at her small feet beneath a long gauze skirt of bold colors and geometric designs. The skirt was thin and would be transparent if she stood in the right light.

Luckily for his peace of mind, they were more in the shadows than not. But that didn't stop him from imagining what he couldn't see. And it pissed him off that he could guess just how she'd look.

Twin ankle bracelets of miniature silver bells had produced the music when she moved. Dainty silver rings with intricate designs circled her painted toes.

On her hands, each finger was adorned with a silver, pewter, or gold ring. A multitude of bracelets with inlaid colored stones hung on her slender wrists and jingled when she clasped her hands together.

Around her neck, and disappearing into the neckline of her midnight blue peasant blouse, were strands of small beads: jet black, bright amber, ruby red.

He noticed the necklaces, then immediately noticed that she wasn't wearing a bra. Her breasts lay soft and full beneath her blouse.

An invisible fist squeezed Zane's lungs, stealing the oxygen from his body, making him light-headed. For God's sake, they were only breasts—and not all *that* impressive. But he could see the faint outline of her nipples beneath the dark, thin material, and it set him on fire.

He wanted to curse, but that would give too much away, so he refrained.

When he took a deep breath, trying to relieve some of his tension, that musky, earthy scent of incense filled his head. He stared at her hard, intent on keeping his gaze on her face. "I'm waiting."

She glanced at the surrounding crowd. Her large, heavily lined eyes looked mysterious and sensual. No one paid any attention to them. She said low, "I want you for sex."

Her gaze melted into his, touching his soul, reawakening those hot, taunting dreams that had plagued him nightly. In his sleep, he'd already taken her every way known to man. Now she offered to let the dream become reality.

Breathing was too damn difficult. He was nearly panting.

"I want you," she boldly continued, fanning the flames, "to share your body with me, and let me give you mine."

Slowly, hypnotically, she lowered her lashes and added, with a small shrug, "That's all."

That's all? That's all. Urgency throbbed through his veins, as if he'd spent hours on leisurely, detailed foreplay. Zane wanted to smack her.

Even more than that, he wanted to drag her into the backroom and lift her long, flirty skirt and take the body she so willingly offered. He wanted to inhale her scent, wanted to taste her in all her hottest, sweetest places. And he wanted to bury himself deep inside her.

Damn it all, he had a hard-on to end all hard-ons, and here he stood in the middle of his shop with hordes of people ready to spend money and purchase his wares.

Nostrils flared, and with as much disdain as he could

muster, given his acute state of arousal, Zane growled, "Thanks, but no thanks."

Her gaze clashed with his, startled, upset. Her lips drew in, got caught by her teeth, and color scalded her cheeks. She took two slow breaths, then asked in a wavering voice, "You're certain you're not interested?"

He was so damn interested it wouldn't have taken much more than a few touches to make him insane. Zane locked his knees, clenched his fists, and hardened his resolve. "Positive."

Her long, silky hair hung to her thighs as she bowed her head. For a suspended moment, Zane feared she might actually cry—or cast a hideous spell on him. He wasn't entirely sure which would be worse. Not that he normally believed in such things as spells and incantations. But there was the Winston curse. He believed in it, had seen its effects on his brothers as one by one they'd been caught and married off. Happily.

One curse per family was more than enough. Little Gypsy could just take her mesmerizing voice and her intrusive sexuality and leave him the hell alone. He liked his life just as it was, just as he'd made it.

Without looking at him again, she turned and left. Her departure struck him like a punch in the gut. She hadn't been crying, he thought with concern, but she'd been so silent. . . .

Oh, hell, she was always silent. She used it as part of her mystique. He refused to be drawn in by her and her feminine cunning and what amounted to no more than theatrics to shore up her ruse as a Gypsy.

The gentle, enticing sway of her skirts as she slowly retreated held his attention. She might be leaving, but her scent remained, circling around him, filling his head and his heart. Her effect remained, too, keeping him hot and tight and far too aware of his physical needs. And that last look on her face remained, making him curse himself for being such a bastard.

He was good with women, damn it. *Great* with women,

in fact. He always treated them gently, whether he was interested or not. So why the hell had he been so rude to her? Why had he felt compelled to grind her down with his rejection? He'd been out to prove . . . what? That she didn't affect him after all?

Zane snorted at that. The tent in his pants proved otherwise, no matter his behavior toward her.

Now that she was gone, only the essence of her remaining without the threat of her appeal, he was ashamed of himself.

A customer touched his arm, causing him to jump. With great effort Zane brought his mind back to the job at hand. Even with two employees in to help, they were swamped. The line at the register was long and continuous. People had questions, and the shelves constantly had to be restocked. He couldn't afford to be distracted by his witchy neighbor. He would run the register—where he could hide his arousal behind the counter—and do his job.

But for the rest of the day, she lingered in his mind, an unwelcome invasion that kept him jittery and taut, the same way he felt when he'd gone too long without sex.

He hated what he knew he would have to do.

But since he was resigned to doing it, he'd damn well put himself in charge. No more letting her toy with him, no more letting her overwhelm his senses. It was Thursday, the weekend fast approaching. He'd have time to spend with her, and on her. And if anyone would be overwhelmed, it'd be her.

That thought finally had Zane smiling.

In anticipation.

Tamara Tremayne flipped over the CLOSED sign in the front door of her shop and turned all the locks. Luna, her assistant, had left an hour ago. Her relatives had called a few times but hadn't come by, which was strange. But she was thankful for the quiet. She was finally alone.

For a moment, she leaned her forehead against the glass

in the door and looked at the FOR SALE sign stuck in the scraggly strip of lawn in front of the old building.

She didn't want to sell, but she had no choice.

Walking around the shop, she pinched out the many candles she always kept lit, and snuffed out the stems of incense that continued to smolder, filling the air with sweetness. Smoke clung to the ceiling, giving added ambience to the small shop with its colorful cloths over every tabletop and the glittering beads on lampshades and curtain trims. A dark drape separated her reception area from the two small rooms she used for her sessions. She pushed it aside and made sure all the lamps were turned off.

One of her favorite estate sale finds, a polished, curving mahogany countertop with ornate trim, concealed the traditional and quite modern CD player. Tamara clicked it off, killing the sensually stimulating New Age music. It felt like her heartbeat died with the last strumming note. The silence lay heavy in the air.

As she strolled away, feeling lazy and defeated, Tamara trailed her hand over a large crystal ball, wishing it could, indeed, predict the future, wishing she could see if Zane Winston would ever give her the time of day. But the beautiful glass was empty. And she already had all the answers she needed.

Thanks, but no thanks.

Four little words had never hurt quite so much. Each one had felt like a sharp dart piercing her heart, stealing her breath, making her lungs constrict. They'd dashed her dreams, her fantasies. They gave her nothing to look forward to but a continuation of the long, sexually frustrating nights and her endlessly hopeful dreams.

Zane was known for his seduction successes. Out of the four Winston brothers, Zane was the most blatantly sexual, the most outrageous, the most . . . wanted. At least by the ladies. There was an earthy wildness about him, a primal masculinity that drew women in, a hot sexuality that kept them coming back.

Intelligent, driven, Zane was, in her mind, the most

handsome of the brothers. And that was saying a lot, considering the Winstons were a virile and sinfully gorgeous clan.

Cole, the oldest, struck her as the most somber. He took his responsibilities seriously and loved with a depth of emotion Tamara had never seen before. And she didn't need to be a mind reader to figure that out. It was there on his face whenever he looked at his brothers, and especially when he looked at his wife or his new baby daughter.

It was a look that made her long for things she'd never have—a husband, a family of her own. A normal life.

Tamara had visited the Winston Tavern a few times, and she loved it there. She loved blending in with the rest of society as if she were just a woman running a shop, just a woman out for a relaxing evening.

Not a Tremayne.

Not a Gypsy.

She had so little time for socializing or frivolity.

Chase, the second oldest, was the bartender, and she'd seen through him right away. Tamara smiled. She wasn't a true psychic, as her advertisement claimed. She couldn't read minds, just as she couldn't predict the future. But she was much more intuitive than most people. Throughout her life, there had been certain people whose emotions were clearer to her. Generally, she thought them to be people with acute feelings: loving with their whole heart, or hating with fanaticism.

The Winstons, with their zest for life and open honesty, were often quite clear to her. Chase gave the impression of being quiet and serene, but he was a deeply sensual person and very erotic, maybe even bordering on kinky. His quiet persona hid some of his fire, but Tamara could see the heat in his gaze, and knew that his thoughts regularly focused on the sexual. Luckily, his wife was the perfect match.

Tamara liked Mack Winston the best. He was the youngest, the most playful, a man who knew how to laugh and have a good time. She'd watched him at the bar, moving from table to table, a smile always on his face. He saw joy in everything and everyone, especially those he called family. You couldn't be near Mack and not smile, too.

Yes, she liked Mack best, but it was Zane she wanted.

Even though his driving sexuality scared her just a bit— or maybe *because* it did—she wanted him. She wanted him so much she could barely sleep at night. She'd lie awake for hours, imagining all the ways Zane might want to make love, and all the ways she could enjoy him. Sometimes the dreams were so real, almost as if he were with her, guiding her, telling her what he liked and how he liked it, showing her what she'd like, too.

In her heart, she knew dreams would never compare with the reality.

For the few years that his shop had been there, Tamara had watched Zane open in the mornings, and close at night. She'd watched women fawn all over him. She'd gotten to know his brothers better just by observation, and she'd gotten to know Zane better, too.

He was an overachiever, though he'd never admit it. He preferred the label "playboy." He was a combination of his brothers' better traits with a naughty, rambunctious streak thrown in, a man who prided himself on individuality, a man who struggled to be his own boss in all ways—but especially with women.

When she'd turned eighteen, Tamara had known it was time to settle down, to lay claim to a location and make it her own. The old building had appealed to her on several levels: not only was it perfect for her shop, but the living quarters upstairs were quaint and cozy. She'd been there for six years now.

In that time, she'd seen other shops in the adjacent strip mall try to make a go of it, but they were never able to stay afloat for long.

Zane hadn't let the failures of others keep him from trying. He'd taken the empty store and quickly made a success of a fledgling computer business. He sold products and did repairs, and even built computers to customers' specifications. He worked long hours, sometimes far into the night. From her bedroom window above the shop, Tamara had seen his lights on past midnight. Yet he'd be there bright and early the next morning, looking sexy as ever and not in the least worn down.

He must have incredible stamina, she thought, then shivered as a lustful fever crept into her bloodstream. She'd never get to know, because Zane didn't want her at all. Any other woman might have had a better chance. For some reason, he'd taken an immediate dislike to her. Even over the past year, as she'd tried to be friendlier, that hadn't changed.

Shaking herself out of her melancholy, Tamara pulled a long, thin chain decorated at the end with a silver finial displaying a couple entwined in a sensual embrace. It was another of her finds that added to the mystical illusion of the shop.

The mellow, overhead light flicked off, leaving the shop in moonlight and shadows as she made her way to the back stairs and her apartment above. There was also an outside entrance, but Tamara rarely used it unless she went out at night. Tonight, all she wanted to do was shower and go to bed and try to figure out where she'd gone wrong with Zane. The software manuals she usually worked on in the evening to give added income to the family and to help add balance to her crazy lifestyle, could wait. It looked like she might have the whole weekend to sit home and work on them.

She wanted to read the journal again, to see if she'd somehow mistaken the instructions. It had seemed so clear-cut, almost guaranteed to work. But not for her. Not for a Tremayne.

Even before Tamara had opened the door at the top of the stairs, she knew the book—and all her fantasies—would have to wait.

The family was there to visit.

She had given Olga a key ages ago, to be used only in

an emergency. To the Tremaynes, everything constituted an emergency, and now they felt at ease to let themselves in whenever they wanted. With her family of self-proclaimed black sheep, counterfeit clairvoyants, and bona fide con artists, visits were seldom a casual thing. They usually meant that the family had ganged up on her with the intent of making her change her mind about something.

Not that they could. She'd been running the family since her sixteenth year, but not necessarily by choice. Someone had to do it.

Pinning a fat smile on her face, Tamara pulled the door open and said with false enthusiasm, "Uncle Thanos! Aunt Eva! Aunt Olga!"

Aunt Eva, at age seventy, the oldest in the group, and the most dramatic by far, was the only one who didn't still help out in the shop on occasion. She visited it, but usually just to criticize. She said, "So we are selling. We're being run out by demons!"

Uncle Thanos, his voice booming to match his great size, disagreed with Eva's sentiment. "It's a good thing to sell! Things'll be changing again. Finally, adventure, excitement, new travels. I'm more than ready."

Both Eva and Olga nodded, and Olga admitted, "It's for the best. We're not meant for the dormant life."

Tamara shook her head as she began removing all her jewelry and placing it on the small mahogany entrance table. So Thanos wanted to move? Ha! Getting the three of them packed up and mobile again would be a chore. Just thinking about it gave Tamara a pounding headache.

Despite the image they liked to project, her relatives were no longer the wandering Gypsies of her youth. As a child, she'd lived in more places than most people did in their entire lives. Tamara had always been grateful to them for raising her after her parents had died. They'd taken her in without hesitation, given her love and laughs, if not stability. Living with them had provided an interesting education.

But Tamara knew for a fact that they liked the settled, mostly sedate lifestyle she'd been able to give them since she'd become an adult. They took turns working with her in the shop, mostly on the busier weekends, and that was about as much excitement as they could handle these days.

Thanos now preferred to tend the tiny garden behind the house she'd bought for them, and amazingly enough, Eva and Olga knitted. They hid their projects from her, but Tamara still knew. She always knew what was going on when it came to her family.

Just as she knew their visit was for bluster. They didn't want to move, but they tried to hide that from her. And Tamara loved them all the more for their consideration.

Aunt Olga, so thin she looked like she could be folded away, announced in tones of premonition, "It's Uncle Hubert. He hasn't forgiven us for not forewarning him of his imminent death." Her frail hands covered her face. "Now we've angered him. You're right, Tamara. We must go. Before it's too late."

Tamara dropped back against the wall, so tired she wanted to collapse. Her colored contacts were starting to burn, and the ridiculous sandals pinched her beringed toes.

In as reasonable a voice as she could muster, she said, "Uncle Hubert died months ago. It was a freak accident, certainly not something we could have predicted."

"It was an omen," Olga cried.

If it had been an omen, Tamara thought with a smirk, someone had a warped sense of humor, because Hubert had expired at an outdoor concert when a vicious storm had overturned the portable toilet in which he was seated. He'd sustained a hard hit to the head and a true blow to his dignity, considering his pants had been around his ankles at the time.

"He was on the West Coast," Tamara reasoned. "We're in Kentucky. It wouldn't make much sense for Hubert to come all this way just for a little haunting over something we had no control over. Besides, it's not like we hadn't all warned him that he needed to quit partying so much.

One less concert, one less drink, one less groupie, and he might have still been with us."

The wig tickled and without caring what her relatives might think, Tamara pulled it off and vigorously ruffled her short blonde hair. Immediately her head began to feel better.

At least it did until Aunt Olga objected to Tamara's rationale.

"Mind powers," Olga insisted, "aren't affected by distance. Ghosts can damn well go wherever they please!"

Throwing up her arms in a display of frustration, Tamara stalked away. None of them had mind powers, much as they'd like to convince themselves otherwise, so there was no way they could have warned Hubert. Hubert knew it, so he had no reason to haunt them.

No, their troubles were rooted in a flesh-and-blood human, not a ghostly manifestation. But not knowing why anyone wanted to cause them trouble was what really bothered Tamara. So far as she knew, she had no enemies, and neither did her relatives. They were cons, but they were harmless cons. And it wasn't like the shop would be of value to anyone but a group of sentimental, aging Gypsies.

"I'm going to shower," she called over her shoulder, needing a few minutes of solace to shore herself up for the rest of the visit. She knew the relatives were night owls, and they wouldn't think twice about keeping her up so they could continue to lament the supposed haunting. "I'll be back in a minute."

More objections followed her down the short hall. Her living quarters consisted of a family room that opened to the outside stairs on one wall, and to the stairwell leading down to her shop on another. Next to that, separated by an arched doorway, was the kitchen, which also opened onto an L-shaped hallway. To the right was the part of the house she'd closed off. To the left was another short hallway that led to her bedroom and the bath.

Tamara could hear the buzz of the aunts grumbling,

along with Thanos's booming contribution, but the closing of the bathroom door mostly drowned them out. Despite her dejection over failing with Zane, a small smile touched Tamara's mouth. *Her demented family.* She should have known they'd find a way to dramatize the problems with the shop and their grief for Hubert. They lived to put on a show.

She loved them so much, even if they were all nuts. And perhaps their visit was propitious after all. She certainly couldn't pine for Zane while dealing with her relatives' extravagant tales of vaporish ghosts and spurious hauntings.

But even as Tamara tried to convince herself of that, her body warmed with the mere thought of Zane. She wanted him, needed him.

One way or another, she'd have to figure out how to have him before the house sold and she left town. She'd study the manual in minute detail until she found a way to win Zane over.

She deserved at least that much.

Two

Twilight had come and gone by the time Zane locked up the store for the night. It had been a great sale, very successful, and he was pleased. So why did he still feel so on edge?

Little Gypsy.

The large, ancient building housing her shop on the ground floor sat across the alley from the newer, more modern strip mall. Zane turned and, as usual, there was a light on in her upstairs window, the room he somehow knew was her bedroom. His stomach tightened, his muscles loosened, his body warmed.

They were extreme reactions that he couldn't control, and he hated that. In part, he'd avoided her for that very reason. She got close, and he felt it in his every nerve ending. He couldn't bear it; it smacked of a weakness he refused to accept.

Even as he told himself that he wouldn't allow her to get to him, he wondered what she'd look like stripped of those ridiculous long skirts and colorful blouses. Her hair was so long, it could easily cover her nudity. And that in itself was hotly erotic.

Except that he didn't like her hair. Normally long hair was a turn-on for Zane, the ultimate in femininity. But on the Gypsy, it seemed overdone, too much along with everything else. Her hair was thick and straight and inky black—and didn't suit her at all.

Without intending to, he walked toward the building, his hands on his hips, his head tilted to stare up at that lit window. He was diagonal with the front of the shop when he noticed the sign.

Zane stared at the bold black words FOR SALE for a long minute, refusing to believe what his eyes told him. She was moving away? Leaving for good?

"Shit." He stood there, feeling dazed and angry as the night breeze drifted over his heated skin, ruffling his hair, fogging his breath. He shook his head, a sharp, decisive movement. "No!" His voice sounded ominous in the quiet of the night with all the shops closed, the street mostly empty. It was an apt reflection of the turbulence smothering him. *"Hell, no."*

With a hard stride, Zane started toward the stairs at the side of the house. He'd prove to himself and to her that *he* was in control; no curse or spell—*no small Gypsy*— could make him do things he didn't want to do, or feel things he didn't want to feel. He wouldn't allow it.

Determined, even a little anxious, he took the metal steps two at a time. What he'd say to her, he had no idea, but by God she wasn't going to walk away without a few explanations.

Like how the hell she'd managed to get into his head when he didn't even know her name.

And how she could dare to proposition him in the middle of a busy sale, as if she'd been asking what time it was. He'd known a lot of bold women, and appreciated them for that very quality. But what the little Gypsy had done really crossed the line.

And now she dared to invade his dreams, to the point that he couldn't sleep anymore for craving her.

If she had cast a spell, she could damn well uncast it.

That's what he'd tell her. That and a little more, like how she was far too brazen, and how she grated on his nerves even from a distance.

And how he wanted her, too.

Each footfall on her steps clanged louder and louder, until Zane was literally stomping up to her door, the stairs rattling and shifting beneath his feet. He lifted one fist, rapped hard, and waited. He didn't realize he was holding his breath until he saw the curtain covering the door window move, and a pale face peeked out.

The curtain dropped immediately.

Anticipation, charged and smoldering, sizzled in the humid evening air. It shot through his veins and made his skin prickle. Zane sucked in a deep breath, and he was just about to knock again, through with waiting, when he heard the lock click.

The door opened a crack and a thin, small, blonde woman slipped out, pulling the door shut tight behind her. The landing at the top of the stairs was narrow, partially covered by a thick welcome mat. They stood close by necessity, her nose even with his throat, her hands still behind her, clutching the doorknob.

In utter silence, Zane looked her over. She wore slim jeans faded nearly white, a loose, untucked shirt, and no jewelry.

He didn't understand, didn't know who she was or why she was staying with the Gypsy—and then the breeze shifted and her scent, hot and sultry and compelling, filled him up and he went rigid.

The sweet smell of incense was gone, but the more basic aroma of woman remained, unique and tempting. Like any alert male animal, Zane drew it in, savored it, and recognized her by scent alone. Confusion swamped him, and then she looked up at him.

Large, dark green eyes fringed by impossibly long brown lashes ensnared him. Even the air he breathed seemed heated.

Zane shook his head. He knew, and yet he whispered, "Who the hell are you?"

"Tamara." She released the doorknob and shifted nervously. Her gaze never left his; like him, he doubted she could look away. "Tamara Tremayne."

Zane watched a soft, pale curl blow across her cheek. She quickly tucked it behind her small ear. His heartbeat stuttered.

"I'm sorry," she murmured, "I never introduced myself properly. Then again, you never really gave me the chance." Her voice was shaky, husky, and oh so familiar.

Zane watched her lush mouth move, now clean of the shiny red lipstick. The corners tilted up in an uncertain smile that he felt clean down to his groin.

Jesus. He knew lust, knew what it felt like, had wallowed in the intensity of it, the fiery pleasure of it.

This was something more.

This was so damn powerful he shook.

"Tamara." He touched her cheek, still staring into her eyes, unable to look away for more than a few seconds at a time. She looked so different. His mind was alert to deception, not understanding why or how she'd changed so quickly, but his body had immediately known her— and reacted to her. The erection he'd fought since her visit to the store was back in full force, straining against his slacks.

Tremulous, she smiled again, and that was all it took. She was as irresistible as the air he dragged into his lungs. Zane meant to kiss her gently, to let her get used to his deep sensuality and his agreement to her proposition by small degrees.

It didn't quite happen that way.

As he leaned toward her, her lips parted, and with a groan Zane took her, his mouth hungry, starving. She made a small sound of surprise, of acceptance, and her eagerness licked over him. He felt ready to ignite with the pleasure of it.

Insane, he insisted to himself, even as he held her face

still and, with one hard move, pinned her to the door with his hips. She was small, delicate, *pretty* . . . and she tasted better than anything he could remember. Her mouth was sweet and damp, her tongue stroking against his, accepting his, as eager as his own yet less practiced.

Her hands clutched the front of his shirt, then drifted lower to his waist, sliding slow and easy, exploring with a hunger that fueled his own. As if relishing the feel of him, her fingers spread and her small, hot hands teased. Zane threw his head back, panting, praying she'd touch him where he craved it most, trying to encourage her to do so.

And the door opened behind them.

Zane tried to catch her, but his sluggish brain was slow to react, his body too overheated to be cooperative. Tamara fell flat with a small yelp, and Zane tripped over her. He was barely able to keep from landing on top of her, smashing her into the carpet. He stumbled hard against an enormous solid object, and then was lifted off his feet and dangled in the air.

Confused, he stared down into the most ferocious face he'd ever seen on human or animal.

The man—if this was a man and not a damned yeti—sported a full, black bushy beard, a gold earring in one ear that matched a gold front tooth; his eyes were black as midnight.

Mean black eyes.

Immediately concerned for Tamara and intent on protecting her, Zane reacted on instinct. He brought his knee up in a sharp, solid blow, forcing the giant to gasp and drop him. As the man bent forward, holding his gut and wheezing, Zane grabbed him by his bushy head, ready to bring his knee up again, this time to smash a nose or break a jaw.

Zane's leg flexed, readying for impact—and something wiry jumped onto his back, clawlike fingers digging in for a good hold.

Twisting around, Zane saw a small, wrinkled face, wild,

gray hair pulled loose from a bun, and another set of fathomless ebony eyes. Their gazes locked; the wizened face scrunched up, then let out a screeching war cry that made the skin on Zane's body crawl and his eardrums reverberate with pain.

Before he could figure out how to get the demon off his back, Tamara had crawled around in front of him. She threw her arms around his thighs and pressed her face to his abdomen.

"Don't hurt him, Thanos!" she pleaded.

Don't hurt him? Indignant, Zane heard her words, and everything male in him rebelled. *He* was protecting *her*, not the other way around! Hadn't he already felled the giant? Why the hell was she worried for him? Or was Thanos a name for the witch on his back, yanking at his hair and bellowing into his ear until he thought he'd go deaf?

It was a miracle he could think at all with Tamara on her knees in front of him. Her supplicating position registered with the force of a thunderclap, and he nearly lost awareness of everything else. Even the pain in his scalp as the witch continued to yank on his head couldn't quite dispel the lascivious images.

Through the cotton of his pants, Zane could have sworn he felt the warmth of her breath.

Damn, he was in deep.

Zane touched the back of her head with one hand, amazed at how soft her blonde curls felt, and heard her say in an evil voice, "I mean it, Uncle. Put the cane down."

Cane? Zane looked up from Tamara, still in her imploring position, and observed that the giant now held a cane in one meaty fist, and the cane had a lethal blade on the end. He was also rubbing his stomach where Zane had kneed him, and he looked mad as hell.

Oh, shit.

Well, yeah, maybe he could use her intervention after all, especially since she seemed to know these lunatics.

"Tamara?" He deliberately tried to ignore the heaving behemoth ready to skewer him, despite Tamara's pleas. Zane tangled his fingers in her hair and urged her face up to his.

She blinked at him, and those green eyes nearly did him in once again. *Green, not black.* "Yes?"

Uncertain how to deal with such an overwhelming craving, Zane concentrated instead on the bizarre circumstances. "Do you think you can get this monkey off my back? I prefer my hair to stay on my head, rather than being strewn around the floor."

Gasping, Tamara leaped to her feet. She snatched the cane away from Thanos—*thank God she, at least, was thinking straight*— and ran behind Zane to remove the old lady who grasped him so tenaciously. It took Tamara a few minutes to get the old woman to disengage, and during that time, Zane lost a little more hair, even while he tried to hold perfectly still.

Thanos no longer held the cane, but he looked more than capable of removing body parts with his bare, ham-sized hands. Zane silently took the giant's measure; he didn't want to hurt anyone unless he was forced to.

"Aunt Olga," Tamara scolded in that beguiling voice he knew all too well, "what were you thinking, attacking him that way? You could have been hurt."

Olga waved a fistful of hair. "Ha!"

It was a cry of triumph. Zane rubbed his head and winced. He was lucky he wasn't bald.

Somehow he'd walked into a circus. Tamara wasn't Tamara anymore; she was better, and more mysterious than ever. And she had giants and witches for relatives. The best thing to do would be to walk right back out, to forget this day had ever happened.

But he wasn't a weak-spined coward, ready to turn tail and run at the first sign of mental instability. So her relatives were certifiable? He wouldn't let that stop him. Not when there was something, or someone, he wanted.

And right now, at this moment, he wanted Tamara Tremayne bad. That fact had been driven home to him in no uncertain terms.

Even in the midst of bedlam, he was aware of the vibrating tension in his muscles, and the sexual fever pulsing in his blood. He was too drawn to her to walk away now. But he could handle things his own way, refusing to give her the upper hand.

Zane raised one brow, keeping a close eye on Thanos-the-missing-link, and said, "Tamara, would you mind telling me what the hell is going on here?"

The giant stepped forward and thundered, "You were mauling her! We all saw you."

Zane couldn't very well deny that, because he had been all over her—never mind that she seemed to be going along with it, even enjoying herself. And perhaps doing a little mauling of her own.

Not since his second woman had Zane abandoned all finesse during a seduction, but with Tamara, for that brief moment, he'd been aware only of his need for her. Nothing else had registered. They'd been on a stair landing, for God's sake, but if no one had interrupted them, Zane suspected he'd have taken her right there, with only the night shadows to conceal their activity.

And from all indications, she'd have let him.

As he started to nod in assent, ready to accept the truth of Thanos's claims, Tamara gasped and said loudly, "I *wanted* him to."

That sure got things quiet.

While they all, Zane included, stood there staring at her with their mouths open, she asked, "What were you all doing watching, anyway? I specifically told you to give me a few minutes of privacy."

"Your apartment isn't big enough for privacy," Thanos told her.

"It's big enough if you don't press your nose to the door window and snoop."

Zane was surprised not only by what she said, but also her vehemence and the number of words she'd used to say it. In the time he'd known her, Tamara had managed to be mysteriously soft-spoken and far from chatty.

Olga, brushing Zane's hair from her hand, shrugged her narrow, frail shoulders. "We heard you hit the door. We thought he was attacking you."

Another woman, a bit older but looking just as mean, harrumphed as she came up next to Olga. "He *was* attacking her."

Olga narrowed her eyes. "Now that I think about it though, she didn't seem to be fighting him off."

Zane rubbed the back of his neck. This was too much for him. Way too much. It had been a long time since he'd had to deal with a woman's relatives. "Look, I'm sorry I jumped on her that way. I've never done that before."

Tamara took immediate offense. "Don't you dare apologize, Zane Winston. You didn't jump on me, you kissed me." She stepped closer to him, pointing that lethal cane at his chest. "And it was wonderful." Her fierce expression was enough to melt his insides.

Zane's libido stirred, and he fought to keep his responses at bay. Not here, not now. It had been bad enough dealing with an erection in the store, with swarms of customers moving around him. In front of her less than reasonable relatives, it would be impossible.

Zane didn't move except to let his eyes shift, taking in all the curious faces surrounding them. Thanos looked bemused. Olga and the other woman were pressed together, eyes wide, staring at Tamara.

"Uh. . . ." Zane knew he had to regain control somehow. "Care to introduce me, Gypsy?" He figured if he was to be accosted and threatened and put on display, it should at least be on a first-name basis.

Tamara clapped a hand over her luscious mouth. "Ohmigosh. I'm sorry, Zane. Of course I should introduce everyone."

She stepped to his side and clasped his arm, providing a united front against the others. Zane refused to dwell on the emotions that her action stirred, how her stance pleased him. Plenty of women had stood at his side throughout his life, but none had ever seemed quite so *right* there. That realization disturbed him.

"Zane Winston," she said, now smiling, "this is my uncle, Thanos, and my aunts, Olga and Eva Tremayne."

The relationship was easy enough to see. Though they didn't look anything like Tamara now, they certainly looked like her when she wore her Gypsy getup. And while their eyes were black, and hers were green, the slanting, cat-eyes shape was the same.

"You called her Gypsy," Eva accused with a smile. She looked very pleased by it.

Zane shrugged. He wanted to touch Tamara again; he wanted to find out what the hell had happened with the long black hair, the penetrating black eyes. In the most basic ways, she was the same woman without the unusual clothes and makeup, yet she was also doubly intoxicating.

Now she seemed more real, more attainable, and that played havoc with his senses. She wasn't that gorgeous, and she certainly wasn't stacked. But she was still so intrinsically sexy that his temperature had automatically gone up three degrees the second he'd seen her.

He was starting to sweat.

"She claims to be one," Zane explained, and hoped he was the only one to notice the gravelly, aroused tone to his voice. "But seeing her like this, I have to wonder."

"There, you see," Olga said with satisfaction. "Without the right props, no one would know your heritage. You're far too fair, too slight, and plain. We were right. You need the enhancement."

Tamara frowned at Zane, and her eyes were lit with a touch of disappointment. At him?

"They insist I wear the dumb costume—"

"Not dumb," both women exclaimed, obviously appalled that she'd utter such sacrilege.

"—otherwise, I'm like the white sheep in the family."

Thanos shook his huge head and laughed. The windows

rattled at his exuberance. "Little Gypsy, even without the costume, you're still a white sheep." To Zane he added, "She's too good, too tenderhearted. She has a conscience as big as the moon. How she came to be in our family is a miracle."

Eva added, "It's amazing she plays the game so well, considering her romantic nature."

"The game?"

Nodding, Eva said, "Fortune-telling, palm reading, and the rest."

Olga went on tiptoe to murmur into Zane's ear, "She comes from sure stock, yet doesn't like fooling people. Can you imagine?"

Zane wasn't exactly sure what they were all prattling on about, but he could feel Tamara's distress. He knew he was partly responsible, and regretted it. The last thing he wanted to do was hurt her.

Didn't these people—her own family—know they were upsetting her? It angered him, and made him feel not only protective, but defensive. They weren't emotions he normally associated with anyone other than his family. He frowned with that realization. "I'd like to talk to Tamara alone now, if you wouldn't mind."

Thanos barked a rough laugh. "It's not talking you have thoughts for, man. Your lust is there for all to see."

Olga sighed dreamily. "For our little Tamara."

"It's about time," Eva added.

About time? What the hell did that mean?

Tamara, her face coloring hotly, whirled on them all. Zane had never seen her angry, never heard her loud.

Never seen her blonde.

"Don't any of you even *think* of interrupting me again, do you understand?" She pointed toward a hallway and said, "We're going to my room, and if I hear even a creak of a footstep"—her voice dropped to a demonic growl—"I'll make you all *so* sorry."

As far as threats went, it wasn't specific enough that

Zane would have worried. She was one small woman. What could she possibly do to them?

Thanos gave her an approving nod, unmistakably pleased with her show of anger. "The Tremayne temper. She has it in spades."

The two old women twittered.

Exasperated, Tamara grabbed Zane by the arm and practically dragged him down the hall. He felt the gazes of her aunts and uncle boring into his back like fiery brands. Without any of them uttering a word, he heard *their* threats loud and clear, and they were a lot more specific than Tamara's had been.

If he hurt her, they *would* make him sorry.

Zane shook off his uneasiness. He was about to be alone with her, and that filled him with undeniable expectation; there was no room for anything else.

Tamara dragged him inside a room and shoved the door shut. Bright, overhead lighting, centered above a huge, modern computer desk, nearly blinded him, drawing his attention first.

She flipped a wall switch, and there was only moonlight filtering through her window, and light from one small lamp on a table beside her queen-size bed.

Zane stilled. He was in her bedroom. They were relatively alone. He looked at Tamara and caught her bewitching smile.

Oh, no. He wouldn't make it so easy on her. She'd led him in here, and now she was smiling at him, her eyes filled with promise. Teasing, taunting, using her Gypsy tricks and her curses. He was on to her.

Now was as good a time as any for him to take control. She claimed only to want sex. Fine. He'd give it to her, in abundance. He'd brand her in the best way known to man.

His gaze raked over her, seeing the thrust of her pretty breasts beneath her top, the gentle slope of her belly, and the curve of her hips in the snug jeans. There wouldn't be a single part of her he left untouched.

He'd see to it that she experienced the best damn sex she'd ever had. When all was said and done, she'd be as emotionally raw and hotly wired as he now felt.

Having made his decision, Zane gave Tamara his own slow smile, and watched her eyes widen in wariness. She swallowed, and said softly, "Oh, my."

Zane had the awful suspicion she'd just read his mind, and anticipated his intent.

Christ, what had he gotten himself into?

Three

"Oh, my, what?" Zane demanded.

She licked her lips, tried for a negligent shrug, but her eyes told it all. She had beautiful, incredible eyes, the green much nicer than the darker contacts had ever been.

"I was . . . just. . . ." She gestured with her hand. "You look so . . ." Clearing her throat, she said, "Never mind."

Refusing to let her see his unease, purposely shifting the mood, Zane glanced around the room and was amazed by what he saw. In direct contradiction to what he'd seen of her shop through the large front window, her private room was plain—and modern.

Neither the desk nor the computer fit his original image of her. As a Gypsy, she used candles and incantations as her tools, not a state-of-the-art computer complete with fax and scanner and copier. Yet the system arranged neatly on her desk was most impressive. Zane eyed it with appreciation, wondering what she did on that computer, if she'd learned to cast spells through the Internet.

There were no ornate fixtures or candles or lace overlays. No smoldering incense, no colored lights. Her bedspread was plain blue, her carpeting a solid beige, her furniture sturdy light oak in a style of clean, simple lines.

There was no clutter anywhere, nothing fancy, nothing exotic or seductive. It amazed Zane, and further confounded him.

This room matched her as she was now, a petite blonde scrubbed clean of makeup, barefoot, wearing well-worn jeans. An innocent earth child, and doubly sexy because of it.

Tamara took in his frown and stepped away. For the moment, Zane let her retreat, knowing if he reached for her, they'd be back at square one, with her body flush against his where he most wanted it to be. He needed some answers first; he needed to know her at least a little more.

Zane watched her pace the length of the airy room. She went to the window that faced his store and moved the curtains aside to look out. How many nights had she done that? How many nights had she watched him from that window? Maybe he'd felt her gaze, maybe that accounted for his sleepless nights and vivid dreams.

In a soft, agonized whisper, she said, "I'm so, so sorry."

Zane's chest constricted tightly at her low apology, at the embarrassment and upset he could hear in her tone. "For what?" he asked, keeping his tone gentle, hoping to soothe her, to gain her confidence.

"Everything." She shrugged helplessly. "Shocking you as I look now, letting my relatives attack you, even my bold proposition this afternoon."

Panic ripped through him, and he growled, "I won't let you take it back."

She turned to face him, lips parted in surprise.

In three long strides, Zane reached her. *"I won't let you take it back."* He clasped her shoulders, drew her up to her bare toes. "You said you wanted to sleep with me."

Her chest rose and fell, her eyes widened and glittered with moonlight. "I do."

"You said you wanted sex with me." Zane didn't want

any misunderstandings. He wasn't sure he could survive a misunderstanding.

Tamara licked her lips slowly, cautiously. "Yes."

Rather than easing his tension, her confirmation drew him tighter until his every muscle strained and he could count the hard beats of his heart. Knowing he was close to losing it again, Zane forced his fingers to open, to release her, and he stepped away.

He felt like a damn fool. How did she keep doing this to him, pushing him over the edge, making him act like a man he didn't recognize? How did she make him so aware of her every thought and emotion, until they became his own? He didn't want any woman to affect him that deeply.

"Good." He gave a sharp nod. "Then that's settled."

"Is it?" She looked him over, taking in his features with a kind of hopefulness that nearly made him groan aloud. "Is it, really?"

"Oh, yeah." Zane couldn't quite get over his amazement at her appearance. He could have looked at her all night long and it wouldn't have been enough. "There's no backing out for you now."

Her blonde curls bounced silkily as she shook her head. "I don't want to back out. I want you."

In that moment, Zane decided Tamara would have been a valuable addition to the Inquisition. "Damn, don't say that."

"Don't say . . . what?"

"That you want me." He scrubbed his hands over his face, paced up and down. "I don't know why, I don't understand this at all, but I'm hanging on by a thread." He stopped and glared at her. "A real thin thread."

Tamara came a tiny bit closer. It was too close. He could detect her scent again, and it called to him in some primal way, tightening his testicles, filling him with a surge of hunger until his vision blurred and narrowed on her features.

"You want me, too?" she asked.

Her naïveté would have made him laugh in different circumstances. Plainly visible if she only looked, his cock filled his pants, straining for release, straining for her. And even if she missed that rather obvious sign, lust was written all over his face. Hell, even Thanos had seen it, and that's when Zane had thought he was successfully hiding it.

"I want you," he confirmed, then added, "And I intend to have you, since you were gracious enough to offer."

"Thank you."

He knew women, knew all their tricks, all their ploys. But he had no idea what Tamara was up to—or, for that matter, who she really was. A blonde who pretended to have raven hair? A modern woman who gave the illusion of Old World values? A wild temptress who now looked too sweet to bear?

Slowly circling her, Zane studied Tamara from every angle. Wearing a loose pullover shirt and trim jeans, her blonde hair mussed, her extreme makeup and the abundance of jewelry gone, she looked like innocence personified.

Yet she'd liked being mauled by him on the stairs when he'd only just learned her name. Her sexual nature matched his, or at least came close enough that she'd been as unaware of the surroundings as he had. All that had mattered was getting closer.

But there was something he was missing. Since he'd known her, which had always been in a peripheral way, Tamara had presented herself as a free-spirited Gypsy wrapped in mystery and superstition. Her clothes said as much. Her shop said as much. Her every smile and teasing glance said as much.

And now, by pure chance Zane had caught her looking entirely different. Not like a Gypsy siren, but like a damn schoolgirl.

"How old are you?" he asked abruptly, suddenly uncertain—she appeared so young, so inexperienced, so hopeful.

She tucked her fair hair behind her ears, inadvertently shoring up his perceptions, then said, "Twenty-four. And you?"

"Twenty-seven," Zane answered, distracted by his thoughts. She didn't look twenty-four. Of course, she hadn't really looked like a black-haired Gypsy either. Perhaps that accounted for his edgy reaction to her. He'd suspected she was hiding behind a dark façade.

Would she have gone on deceiving him if he hadn't made his impromptu visit tonight?

Was she deceiving him even now?

"This is your natural look?" At her blank expression, he clarified. "The blonde hair is natural?"

She touched her hair. "Yes."

"There are ways I can tell, you know."

Her brow lifted. "How?"

"When I see you naked."

She blinked at him, and then, as realization dawned, her face heated and her hand dropped to her side. "I'm a . . . a natural blonde."

Zane sensed her discomfort as he continued to circle her, continued to study her in minute detail. "I *will* see you naked, you know."

Nodding, she asked, "And I'll see you, too?"

Zane hesitated, taken aback by her question. "Did you think I made love fully dressed?"

"Have sex."

"What?"

He stood behind her, paused momentarily. She replied without looking at him, "We'll have sex, not make love. We . . . you and I barely know each other, so there won't be any love involved."

She annoyed him. Zane narrowed his eyes and said through his teeth, "Yeah, I'll be naked. And it's fine with me if you want to look your fill."

Again she said, "Thank you."

"I'll be looking my fill, too. Will you like that, Tamara?"

She nodded, but said, "I don't know."

Because she had something to hide? For certain she didn't have a shy bone in her luscious little body. Zane began circling again.

Her fair skin and glittering green eyes went along with the golden hair, so she was likely telling the truth about that. But he wasn't quite satisfied; there were too many things that didn't add up.

Would she have worn that black wig to bed with him when he made love to her? Would black eyes have smiled up at him when he was inside her, riding her slow, stroking deep?

Eyes like green fire watched him now, wide and wary at his prolonged silence. Zane stopped in front of her and smiled.

"Just like that?" he asked, keeping his voice silky and smooth. "You ask me to have sex with you, I agree, and you're . . . grateful?"

Her gaze wavered, embarrassed, then bravely came back to his. "Well, you did say no at first."

That wasn't the answer he had expected. It wasn't practiced or flirtatious or challenging. It was . . . honest.

It threw him off. Zane stared at the ceiling, trying to organize his thoughts. It was a mistake. Tamara took swift advantage of his preoccupation and moved against him. Her arms slipped around his waist, squeezed him tight.

"I've wanted you," she whispered, "since the first time I saw you."

His knees nearly gave out. "Did you cast a damn spell on me or something?" he growled, needing to know.

Her cheek rubbed his chest as she shook her head. "No. I can't do that." She glanced up at him. "But I probably would have if I was able."

Too much honesty, he decided. He wasn't used to it, didn't know how to deal with it. Thoughts warred with his instinct, and instinct won. He couldn't resist cuddling her closer. Everything about the embrace felt right: the way the heat of their bodies melded together, mingling their scents; how her head tucked neatly into his shoulder; how her breasts crushed against his ribs. And that bothered him even more. It shouldn't feel so right. No embrace had ever felt like this before.

If she hadn't done something magical to him, then what was going on?

"Why have you waited to say something?" Zane asked. "Why ask me now?"

Her arms tightened. "Every other woman in town has had you," she complained softly, "So why *not* me?"

She sounded logical, a woman utilizing a sensible argument. Only there was nothing sensible about Tamara Tremayne or the circumstances.

"So now, today, you decided to pull out the big guns?"

"Big guns?"

He rubbed his chin against her hair, feeling the warmth and softness of it. He wanted to devour her, and he wanted to hold her gently all night. "No man can resist a direct attack. You said you wanted me, which made me want you." That was only a partial truth. In his dreams, he'd wanted her for a long time.

"You've always ignored me," Tamara said, tilting her head back to see his face. "And I hated it. I tried everything to get your attention, but you always looked through me, or past me." She drew a deep breath. "Now I'm going to have to leave, and my biggest regret was that I wouldn't have another chance to be with you, to fulfill a few of my fantasies. So yes, I felt a direct attack was my last resort."

Zane was still aroused, but now some other emotion prevailed. He didn't know what it was, so he couldn't fight against it. "I haven't been with *every* woman in town." For some reason, he wanted her to understand that.

She laughed. "Okay, so there are a few you're not interested in. I've been to the Winston Tavern. I've seen the women hanging on your every word. And I saw how much you love it."

Zane pushed her back a bit, frowning. "You've been to the bar? When?" His oldest brother, Cole, ran the bar, and

Chase was the bartender. He and Mack worked there part-time, more so back when they were in college. Now Mack was teaching and Zane spent the majority of his hours at his computer store. But the bar was a comforting haven when he wanted to be with friends and family, and it still seemed natural to serve drinks or wipe tables whenever he was around.

Not once could he recall seeing Tamara there.

"Off and on," Tamara hedged.

"Off and on when?" A thought occurred to him, and his hands tightened on her shoulders. "You were there dressed as you are now, or as the Gypsy?"

As if his question had somehow insulted her, her chin lifted. "Neither. I dress the Gypsy when I work. You heard my relatives. I'm not a very convincing fortune-teller as I really look." Her upturned nose wrinkled. "I look too young and gullible. So it's necessary."

Zane wanted to tell her she was a pretty damn convincing femme fatale no matter how she dressed, but he held the words back.

"You caught me getting ready for bed," she explained, "so I'm sort of a mess right now. But when I go out, I do know how to clean up proper."

Zane stared down at her. He was very aware of her body against his, but he had control of himself, and he meant to keep it that way. Talking with her seemed like a good way to maintain that control. "The ghastly makeup?"

"Is like the jewelry and the dark contacts and the wig. I wear makeup, just as most women do, but it's not so dramatic."

Zane looked at her mouth, naked and full and so sexy. He touched the corner of her lips with his thumb, brushing softly until she opened, until he could hear her accelerated breathing and see the tip of her pink tongue. "You don't need makeup."

Carefully, he lifted his hands to her hair and tangled his fingers in the fine, silky curls. She was baby soft, and it made him wonder about other parts of her, if she was so damn soft all over. His blood surged hotly.

"Answer me this." His large hands easily held her immobile. "If I had agreed this afternoon, how would you have come to me?"

Her lashes lowered, hiding her eyes. "I don't know what you mean."

Zane gently tugged on her hair until her face tilted up at him. Restraining himself, he kissed her—a light, teasing kiss—then whispered against her lips, "Yes, you do. Would I have been sleeping with the sultry Gypsy or the sweet little blonde?"

Tamara strained closer, trying to gain full access to his mouth again, but Zane stayed just out of reach, only his breath caressing her lips. She made a soft sound of frustration. "I don't know. I hadn't thought that far ahead."

"Tamara. . . ." He loved saying her name, loved the lyrical sound of it, the suggested eroticism, the mystique. It suited her perfectly. "Don't ever lie to me."

"A . . . a book said I should be bold, that men love boldness in a woman." She waited for his nod of agreement, then continued. "Especially men who are slaves to their primitive nature."

"Primitive nature?"

"Men who are ruled by their libidos." She said it against his mouth, then licked his bottom lip in a suggestive way that made his erection swell and strain against his fly.

Holding himself in check had never been so damn difficult.

"I'd have been the Gypsy," she whispered, "bold and sensual." Her green gaze snared his, mesmerized him. "And you'd have loved it."

Zane took her mouth hard, further scattering her wits, doing it deliberately. It was a great effort not to give in to the demands of his body, but her comment about a book, about slaves and boldness, swirled in his head. He wanted explanations, and he intuitively knew the best way to get them would be to keep her off balance.

She gasped when he ended the kiss. "You think I'm a slave to my sexuality?" As he spoke, he pressed hot, damp kisses against the tender skin of her throat.

Her head tilted back, exposing her to him. "I know you are."

Zane smiled, nibbling his way down to her shoulder. He was the master, not the slave; she'd understand that soon enough. Spells and curses be damned, he would do as he pleased, and not be caught.

It was what she wanted anyway, what she'd asked for, so there would be no call for him to feel guilty.

Impatience rode him hard, and he decided to get this interview over with. He wanted to take her to his place, where they could be alone, without the twin banshees and a dark behemoth waiting outside the door.

He wanted her naked, stretched out on his bed. With nothing between them except excitement, it wouldn't matter who she chose to be, the Gypsy or the innocent. He'd take either one.

And listen in satisfaction while she screamed his name, begging for more of the pleasure he'd give her.

Zane nuzzled her throat, inhaling her increasingly potent scent. "Tell me about this book, Tamara."

Suddenly she stiffened. A second later, before Zane could reclaim her thoughts, she pushed away from him. He let her go rather than chase after her. Her reaction to a mention of the book was interesting, even if his body rebelled at the distance now between them.

Looking horrified, Tamara backed up and shook her head. Moonlight poured over her in a silver glow, showing her wide eyes, the gentle slope of her narrow nose, her rounded chin. When she was several feet from him, her back to the wall near the door, she said, "The book is—"

A crash from far away echoed in the room. Zane heard the relatives just outside the bedroom door, scrambling around and muttering obscenities. A fist—likely Thanos, given the way the door frame rattled—demanded their attention.

"He's back," Thanos thundered.

"Hubert is downstairs," Olga wailed. "Lord almighty! He's come for us!"

Tamara flipped on the bedroom light and opened the door. *"Hubert is dead!"*

"It's his ghost," Eva insisted, her hands clasped to her chest, her black eyes filled with dramatic horror.

"There's no telling what he's capable of doing in this form!"

"Oh for the love of . . ."

Tamara, still muttering to herself, started away. Zane rushed after her. He wondered who Hubert was, and what he had to do with ghosts and the racket that had come from downstairs.

Like a parade, the other three hustled into line behind him.

"What the hell is going on?" Zane asked to Tamara's retreating back.

She kept moving, forcing Zane to keep up as she raced on light feet for the stairwell that would take her to the main shop.

"Shh," she cautioned, and then quietly opened the door. It gave an ominous creak, as if tuned for the effect. "I have an intruder, a live one, though my aunts insist on thinking it's my deceased uncle Hubert."

He knew he shouldn't have been surprised at this new turn of events, but just when he thought things couldn't get more bizarre. . . . "Your deceased uncle Hubert?"

"Tragic," Olga whispered from behind Zane's right shoulder. "Just tragic how he died."

"And now he wants revenge," Eva predicted in mournful tones while edging close to Zane's other side.

Tamara turned. "Stay back, all of you." Incredibly, she included Zane in her order. Her uncle and aunts obediently stopped in midstep. Zane gave her a ferocious scowl.

"This time," Tamara said with relish, "I'll catch him for sure."

Zane snared a fistful of her shirt and jerked her up short just as she started to turn away. "The hell you will!"

She tried to shush him, which only made him angrier. "You mean to tell me," he growled, his other hand now wrapped securely around her upper arm, making sure she wouldn't slip away from him, "that you think someone has broken in downstairs and you're determined to go investigate?"

"Someone *is* downstairs," she whispered anxiously, "unless your big mouth has just scared him away."

His big mouth? Zane couldn't remember a woman ever outright insulting him before. Usually they showered him with sweet compliments.

He'd never met a woman with a more stubborn independent streak, either. Most females would have had enough sense to send an available male downstairs to check things out. But not Tamara. No, she ignored Zane's presence—except when it came to the subject of sex.

His scowl turned a little blacker. He glared at Tamara, then thrust her toward Thanos. "Hang onto her. I'll be right back."

Olga and Eva looked at him like he was true hero material.

Thanos, beaming at him in approval, asked, "What will you do if it is a ghost?"

Knowing the big man deliberately baited him, Zane said, "I'll kick his ass," and he trotted down the steps. "Just keep the women upstairs."

He was surely in bedlam, Zane decided, hearing Thanos laugh as Tamara insisted on being turned loose. But with the mood Zane was in, any intruder, ghost or otherwise, would be smart to get the hell out of his way.

Zane fully expected to walk through the downstairs without a single disturbance.

Unfortunately, things didn't quite turn out that way.

Four

Tamara heard a loud thump, then a husky groan. Her heart shot straight into her throat, nearly strangling her. "Zane!"

In his sudden concern for Zane, Thanos became preoccupied and loosened his grip just enough. Tamara didn't even think twice; she bolted away, intent only on getting to Zane.

"Damn it, Tamara," Thanos groused as he made a wild grab for her and missed, "come back here this second!"

Tamara ignored him, leaping down the stairs two and three at a time. Behind her, she heard Olga chanting and Eva cursing.

Zane hadn't flipped on any lights, but the moon was bright enough that the shadows were gray rather than black, and large objects were outlined by an opalescent sheen. Tamara knew her shop—every knickknack, curio, and tattered rug—without the benefit of lights.

She also knew Zane Winston, much better than she'd thought. Her intuitive abilities were far from psychic, but every time Zane had looked at her, she'd felt him. She'd shared his feelings.

She'd known his desires.

And boy, was the man hot-blooded! Tamara hadn't expected to be wanted like that—in fact, Zane's graphic, blatant hunger alarmed her. She'd hoped he would agree to share sex with her, but she hadn't expected him to crave her. She wasn't exactly afraid of him, but his intensity was startling. And exciting.

No way would she let some blasted intruder hurt him.

Crouching by the long counter, she stopped and listened, but it was difficult to hear anything over the pounding of her heart and the racket of her relatives upstairs.

Then a faint grunt reached her ears. *Zane!* She felt his pain, slight but nagging, and she accepted it, took it in, made it her own.

Without hesitation, she followed her senses toward the backroom. She slithered past the counter, slipped through the partially open curtain.

There was only one narrow window in the backroom, shadowed by the other buildings, and she didn't dare turn on a light. It was so dark she couldn't see her hand in front of her face.

Reaching out, she felt for the wall, then the door frame. The door was wide open, and she darted inside—and promptly toppled over a large, hard object sprawled out around her feet.

With a grunt, she landed hard. One of her elbows cracked on the concrete floor, making her wince, and the other. . . .

The lump on the floor reared up with a bellow, then collapsed with a long, shuddering, pain-filled moan.

"Zane?" Tamara twisted around, trying to find his head so she could see how badly he was hurt.

His hand caught her bare foot, stilling her movements. "Christ almighty, woman! Are you trying to make me a choirboy?"

Tamara's eyes adjusted to the dark, and she realized she was facing the wrong end of Zane. He was the hard thing she'd tripped over, sprawled flat on his back in the middle of the floor. "Zane? What in the world are you doing? Are you hurt?" Then, with extreme menace: "Did someone hit you?"

Zane laughed. "I'm just bruised." His fingers were still around her foot. "There's no one here. I fell over a damn box of books."

"You're bruised?" She tried to turn so she could evaluate his injuries.

Zane tightened his hold. "Bruised, and getting more so by the second. Will you hold *still*?"

Tamara froze. She'd just realized her head was directly over his lap.

Her hands twitched. She squinted hard, trying to see more clearly through the inky blackness. "Um . . . I guess that wasn't your stomach I elbowed."

He growled. "My stomach is *not* soft."

No, she knew it wasn't. She'd seen his washboard abs a few times when he'd been helping unload a truck behind his shop. Watching Zane Winston lose his shirt, seeing the sweat dampen his upper body as he worked, had been a particular kind of provocation, doing much to embellish her fantasies. His chest was lightly covered with springy dark hair, and his jeans always rode low, showing off his navel, occasionally even his hipbones.

Groaning, she gave in to temptation and put both hands on his fly. He jerked, and a low, raw groan reverberated softly in the room. Tonight he wore casual khaki slacks, which did nothing to hinder her inquisitive fingers.

He filled her hands.

Eyes closed so her senses could fully absorb him, her stomach flip-flopped, heat pulsed and swelled beneath her skin. He was soft down low—probably where her sharp elbow had landed—and hot and hard and heavy above. She traced the rigid length of his erect penis with her palm and felt his legs flex, shift. Her breath shuddered in and out. So hard, so long. So very nice.

Zane lifted his hips just a bit, then made another low sound, this one more pain-filled than any of the others. It struck Tamara that she was copping a feel off an injured man! She wanted him, but she didn't want to take advantage of him. Not like this.

Mortified by her uncharacteristically brash behavior, she was just about to lever herself up—never mind that his hard body felt very nice beneath hers—when the bare lightbulb overhead clicked on.

There was a startled moment of silence before Thanos roared at Zane, *"What the hell do you think you're doing with her, man?"*

Tamara started to object, but Zane just dropped his head back and laughed. He still held her foot, his long fingers fastened around her ankle so tightly she knew she couldn't do a thing until he let her.

She looked down at his erection, appreciating the bird's-eye view now that she could see him, and regretting the interruption.

Thanos took a step forward, his eyes almost red. Zane said, "She's on top, Thanos. All I'm doing is trying to protect my more vulnerable body parts from elbows and knees."

No sooner did he say it than she moved again and her heel made sharp contact with his chin.

Thanos chuckled.

Zane didn't find anything humorous in the situation. He sat up and used her leg to drag her around to face him, then held her cradled on his lap. The new position effectively hid his arousal from her uncle, and it felt really nice against her backside.

Using the tip of one finger, Zane brought her gaze around to his. His brown eyes, shadowed by his lashes, were dark with annoyance. "Do you have a problem following orders?"

Unsure whether she should be outraged or incredulous, Tamara leveled a look on him. "You've got to be kidding, right?"

His brows snapped down. "I specifically told you to wait upstairs."

Tamara leaned back to stare at him in disbelief. "Surely

you never, for one second, thought you could give me orders?"

Zane glanced up at her uncle, who held out both hands, wisely refusing him any help. Tamara waited.

With an exaggerated sigh, Zane said, "I can see we're going to have to work out a few ground rules."

"Absolutely, but later." She was beginning to notice the mess around her. An enormous box of erotic books she'd purchased from an estate sale had fallen from a top shelf. They were everywhere, a few of the spines broken, some pages torn.

She hadn't had a chance to assess the value of all the books yet. Some of them seemed very old, maybe even antique. A collector might pay a high price for them—if they hadn't been destroyed by the fall.

Thank God she'd already moved the journal upstairs. In truth, it was probably worth less than any of the other books. But Tamara found it fascinating reading, and beyond value to her personally. "What happened here? Are you sure no one hit you?"

Zane worked his jaw as if only the clench of his teeth held his temper at bay. "No, there was no one here. No intruder, no spirit. You must have put the books too close to the edge of the shelf, and they fell. That's the racket you heard. I tripped over the damn things, and you tripped over me."

It seemed very unlikely to her that the books would have fallen suddenly. She'd bought the box of books almost two months ago, and they'd been on the shelf ever since. They hadn't shown any sign of toppling before now.

Tamara rubbed her bruised elbow. "Where are you hurt?"

"I conked my head is all. It dazed me for a second." Zane took her hand and pulled her arm straight so he could examine her elbow. "At least you landed on me rather than the hard floor."

Tamara blinked at him. "News flash, Zane. You're not exactly cushiony."

To her amazement, he brushed off her elbow, ran his thumb over it twice, then pressed a soft kiss to the red spot. In a voice far too intimate, considering her uncle stood close by at full alert, he asked, "Does it hurt?"

She nearly melted on the spot. Her insides turned to liquid, problems faded away under the impact of his touch.

The intruder had been at it again, she just knew it. But for the first time since the trouble had started, she really didn't give a damn.

Zane Winston wanted her. For tonight, that was enough.

Thanos hauled them to their feet. *"None of that, now,"* he said to Zane. "You keep your lips to yourself until Tamara's aunts and I have had time to consider this."

Zane raised a brow at Tamara, who sighed theatrically. "There's nothing to consider, Uncle Thanos, so back off."

"Not this time, sweetie. There's a lot going on here, what with the trouble and ghosts." He eyed Zane. "How do we know who's involved and who isn't?"

"Thanos!" Tamara looked prepared to have a full-fledged fit, and Zane meant to forestall that occurrence. Already his head ached from connecting with the concrete floor, and other parts of him ached, thanks to Tamara's bold curiosity and soft little hands. He couldn't take a family brawl right now.

"I'm here because she asked me to be," Zane pointed out, "and I wouldn't do anything to her that she didn't want me to do." He hoped to reassure Thanos, and at the same time spoke only the truth. From what Tamara had said to him, she wanted a lot, all of it sexual. That suited Zane just fine.

Tamara gasped as if she'd known his exact thought, but Thanos laughed out loud. "Ah, now there's the rub. What our little Gypsy lacks in dark looks, she makes up for with darker passion and an imagination that boggles the mind."

Zane eyed her. "Dark passion, huh?" He wasn't sure he liked hearing that. How many men had come before him? Had she seduced them as the Gypsy, or as the angel? And exactly what had her imagination dredged up that could boggle the mind? His mind was pretty damn creative, all on its own.

"That's enough out of both of you!" Tamara looked beyond Thanos, then put her hands to her head. "Here come Eva and Olga. This night is never going to end."

Zane felt his smile slip. Did she mean her relatives intended to hang around a little longer? That wouldn't do. He wanted her now. Right this instant. He was willing to wait a few minutes more ... but the whole night? He snorted.

Tamara gave him a pathetic, helpless look, and nodded. Damn it, if she didn't stop reading his thoughts, he'd—

Olga suddenly came around Thanos and threw her skinny arms around Zane with an exuberant hug. "Zane! Thank God you were here, young man." Then she thrust him back and demanded shrilly, "What did you see? What did Hubert look like? Is he well?"

Eva shook her head. "Olga, Hubert is *dead*. How can he be well, for pity's sake?" Then to Zane, "Was he ethereal? Wispy? Or was he as solid and substantial as ever?"

She turned to Tamara without waiting for Zane to answer. "You know Hubert always was a stocky man. Thick in the chest."

He'd landed in bedlam, Zane decided. In precise tones, so no one would misunderstand, he said, "There was no ghost. No Uncle Hubert. No intruder." Waving a hand, he indicated the books scattered everywhere. They were dusty and old, some of the yellowed pages lying loose. "The books fell, that's all."

Olga peered at the books. "Wonder if Hubert pushed them down."

Eva nodded enthusiastically. "Probably did. Hubert never was one much for reading."

"No." Tamara stood like a small amazon, hands on her hips. "For the last time, it's not Hubert. It's a . . . well, a man, probably, though I suppose it could be a woman."

Zane surveyed her serious expression and swallowed his impatience. "What makes you think a man would break in here? For what purpose? To steal your books?"

"No, of course not. But. . . ." She hesitated, then shrugged. "Never mind. It's not your concern, and I don't want to involve you."

Zane felt like he'd been slapped. Damn her, he hadn't even wanted to be involved, not until she tried to exclude him. First she'd propositioned him, then insulted him, and now she was shutting him out. He matched her stance, fists on his hips, legs braced apart. "I'm making it my concern."

"No."

That did it. Zane's temper exploded and he glared down at her. In a near shout, he said, "You're saying that cursed word more and more! I think I liked it better when you stayed quiet and mysterious."

Eva clapped her hands together. "That's what we keep telling her! She's not nearly mysterious enough."

Olga agreed. "She's too . . . blonde."

Laughing to himself, Thanos added, "And green-eyed."

Zane wished her meddlesome relatives elsewhere, but obviously his wishes meant very little.

"That's enough on my appearance." Tamara's tone was stern, bordering on brittle. She started to smooth her wayward curls, then caught herself and sent Zane a crooked smile meant to placate. "I guess you should be going." She nodded toward her aunts. "The family and I have a lot to discuss."

Now she hoped to dismiss him. Crossing his arms over his chest, Zane propped himself against the door frame and stared impassively.

Tamara frowned. She turned and took two steps toward

the door. "C'mon, Zane." She sounded like she was enticing a pet. "It's time to go." She took two more steps.

Zane yawned, then asked Thanos, "So what's been going on?"

"Mischief," Thanos told him without hesitation. Tamara
rushed back to her uncle's side.

"Uncle Thanos, our family problems don't concern
anyone else. I'll thank you—"

Thanos threw a meaty arm around her shoulders and
squeezed her till she squeaked. Zane started to protest, but
Tamara had a long-suffering look on her face, as if she
was quite used to the rough affection. "You can thank me
later, little one. For now, why don't you take your aunts
upstairs and get them settled while Zane and I talk things
over? They've had an upset."

"Tea," Olga hinted elaborately, "would be just the thing
to settle the nerves."

"Oh, no." Tamara pried herself out of Thanos's embrace and glared at him. "I'm not going to be dismissed
like a . . . a. . . ."

"Female?" Zane supplied.

"That's right!" Going on her tiptoes, she poked a finger
into Thanos's chest and said, "You can take them upstairs.
I'm sure the three of you can manage a pot of tea. I'll
pick up this mess."

"I can't leave you alone here with the young lothario."
Thanos shrugged. "He's looking at you like a hungry man
looks at a juicy tart."

"He is?" Tamara turned to Zane and examined his gaze.
Now that she was the one feeling rattled, Zane relaxed a
little. In fact, he tried for a leer so she wouldn't be disappointed.

Tamara blushed as she turned back to her uncle and
pushed on his shoulder. "Yeah, well, I can take care of
myself, you know that."

"Right." Thanos, ignoring her meager effort to shove
him out of the room, looked over her head at Zane. "Give

me your word there won't be any hanky-panky going on down here."

Zane smiled lazily. He and Thanos were off to a fair start. "I never begin things I can't finish properly."

For a moment, Thanos looked outraged, then his frown lifted and he laughed heartily. He thwacked Zane, nearly knocking him off his feet. "A man after my own heart."

Catching Tamara under the chin, Thanos lifted her face and said, "I think he may just do for you, little one." He kissed her forehead. "But you do as I say. Mind your manners, and remember that your aunts and I will be right upstairs."

Zane thought it would be near impossible to forget, considering they butted in more often than not. He imagined if they were anywhere in the vicinity, he wouldn't have guaranteed privacy. Which meant he'd have to wait tonight, no matter how it pained him. When he took Tamara, he wanted the whole night to enjoy himself, to indulge her every need. *Soon*, he promised himself. *Very soon*.

Tamara gazed at him, her eyes burning.

Zane waited until Thanos had escorted both women from the room, then caught Tamara's arm and turned her toward him. "Are you reading my mind?"

She looked startled, laughed a little too exuberantly. "First you accuse me of casting spells, and now I'm a mind reader?"

Put that way, he felt just a little foolish. Until he looked into her eyes.

She had the most incredible green eyes he'd ever seen. They were both sharp with intelligence and soft with innocence. It was a potent combination. Her lashes, a dusky brown, were thick and long, leaving exaggerated shadows over her high cheekbones. Her skin looked and felt incredibly soft, and her mouth. . . . Zane groaned softly and bent to kiss her.

She opened her mouth right away, but Zane kept the kiss simple, light. He'd promised Thanos—and besides, he'd meant what he said. There was no point in making this more difficult on either of them.

Against her lips, he said, "Tell me about this imagined intruder."

Her small hands clung to his shoulders. "Not imagined."

He let that pass. "Tell me, Tamara."

She sighed and laid her head on his shoulder. "I can think of a dozen things I'd rather talk about."

"Such as?" Zane coasted a hand up and down her slender back. She was so sweet, so delicate. Her curves were subtle, but *there*, and very enticing.

With his fingers spread, Zane's large hand spanned her back from shoulder blade to shoulder blade. That fact was oddly exciting, exemplifying his harsh maleness to her elegant femininity. He imagined his rough hands on her breasts, her smooth belly, her silky inner thighs.

Damn! Zane stroked her, his fingers barely touching her rounded hip—and he forced himself to stop. He drew a deep breath. "Tell me what you'd rather talk about."

Tamara kissed his collarbone. "I'd like to talk about all the things I want to do to you." Her fingers felt cool on his heated skin, slipping over the nape of his neck, the top of his shoulder. "I've been lying awake at night, thinking about how I'd like to—"

To save himself, Zane pressed a finger to her lips. His forehead touched hers. "Shh. Baby, if you talk like that, I'm not going to be able to keep my promise to Thanos."

Tamara clutched at him, urging him on without even realizing it. "He shouldn't have asked for such a horrible promise."

Zane laughed. "A *horrible* promise, huh?" He stroked her lips, then sighed. "Unfortunately, he's right, and you know it. Your downstairs is no place for an orgy when the upstairs is overloaded with relatives."

A delicate little shudder went through her, and Tamara breathed, "Orgy?"

Zane couldn't resist one more small kiss. He had a feeling he'd be dreaming about kissing her, and more, all night long. "An orgy of pleasure," he explained. "Any thoughts you've got, any sexual curiosities you want to appease, I'm all for it. Remember that."

He deliberately stepped away from her and temptation. "But for now, I'll help you pick up this mess while you tell me why you're so set on believing an intruder is responsible. And don't leave anything out."

Five

Zane glanced at Tamara as he began gathering books. Her quick mood swings were almost amusing. Contrary to what he'd told her, he liked her honest reactions far more than the mysterious silence of her Gypsy self.

Right now, she looked disgruntled and rebellious, but he knew in the end he'd win. He always did. His feelings for Tamara were too extreme for him to do less than maintain absolute authority. Considering the nature of their involvement, it'd be best for both of them that way.

He had a stack of books back in the box before Tamara reluctantly began helping. "I don't have any positive proof of an intruder," she admitted, "or else my aunts wouldn't be convinced that it's Uncle Hubert come to haunt us."

"Why would your uncle want to haunt you?" Zane gathered up one old relic that had more torn pages than not. He tried to get them back inside the cover in order, then gave up and just held them in his hand.

"Uncle Hubert strongly believed our family has psychic power." She made a face. "Like the rest of the family, he was really into that sort of thing. We don't, of course, but he thought we did. My aunts are assuming he's haunting us because he thinks we could have predicted his death—so that he could avoid dying—but we didn't."

Zane sat down and propped his back against the shelf where the box of books had been stacked. The shelf shifted slightly, obviously not sitting level. The old floor had sloped with age, and large cracks ran along the outside wall. "How did he die, if you don't mind me asking?"

Tamara sat, too, crossing her legs tailor-style. "Hubert was a ladies' man, sort of a guru with a following. He got stuck in the sixties and never quite came out."

"Ah. A flower child?"

"Sort of. He was into tie-dye and tattoos and piercings and sex and . . . whatever felt good." She shrugged, but her disapproval was plain on her face. For a Gypsy, she was a prim little thing. "I told him time and again that he'd come to a bad end if he didn't clean up his act. My aunts think I cursed him somehow by saying it."

Zane held himself very still. "But you can't curse anyone?"

"Nope." She held up both hands. "You can stop fretting," she said with a frown. "I already told you, I'm incapable of any real powers."

Looking at her, Zane wasn't at all sure he believed her. Whether she admitted it or not, she'd done something to him. Figuring out what was going to take some time.

Tamara barely managed to control her annoyance. He silently applauded her restraint.

"Still," she said, "they think Hubert believes he was cursed, because he was at a rock concert by his favorite group when a freak storm blew in."

"He died in the storm?"

"Actually, he died in a portable toilet, one of those little plastic houses they use on construction sites. The wind was fierce and knocked it over. He was inside and well . . . when they righted the Porta-Potti the next day, they found Hubert."

Zane tapped the crumbling book on his knee. It wasn't really funny, yet he had the nearly uncontrollable urge to smile. Part of his mood was due to Tamara's expression. She looked so disapproving of her uncle. "Not exactly an auspicious way to go, huh?"

"No." She glanced down at the book literally falling apart in his hands and reached for it. "I guess this one didn't hold up through the fall."

An illustrated page fell out, and she stared. Zane released the smile he'd been holding, and grabbed the page before Tamara could. He lifted it for a closer look. "Ah. Exactly what have you been buying, Miss Tremayne?"

Though her cheeks were bright pink, Zane gave her credit for trying to brazen out the situation. "I buy at estate sales in bulk, so sometimes I get things I hadn't planned on. Obviously what I got this time is erotica, as you can see."

He turned the page, holding it eye level for her, and asked silkily, "Is this something you're interested in trying?"

The illustration was an exaggerated depiction of a man and woman stretched out in the woods atop leaves and flowers, sharing oral pleasure. The ink sketch showed legs and arms in impossible positions, but there was no question about the enjoyment each derived; their eyes, the only facial features visible due to their carnal activity, were glazed with rapture.

Tamara looked like she couldn't breathe, but then her gaze darkened and she peeked up at Zane. Before the words left her mouth, he knew what she would say. And still, hearing her say it, hearing the deepened timbre of her voice, shook him.

"Would you . . . be interested in that?"

Hell, yes, he'd be interested. The thought of tasting Tamara, of her tasting him. . . . Thinking it had almost the same effect as doing it. He felt burned.

Zane stuck the picture inside the book and closed it. His heart thumped wildly in his chest, annoying him with the proof of his weakness where she was concerned. She left him breathless with just a few words. What the hell would it be like when he got inside her, when he could feel her squeezing him, hear her moaning, taste her excitement?

"I already told you," he rasped, hoping she wouldn't detect the dark hunger in his tone, "anything you want to do is fine with me."

Her gaze sharpened at his agreement, devouring him, easily sharing with him the images going through her mind.

Her sensual curiosity engulfed him. Everything with Tamara, every word, every conversation, somehow seemed more acute.

She picked up a few more books and packed them away. Idly, as if she wasn't anxious to hear his answer, she asked, "Do you read a lot of erotica?"

He laughed, he couldn't help it. "No. Not since I was a kid and stole Chase's stash to share with Mack." His grin lingered as memories crowded in. He and Mack had spent a week hiding out in the woods behind their home, engrossed in the books—the most reading either of them had ever done—before Cole busted them.

"Chase had some pretty . . . risqué stuff. I remember Mack and I had a hard time not snickering around him after that."

Tamara smiled. "You were young, I gather."

"Old enough to appreciate what I'd found."

"Was Chase mad when he realized you'd gotten into his personal belongings?"

"Mad?" Zane could barely recall ever seeing Chase really angry. He was usually the quietest, but not when it came to Allison. Around his wife, he was an entirely different man. "No, I'd say he was more disgruntled, and determined to make Mack and me understand the differences between fantasies and reality." Before she could ask, he said, "Fantasy is *anything* that gets you hot, no matter how raunchy or ribald it might be. But reality is only what your partner will accept, what will make her happy, too."

Her green eyes glittered at him, filled with questions. "Do you . . . have any fantasies that your partners haven't accepted?"

"A few." Zane shook a finger at her. "And no, I'm not listing them for you."

Tamara bit her lip, then nodded. "Maybe later?"

"Maybe." Damn, but she was killing him in small degrees. A change of topic proved vital. "Chase is pretty laid back most of the time, but Cole, well, he's another matter entirely."

Tamara settled herself comfortably and asked, "What did he do?"

"You have to understand, after our parents died, Cole took over raising us, and he was pretty serious about the whole thing. Whenever he thought we'd gotten into mischief, he lectured. Annoyed the hell out of us, and we'd do our best not to earn a lecture. But God, when Cole got to talking about sex and women, he could go on for hours. And it always came down to the same thing, so most of what he said wasn't even necessary. He could have summed it up in a few sentences, but we always suspected that Cole liked to lecture."

"What did he tell you?"

"Nothing you need to hear."

She straightened. "That's not fair! Why bring it up if you won't tell me?"

Zane leaned forward. "I'll tell if you'll tell."

"You did it on purpose!"

He shrugged. "You answer my questions and I'll answer yours."

Tamara huffed, "Well, since I have a feeling you're going to badger me until I do, sure. Why not?"

"Don't be mad, sweetheart." She ignored him, gathering up more books. Zane didn't like being ignored, not even a little. "Respect women," he said abruptly, determined to regain her attention. "No matter what, no matter where you met her, or what she's done in her past, or who she's been with or why, you give any woman you're with respect."

"That's it?"

"Pretty much. Cole made it clear sex was well and good—"

She smiled.

"—but that sex should be for a reason beyond the physical." Zane laughed, remembering how Cole had always harped on that point. "If you can't at least respect a woman, you have no business being around her. It makes a man look pathetic to go screwing around with a woman he doesn't even like, just to get laid. Cole always said you might as well be paying a prostitute, which definitely smacks of desperation. Since Mack and I never wanted to look desperate, we listened."

"Until now."

"What does that mean?"

"Nothing." Her lashes lowered, hiding her eyes. "I like your brothers."

"Everyone does." She'd said it matter-of-factly, as if she were well acquainted with them, which made Zane frown. "How do you know them?"

"I know *of* them. As I said, I've been to the bar. I've watched them." Her brows lifted. "Your brothers would be pretty darned hard to miss."

"They're all married." His frown became more severe.

"I know. Their wives always look very happy, even when they're arguing with them."

She seemed pleased by that, not at all covetous. Zane nodded. "Yeah, happy about covers it."

"I have another book," Tamara suddenly blurted, "one I took upstairs already."

Zane paused. Her quick switch momentarily threw him. "Erotica?" he asked. He wasn't sure he could handle another conversation on positions. He was already struggling with the last tenuous hold on his discipline.

She glanced at him, then away. "Not exactly."

Aha. The book she'd mentioned earlier. Zane gentled

his tone, anxious to hear this tale. "The book that told you to be bold? The one that stated men were slaves to their basic natures, or some such rot?"

"Yes." Tamara picked up the last of the spilled books and shoved them awkwardly into the box. "Only it's not rot. It's a journal of sorts. Written by this amazing woman."

"Anyone I know?"

"Well, I seriously doubt it! She was an elderly woman, and the journal was something she kept hidden from everyone. Not even her family knew about it. She says in the very beginning that what she's writing will be of use to women with aggressive sexualities, women who want to be free, but that not everyone would understand. Certainly not anyone in her peer group. Though her name is nowhere in the book, I gather from what she said that she was from the social elite, and didn't want her affairs to become public knowledge. She explained that her family had already disowned her and that in her social group such things, if they were ever discovered, would be broadcast in the scandal rags."

Zane leaned forward. Much of what she'd just told him was intriguing, but one comment in particular drew his interest. "You fit in the category of 'aggressive sexuality,' do you?"

She floundered. "I . . . well, I don't know."

"You don't know?" What the hell did that mean? Zane wanted to come right out and ask her how many men she'd been with, but at the same time, he wasn't at all sure he wanted to know. He'd always made it a rule not to get overly involved in women's personal lives. Keep it light and friendly—that was his motto.

Her chin lifted. "I feel aggressive about wanting you. And since you were resisting me, I figured I could use some help."

Zane snorted at that, seeing it as a deliberate avoidance of his question. "So you're reading about the private, and evidently racy, sex life of some deceased old lady?"

"It's not like that!" Obviously affronted, Tamara said, "It's sort of a guide, explaining things that she found instrumental in building a wonderful sexual and emotional connection. The journal is divided into sections that detail ways to accomplish different relationships.

"She wanted to share what she'd learned with others, but she didn't dare write a book that would be published, for fear of how society would react." She stood and propped her hands on her slim hips, her expression challenging. "According to this woman, making an emotional connection helps amplify the sexual connection."

"I'll buy that."

"You will?"

"Sure." Zane smiled up at her, and admitted, "I never have sex with strangers. It'd be cold. And I have to at least like a woman to want to be with her, not just find her attractive."

"But. . . ." Tamara hesitated, then went on boldly, "You agreed to have sex with me, and you don't like me. And for the most part, I'm still a stranger to you."

Zane considered that for a long moment. "You figure all Cole's preaching went in one of my ears and out the other?"

She shrugged. "At least where I'm concerned."

"Well you're wrong. I like you just fine." He realized it was true, frowned. "You know, you don't feel like a stranger to me. On some level it seems like I've known you ever since I opened my store. I know we never talked much—"

"You avoided me."

"I didn't exactly avoid you," he said, annoyed at her insistence. Avoidance sounded like the act of a wary man. And he sure as hell wasn't wary of her. He wasn't wary of any woman.

"Yes, you did. Because you didn't like me."

Zane locked his jaw. Through his teeth, he said, "I didn't know you well enough to like or dislike you. It's just that you. . . ." *Affected my brain and made me antsy and hot and excited.* "I was just busy getting my business started."

"You found time to date a lot of other women. I saw them with you."

"At the bar?"

"And at your store. You meet a lot of your women there."

His annoyance peaked. "They're not *my women.* We just date. You make it sound like I maintain a harem or something."

She shrugged, unconcerned at insulting his finer sensibilities. "I thought you were proud of your way with women. It's nothing to be ashamed of, you know. I haven't seen any of the women complaining."

Zane pulled himself together once again. It seemed he did that a lot around Tamara. "How'd we get onto my dating habits? We were talking about you and that ridiculous journal."

"It's not ridiculous. In fact, it was the words in the journal that encouraged me to approach you. If I hadn't found that book, we wouldn't be here now."

That was an unbearable thought, and he immediately rejected it. "I'd have approached you."

"Ha!" She tossed her head, flipping her bangs away from her forehead, and glared up at him. "I doubt you'd have even noticed I was leaving until after I was gone—if you noticed even then. I'd have sold my place and moved away and we'd never have shared a kiss, much less anything else."

"You don't know that for sure."

"If it wasn't for that book," she went on, "we'd never have had a chance to enjoy each other. I'd say the book is far from ridiculous. In fact, I'd say we should use it as a guide."

Zane drew back. "A guide? You think I need a goddamn guide to make love to a woman?"

"Don't shout at me. And we're going to have sex, not make love."

Her insistence on that point infuriated him. "I'm not shouting," he shouted.

"You need something," she said, ignoring his temper, "at least where I'm concerned, because it's for certain you hadn't made a move on your own."

Zane growled. Now that he had kissed her and touched her and planned to do so much more, he couldn't believe he'd ever overlooked her. And he damn sure didn't like having her remind him of his oversight.

But he wouldn't admit that to her. He was used to being the one calling the shots. He was used to wielding all the power. But she *had* instigated things, damn it. She'd been quiet and intriguing and she'd lured him in with three little words. *I want you.*

She was far from quiet now. In fact, he'd call her argumentative. Perhaps if he got her back into costume, she'd revert to form and settle back into her mysterious silence. Zane shook his head. He actually liked her much better this way.

In an effort to draw her fire away from him, Zane asked, "Why the hell are you moving, anyway?"

Tamara hesitated, and he said quickly, "Oh, no, you don't. Don't lie to me."

When she looked surprised, he said, "I can see the intent plain in your eyes."

"That's ridiculous."

"Like hell it is." He caught her shoulders and pulled her close. "You don't want to tell me what's going on." He kissed her pursed mouth hard, leaving her bemused, then added, "But I'm afraid I'm going to have to insist."

Tamara pulled away and turned her back on him, her spine rigid, her shoulders stiff. "You can't get around me with sex, Zane."

"Wanna bet?"

She flashed him a glance, then narrowed her eyes. "My problems are my own," she insisted. "I don't want or need to drag you into them."

"You just want me for physical pleasure?" There was

a slight acerbity to his tone that he couldn't hide.

"That's right. And I haven't even gotten that yet, so there's nothing more to talk about."

Zane stepped up behind her, close enough that his groin nestled against her soft, rounded bottom. He clasped her shoulders and squeezed gently. "We'll get there soon enough, honey, but not until you tell me what's going on. Fair's fair. We agreed, remember?"

Almost against her will, she leaned into him. "Blackmail? You'll hold out until I 'fess up?"

It was his turn to shrug. "Think of it as concern, not coercion."

"I'm not used to sharing with anyone. I've been the leader of the family for a long time; my aunts and uncle depend on me, not the other way around."

"Your parents died?"

She kept her head down, her face averted. "Yes, like yours, when I was young. Thanos and my aunts took me in."

He noticed that she hadn't claimed they raised her. Because he'd met them, he had to wonder if Tamara hadn't always been the logical, responsible one. "What happened to them?"

Shifting, she finally looked at him. "From what I remember and from what everyone has always told me, they liked to live on the edge. They were daredevils, true Tremaynes, and they got a rush from taking risks and accepting challenges. One night after a celebration, my father raced his car against a friend on a deserted road and. . . . Well, it was dark, and rainy. He crashed." She looked wistful, and resigned, as if she still couldn't understand it, but had long ago accepted it. "Thanos is the one who told me."

"Thank God you weren't with them." A sizzle of anger stirred along Zane's nerve endings. How could any parent behave so irresponsibly? He imagined what Tamara must had felt, felt a little of it himself, and it nearly smothered him with compassion.

"Oh, no. They realized when I was very young that I was different—the white sheep, as you've already heard Thanos call me. They never took me with them when they . . . did dangerous things. Thanos explained that they had wild blood, and that's why they died. He and my aunts were there for me from that moment on."

There was an indefinable sorrow in her eyes as she told that story. The people who should have put her welfare first had instead been out partying and playing with their lives. It sounded to Zane as if they'd totally shirked their duty to her, and in the end, they'd left her alone. He discounted Thanos and the aunts as appropriate supervision. "How old were you?"

"Ten." She shrugged. "But Thanos likes to say I was ten going on twenty-five. He says I no sooner got over my grief than I started organizing everything."

She gave him a small smile. "Try to understand, Zane. I've always been the one in charge, the one who handles problems. It's my way, and Thanos understood that. He helped me to find my place in my new family by letting me take charge. As a child, it made me feel useful, less of a burden. As an adult, it's what I'm used to. My relatives come to me to fix things. All this . . . sharing stuff, your concern, it's not what I was asking for."

"And it's not what you wanted?" He wondered then if she was afraid to share. That possibility struck him deep in his soul.

She looked uncertain. "That's right."

Zane turned her around and looped his arms around her waist. There were some things he intended to be firm on, so she might as well understand that right now. "It's all part and parcel with involvement, sweetheart, at least as far as I'm concerned, so you might as well get used to it. Until you do move, we've got something going on, and I'm not good at standing in the background. Understand?"

She shook her head in exasperation. "You don't have to act like a caveman."

There she went, insulting him again. "Tamara—"

On impulse, she kissed his chin, licked her lips, then kissed his chin again. "Mmmm." Her voice softened, but her meaning didn't. "Spare me the threats, Zane. They won't work."

The spot tingled where her lips had touched, and it was no more than two simple pecks. *On his chin.* "I do not," he stated emphatically, ignoring how intimate those innocent little pecks had felt, "threaten women."

She patted his chest. "Then what would you call it?"

With ruthless determination, Zane reined in his temper and managed to say—with only a partial growl—"You're reneging on a deal. We agreed that if I answered your questions, you'd answer mine."

"I answered your questions on the book."

She was right, damn it. "You're just trying to distract me."

This time her patting was a little harder, tinged with her own temper. She glared up at him. "I can't believe you're being so insistent! It has nothing to do with you."

His control slipped another notch. "As long as we're sleeping together, anything that concerns you, concerns me."

"We're not sleeping together yet."

"Stop stalling and tell me."

"Oh, all right." She wrenched herself out of his hold and paced three steps away.

Zane thought about hauling her back; he *liked* holding her, liked having her snuggled in his arms.

He was just reaching for her when she spoke. And her first words stopped him cold.

Six

"Someone has been trying to drive us away."

Zane stared at Tamara, not sure he'd heard her correctly.

"I don't know who," she explained hastily, "and I don't know why. But there's been too many small crises for me to write them off as coincidence the way the police have."

"You're not just moving to . . . move?"

"No, why would I? I love it here." A poignant yearning colored her words. "I had a small inheritance from my parents, money they'd earned in the circus and on the road. My uncle put it away for me until I turned eighteen. As my guardian he could have used the money, and there were plenty of times through the years when we needed it." She smiled at that, as if being broke was part of a series of fond memories.

"I used it to buy their small house. They griped about that, because they'd always considered the money mine and they wanted me to spend it on myself." She glanced at Zane. "They never realized that I wanted to be by myself for a change, so buying the house for them was for me, too."

"How old were you then?"

"Eighteen. Plenty old enough."

Zane shook his head. Hell, at eighteen he'd still been living with Cole, working for him and getting a lot of help as he started college. He couldn't imagine being so completely alone at that age. "How'd you buy this place?"

"I'd saved up money from the jobs we did. I used all my savings for the down payment, and it was just enough."

He imagined she had a very frugal lifestyle, without a lot of room for luxuries or extravagance. Yet, she didn't seem to want for anything—except him. That thought caused a tightness in his chest, and in his groin.

Unaware of his private turmoil, she continued matter-of-factly. "My family is settled and this house is perfect for me. When I was younger and we were on the road so much, I used to dream of a house just like this. I love the wooden floors and the rusty pipes and the high moldings." Sadness invaded her expression before she shook her head, as if bringing herself back to reality.

She clearly thought she had no option except to sell, and just as clearly wasn't going to dwell on what couldn't be. She was too sensible to bemoan things she couldn't change. It was that sensibility, Zane thought, which had enabled her to get a band of loony Gypsies settled in the first place.

"I'm leaving," she told him, "because I don't know what else to do. Everything that happens costs money—money that I can't spare." She shrugged. "So we're . . . moving."

Zane crossed his arms. If there was any way to help her, he damn well would. But first he had to know all the details. "Start with the first crisis."

"A fire."

He cocked a brow and waited.

"That's right. A fire here in my shop. It had been a busy day with people in and out, so I hadn't had a chance to eat all day. When I closed the shop, I went to your bar to get a sandwich and a drink. But you weren't there. I guess you had a date or something, because you weren't at your store either."

"You were looking for me?"

She shrugged and waved a hand in airy explanation. "I've admired you from afar for some time now. But as I said, you weren't at the bar, so I wrapped up the sandwich, finished my drink, and came home early."

"You've *admired me from afar*?"

"Do you want to hear this story or not?" she demanded.

"Yeah." A feeling of contentment settled over him. "I want to hear the story."

"Then stop interrupting."

Bossy little woman, Zane thought, this time with humor. He realized he was starting to get used to her. And he was liking her more with each minute that passed.

Wondering if she'd be that bossy in bed, he smiled and said, "Yes ma'am."

She eyed him, and must have decided he was sincere, because she continued with her tale. "I always use the outside stairs when I'm going straight home instead of into the shop. But this time I felt that something was wrong."

"You *felt* it? Like a premonition or something?" She kept claiming she didn't have powers, but Zane was sure she did. How else did he explain his obsession?

"I didn't mean it like that! I already told you I'm not psychic." She looked flustered, then went on. "I just used the shop door this time is all. And as soon as I stepped inside, I smelled the smoke. It came from this room, which was a good thing since the door was shut and it kept the damage from reaching most of the rest of the shop."

Zane looked around and only then noticed the blackened corners of the ceiling. The room was small, square, with a shallow closet where Tamara had hung a jacket, and a minuscule bathroom that boasted a plain white toilet and white enamel sink with the pipes exposed. A single bare bulb, hanging in the center of the room, supplied light. It was a storage area in every sense of the word, and at the moment it was packed full of boxes and bags and odds and ends. A fire could have really taken off, with plenty of paper and cardboard to feed on. "Do you know what started it?"

"An old chair that I'd bought at an auction caught fire. The material was threadbare and dry so it went up like kindling. I had planned to reupholster it because I liked the wood trim. It was dark and ornate, and went well with the rest of the decor."

"Eclectic hodgepodge?"

"Exactly."

Zane shook off another smile. He'd have to quit smiling like a fool over every inane thing she said. Otherwise, she'd think he was besotted. And that would never do. "How'd it catch on fire?"

She shrugged. "Supposedly a cigarette. The fire department found a butt down in the seat. Only I don't smoke and no one who works for me does either. I don't allow it."

"A customer?"

"Not that I know of. I have a prominent NO SMOKING sign. Besides, customers aren't allowed in the backroom and they're never left unsupervised, so it's not likely someone could have snuck in there to take a cigarette break."

"Could someone have asked to use the bathroom?"

She shook her head. "I send them to the diner across the street." She began pacing again, her movements punctuated by her explanations. "Luckily I caught the fire early because I can only imagine the amount of damage that might have been done otherwise. As it was, it took me a week to get things cleaned up and the smell out."

She could have been killed, Zane realized. What if she hadn't gone out that night? Or what if she hadn't come home early? If he'd been at the bar when she was there, would she have hung around *admiring him from afar* and then gotten home too late to stop the fire—or perhaps even been caught in it?

A sick feeling stirred in his stomach; it felt remarkably like fear. *For her.*

Damn it, it had to be just a fluke. He couldn't think of a single reason why anyone would want to burn down her small establishment. She wasn't a threat to anyone, didn't offer any great competition to the other businesses in the area. None of it made sense, unless it was all personal. "You're certain your assistant—what's her name?"

"Luna Clark."

Zane did a double take. "Luna?"

Smiling, making her voice deliberately mystical, she said, "Luna, goddess of the moon."

Zane stared. "Uh-huh. Right. So you're certain your assistant goddess doesn't smoke?"

"Just because Luna is a little different doesn't mean she'd lie to me."

"Don't get in a snit. I didn't mean to suggest she would." Then he asked, "Different how? I've never met her."

Tamara grinned. "Except for her coloring, Luna could have been born into my family. She fits right in with them. She believes all the crazy stuff they believe about fortune-telling and fate and ghosts. She's beautiful, naturally flamboyant without a wig or contacts. Half the time I believe she's got mind powers. She usually knows what I'm thinking."

"Does that bother you?" Zane figured one mystical woman was more than enough for him. He'd be happy never to meet Luna face-to-face.

"No. Being around Luna is a riot. The customers love her."

Luna, Zane thought, sounded more than a little flaky. "How long has she worked for you?"

"Around a year. I trust her completely. Besides, she wasn't here that day. She's only part-time."

Zane strode toward her, inexplicably drawn nearer. "Who did work that day?"

"Just me."

"All day?" The sense of fear intensified, only Zane didn't know where it was coming from, or why. He just knew that it was very real, as real as the need to protect Tamara, to claim her. "By yourself?"

"You don't have to say it like that." She rolled her eyes. "My shop is hardly as busy as yours. I can and do work alone quite often. It's no big deal."

A deep breath didn't help. Silently counting to ten didn't help, either. "Are you telling me," Zane asked quietly, "that you *still* work alone? Even though you think someone is out to hurt you?"

She inched back, warily moving away from the bite of his restrained temper. "I never said anyone wanted to hurt *me*. The problems have all been related to the shop somehow. The fire, a dead rat in the toilet that caused all the plumbing to clog up and overflow—"

"Whoa." Zane held up a hand, halting her in midsentence. "A dead rat in the toilet?"

She shifted on her bare feet. "The police said it crawled into the pipes and died somehow, but . . . well, if you'd seen it, you'd know that rat was roadkill. It was disgusting, and I'm convinced it was put there deliberately. Same as the cigarette."

"How?"

"I don't know. That's just it. The window in here is too small for a man to crawl through, and the rest of the place is always locked up."

Zane looked at the window. It was high, narrow. "A kid could probably fit through."

"Maybe. But why would a kid want to?"

He shrugged. Kids did a lot of stupid things, like taking a bet, or agreeing to vandalism for the thrill of it, or for a few bucks. Someone might have hired a kid for the job. It made as much sense as anything else. "Your problems could just be childish pranks."

Tamara bristled. "Childish pranks have ruined my savings account. Repairing the plumbing cost a fortune, not to mention all the cleanup and the fact I had to close for nearly a week. And it wasn't long after the fire had forced me to miss some days, too."

"Do you have a better explanation?"

She sighed in defeat. "I think somehow, someone is getting in without me knowing it. That's why my aunts insist—"

"On Uncle Hubert's ghost." Zane shook his head. "I suppose they choose to believe that because it's less threatening to them than a flesh-and-blood person skulking around, getting in unnoticed."

"I think so." She frowned as she looked up at him, as if she didn't understand him or his level of concern. If it had been up to her, she wouldn't have told him anything—except that she wanted him.

He drew a deep breath. Truth was, Zane didn't understand himself. Never before had he felt so drawn in by a woman's problems. Especially when he'd only kissed her, and most of the time in between those kisses had involved her insulting him. And there was the fact that part of her problems included an eclectic group of relations who had taken turns trying to do him bodily harm.

All in all, Tamara Tremayne shouldn't have been such a temptation. If he had any sense at all, he'd be running in the other direction.

But now he was involved up to his eyebrows. He was worried, damn it, when he didn't like to worry. He felt . . . connected to Tamara and everything that surrounded or touched her, including her problems.

Tamara cleared her throat. "I lost three nice rugs because of the water damage, and several boxes of things that had been on the floor."

"It was the toilet in here?"

"Yes. It's the only one on this floor. There are two bathrooms upstairs, but I only use the one that connects to my bedroom. The other is in the hall in the part of the house that I've shut off."

"You don't use all the rooms upstairs?"

"No. Uncle Thanos and my aunts live in their own home, and I certainly don't need all this space."

He hated to say it, because the idea of an intruder being near Tamara while she slept filled him with rage and helplessness. But the thought wouldn't go away. "Maybe someone got in through that part of the house."

"Upstairs with me?" She looked taken aback by the idea, and damn if Zane didn't feel her anxiety as if it were his own. Then she shook her head, the stubbornness he was beginning to recognize apparent in her expression. "No, the windows are all too high for someone to climb through, and they're locked besides. I even have the hallway door leading to that part of the house locked."

"You put a lock on it?"

"No. It's not uncommon for older houses to have key locks on all the doors."

"A skeleton key?"

"Yes. But the locks are sturdy and I'm a light sleeper. I'd hear if anyone was prowling around."

It was an attempt to convince herself as much as him, and it didn't work. Zane didn't like thinking about her being alone. He wasn't entirely convinced that her prowler was anything more than coincidence and pranks, as the police apparently thought, but just in case, he'd have felt better if she had company.

He'd always written off intuition as coincidence, but now he couldn't rid himself of the feeling that something was very wrong. Tamara wanted him, but he was almost certain that she needed him, too.

It was far too soon for him to propose that he stay over; that would suggest an intimacy that she'd claimed to want no part of. He tried doing the next best thing. "You have a phone by your bed?"

"Yes."

"Call me if anything happens, if you hear anything at night or if you just get nervous."

"Zane. . . ."

"Whatever you do, do *not* try to deal with an intruder on your own." He broke out in a sweat as he thought of how she'd tried to race down the steps alone earlier. She hadn't known that only a box of books had fallen; she'd been fully prepared to confront an unknown assailant.

"Zane. . . ."

He could tell she was going to refuse. She was an independent woman, doggedly so, and she wouldn't like the suggestion that she might need him. "Promise you'll call me, no matter how silly the reason might seem, or I'm going to suggest to Thanos that he spend the night."

Her eyes flared. "Good God, if you do that, my aunts will want to stay, too!"

He shrugged.

"Do you have any idea how hard I had to fight for my privacy? It wasn't easy getting them settled in their own home!"

He'd want to hear more on that later, he decided. Since he valued his own privacy, and protected it fiercely, he could understand. But this was too important to let go. "Then promise me."

Angry color darkened her cheeks. She didn't like being manipulated any more than he would.

They had more in common than he'd ever suspected.

"Do it for me, Tamara," he insisted. "I know you can take care of yourself, but I'll still worry."

"You're supposed to be a playboy, not a mother hen."

Thoroughly exasperated, Zane asked, "Do you always resort to insults when you don't get your own way?"

Looking contrite, she bit her lip. "There's no reason for you to worry."

"I'm male and you're definitely not. That's all the reason I need."

For several seconds she glared at him. "Oh, all right." After she gave that grudging promise, she actually smiled.

"I can tell dealing with you is going to be more difficult than I'd expected."

"You thought things would be simple when you propositioned me?" Zane asked. "No messy involvement or unsolicited caring, just sex? I'd show up when you said, leave when I finished, and not talk to you much in between?"

She looked uncertain, started to say something, then pinched her mouth together and shrugged.

Indignation nearly choked him.

In the past, a no-involvement relationship had always suited him just fine. But at the moment, he wasn't really sure what he wanted. He decided things would last as long as *he* said, and she could just deal with it. Not that he'd tell her so.

Zane turned away from her before she could sidetrack him again.

Hefting the box, he put it back on the shelf. He made sure it was securely stationed this time and wouldn't fall, then took Tamara's hand and started her out of the room. He had more important things to do than moon over his unaccountable feelings for a little Gypsy with too much backbone.

Keeping her safe was first on the list. And to do that, he had to figure out what the hell was going on. He could probably use a little help with that. He'd see his brothers tomorrow, and maybe they could all come up with a logical explanation.

Thinking of the razzing he'd take pissed him off, but he could live with that. He *couldn't* live with leaving Tamara in danger.

"Okay, before I head home," Zane growled, "tell me the rest, and don't leave anything out."

"Zane. . . ." She trotted along next to him as he headed upstairs, where her relatives waited. "You're . . . upset?"

She was good at reading him, and he didn't like that much either. He gave her one sharp nod, unwilling to discuss it. He should have known that wouldn't be enough for Tamara.

She pulled him to a stop in the middle of the stairs. One step above him now, she was on eye level. Her expression turned serious, and curious, and warm. "Why?" she whispered. "Is it because we can't start our new . . . association tonight? Or is it because of that insult business? I didn't mean to make you angry, you know."

It didn't matter this time if she saw his hands shaking. Zane cupped her face and drew her closer until their breaths mingled. "You could have been hurt, Tamara. If you're right, and it is an intruder deliberately preying on you, you could have been killed."

Her eyes widened, in shock both at his vehemence and at the fact that he obviously believed her. Her emotions—relief, confusion, lust—rolled over him in suffocating waves.

"I'm not just upset, honey. I'm goddamn furious." Zane kissed her, to try and block the unwelcome connection, to replace it with pure lust, something he could understand and deal with.

His time as a free man was slipping away, and he knew it.

Cole was at the bar when Zane wandered in much later that night. He hadn't meant to go there. Hell, he'd meant to go home and think about things, maybe get some needed sleep. He'd spent a long while talking to Tamara, hearing about the more recent problems. Before he'd left, they'd made plans to have dinner the following day.

But Zane hadn't gone home afterward, knowing he'd only have stayed awake thinking of Tamara. And so he found himself at the bar. It was a place of comfort, a place to let his brain rest.

Women greeted him as he walked in. They didn't insult him—far from it. They ogled him and smiled suggestively, and his world felt right again.

Dropping onto a bar stool, Zane asked his brother, "Been busy tonight?"

Cole glanced up while filling a mug with beer, then continued to look. With a sudden frown, he demanded, "What'd you do?"

Startled, Zane glanced around, realized Cole was speaking to him, and said, "Nothing. I just got here."

Cole slid the beer to the customer, wiped his hands on a dish towel, and propped his elbows on the bar. He studied Zane suspiciously. "You're up to something."

"I am not!" Zane shifted uncomfortably, laughed a little nervously. There was no way Cole could know what he had planned for Tamara.

"You look just like you used to when you got into trouble."

Zane managed a credible snort. "I never got into that much trouble."

"Ha! I had outraged mothers calling me all the time."

"That's an exaggeration." Zane refused to feel guilty about things he'd done in his teens. More often than not, it had been the females asking him out, anyway.

"You'd stay out too late," Cole continued, on a damn roll for some reason, "go places you shouldn't, like parking, and then break things off as soon as she got serious. . . ."

As if a light went off, Cole straightened. "That's it! You're after a new woman, aren't you?"

"No!" He wasn't after Tamara. Good God, just the opposite. *She* was after *him.* Of course, he was the one who'd been insistent. . . .

"I can see it in your face," Cole said with a nod. "She's got you hooked, doesn't she?"

"*No.*" That was just plain laughable. No way did Tamara have him hooked; he wouldn't let himself be hooked. No woman could affect him to the point that it'd be plain on his face, to the point his brother could take one look at him and. . . .

"If she's a nice woman, Zane, leave her alone."

Leave her alone! Zane couldn't quite hide his irritation. "I know what I'm doing, Cole." At least, he thought he did. But Tamara had a way of keeping him guessing, keeping him on edge.

Affecting him, damn her.

God, maybe he *was* hooked.

"There are plenty of interested females around without seducing one who's hesitant." Cole nodded to the room at large. "Just look around you. Hell, half a dozen are ready and waiting as we speak."

Zane peered over his shoulder and was met with a lot of seductive looks. Beyond feeding his ego, however, they didn't move him one bit. He plain wasn't interested. The only woman he could think of right now was Tamara, and he wanted her bad.

He turned back to Cole and caught his brother's speculative gaze. "Now you can just stop that."

"Stop what?" Cole asked innocently.

"Stop imagining things." Given half a chance, Cole would come up with all kinds of ridiculous notions.

Cole laughed, forced a shrug, and began wiping off the bar. "If you say so."

Gritting his teeth, Zane said, "I am *not* hooked, damn it!"

Several people looked up, making Cole lift his brows and Zane cringe. Zane ran a hand through his hair and then stood. "I'm heading home."

"Don't leave mad," Cole admonished.

"I'm not mad."

This time Cole laughed. "Not hooked, not mad, and not protesting too much, huh?" He hesitated, then said, "Bring her around. I'd like to meet her."

"Not yet." Zane realized what he'd said the second the words left his mouth. He scowled at Cole.

"Well, at least remember what I told you."

"About seducing the unwilling? Ha! I . . . no, forget that." Zane frowned. No way in hell would he explain to his oldest brother that Tamara only wanted him for sex.

Not only was it none of his business, it was embarrassing besides.

Cole took pity on him and leaned across the bar to clap him on the shoulder. "You look exhausted. Get on home and get some sleep."

"Yeah, I think I will." If he stayed any longer, he'd be making confessions and telling more than he should. "Give Sophie a hug from me."

Zane made his way out, dodging women and suggestions and invitations. The fresh air felt good, and the thought of his bed sounded great. But Zane knew he wouldn't sleep. He knew he'd think about Tamara, and if by chance he did doze off, he'd dream about her. He had to get a grip.

Tomorrow he'd prove to her that he was still in charge. And before the day was over, they'd both believe it.

Seven

They had made plans to get together for a late dinner that night. Because she closed up earlier than Zane, she could take care of a few errands first, shower and change, and replace her garish makeup with something more suitable. She could hardly wait.

Tamara couldn't remember floating through a workday before, but no matter how busy it got, no matter how harried, she felt elated.

Zane had said he wanted to discuss things. She didn't know if he meant her proposition or her problems, but she'd vote for the first. The last thing she wanted was to involve him further in her problems. It was humiliating for one thing; she'd worked long and hard to find a settled life, and she didn't want him to know her financial position was still precarious. A few more setbacks, like the fire and the water damage, could wipe her out completely.

And for another, the book had said to be independent. A man should know you want him before he thinks you need him, otherwise you give him an edge. Tamara thought the book was right, and she intended to keep every edge she could; that was the only way she could deal with Zane Winston and not get her heart permanently squashed.

Luna, who had worked with her that day, eyed her suspiciously. "You've been grinning ever since I arrived."

Tamara tried, and failed, to suppress another smile. "Have I?" She felt like laughing out loud. After all the recent troubles, it was good to be able to concentrate on something else, something positive, especially when that something was tall, dark, and outrageous.

"Uh-huh." Luna looked her over. "Whatever it is, you're glowing—and impatient. You want me to take the money to the bank for you, so you can get freed up a little earlier?"

It wasn't something Luna did often, and Tamara shook her head. "No, that's okay. I can do it. You probably have a date or something tonight, don't you?"

Today Luna had red hair in three stubby braids. The last time she'd worked, her hair had been brown and gelled into a severe bun. Luna changed her appearance from day to day, and the regular customers found her fascinating.

"I have a date," Luna said with a wink, "but waiting is good for him. Keeps him on his toes."

Tamara wished she could be so cavalier. She had no intention of keeping Zane Winston waiting for her. Not only was she far too anxious to stay away from him longer than she actually had to, but she just didn't have the time to waste playing games.

Smiling like a devout sinner, Tamara said, "I have a sort of a date, too."

"What the heck is a sort of a date? You meeting a guy in an alley or something?" As she spoke, Luna went through the routine of snuffing out candles and incense while Tamara took care of the cash register. After counting out enough money for the next day and locking it away, Tamara stuffed the checks and excess cash into a zippered plastic bag. Luna had already run the credit slips and closed out on them.

Keeping her gaze on the money bag, Tamara admitted, "I'm having dinner with Zane Winston tonight."

Luna halted, then let out a long, low whistle. She propped her hands on her rounded hips and fought with a grin. The grin won. "I'll be damned."

"You know who he is?"

"Honey, there isn't a woman alive in or around Thomasville who doesn't know the Winstons, especially *that* one." She crossed her arms and leaned against the counter. Her black leather pants gleamed in the dimmed light. "It's Zane's antics that have given the Winstons celebrity status."

"Not entirely. Heck, they're all gorgeous, and that's probably reason enough for them to be so popular."

"Maybe," Luna conceded. "But I saw the article the local paper did on him recently. He made the family tavern topless when he stripped off his shirt to serve drinks to a group of women organizing a wedding shower."

"They goaded him into it!"

Luna's eyebrows bobbed theatrically. "The guy's got a stellar chest."

Tamara knew that. She blushed just thinking about how great that chest had felt against her hands and her breasts. "Yeah, he does. His brother assured the reporter that from now on, Zane would be wearing a shirt when he worked there." She couldn't help laughing. "I have the feeling keeping Zane in line is a full-time job for his brothers."

"You know those women asked him to be a stripper at the wedding shower, to surprise the bride."

Tamara had read the whole article—which wasn't the first one on the Winstons. She'd saved them all in an album. "Yep, and Zane refused, saying the bride would never go through with the wedding if she viewed him in the buff."

Both women laughed out loud. Luna pushed away from the counter. "You be careful with him tonight, okay? Guys like that are walking, talking heartbreakers."

"I know what I'm doing."

"Yeah, right." Luna sent her a knowing look. "Honey, *I* know what I'm doing. You're still trying to figure out what it is you want to do."

"I want to do Zane Winston."

Luna did a double take at that bold statement, then chuckled. "I'd wish you luck, but I doubt you'll need any. That one would jump any female who held still long enough."

Tamara didn't bother to explain that at first Zane had unequivocally turned her down. It was too mortifying. She tucked the money bag into the pocket of her long skirt and patted it. "Well, I better get going. I have to get back in time to do a makeover before I go over there."

"He's open late tonight?"

"Nearly every night. He's a workaholic, if you ask me."

"Oh, speaking of work." Luna plucked the appointment book from the counter. "Arkin Devane called and wants to come in again tomorrow. I think the guy is hooked— on you."

Tamara halted on her way to the door. "Me?"

"He insisted on having an hour and a half of your time."

"But . . . that's triple the time I usually spend with a customer."

"According to him, there's a lot he wants to talk about." Luna bobbed her eyebrows suggestively. "And he's willing to pay for it."

"Hmmm."

"Hmmm nothing. Looks like Zane might have some competition."

That comment didn't deserve a response. No one could compete with Zane. Not that Arkin was a bad-looking man, just not in the same league with Zane.

Tamara pictured Arkin: mid-thirties, rangy muscles, light brown hair and light blue eyes. He was somewhat bookish and overly intense. But she'd liked him on sight and felt a strange affinity with him. He hadn't said as much, but she knew he was in love and was desperately hoping to find a way to win his lady.

She also knew she wasn't that lady.

"I feel a little guilty," Tamara said, "taking money from the sincere ones, you know?"

Luna slipped on her jacket, then gave Tamara a hug. "Deny it all you like, sweetie, but you're a sincere one, too, so I know he's in good hands."

Luna had the annoying habit of seeing through everyone. She insisted endlessly that Tamara had real intuitive abilities. It bugged Tamara that she was partially right, even though she'd never admit it.

Luna grinned her *I know all, I see all* grin, the one the customers ate up. "Don't forget your umbrella. It looks like rain."

Luna went out, leaving Tamara alone with her thoughts. Seconds later, a crack of thunder intruded, proving Luna did at least know her weather. Shaking herself out of her reverie, Tamara slipped on her slicker and grabbed her bright green umbrella. After one last look around the shop, she stepped outside and secured all the locks.

Bloated purple clouds rolled across the sky and the streetlights flickered on. The sharp nip of cold damp air that almost always accompanied a storm made Tamara's slicker insufficient. The first drops of rain began to fall— and Tamara felt an unwelcome gaze watching her. Chills tingled up her arms, her spine.

The bank was only a short walk away, so she never drove there, but today she wished she'd gotten the car from Uncle Thanos.

With the rain coming a little harder now, the sidewalks were slick and all but deserted. Tamara kept a tight grip on the umbrella as wind tried to tear it from her hands. The bottom of her long skirt was quickly soaked, as were her sandals. She cursed the weatherman who had predicted no more than the possibility of a sprinkle.

The bank was in sight when she thought she heard footsteps behind her. Just as when she'd sensed trouble in her

shop, an eerie foreboding raced over her nerve endings.
She jerked around.

There was no one there, but the feeling didn't abate.
Tamara searched the darkened street, trying to see behind
parked cars and into the shadows of alleys between tall
buildings. Heart racing, lungs compressed with nervousness, she finally turned and jogged the rest of the way to
the bank. She was panting by the time she came through
the doors.

She did her business quickly, constantly peeking out
the wide front window, but she perceived nothing more
alarming than hot bright lightning licking across the dark
violet sky. Briefly, she considered calling Thanos to come
pick her up, but it was almost six and the bank would be
closing in just a few minutes. By the time Thanos could
arrive, she'd be left standing outside anyway.

Thoughts of Zane whispered through her subconscious,
but she shook them off. She would not start imposing on
him. He was busy with his own work and he wouldn't
close his shop for at least another hour. Somehow she
knew he'd come if she called him, but that would seem
so cowardly on her part. And she didn't want to start off
with Zane seeing her as a coward.

Holding the umbrella steady, she stepped outside. Other
than a few people racing to their parked cars, there was
no one around. The sidewalk was well lit by streetlamps
and security lights at the various businesses; they reflected
brightly off the wet pavement and windows. She was not
psychic, Tamara insisted to herself, and her premonitions
tonight were nothing more than female foolishness. There
was no reason to be on edge, to continue standing in the
downpour, getting more sodden by the second.

She drew in a deep breath and started off. Despite the
assurances she'd just given herself, she couldn't stop her
gaze from darting left and right as she walked. Lucky
thing, too, because she was only a few yards from her
shop door when she saw the man move out of the shadows
at the side of the building. He wore a dark ski mask over

his face. Despite the gloom of early evening, his eyes shone bright—and he was looking right at her with an arrested expression.

Panic slammed through her.

Tamara didn't think twice; instincts insisted that she run, so she did just that. The opposite side of the street seemed her best bet, so she managed to zigzag across the wet road, then angled back, giving the man in the mask a wide berth. A slick spot on the sidewalk made her stumble, and she dropped the umbrella as she fetched up against a parked van. Pain shot through her upper arm, but it didn't slow her down. She quickly righted herself, darted a look over her shoulder, and took off again. She hadn't seen anyone in that brief glimpse, but the sense of being followed, watched, was still a pounding beat in her heart. Had he followed her? Was he still after her?

She was so anxious, she knew she couldn't begin fumbling with the locked door of her shop; her hands, her entire body, shook uncontrollably. Besides, that would bring her entirely too close to where she'd seen him. She sprinted right past her shop to Zane's. Because of the rain, his door was closed, and she jerked at it, too afraid to look back, for what felt like a lifetime before it opened and she threw herself inside.

Breathing hard, her heart galloping wildly, she collapsed back against the door. Her gaze sought Zane, and then locked on him in stunned disbelief.

He stood by his counter with a beautiful blonde woman in his arms. They both stared at Tamara, shock replacing whatever expressions they had worn before her entrance.

The furious drumming of her heartbeat slowed and then almost ceased entirely as she took in the incriminating sight before her.

Zane's hands were on the woman's shoulders, her arms were around his neck, her fingers laced in his dark, silky hair. They stood very close together, upper bodies touching. Intimate. All but embracing.

Shoving hanks of the wet wig out of her face, Tamara

searched Zane's eyes. She felt his confusion first, then his annoyance, and finally his unease.

"Tamara. . . ." He moved the blonde aside and started forward.

He hadn't been a willing participant in the embrace. Tamara suddenly knew that with a clarity that defied description. Never had an emotion from someone else hit her so strongly. She heaved a relieved sigh, and turned to look out at the darkened parking lot. Rain drubbing against the glass door made visibility difficult. She couldn't see anybody, yet she knew he was still there, knew he was still watching. She felt his panic mixing with her own, confusing her, making her thoughts jumble. Oh God. What did he want?

"Tamara," Zane said again. He caught her shoulders, trying to turn her. "You're early."

Tamara barely paid him any mind. She scanned the surrounding area—was that a shadow there? No . . . well, maybe.

"It's not the way it looked," Zane insisted, his hands tightening just the tiniest bit, caressing. Warmth radiated from him into her chilled bones. Having him close comforted her, and that was almost as scary as being pursued. She could not begin relying on Zane. He wasn't the reliable sort. Oh, he was a good man, she had no doubts about that. But he wasn't a man who would appreciate having a woman cling to him. She had to remember that.

The blonde cleared her throat—loudly. Zane and Tamara ignored her.

"Tamara, listen to me."

She allowed herself to be bodily shifted away from the door. Her breath was still coming in pants, from both nervousness and exertion. She could barely get her fractured attention to focus on what Zane said. She stared at him, wishing she knew who had been following her and why.

She shivered.

Zane made a disgusted sound. "Don't look like that,

damn it." He lightly shook her. "I was just telling Claire that I was busy tonight. With *you*."

He sounded so . . . concerned. Distracted, Tamara patted his chest while her thoughts spun off in different directions. Would the blasted police believe her this time? There was little enough she could tell them, really. She'd seen a man wearing a ski mask. So what? It was cool tonight, raining, miserable. Lots of people had probably bundled up.

Doubt intruded, edging past her fear. Had he really followed her? Or was he just there, out on errands the same as she was? Tamara couldn't be sure. She thought she'd heard his footsteps behind her, but mostly what had alarmed her was her feeling of being watched, of the man's frustration—and no way would she try to convince the police that she'd been in danger based on a feeling. She could just imagine their reactions to that.

For most of her life, she'd heard the jibes—Gypsies were charlatans, ripping off customers with no more than parlor tricks. And the jibes had been correct.

No, she couldn't tell the police. Something was wrong, she knew that for a fact. But if she went to the police now, they'd write her off as a nut. And then, if she needed their help later, they might think she was just crying wolf. Besides, what could they do now?

Tamara rubbed her forehead, wondering how to proceed.

Zane released her and stepped back. She heard him speaking to the other woman. "You should leave, Claire. Tamara and I have some talking to do." He didn't sound pleased.

Claire said, "You can't be serious. You're turning me down for . . . for this?"

The insult was too blatant for her to miss, even in her distraught state. Eyes narrowed and mean, Tamara focused on the other woman. Oh, her relatives might tease her about being a white sheep, but she knew the power she had when she caught someone in her sights, when she locked her Gypsy eyes on them. The black contacts were great for effect, especially when they accompanied her present dark mood. And no matter what the color of her hair, she was still a Tremayne through and through.

Claire took an alarmed step back.

Though Tamara didn't say a word, the woman quickly donned her raincoat and fled. Tamara briefly wondered if it was safe for Claire to be out there, what with some nefarious type person lurking around in the shadows wearing a ski mask, but the blonde made it safely to her car and drove away. Tamara watched her leave, just to be certain.

Zane made a rough sound behind her. "Terrorizing the locals, Tamara?"

She continued to study the parking lot. There weren't too many places for a grown man to hide. If he was there, she'd have seen him by now. Had she imagined the whole thing? It sickened her to consider that possibility.

"If you think I'm going to apologize, you're sadly mistaken."

Zane's tone drew her away from her concerns. She met his unwavering gaze as her nervousness began receding, replaced by awareness of him. "Okay." Their relationship wasn't the type that required explanations or apologies. She would force herself to remember that, no matter what.

Then she realized that her slicker had blown open when she ran. She was soaked through and through and her makeup was badly botched. No wonder the blonde had been so disbelieving! "I don't suppose you have a towel or anything handy?"

Frowning at her, Zane retrieved a roll of paper towels from behind the counter. "Where the hell is your umbrella?" he asked, as he watched her remove the slicker and drop it by the door.

With the sleeve torn and the lining soaked, it would do nothing to protect her from the weather. She mopped at her dripping face and throat.

"Don't you have enough sense not to run around in the rain?"

She understood him now. He was disgruntled with her and being foul-tempered because of it.

"I dropped my umbrella." Tamara gently wiped away most of the smudged makeup around her eyes and then got a new towel to blot her arms. "It's pouring out there."

"What do you mean you dropped your umbrella?"

Tamara glanced up and then away. Uh-oh. He looked suddenly . . . angry. And suspiciously alert. The man had too many mood swings for her to keep up with.

When she didn't answer right away, Zane caught her arm and said, "What's going on, Tamara?"

"Going on?"

His jaw tightened. "Don't play games. Something is wrong. I can feel it."

Her brows lifted. Was it possible that he could read her as easily she read him? "No kidding?" It was not a reassuring thought. "Kinda like intuition or something?"

Zane opened his mouth, but nothing came out. His frown turned fierce. "It's clear you're upset about something."

Tamara racked her brain and came up with the obvious reply. "You were here in a heated embrace with another woman. Of course I was upset."

"Bullshit."

Startled, Tamara opened her mouth to reply, but this time it was her turn to play mute.

"Seeing me with Claire didn't bother you a bit." He hesitated as he searched her face, his expression alert. "Did it?"

She didn't understand him at all. His attitude was curious, bordering on hopeful.

"Did you want it to?" Tamara tried to peek over her shoulder again, to look out the door toward the parking lot. It was nearly abandoned. There were no lurking shadows, and even more than that, she had no lingering feelings of danger. Whoever had been there was gone, or at least far enough away that she couldn't sense him anymore.

She couldn't quite muster any relief. In her head she might reason that she'd imagined the danger, but in her heart she knew it existed.

With one finger on her chin, Zane turned her face back to him. "Claire asked me out, I said no because I planned to see you, and she tried to push the issue. That's all there was to it." ·

Now she felt relief, even though she'd already concluded as much. It was still nice to have him admit it so openly. "Okay."

Exasperation laced his tone. "Just like that?"

Now that the threat was over, Tamara felt safe devoting her full attention to Zane. And it looked like he definitely needed her full attention. He was all but demanding she give it to him.

In a soothing tone, she reassured him. "You said it was nothing and I believe you."

How could she *not* believe him? She'd felt his sincerity right off. It had been like that from the first. She read Zane more easily than she read others. Throughout her life, there had been people she'd been able to pick up feelings from. She wasn't a mind reader, so she never knew exact thoughts or expectations. But fear, elation, worry—she could sense those emotions in a few people.

When her parents had died, she'd known Uncle Thanos's grief, as well as Olga's and Eva's determination to make her feel welcome as a member of their family. She'd sometimes felt the curiosity of customers, the hopefulness. The scorn.

But it was more than an inkling with Zane. What he felt, she felt as if it were her own. Right now she felt his anticipation, and that brought with it another thought. "Do you plan to see her when you're not seeing me?"

He started to answer and she whirled away, appalled that she'd ask such a thing. "No! Forget I asked that. Really, it's none of my business."

"Tamara—"

"I mean it, Zane. I have no intention of trying to tie you down." The words were hard to get out, but she knew she had to say them. Tamara swallowed hard and added, "If you want to see other women, that's up to you."

Carefully, as if he'd never said such a thing before, Zane muttered, "That's not how it works, Tamara. For as long as we're . . . involved, it'll be exclusive."

Surprised, she stared at him.

He leveled a harsh look on her. "For *both* of us."

Since she had no other prospects, Tamara just shrugged. She certainly had no one else she wanted to see, and she perceived no downside to telling him so. "Fine."

He looked first relieved, then suspicious. "You trust me on this?"

"No, of course not." Zane wasn't a man who could or should be trusted. He was a man to be savored, but only by a woman who kept her wits and didn't expect too much. Like fidelity.

"Damn it, Tamara!" He ran a hand through his hair and glared at her.

"Zane," she said reasonably, "you dance topless on the tables at the bar. You date a different woman every night. You draw customers to your shop with your gorgeous bod alone. Why should you change all that for me?"

His chin jutted forward. After a heavy silence and a look that could scorch, he growled, "Because I said I would and I'm not a liar."

No, he wasn't lying. His earnestness beat at her, wearing her down.

More than anything, Tamara wanted to ask him *why*. Why would he change his habits for her, especially after he'd first turned her down? He'd avoided her, had made his disinterest clear, and now he wanted their agreement to be exclusive?

She wasn't sure the answer would be one she wanted to hear. Slowly, she nodded. "Okay."

"No more doubting?"

"No."

Zane caught her shoulders. "Now that that's out of the way, tell me what spooked you."

Damn, how had he taken her full circle back to the subject she wanted to avoid? "I never said anything spooked me," she hedged.

"You walked in here, soaked to the skin, your blouse all but transparent—"

Gasping, Tamara looked down, but Zane caught her chin and lifted it. Once she met his hot gaze, her blouse was forgotten. "We'll deal with your distracting state of undress in a moment," he murmured. "For now, tell me what happened. And no more lying."

You just had to throw that last in, she thought, scowling at him. He knew she'd lied about not caring if he saw other women. "I thought someone was following me."

Zane stared at her a second more, then cursed as he set her aside. "Why the hell didn't you tell me right away?"

He stalked over to the door, jerked it open, and marched straight into the pounding rain. Tamara ran after him.

"Zane!" The storm had become more violent, rain coming down in a deluge. "Aren't you the one who called me an idiot for running around in the rain? At least I had a good reason!"

He looked between and behind the remaining parked cars in the lot. Finding no one there, he turned and stalked over to the alley between their buildings. Alarmed, Tamara wondered what he intended to do if he found someone.

Lightning pierced the dark sky, briefly lighting the lot. The air sizzled and popped with electricity, while dread churned in her belly. Zane was safe for now, but what if the man had still been hanging around? She would not let Zane be hurt because of her.

Tamara grabbed the back of Zane's shirt. He was soaked through, and now, so was she. "Zane, whoever he was, he's gone."

"You don't know that," he shouted over a loud explosion of thunder that arrived only seconds after the lightning.

"Yes I do," she yelled back. Zane froze.

Slowly, so slowly it was apparent he had no care of the freezing rain, Zane turned to face her. Water ran in rivulets from his nose to his chin, and dripped off his dark hair, now stuck to his skull. "What do you mean, you know he's gone?"

Tamara twisted her hands together. The rain battered her skin with stinging force. She began shivering. "I just . . . know."

Zane eyed her from top to toes, and his expression hardened. "I'll call the cops." But he didn't move.

"No. It wouldn't do any good." She watched Zane absorb her words, accept them, while her teeth began to chatter. "It's okay now."

Zane looked like a savage, every harshly carved muscle delineated beneath the clinging wet clothes, his dark eyes burning, his jaw tight, his lashes clumped together. Primitive emotions shimmered off him like waves of heat. "That's what I thought," he growled. "Come on."

Despite her assurances and his apparent belief, Zane looked around as he led her into the store, his gaze watchful. This was a side of him she'd never seen, never anticipated, and in a way it was as exciting as it was alarming. He wasn't just a playboy, civilized to the point of urbanity. No, at that moment he was pure, basic male and she couldn't help but respond.

Tamara tried to stop on the welcome mat, thinking to do most of her dripping there, but Zane didn't even slow—and given that he had hold of her arm, she got dragged along with him.

His anger was strong and turbulent, surging against her in forceful ripples. Was it because he realized she was intuitive? Or was it entirely focused on the man who'd followed her? She watched his broad back expand with deep breaths as he led her to a storage room so neatly organized in comparison to her own, it put her to shame.

Tamara was swept along on his emotions, some of them clear, some not so clear. She knew she should be searching her mind for a way to explain the inexplicable, but it was difficult at the moment.

If she told Zane exactly what had happened, would he believe her, or would he accuse her of being a card-carrying swami? His ridicule would he unforgivable. She'd still want him, but she'd never be able to put aside her hurt.

He stopped just over the threshold, shoved the door closed with his foot, and backed Tamara into it. She caught her breath when his hard hips pressed against hers; he was fully aroused, his erection a long, hard ridge between their bodies.

Heat rolled off him, despite the sodden state of their clothes. Tamara followed the progress of a raindrop as it trailed along his firm jaw, down his throat and into the open collar of his shirt. Her belly clenched in sexual awareness—his or hers?

Involuntarily, she licked her lips. Bombarded by sensations, she couldn't quite pinpoint the most prevalent. Desire? Worry? Fear? She tried to draw a deep breath, and drew in the humid smell of Zane's heated body instead. A fine trembling started in her limbs and gained strength the longer she stared at him. "Zane?"

Watching her, holding her gaze captive with his own, he closed his large hand over her breast. His lids dropped to half-mast, his jaw tightened. The feeling was so indescribable, so overwhelming, she tried to flinch away from it. Zane held her secure.

Gently he caressed her, learned her, shaped her in his palm and with his long, hard fingers. When he touched her beaded nipple, his eyes shut briefly. He groaned softly before he opened them again, watching her with a concentration that invaded her soul.

His voice low and rough, he said, "Your blouse and

bra are so wet, I can see through them. I can even see your nipples."

Contentment swelled inside her, because he didn't want to question her about the masked man or her intuition. He wanted her, as savagely as she wanted him.

Relieved of that worry, she was better able to focus on what he did to her, to give her full attention to her body. His hand cuddling her breast felt better than she had ever expected. His touch radiated out to make her legs shaky, her fingers tingly. She arched into the steady press of his hips, blindly seeking more. She rubbed her belly against his erection, and moaned at the pleasure of it. With her movements, his breathing came faster, rougher.

Their clothes stuck, cold and uncomfortable, but not a deterrent to the anticipation swelling inside her.

"That's it," Zane crooned with deep satisfaction. He kissed her throat, her shoulder. In contrast to the cold, wet clothes, his mouth was hot, his tongue hotter, leaving behind a burning trail. The clinging material of her blouse bunched in his fist, then rasped across her sensitive breasts as he peeled it away. He kissed her collarbone, lower, dipped his tongue into her cleavage. "I've been thinking about this all day."

Tamara laced both hands into his dripping hair, urging him toward her nipple. The combination of her excitement, the rain, and the cooling temperatures had caused both of her nipples to tighten almost painfully. She needed his mouth on her. *"Zane."*

"Take it easy." He nuzzled closer while tugging at the blouse and her thin lace bra until he'd bared both breasts completely. She felt physically snared, the material restricting her movements as he pushed it over her shoulders to her upper arms. Her breasts were forced higher by the bunched material and his callused hands.

He continued to kiss her throat, her ear, his mouth open on her as if he couldn't get enough, while his hands caressed and teased. The dual assault was more than she could stand. She made an urgent sound that he responded to by rubbing his thumbs over her nipples and murmuring low, "Damn, you're so soft. I love touching you."

"I can't bear it."

He carefully closed his finger and thumb over one taut nipple and tugged. Her body arched hard as she cried out.

"You like that? You'll like this too." His right arm circled her back and his mouth moved lower. Tamara tilted her head back, breath held in impatience, and still she jumped when his tongue stroked over her throbbing nipple.

She groaned.

"I know." He licked again. "You're very sweet, Tamara."

Even the touch of his breath was a torment. "Zane, please."

His low laugh, gruff with triumph, stroked over her. "Okay, sweetheart." And then he drew her nipple into his mouth with a soft, wet suction that devastated her senses. Her body drew tight, her legs felt liquid.

He sucked, teased. His tongue curled around her, his mouth pulling at her insistently. All she could do was gasp in pleasure and hold on to him.

Zane's arm hooked beneath her bottom and she found herself lifted so that he could reach her more easily. Caught between his solid body and the wall, her stiff, wet clothes tangled around her, she couldn't move. He switched to her other nipple, treating it to the same delicious torment, and just when she didn't think she could bear it a second more, his thick thigh thrust between her legs. With one hand opened wide on her behind, he began moving her against him in a slow hard rhythm that drove her wild. She tried to wiggle away, startled and not just a little alarmed by how quickly she spun out of control. But Zane didn't let her retreat. His dark head stayed bent to her breasts, and his hold on her body was secure, unrelenting, his long fingers pressed deep against her buttocks.

She hadn't been prepared for him, she realized wildly.

She had no idea how to react, how to contain herself. Sensations roiled inside her with unstoppable force, and she accepted that she was on the verge of a climax.

The book had said that the first time, a climax was difficult for a woman to achieve. Zane was managing it with distressing ease, and she could do no more than hang onto him.

Then her feet touched the floor again and Zane's mouth was on her own, smothering her cry of disappointment. She'd been so close!

"I know," he muttered gently, again and again. "I know, baby. It's okay."

He fumbled with her wet skirt, shoving it out of the way. She always wore voluminous layered skirts for work, and now she cursed the excess of material as she tried to help bare herself for Zane. She wanted what he wanted, whatever it might be, as long as he didn't let the incredible feelings fade.

When his hand slid over her thighs, her belly, she stilled, frozen with the newness of it, the excitement of it. He wedged his large hand between her thighs, covering her mound in an almost protective way. He didn't move, didn't stroke her. He simply held her that way, the heat of his hard palm both comforting and more tantalizing, and it was so erotic she felt tears sting her eyes.

"I need you now, Tamara," he growled, nipping at her jaw. "Tell me you're ready."

Ready? She'd almost finished without him. If he didn't get on with it, she'd lose her fragile grasp on her emotions and cry with the wonder of it. "Whatever. . . ." she started to say, then had to swallow and try again. "Whatever you want, Zane."

She caught his face, kissing his chin, his jaw, biting at his throat. "Just touch me again. *Please*."

"Jesus." He panted as he reached for his belt, jerking at it, frenzied—and someone called his name.

They both froze.

"No," Zane groaned, the word slurred. His face pressed

into her neck, his body held rigid as he struggled for control. Their frantic heartbeats mingled, matched. His shoulders looked like sleek steel as he braced himself away from her. "No, goddammit, *no*."

"Zane?" the voice called again. "Where are you?"

"I'll kill him," Zane announced as he pushed himself away from her. Looking at his face, Tamara believed him. His eyes were glittering bright, heavy-lidded, his cheekbones dark with aroused color. His deep chest rose and fell with uneven breaths.

He didn't say a word to Tamara as he turned away.

She watched him jerk the door open and stalk out of the room, menace emanating from every hard inch of his body. She dropped her head back to the wall with a *thunk*, while her heart continued to rap sharply in her chest. Holy moly. *Shew.* She fanned herself, took several deep breaths, but it didn't help. Her body pulsed with unfulfilled need, leaving her shaken and wobbly.

"You better have a damn good reason," Zane all but shouted, "for this impromptu visit."

A different voice, this one amused, said, "What the hell? Did you fall into a puddle, Zane?"

Curiosity was one of her less auspicious character traits. Tamara leaned around the door frame, peeking to see who had come to call. Zane had his back to her, hands on his hips, facing away, but the others weren't—and two male faces locked onto her.

Mack Winston gave a start of surprise, then whistled. "Zane," he asked, "what have you been up to?"

Chase Winston just grinned, a cocky, crooked grin that showed he had accurately guessed the answer to Mack's question. He knew *exactly* what his brother had been doing.

Zane whirled to face her, his scowl dark and deadly, his expression black. She bit her lip.

Busted.

Eight

Zane couldn't believe it. He had a boner that would have made Superman proud, and Tamara had gone up like a flame the second he'd touched her. She'd been ready, damn it, *so ready.*

But now he was stuck with his brothers. Oh, he knew good and well they wouldn't just back out politely, regardless of the fact they knew what they'd interrupted. If anything, they'd be more determined to hang around now than ever. Curiosity, and the perverse need to drive him crazy, would guarantee they extended their visit.

He wanted to kick himself. Hard. He'd been caught romping during business hours, his store unattended, his door unlocked. He'd taken total leave of his senses, no doubt about that. His own disbelief was extreme, but he knew his brothers would love ribbing him till doomsday over his lack of discretion. Damn.

Tamara, her face flushed and her lips swollen, stared at the three of them with wide, dark eyes. Zane wanted to erupt in frustration, but he wouldn't give his brothers the satisfaction. With women, he was always controlled. Now would be no different.

He drew a deep breath that didn't do a damn thing to relax him, and said, "Tamara, you might as well come on out."

Looking horrified by that prospect, she ducked back behind the door.

Mack turned to Zane. "You were hiding her?"

"No, of course not."

Unconvinced, Mack said, "She looks like she's hiding."

Zane knew that'd be enough to bring her out. His independent little Gypsy wouldn't want anyone to think her a coward.

Chase crossed his arms over his chest and leaned back against the wall. "Who is she?"

Waving toward the adjacent building, Zane went for the easiest explanation. "She's the Gypsy next door."

Mack, who had seen her several times in the past, whistled again.

"Will you stop that!" Zane no sooner barked at Mack, than he again drew a breath, reaching for that damn elusive control. But it was too late, both Mack and Chase eyed him with satisfied curiosity.

"A Gypsy, huh?"

Chase was having a fine time of it. Zane reigned in his temper with an effort. "Not a real Gypsy, of course. But she looks the part."

At that moment, the jingling of her bell-laden ankle bracelets drew everyone's attention, and Tamara stepped out. All three of them turned toward her. Zane immediately wanted to hide her again.

She was a wreck.

Her wig was sodden, looking blacker than usual, coarser. It hung in crooked clumps, probably because of his hands when he'd been holding her still for his kiss. He could still taste her, how sweet and hot her mouth had been, how stiff her nipple had gotten when he'd drawn on her. His head had nearly erupted with the pleasure of it. He wanted to taste her everywhere—but now he'd have to wait.

Her nose was red, and her makeup was everywhere except where it should have been. Her clothes had been rearranged and overlapped in an awkward way that at least had her decently covered. But it made her look . . . clumpy.

She stood there, narrow shoulders hunched, shivering, the rain dripping off her to form an expanding puddle around her beringed toes.

Looking beyond miserable, she attempted a smile.

Like mute fools, his damn brothers looked at him in disbelief.

Struggling with himself, Zane tried to figure out how to throw his brothers off the scent. At the moment, Tamara looked more like a drowned urchin than a woman who could make a man mad with lust to the point he'd leave his store unattended. They'd never understand why he had lost his head enough to seduce her in his storage room while his business was still open. Hell, he barely understood it.

Then suddenly Tamara's embarrassment hit him. It was such a heavy wave of awareness, pushing at him, smothering him, that he nearly lost his breath. She was mortified, more by his reaction than anything else, and he knew it bone deep.

He looked at her, and saw that she was ready to excuse herself, to claim to be no more than a friend. Her turmoil shamed him, proving his shallowness. He'd dragged her inside, stripped her blouse away from her breasts and touched her and tasted her, and now he was ready to deny it all. He felt like the biggest bastard alive.

Without giving it another thought, he strode forward and threw his arm possessively, protectively, around her shoulders.

She appeared floored that he'd done so, and that gave him a small measure of gratification. It was nice to be able to take her by surprise now and then. It helped to balance the constant state of shock she kept him in.

"Chase, Mack, this is Tamara Tremayne, my neighbor

next door." The bold way he edged her into his side proved she was much more than a neighbor; he didn't need to say the words.

Her shivers were so severe, they rattled Zane's ribs where she pressed against him. He needed to get her to her place so she could change. Some hot coffee wouldn't hurt, either. "Tamara, these are my pain-in-the-ass brothers."

Mack and Chase's replies were automatic, without their usual charm.

"Hello, there."

"Nice to meet you."

Zane understood; Tamara had that effect on him, too. But it was nothing compared to how she reacted to them.

He'd never seen her tongue-tied before. She'd been deliberately, mysteriously silent plenty of times. But she'd never been speechless. Curving his hand over her shoulder, Zane urged her a step closer and, with a grin, prompted her, "Say 'hi' to my brothers, honey."

"Hi."

Chase recovered first. "I take it you two were caught out in the storm?"

Nodding, Zane said, "Someone was following her— *ooof.*"

Tamara's sharp little elbow surely broke something. Zane glared down at her while he rubbed his midsection, but she just smiled at him.

Then patted him.

Chase and Mack watched with fascination.

"Zane," she said, all sweetness, as if she hadn't just tried to stove in his ribs, "don't bore your brothers with that stuff." Her teeth gleamed briefly in a parody of a smile, and she added, "It doesn't concern them."

Disbelief filled him. "Would you rather they think we were playing in the rain?" She didn't answer, but she looked ready to inflict more harm on his person. Zane narrowed his eyes. He held her elbow this time as a precaution, then said to Chase, "She has this problem with sharing."

"So I see." Amusement flickered across Chase's face.

Mack tugged at his ear. "I have a suggestion. Why don't we take her home and let her change out of those wet clothes before she turns blue? She's shivering so much, her bells are ringing."

Zane looked at her feet and saw Mack was right. Her ankle bracelets quivered, making music even though she tried to hold herself still.

"Her blouse is ripped too," Chase pointed out.

"What the hell?" How could he have missed that? Zane wondered. Then a thought occurred to him. "Damn, I didn't rip it, did I?"

Slapping her hand over his mouth, her face scalded with color, Tamara said, "It was already ripped."

He circled his fingers around her slender wrist and lowered her hand to her side. He had that awful feeling she was being evasive again. "How?"

Casting a worried look at his brothers' rapt expressions, she lowered her voice. "When I was running, I accidentally ripped it."

"Were you hurt?"

"I'm fine." She stressed that in a way that let him know she wanted him to drop it.

Like hell. "Let me see, honey."

She twisted away from him. "It's not a big deal, Zane."

He didn't believe her, but he knew he'd have a battle on his hands if he tried to force the issue in front of his brothers. Nodding, he said, "All right. Then let's get you home."

Tamara slipped away from Zane before he could stop her. "No, really, that's not necessary."

"Course it is," Chase assured her.

"My apartment is right above my shop. You two came to visit Zane, and I don't want to interrupt. I'll just be on my way—alone, of course, which is how it should be—

and you can all have a nice chat." She smiled as if that
was that and turned away.

Zane snagged her by the back of the blouse and pulled
her up short. "Nice try."

"Zane!" She slapped her hands over her breasts to cover
herself as the wet blouse was pulled tight to her front.

He'd forgotten her clothes were transparent. She'd
pulled them away from her skin and rearranged herself
some before coming out to meet his brothers, but once
the blouse touched her skin again, it didn't want to let go.
Every fine edge of her lace bra was clearly visible, as well
as her puckered nipples beneath.

Mack had his coat off in a flash. "Here you go." He
stared at the ceiling as he handed it to her. Chase pretended to be busy examining some new computers on display.

When Tamara didn't take the coat quickly enough,
Zane did the gentlemanly thing and stuffed her into it.
The sleeves fell almost to her knees. He buttoned the top
two buttons, then smiled. Tamara was swallowed up by
the dark brown coat, her slim legs barely showing beneath, and the neckline fell almost to her breasts. It was
all Zane could do not to laugh, despite her angry expression.

Addressing his brothers, he said, "Come on. We'll walk
her over, and we can talk while she changes."

"Zane. . . ."

"Quit growling at me, honey. You'll make a bad impression on my brothers."

She glared at him for that comment, and again started
to turn away.

"Mack."

"Got it." Mack stationed himself in front of the door,
barring the way while Zane found his umbrella and Chase
opened his own. Tamara looked ready to spit, she was so
angry at being thwarted, and Zane decided it was just as
well that she get used to it. He assumed he'd be thwarting
her a lot, as long as she continued to try to shut him out.

Once through the door, they sandwiched her between them, making certain she didn't get any wetter—though how she could get wetter, he didn't know. She was already drenched. But Zane also wanted her protected just in case the man who'd followed her was still hanging around.

He no longer had any doubts that she was, indeed, in danger. Hell, he'd felt the menace himself, as dumb as that seemed. And now that he knew the menace was real, he'd find a way to protect her—whether she wanted his protection or not.

His heart pounded so hard he felt bruised. He was wet, shivering, his teeth chattering from both cold and nerves. He clamped his jaws together hard, trying to keep from making any noise at all.

One second he'd been alone, well hidden by the shadows and the storm, ready to do what he must, what he had no choice but to do, and then suddenly she was there, that damn bright green umbrella announcing her like a beacon.

He didn't think she saw him today, but he wasn't sure. She'd just . . . taken off so suddenly. Running fast, like her life was in danger. He'd immediately changed his plans, of course, unwilling to take any more risks.

It made him nearly nauseous, each and every time he went in there. He hadn't had a chance to get into her place today; he hadn't had the time before she'd shown up, and he'd been too rattled after to do more than hide.

That was sheer luck on his part, because not long after she'd run into the computer store, a man had stormed outside, looking around. It was a good thing he'd stayed hidden. Even when the rain soaked past his coat and ran in an icy river down his backbone, he hadn't moved from his hidey-hole. He'd stay tucked away until they were all gone, un-

til he knew without a single doubt that it was clear.
But damn, it was hard. He wasn't cut out for this,
and he needed to search again—before it was too
late.

Zane locked up quickly while his brothers protected her
from the storm. Then they dashed across the lot and went,
en masse, up the outside metal stairs to her apartment
door. Zane and Chase held her elbows. Because Mack had
given her his coat, he held the umbrella, making sure they
stayed as dry as possible.

The landing was jam-packed with all four of them
there, and for a brief moment Zane wondered if it would
hold up under their combined weight. He and his brothers
each went over two hundred pounds. Add Tamara's one
hundred pounds or so to that, and the stairs felt beyond
rickety, creaking and groaning with their weight.

"Do you have your key?" Zane asked her.

She tried to dig in her skirt pocket, but the chore proved
difficult, given the size of Mack's coat on her and how
wet her skirt was. Finally, Zane reached into her pocket
for her. He could feel the sleek firmness of her thigh
through the material, and it inflamed him all over again.
Damn, but he wanted her, and he wasn't used to holding
back, to pulling away after getting so close.

He needed to get her alone, naked. Under him. He
wanted to ride her so gently she melted around him, and
then not so gently until she screamed out her climax.
When he'd cupped her through her panties, he'd felt how
soft and warm and wet she was.

He shook, he wanted her so much.

He didn't, however, want to take her against the wall
in his storage room. Talk about a lack of finesse. Later,
he might even be grateful that his brothers had interrupted.
For now, he was still quietly seething, his lust barely
banked.

Tamara flipped on the light as soon as they stepped
inside. She faced Zane with her hands on her hips. The

coat sleeves covered her arms and beyond, so she looked more comical than angry.

He said easily, "Don't start complaining again."

"I'll complain if I want to!"

He unbuttoned the coat, easily dodging her flapping hands, then turned her and wrested the garment off her shoulders.

"Damn it, Zane, if you don't—"

He leaned close to her ear, so close he could brush her lobe with his mouth as he spoke. "You're giving my brothers another peep show, babe."

She whirled, turning her back to them. Over her shoulder, she speared Zane with a smoldering look, and said through gritted teeth, "I'll be right back. Don't you dare say a thing while I'm gone."

Tenderness warmed him. She was so damn cute, so determined to refuse any and all concern. For some reason, she was threatened by the idea that he might actually start to care about her. Zane didn't know why, but he intended to find out.

Her eyes, resembling those of a raccoon with the smudged makeup, narrowed on him, waiting. Zane saluted her. "Yes ma'am."

Her bossy disposition, which had once seemed both annoying and intolerable, now struck him as adorable. She marched away, slim derriere swaying, and Zane stared after her, his mind conjuring wonderful, intimate, carnal images of letting her be bossy in bed—until Chase clapped him on the back.

"You're not being very subtle, Zane."

Mack laughed. "Hell, I'm embarrassed to even witness this. I feel like a voyeur."

"Go to hell, both of you."

His brothers thought that was hysterical. When they finally stopped laughing, Zane told them, "You might as well sit down. I'll fill you in while she showers."

"I thought she told you to be quiet," Chase commented helpfully. He looked around her apartment with interest.

"Yeah," Mack said, piping in, "and you looked like you took her warning to heart."

Oddly enough, their taunting didn't bother him. Tamara was different, and what he felt about her was different. He hadn't quite pinpointed his feelings for her yet—there was curiosity because she *was* different, lust certainly, amusement and concern and protectiveness. What those things all meant collectively, he had no idea. For the moment, he could only make plans to get her alone and in his bed. Or her bed. Or hell, the couch would do. And he wanted to make certain she'd be safe. Once those were both taken care of, maybe he'd be able to stop thinking about her. Maybe.

But he preferred that his brothers not see her as just another woman he wanted to bed. He wanted them to know she was . . . special.

"She'll learn," Zane told them thoughtfully, "that I do things my own way."

"If you say so." Mack sprawled out with a groan on the striped sofa, his arms stretched out along the back, his long legs stuck out in front of him.

Chase walked around looking at the photographs on the walls. Zane hadn't noticed them on his first visit, what with her aunt jumping on his back and her uncle threatening to kill him. Then there had been the ghost who wasn't a ghost at all. . . .

"Are these her parents?" Chase asked.

Zane moved closer to examine the old black-and-white photograph in an antique-looking, ornate oval frame of gold and silver. "I don't know. They died when she was young. She was pretty much raised by two aunts and this enormous uncle who could rival Bigfoot."

"No kidding? Sounds like an interesting family."

"You don't know the half of it." The couple in the photo could have been Tamara's parents. The woman had the same features as Tamara and the aunts: exotically shaped cat eyes, high cheekbones. But the photo was so old, he couldn't tell if she had dark or light hair. The man was big, long hair to his shoulders, mustache, an indulgent smile directed at his wife. It was a nice photo—Zane decided to ask her about it. Later.

Mack clasped his hands behind his head, and his eyes looked drowsy. "She's not your usual type."

The shower started, and Zane moved to the doorway so he could stare down the hall. He pictured Tamara tossing aside the hideous wig, removing her rings one by one, peeling the wet clothes off her body. His heart gave a lurch at the image of her soft skin exposed, those small, plump breasts completely bare. He throbbed.

Shaking his head to clear it, Zane looked at Mack. "What did you say?"

Mack smiled.

"Stop needling him, Mack." Chase sat in the chair facing his youngest brother. "And Zane, stop staring down the hall with such a pathetically lustful expression. Mack's right. It's embarrassing."

Zane sat. There was a lot he needed to discuss with his brothers. And now, while Tamara was busy, seemed like the best possible time. He leaned forward, elbows on his knees, to address his brothers. "I may need your help."

Nine

"*You definitely need help,*" Mack informed Zane, referring more to his lovelorn expression than to the real issue at hand. "But what can we do?"

Rather than strangle his brother, Zane explained the situation. He told them all about Tamara's troubles, the skeptical police, her nutty family. He skipped the finer details and merely hit the highlights. It was enough. Both Mack and Chase looked incredulous.

Zane heard the shower turn off and the blow-dryer start. He was running out of time. "So what do you think?"

"You're sure she's not just imagining the vandalism?" Chase asked. "I'm not suggesting she'd lie. But the police have a point. Everything that's happened could have been simple pranks or happenstance."

"I had a few lingering doubts myself, until today," Zane admitted. "But when she came through my door—well, I knew then that she was right. Someone was out there. She was really afraid, and from what I've discovered about her so far, she's not exactly a faint heart. She's got a backbone made of iron."

Mack had lost his casual pose and now frowned. "What do her relatives say?"

Zane shook his head. "They think it's a ghost. Their deceased uncle Hubert. Can you believe that crap?"

To his surprise, Chase straightened. "Well now, I wouldn't rule out the possibility."

Both Zane and Mack stared at Chase.

"What?" Chase shifted. "Ghosts exist."

"Whatever you say, Chase." Zane sent a look to Mack which clearly said, *Yeah, right.*

"I'm just saying not to rule it out."

"Trust me, this is a flesh-and-blood person. I'm positive of it." He went on to explain about Hubert and the eccentricities of the relatives, why they might prefer to believe in a ghost than any tangible threat.

"Yeah," Chase said, nodding, "sounds like they fabricated the ghost."

"Don't sound so disappointed, damn it." Sometimes, Zane didn't understand his second oldest brother at all. Chase was the quietest, the most thoughtful—and what ran through his mind was anyone's guess. More often than not, Zane suspected, his thoughts were occupied with his wife, Allison.

"The thing is," Chase explained, "if her relatives really do believe it's a ghost, I wouldn't alienate them with ridicule. Believe me, if you piss off the relatives, you could piss off Tamara, too. They obviously mean a lot to her, given how she's taken care of them."

Zane curled his hands into fists. "How do I help her, damn it, especially when she doesn't want my help?"

They all grew silent, thinking. Finally, Mack leaned forward. He didn't quite look at Zane when he said, "You know who you need to call."

It wasn't a question, but a statement. And Zane did know, damn it. But still he tried to refuse. "No way. I've considered him, but he's usually more trouble than not. And more trouble is something I don't need right now."

"Joe is trained for this sort of thing," Mack argued.

"Joe is trained to seduce women." Their cousin, Joe Winston, was a big, mean son-of-a-bitch. He was between Cole and Chase in age, almost thirty-six now, but age had only made him leaner, harder, stronger. *Nastier.*

He'd given up on law enforcement after a stray bullet had damaged his knee. But even when he'd been on crutches, the women had flocked to him. He had danger written all over him, and for some reason, women seemed to love it.

Joe had played at being a bounty hunter for a few years, a private dick, a bodyguard, and he'd been successful at each job. But he'd been a ladies' man almost from birth.

"He could look out for her," Mack continued, "and she'd never even know he was there."

"Forget it." The thought of his disreputable cousin spying on Tamara, possibly seeing her at vulnerable moments, made him want to howl with possessive fury. Joe would go after her simply because she was different, and because she'd be a challenge.

Chase started laughing and almost couldn't stop. "Oh, this is priceless, Zane. You're worried your little Gypsy will succumb."

Shooting to his feet, Zane barked, "I am not!"

Mack said very softly, "Am too."

Zane squared his shoulders and pointed a finger at Mack. "I'll have you know—"

"What," Tamara said from the doorway, "is all the yelling about?"

Chase and Mack looked up, then their expressions went comically blank, before turning warm and admiring. Zane wanted to groan. He most definitely didn't want to look. But like a magnet, his gaze was drawn to her.

He turned, and there stood Tamara, hair brushed into soft golden curls, exotic green eyes bright. She wore a pair of skinny beige jeans and a long-sleeve, emerald green shirt. A narrow strip of her belly showed between the waistband of the pants and the shirt's hem. Her makeup was gone, her jewelry was gone. He gulped.

Zane was vaguely aware of Mack and Chase slowly coming to their feet. He wanted to knock their heads together. They acted like they'd never seen a woman before. He could almost feel them sorting through their thoughts, trying to decide if the bedraggled, rain-washed Gypsy and the adorable woman before them now could really be one and the same.

It wasn't that she was beautiful, Zane reasoned, attempting to study her dispassionately, from a purely male perspective rather than that of a man already involved.

True, she was cute. Especially now with her expression so disgruntled, her soft mouth set in mulish lines. But her appearance certainly wasn't enough to turn his grown brothers into leering idiots.

Yet there they stood, ogling her.

Zane cleared his throat, but the only one to notice was Tamara.

"Well?" she asked, eyeing him with accusation and suspicion.

Zane shoved Mack in the shoulder, which made him stumble into Chase. Neither of them fell, but it was a close thing.

Returned to his senses, Chase said, "I'm sorry. It's just. . . . You look so . . . different."

Mack bobbed his head. "Different."

Tamara scowled at Zane. "You didn't tell them I wear a costume?"

He rolled one shoulder. "Hey, you told me to sit quietly, so I did."

Mack choked over that tale, and while Chase pounded him on the back, Zane moved to stand at Tamara's side.

"Are you okay?"

She bristled, casting conspicuous glances at his brothers. "Of course. Why wouldn't I be?"

Zane wanted to shake her. "You were chased by a guy in a ski mask."

"Zane. . . ." She attempted to give him a *shut up* look. He ignored her. "And drenched to the skin."

"Zane. . . ."

"And scared half to death—"

"Get out."

"What?" He couldn't believe she'd ordered him out. He was worried. He wanted to hold her and comfort her.

"You heard me." She shoved against him, trying to make him move. He didn't budge, except to blink in disbelief.

He stared down at her, his temper starting to heat. "I'm not going anywhere."

"Oh, yes, you are. I've had it with your bulldozing."

He leaned down to go nose to nose with her. "Hey, *you* came to *me*, remember?"

Her eyes widened, and she looked devastated. *"You told them?"*

Zane drew back, then realized how she'd misunderstood. "Not that, damn it!" He felt the searing intensity of his brothers' interest. The nosy bastards. "I meant today, at the shop. You got scared, so you came to me."

"Oh, that." She shook her head and quit trying to shove him away—probably because she wasn't making any headway. "I didn't think I'd be able to get my door unlocked in time, and I wasn't sure if any of the other stores in the mall were open."

His teeth ground together. "So I was the most convenient?"

"Well, you *are* right next door."

She sounded so logical, his temper ignited. "When I get you alone. . . ."

Chase cleared his throat. "Hold that thought, okay?"

Mack made a face. "You're a spoilsport, Chase, you know that? I was all set to hear what grand retribution he had planned."

"You're too young to hear whatever Zane has planned, and you know it."

Zane had all but forgotten his brothers' presence. Tamara could so easily twist him in knots and make him forget himself and his surroundings. He glared at her, letting her know where he placed the blame for his social faux pas.

"We'll discuss this later," he told her, in what he hoped sounded like a calmer, less emotionally charged tone.

Rubbing the back of his neck, Chase said, "Yeah, well, as to that. . . . It might need to be much later. That's why we're here. We were hoping you could close up the bar tonight."

Zane's expectations for the immediate future did a nosedive. "Tonight?"

"I wouldn't ask, except there's no one else."

Zane propped his hands on his hips. "Meaning I can't very well refuse?" Man, he hated it when family loyalty forced him to be noble.

Mack tried and failed to control a grin. "Sorry about that. It seems to be the night for kid distractions. Trista is having a sleepover, and I hate to leave Jessica to deal with that on her own."

Tamara politely asked, "Trista?"

"My daughter. She's fourteen, and her birthday is in a few days. She's celebrating with friends tonight—ten of them—and I don't want to miss it."

She blinked at him. "You have a fourteen-year-old daughter?"

Beaming with pride, Mack said, "Yeah. Smartest kid around, and beautiful to boot."

Zane put his arm around Tamara. He was well used to Mack's bloated pride. "Mack would never volunteer the information, since he thinks of Trista as his own, but she came part and parcel with his wife. Jessica had Trista from a previous marriage. I gotta agree with him on the smart and beautiful part, though. And she's so damn mature it's scary."

"Oh."

She still didn't sound like she understood, but Zane figured he could explain that Mack married an older woman later. When Mack wasn't around to object. Zane smiled. He liked Jessica a lot, and she certainly kept his goofy brother on his toes.

"So what are you doing?" Zane asked Chase, still hoping there might be some way out for him.

"Sammy's cutting teeth."

Zane winced in sympathy. "Rough. Did you try giving her something cold to chew on? That worked for me when Nate was doing the same."

"Yeah. It helps, but not for long. Allison hasn't had a quiet minute all week. She's made plans to go out with friends tonight, while I keep the little imp happy—and believe me, closing the bar would be easier than keeping a teething, bossy, female baby in good spirits."

Tamara, looking a little dazed, said, "Sammy?"

"Samantha Jane Winston, five months old and a hellion already." Zane grinned as he said it. He adored his niece, and his nephew. "When she wants to be held, you hold her. When she wants to be fed, it better be right now. She has a yell that could pierce your eardrums."

"Not that anyone lets her yell much," Chase explained. "Especially not Zane. She already knows she has him wrapped around her very tiny finger."

"She likes me the best," Zane confided, earning a scowl from Chase. It annoyed his brother no end that the second Sammy heard Zane's voice, she started squealing for him. "So let me guess," he said, before Chase could get really put out, "Sophie is going out with Allison, and Cole is watching Nate."

And before Tamara could ask, he told her, "Nate is Cole's little boy, eleven months old now, and not only walking but running—straight into trouble whenever he can accomplish it."

Mack leaned forward in a conspiratorial tone and said to Tamara, "He gets that from his uncle Zane."

Zane reached for Mack, but he ducked away. "Trista and the babies have been to the bar, but usually during the afternoon, which is probably why you haven't seen them. You only go there at night, right?"

Mack and Chase looked at her again, frowning in concentration.

"You've been to the bar?" Chase asked.

"I don't remember seeing you," Mack said.

Tamara muttered, "I try to . . . blend in."

No one knew what she meant by that, but Zane was beginning to understand her. She felt isolated by her family's eccentricities and her occupation. He could only imagine what her life as a child had been like. His arm around her shoulders tightened, and he gave both his brothers a look to let them know to drop it.

Chase was the first to catch on. "Actually," he told Zane, now smiling widely, "Sophie isn't going out with Allison. But we do have some other news for you."

Mack bobbed his head in agreement.

Warily, Zane eyed them both. "What?"

"Sophie is pregnant again."

"What!" A grin caught him by surprise. Another niece or nephew was on the way—it didn't matter to him which. He'd never suspected how incredible babies could be, but he'd found he liked being an uncle. "When's she due?"

"Around October." Chase chuckled. "Cole is a wreck, of course, and so we figured he deserved the night off."

Zane turned to Tamara and lifted her off her feet into a huge bear hug. She clung to his shoulders in startled surprise. "My oldest brother is like a mother hen at times," he told her as he set her back on her feet. The look on her face was priceless.

This time it was his family overwhelming her.

"Especially now that Sophie is expecting again," Mack added. "Her last delivery wasn't exactly easy, and Cole had swore one kid would be it. But Sophie won that argument."

Zane laughed. "Sophie wins all the arguments." He suspected that was because Cole, like the rest of them, hated to disappoint her about anything. "When did she find out?"

"Just this afternoon." Chase chuckled. "She came

straight to the bar when Cole was opening up and gave him the news. He's been walking into the walls ever since then."

Glancing at his watch, Zane said, "Damn. I guess I better be heading over that way. I'm surprised he managed to stay there this long. I figured he'd be home, hovering over Sophie, fretting."

"He wanted to follow her out after she told him, but Sophie said she had stuff to do, and made me promise I'd keep him there until eight."

"She's planning a. . . ." Mack glanced at Tamara and coughed. "A private celebration, and didn't want Cole home until she was ready."

"Sophie owns a lingerie shop." Zane winked at Tamara. "When she plans a private celebration, no telling what goes on."

Chase added helpfully, "You know, you have about fifteen minutes yet before you'd have to leave, if you want to—"

Zane looked at Tamara, observed her hopeful expression, and shook his head. Without looking away from her, he said, "You two go on. I'll be right behind you."

To Zane's annoyance, Chase walked right up to Tamara and folded her into a big hug. "It was very nice meeting you, Tamara."

Mack kissed her cheek, and even went so far as to bob his eyebrows suggestively. "Very nice."

Flustered, she stammered, "It was nice meeting both of you, too."

It was still raining hard when they opened the door and went out, immediately popping open their umbrellas and pulling up their collars. Cool, damp air blew into the room, and then the door was closed and they were alone again.

Tamara touched his arm, her brows lifted in question. "Fifteen minutes . . . ?"

"Isn't near enough time." Looping his arms around her waist, Zane pulled her into his embrace and kissed her, a kiss of regret, gentle and undemanding. "I'm not a fifteen-minutes kind of guy, honey. When I get you naked, it's going to take me at least twice that long just to get my fill of looking at you."

Her eyes widened. Zane waited for her to blush, for her modesty to kick in. Instead, she blurted, "The book said we should do that."

"Do what?"

She ran her fingers through the hair at his nape. "The journal I told you about? It said new lovers should spend a day just looking at each other, getting used to being naked together."

Zane nearly choked. It made him hot—and more frustrated—just to talk about it. "When you're naked," he informed her, "I can guarantee you I'm going to do more than just look."

Her smiled was pure female mischief. "Like what?"

Eyes gleaming, he whispered, "Like kiss you all over."

"Oh." Her head dropped to his chest and her arms tightened. Zane rubbed her back, wishing that he could stay, and not just to satisfy his lust. He was worried. Despite her show of bravado, he was certain she was a little worried, too. He wanted to hold her, to talk to her. To reassure her.

After a moment, she said, "I like your family a lot."

"They have their moments." *Tonight definitely wasn't one of them.* Knowing he had to go, he reached into his pocket and pulled out an ultrasmall cell phone. He pushed the buttons a few times, setting the phone, did a check, then tried to hand it to her.

She looked at it without taking it. "What is that?"

"Obviously it's a phone." She still didn't reach for it, and he sighed. "I want you to keep it with you." The phone was so slim and small, keeping it next to her person shouldn't be a problem. And that was where he wanted it—on her at all times. "You can push the talk button, and it'll automatically dial me."

Pulling away from the phone as if it might bite her, she asked, "Why?"

He'd expected an argument; everything with Tamara was an argument when she felt he was trying to protect her or help her. He respected her self-reliant nature, especially since he knew it was so important to her. But at the moment, he wished she were just a little less stubborn.

"I don't feel right leaving you after what happened." She shook her head, and he added, "I had planned on spending the night. Tomorrow we could have discussed how to handle this problem."

"*My* problem, not yours."

Zane curled his free hand around her nape and held her still as he bent to kiss her. Her mouth immediately softened and he thrust his tongue inside, tasting her deeply, stealing her breath. Branding her.

When he pulled back, her beautiful green eyes were heavy, and her lips were wet, open. "I'm not taking any chances with you, sweetheart. Now promise me you'll call me if anything happens, or I'll let Cole know I won't be closing the bar after all."

Slowly the fog of desire cleared from her gaze. She heaved a disgruntled sigh, then held out her hand.

Zane placed the phone in her palm and curled her fingers around it, holding her hand in his own. "Keep it with you," he insisted. "In bed, if you go to the bathroom, if you. . . ."

"I got it. Keep it with me."

"If you hear anything, anything at all, just push the Talk button."

"You won't be at home."

"I set it to automatically dial another cell phone I have. It's one I normally keep plugged into my car, but I'll carry it with me now."

Tamara nodded, then slipped the tiny phone into her back jeans pocket. "You should go."

"Yeah." He didn't want to leave, damn it.

Staring at her feet, she asked, "What time will the bar close?"

"Tonight? Not until two."

She groaned, then offered suggestively, "I don't open my shop until ten on Saturdays."

Zane almost smiled. "You need to get some sleep. If I come back here, neither one of us will sleep tonight." He again thought of Joe. His cousin would be able to keep her safe when Zane was busy—like tonight. But damn, Joe had always rubbed him the wrong way.

He clasped Tamara's arms just above her elbows and lifted her up, promising himself it would be the very last kiss, and then he'd go.

Though she tried to cover it, he caught her small wince of pain.

He instantly gentled his hold. "What is it?"

She shook her head. "Nothing, I just—"

"I hurt you."

"No you didn't!" She shifted her shoulder, her expression sulky before she admitted, "I kind of bumped into a van when I was running to your shop."

Going rigid, Zane demanded, "Where are you hurt?"

"It's just a small scratch."

"Where, Tamara?"

"On my arm."

He'd specifically asked her about the rip in her blouse. Why hadn't she told him she was hurt? *Dumb question.* She would consider it none of his business, something to be dealt with on her own.

He stared at her, trying not to let his anger show. "Let me see."

Smug, she told him, "I can't. I'm wearing long sleeves."

No doubt so he wouldn't see her injury. Zane locked his jaw, and solved that problem by catching the hem of her shirt and pulling it up over her head. Tamara tried to stop him with a lot of squawking and complaining and slapping, but she wasn't a match for him. As gently as he could, he relieved her of the shirt and left her standing there in her bra and jeans.

Damn, she was a temptation. Her jeans fit her body perfectly, and her bra, though plain, white cotton, was low-cut and very enticing.

Tamara protested her unveiling, until she realized he was bent on ignoring her luscious little breasts to center his concentration on her injury.

Then she became indignant.

Zane took one look at the long red scratch and bruised skin on her upper arm and wanted to bellow. Someone had hurt her, whether deliberately or inadvertently, and there was no way Zane would let it happen again. He made up his mind. He'd call Joe. Tonight.

But he'd also give his disreputable cousin a warning. Tamara was off-limits—and there'd be hell to pay if he forgot that.

Ten

How dare he ignore her when she was half-naked?

Tamara stalked through her quiet house, holding her shirt bunched in her fist as she made certain everything was secured. The latches on the windows were loose and rusted, but thanks to how warped the old windows were, they were tough to open even when they weren't locked. Cold air seeped in around the wooden frames, and made goose bumps rise on her exposed shoulders and midriff as she pulled down every shade.

She barely noticed, she was still so annoyed.

Zane had stripped her shirt off as if she was a child. That had been bad enough, and she fully intended to raise hell with him about it when she saw him again. But worse, he'd ignored her partially exposed body to examine one measly scratch.

Annoyance and stung pride carried her through her house with a stomping gait.

The living room door had a dead bolt, and Zane had listened from the metal landing until he'd heard her click it into place. The door leading to the downstairs, and the door closing off the part of the house she didn't use, both required a skeleton key. She jiggled each of them, making certain they were closed tight.

It had taken her almost five minutes to convince Zane she was fine and she could damn well tend to a scratch without his help. She'd never expected him to be so . . . mollycoddling. Not that she disliked it, because she didn't. And that was part of the problem.

It felt so nice to be tended to, to have someone care.

Zane had surprised her at every turn. She was no longer certain what she'd expected, what she'd hoped for. He seemed so genuine. So concerned and sincere. He wasn't at all like the man she'd read about in the local papers, the outrageous man who bordered on being an exhibitionist, the lady-killer, and the risqué brother. He *was* those things, no way around it. But he was so much more than that.

His happiness over the thought of a new nephew or niece had astounded her. She'd never pictured him with kids, never considered that he might know how to handle himself with children, or be comfortable around them. Yet both his brothers had agreed Zane was a favorite uncle. Sammy squealed at his presence, and Nate emulated him.

Kids were a good judge of character. They knew when someone was innately kind, generous.

Oh damn, she was falling in love with him. She squeezed her eyes shut and tried to deny the truth, but it was impossible. She'd probably been half in love with him even before he'd accepted her proposition. She knew her heart had always thumped erratically whenever she caught sight of him. His laugh had the power to make her stomach flip-flop. And his eyes . . . she often felt like she was melting when she met his eyes.

She'd written all that off as sexual attraction. Every woman who looked at him wanted him, so why should she have been any different, except that he hadn't wanted her in return?

But now she knew it was more. Damn and double damn!

Tamara stopped dead in the hallway and stared blankly at a wall. Love Zane Winston? It was beyond foolish, yet. . . . Yet how could she not?

No one had ever tried to take care of her before. She could take care of herself, so it had never been necessary. But it felt nice that he wanted to, that he tried.

Her aunts and uncle had accepted her with open arms, but they were like overgrown children, wallowing in the freedom of their Gypsy spirits, disinclined toward anything that hinted of normalcy, while she'd always craved the mundane. She'd quickly adopted the roll of caretaker, and that setup had suited them all.

But now Zane coddled her, wanting to protect her, worrying about her. He touched her and set her on fire, making her experience things she hadn't even known were possible. He argued with her, but didn't hold a grudge. He put his brothers above his lust, and loved his niece and nephew.

He ignored her body to fret over a scratch.

Oh, he was a very lovable man, and she wasn't immune. Hiding her feelings from him was the key, if she wanted him to stick around. Zane was a bachelor with a capital B. It had taken quite an effort just to get him to agree to have sex with her. If he ever suspected what was in her heart, he'd bolt, she was sure of it.

A clinging woman spouting words of love was guaranteed to drive him away.

Tamara sighed and forced her feet to unglue themselves from the carpet. She couldn't solve any of her dilemmas about Zane tonight, so she might as well quit fretting over it. She had more important things to take care of.

It was still fairly early, but she wouldn't be going back out, so she changed into a sleep shirt and eyed the pile of work on her desk. The sooner she turned in the work, the sooner she'd get paid. It would be a few hours before she could go to bed.

She headed for the kitchen to make a sandwich. On her way past the family room she noticed the blinking light on the answering machine. She pushed the Replay button and listened while she opened the refrigerator.

The voice of her Realtor came on the line. Tamara froze, turning to stare at the machine in horror. There had been an offer on the building. A good one. The Realtor expected her to show up at his office the next day, during her lunch hour, to look it over.

Her hunger gave way to cramps, caused by distress. If the building sold now, she wouldn't have time to spend with Zane. There might not be an opportunity for intimacy.

Could she have gotten so close, only to miss getting to love him?

Zane entered the bar in a rush. He was a few minutes late because he'd had to go home and change. As he darted past the tables to the bar where Cole played bartender, several women whistled to him, a few even reaching out, trying to get hold of him. He was too distracted to pay them much mind, and barely managed a smile.

Cole eyed him as he slipped around the bar. "You just disappointed a lot of ladies."

"What?"

"Your admirers. They're not too pleased to have you breeze by without a notice. First last night, then again today. You ready to tell me what's going on?"

Glancing over his shoulder, Zane eyed the table of sulking women. They waved to him, and this time he winked. When he looked at Cole again, he shook his head. "Sorry, I guess I'm distracted. I've been rushing like hell. I got here as quick as I could."

He hated that he'd kept Cole waiting on such a special night. He knew his brother well, and Cole was likely going nuts wanting to be home with his wife. "Go ahead and take off. I've got it covered."

The place was packed, but that wasn't unusual for a

Friday night. They did a hell of a business on the weekends.

Cole finished filling an order, then turned as Zane hung his coat on a hook. Leaning back against the wall and crossing his arms over his chest, Cole said, "Chase and Mack filled me in."

Zane wanted to groan. Instead, he kept his expression carefully impassive. "They told you about Tamara?"

"In great detail." Cole looked Zane over, and smiled. His most outrageous brother was doing his best to look indifferent. Zane obviously didn't realize it, but that in itself was telling. "They took turns grabbing the phone from each other and shouting into my ear. Around all the laughing, I gathered the Winston curse has taken a nibble out of your stubborn hide."

More like it had bitten off a huge chunk, but Zane wasn't about to admit that. He said noncommittally, "Maybe."

"So that's what had you acting so odd last night."

"I was *not* acting odd." Zane shifted, his tension growing. "I was just. . . ."

"I know, distracted."

Chin out, hands fisted, he said, "Yeah," and his stance dared Cole to press him on it.

Far from intimidated, Cole appeared to be barely holding in his laughter. "She sounds . . . unique."

There was just enough inflection in his brother's tone to set Zane's teeth on edge. "You all don't have to keep referring to her as if she's an oddity."

Giving up with a chuckle, Cole held up both hands. "Ho! I didn't mean it that way."

"The hell you didn't. Mack and Chase acted the same." Zane glared at a customer who loudly demanded service, then turned back to Cole. "She *is* different, okay? But in a really nice way."

"That's exactly what Mack and Chase said."

"Bullshit. I bet they told you about the wig, didn't they?"

The customer leaned over the bar. "A wig?"

Zane filled his beer glass and shoved it at him with a glare. "Mind your own damn business."

Still grinning, Cole said, "That's a great way to keep the business healthy, Zane."

Zane was just harassed enough to growl, "Would I be seeing a woman who was odd, damn it?"

"Of course not." Cole's tone was soothing—and filled with barely suppressed humor. "You did say a wig?"

Zane felt his face heat. He hadn't blushed since he'd been a boy. "Sophie's plans for the night are going to be ruined," he growled, "if you don't stop needling me."

In a stage whisper, Zane heard the nosy customer grumbling about women and wigs and curses. Great. Now he had everyone gossiping.

He barely stifled a groan. "Go home, Cole."

"In a minute." Cole refilled two more drinks. He'd hired a couple of new guys, but they hadn't quite gotten a handle on things yet, and were slow to fill orders.

When Cole finished, he reached for his coat. Zane put a hand on his shoulder. "Damn it, I didn't mean to act like a bastard."

"No?" Cole looked amused, not insulted.

"No. I meant to tell you congratulations."

Shaking his head, Cole said, "I swear, Zane, I don't know if I can live through this again."

Zane knew exactly what he was talking about. "You'll be fine. And so will Sophie. She's a trooper."

"Hell, she doesn't even remember how much pain she was in. She talks about the birth like it was a breeze. And I'll be damned if I'm going to remind her otherwise."

Zane felt sympathy for his oldest brother. "You're happy about the baby, aren't you?"

"Hell, yes!" Then he looked around, realized that he'd shouted, and rubbed his hands over his face. "Yes, I'm happy to have another baby, but you can't imagine what it's like to see someone you love hurting that much."

Tamara had only had a scratch, and he'd wanted to beat

someone to a pulp. The thought of her going through la-
bor . . . . Zane broke out in a sweat and quickly shook off
that thought. "Now they know she delivers fast," he assured Cole. "They'll be ready for her."

"They better be, or I'm going to knock some heads
together."

Zane patted him on the back, giving in to a reluctant
grin. "You know what you need?"

Cole eyed him. "What?"

"To go home and let your wife soothe you."

Smiling, Cole said, "Yeah." Then, "I *am* sorry I interrupted your plans tonight."

Zane was sorry, too. "Are you kidding? I interrupted
your plans for most of my life. You were always there
for me, so I'm glad to get to pay you back a little now
and then."

"Ah, shit." Cole looked away and grumbled, "I just
found out I'm going to be a father again, Zane. If you
start getting all emotional on me, tonight of all nights, I
may have to flatten you just to keep my manly conse-
quence."

Zane laughed. His brother was about the best man he
knew. When their parents had died, Cole had taken over
without a single complaint. It wasn't until the rest of them
were in college that Cole started taking care of his own
needs—which included falling in love with Sophie.

Long before he and Sophie had their first child, Cole
had learned all the parenting skills he needed by raising
his brothers single-handedly.

Zane gave Cole a slight shove. "Get out of here. You're
embarrassing me."

Cole turned up his collar. "I'm embarrassing myself."
He started to walk away, but paused. "Don't let her get
away, Zane."

Zane played stupid by saying, "Who?"

Not in the least fooled, Cole pointed at him. "I didn't
raise any dummies. Judging by last night and tonight,

you're hooked. Don't do something stupid to blow it." He strode away.

Zane was busy for the next three hours, nonstop. He sometimes missed working at the bar, the activity and loud camaraderie, even though he loved having his computer store. Cole had never expected any of them to stay on at the bar, but he'd made it a very welcome place to be.

The second things slowed down, Zane called Tamara. He didn't think she'd be asleep yet, and he wanted to make certain she was okay. Fretting over a woman was a new experience, and he didn't like it worth a damn.

She answered on the third ring.

She sounded weary, and a bit uncertain. "Zane?"

"What took you so long?" Zane demanded, thinking here he was, worrying like an old woman and she couldn't even be bothered to do as he'd asked.

She yawned into his ear. "Sorry. I was working on some stuff and the phone was buried under papers."

"I thought I told you to keep it on you."

"I can't."

"Why?"

"Because. . . ." She sighed in exasperation. "Zane, I'm almost ready for bed."

"So?"

"So I'm . . . not wearing anything with pockets."

Awareness kicked in, and he lowered his voice to ask, "What *are* you wearing?"

Her voice lowered, too. "Just a T-shirt."

His heart punched hard. "Panties?"

"Well, yeah."

His thighs tightened. "What color are they?"

She laughed. "Zane!"

"Tell me. Otherwise I'll go crazy all night wondering."

"They're beige."

"Same color as your skin?"

"Almost."

He groaned, picturing her curled in her bed, the sheet

gone, maybe in his T-shirt instead of her own. "Have you been thinking about me?" he whispered.

"You want the truth?" He heard the smile in her voice. "I'm having a hard time doing anything else."

"Good." A slow heat began filling him. "It's crazy here tonight. Cole's hired two new guys, but they're green-horns and slow as molasses. I've about run my ass off or I'd have called sooner."

"Zane." She said his name in soft rebuke. "I don't need you to call and check up on me."

"But you'll let me do it anyway," he said with insistence.

There was a long hesitation before she answered, resigned. "Yes. I'll let you do it anyway."

"Good girl." Damn, he should be with her. Regardless of what she said, she still had to be a little rattled after what had happened. Zane wished like hell he could get his hands on the man who'd chased her. Every time he thought of her running in a panic—*to him*, despite her protests on that—it made him nuts.

"You know, honey," he said with gentle persistence, "you don't have to be tough with me."

"I'm fine," she said again, and Zane gave up. Sooner or later, he'd get her to let down her guard, to stop shutting him out. He refused to accept any other possibility.

"All right. Go get some sleep."

"Good night, Zane."

"Dream about me." He laughed when she groaned again. She hung up without answering. Zane looked around the bar and decided it was a good time to make another phone call. Things had slowed down a little, the first rush hour over, and he knew if he didn't make this call now, he might not make it at all.

Joe Winston stretched out naked on the top of the quilt and yawned. A cool night breeze whispered through the open window to dry the sweat on his body and lighten the scent of sex. Except for his bum knee, which throbbed like a son-of-a-bitch, he felt good, damn good. About ready to sleep.

The woman next to him immediately rolled into his side. Her hands were graspy, her attitude more so. Belatedly, he realized he never should have slept with her again. Not only had her "harder, harder" demands about taken out his knee, but she was the type to read too much into a second tumble. She'd see it as keen interest rather than the boredom it had been.

Joe held himself still, not about to encourage her.

"I want you to come meet my folks," she whispered significantly, then licked his ear.

Damn, damn, damn. He'd known her only a few weeks, for Christ's sake, slept with her only twice—and this time was an accident, a case of her catching him off guard. But then she was good at that. He'd made it clear he had no intentions of getting serious with anyone, yet she was already making plans for him. Why did women never listen?

Her cool, soft palm moved over his chest, tangling in his body hair and slowly sliding downward. Hell, he'd just finished giving her the ride of her life, and here she was, begging for more!

Her fingers curled around him and she purred triumphantly.

In disbelief, Joe reared up to stare at his cock. He was hard again, damn it, straining against her pale, slender fingers. Unbelievable. He dropped back on the bed with a groan. Done in by his least intelligent body part.

"Joe?" She stroked him with slow, thorough expertise. "Will you come home to meet my family tomorrow? My dad is planning a special dinner for us."

Her dad! Special dinner? He groaned, the sound of mortal man in excruciating pain. It had no effect on her that he could tell.

Someone should have explained the rules of warfare to women. It surely wasn't fair to ask a man such questions while pleasuring him. Everyone knew the male brain couldn't function properly under such provocation.

The ringing of the phone saved him. Joe decided he'd kiss whoever was calling so late. "Hold up, baby," he told her as he coerced his throbbing leg over the side of the bed and his sluggish, aroused body into a semi-sitting position, which forced her to release her death grip on his traitorous member.

She sat up, too, and pressed her lush, naked breasts into his shoulder blades.

"Yeah?" he said into the receiver, trying to ignore the feel of stiffened nipples grazing his heated skin.

"Joe?"

"Right on one."

There was a muttered curse, then, "This is Zane."

"No shit!" He tried to squirrel away from the woman, but she stayed glued to him, disregarding his not-so-subtle hints. "Zane, how ya doing? Everyone okay?"

"The family is fine." A moment of silence, another curse, then grudgingly: "You still up for hire?"

The woman raised herself to her knees, and Joe felt her crisp feminine curls on his spine as she ground herself against him. He squeezed his eyes shut, determined to block her out. "Yeah, yeah. Why?" He laughed. "You got someone you want me to kill?"

"Very funny."

The woman behind him paused. Good. Maybe he could convince her of what Zane had once believed. She started moving again, sinuously rubbing against him, and Joe gave up on that idea.

"You're a real comedian, Joe, you know that?" Zane's tone was so dry, it worked as a distraction for just a minute. His cousin had always been a source of amusement. Joe hadn't forgotten the time Zane had accused him of being no more than a hired killer.

At the time the accusation hadn't been so far-fetched. He'd been in a murderous mood, and if he'd caught the bastard he was after then, instead of over a year later, he might well have beaten him to death with his own hands.

Instead, he'd turned him over to the authorities. Stupid.

"So what's up?" The woman started chewing on his neck while her hands reached around to the front of him. One tapered, painted nail dipped into his navel. Almost desperate, Joe snapped, "Tell me quick, man."

"I need you to keep an eye on someone."

"Family?" he demanded, feeling a surge of rage that anyone would dare to threaten a Winston. Of course, they threatened him all the time. But that was different. He was in the business, and usually the person threatening him had good reason.

"No, a woman."

Joe held the phone away from his ear to stare at it in disbelief. Zane had more damn women than an Arab sheik, but he'd never wanted to protect one of them before. At least, not that Joe had ever heard about.

Putting the phone back to his ear, he remarked, "I'm not a damn baby-sitter."

"Fine," Zane snapped right back, "I'll hire someone else."

"Now wait a minute. . . . Damn it!" Joe reached behind himself, caught the woman by the shoulder and moved her to the side. "Will you stop raping me?"

"What the hell does that mean?"

It could have been funny, Joe thought, if he wasn't so tired. "I wasn't talking to you, Zane."

Another silence, then a laugh. "I should have known you wouldn't be sleeping alone."

"I wish."

"Ah ha. Like that, is it?"

"Yeah." Joe didn't go into details, didn't admit he'd been stupid enough—and lonely enough—to let a woman work her wiles on him. That would have ruined Zane's image of him. "So you need me there tomorrow, huh?"

Zane's surprise was obvious. "Well, it doesn't have to be—"

"All right, all right," Joe said, sighing as if he were put

out. The woman sprawled on the bed next to him, then stuck her bottom lip out in a rather fetching pout. She was naked and warm and open to him . . . his resolve weakened the tiniest bit, but he brought it ruthlessly back under control.

He looked away and held the phone a little tighter. "If it has to be tomorrow, then it has to be tomorrow."

"You're ditching her, I gather?"

"Oh, yeah."

"You're a real bastard sometimes, Joe. You know that?"

He laughed. "I've known it a long, long time." Bastard was one of the least insulting things he'd been called in his lifetime.

"A woman will kill you someday."

"It wouldn't be the worst way to go," Joe said, and then smirked because his companion had just flounced out of the bed. Obviously, if he wouldn't come home with her to perform dutifully for Mommy and Daddy's approval, he wasn't worth screwing. Joe saluted her naked backside as she yanked on her dress, snatched up her shoes, and stormed out of the room.

"What time will you be here?" Zane asked.

The clock on his nightstand told Joe it was creeping toward midnight. He wasn't at all tired now, and though his front door slammed loudly, he didn't trust her not to come back. And he didn't trust himself to refuse her if she did. "I'll get out of here tonight."

Zane laughed. "So she's got you on the run?"

"Avoidance is the better part of valor." Naked, Joe stood and limped to the open window. He was just in time to see the taillights of her car disappear from sight. He scratched his stomach and stretched. "Wanna take me to breakfast in the morning?"

"If you can drag your sorry ass out of bed before noon."

The nightstand drawer held a pen and paper. Joe caught the phone between his shoulder and ear and said, "Give me some details. Who's the woman, where's she live, and what the hell am I watching her for?"

"It's more than just keeping an eye on her, though knowing someone else has her in sight will give me some peace of mind. It seems she's being vandalized regularly, only the cops don't quite buy it."

"Why not?"

Zane sighed. "At best, they're writing it off as coincidence, as unrelated mischief."

"And at worst?"

"They think she's imagining the whole thing." Zane told him about the rat and the fire and even about the toppled box of books, which he had once dismissed. Joe jotted down everything Zane told him, frowning thoughtfully.

"So what do you think?"

Being truthful, Joe said, "I think the lady's got a problem."

"Damn. I was afraid you'd say that."

"Yeah, well, for the record, I don't believe much in coincidence." Once he might have, but he'd learned the hard way that when things seemed off-kilter, they generally were.

"Today," Zane admitted in guttural tones, "someone was hanging outside her shop. In a ski mask. She found the guy when she came back from the bank."

Joe heard his cousin's fury and whistled low. "And that's why you need me to keep an eye on her? Because you can't be with her all the time?"

"That, and I want you to do some snooping. Discreetly. She doesn't know I'm calling you."

"Stubborn?"

"Like a mule. But if you're right, someone is getting into her place. I have no idea how, or why they'd even want to."

Joe felt the tingle of the challenge. It sounded like mixed messages to him. Fires could be deadly, but rearranged boxes of books were the act of a snoop. Rats in the toilet were vandalism, and a man in a mask could be an outright threat. He understood why the cops might be baffled, but then he wasn't a cop. Not anymore. "I'll see what I can find out."

"Great. I appreciate it."

Joe smiled in amusement when Zane added, now with his own dose of menace, "One more thing, Joe. Keep your hands off her, understand?"

Deciding to tweak Zane a bit—just because it was fun—he asked, "A real looker, huh?"

Zane hesitated. "Well. . . ."

"She's not?" Joe had to bite his lip to keep from chuckling. "Don't tell me you've fallen for a plain Jane."

"She's not plain!"

"Tall?"

"Not exactly."

"Nice bod?"

"None of your damn business!"

"Let me get this straight now." Joe pretended to be very serious, while his shoulders shook with suppressed laughter. "She's a short, stubborn, not quite plain woman with a body type you don't care to discuss. Hell, Zane, that's a perfect description. I'm sure I'll recognize her right off."

The grinding sound he heard was likely Zane's molars.

"I'm going to kick your ass when you get here."

"I could use the exercise." Then, because he obviously had a real job to do, Joe asked, "Seriously. What's she look like?"

"That depends. And if you laugh, I'm hanging up."

Zane was hedging, and that in itself was unusual. In Joe's experience, a more outspoken, up-front guy didn't exist. Zane was also threatening, but that was nothing new. They'd always gone head to head—which was one reason Joe liked him so much. He could always count on Zane to keep him humble.

"No laughing, Scout's honor."

"You were never a Scout."

Pretending to be wounded, Joe said, "But I wanted to be."

A long groan issued through the phone. "Shut up and listen. Tamara works as a Gypsy."

Another surprise. Joe tried to conjure up an image of what a Gypsy looked like, but the only thing he could think of was the old woman in *The Wolfman*. "You mean like with crystal balls and palm reading and all that crap?"

"Yeah," Zane ground out, "all of that. When she's working, she dresses the part, which includes this long black wig and a good dozen or so rings and dark contacts. Very exotic look."

"Sounds like an interesting woman."

Zane made no response to that, but Joe could practically feel his annoyance. "When she's not working, she's blonde, with green eyes. Cute."

"Cute, huh?" For Zane to be so interested, she had to be more than cute. Joe wouldn't be at all surprised to find a model-perfect woman.

"I'm hanging up now."

Joe picked up a balisong knife from the nightstand and sat on the edge of the bed. He flipped it open one-handed, exposing the razor-sharp, lethal blade, then flipped it shut again, almost in the same motion. "Don't you want to know what I charge?" Open, shut. Open, shut. The knife made a quiet, clinking sound each time he flipped out the blade.

Truth was, he could use a vacation, and this seemed like a perfect time. The woman's trouble sounded like a puzzle, and he was always up to solving a puzzle. Besides, he would enjoy a visit with his cousins, even Zane.

"I don't know. Can I afford you?"

"Helluva time to ask! What were you going to do, wait until I'd finished, then stiff me? Would you have claimed I was too expensive?"

"I have no idea why Chase and Mack thought I should call you."

So it hadn't been Zane's idea to call? Yet, obviously

Zane was involved enough that Chase and Mack had thought he could use the help.

Joe opened the knife one last time and examined the edge of the blade. "Cuz they love me, cousin." He chuckled, then said, "Hey, don't sweat it. How about just expenses?"

"I'll pay you the going rate."

He snapped the knife shut and put it back on the nightstand. "No way. You're family. Besides, after hearing about this woman, you couldn't keep me away. The curiosity is killing me."

"*I'll* kill you if—"

"Yeah, yeah, I know. You'll kill me if I touch her, if I sniff her. If I even look at her too hard." He dropped back on the bed with a groan, then stared at the moon shadows on the ceiling. "You know I don't poach, so quit worrying."

It was a novel thing, having Zane jealous over a woman. He'd told the truth when he said his curiosity was stirred. She must be a hell of a babe, regardless of what Zane had said.

A thought occurred to him. "Hey, Zane, you in love with this woman?"

A faint click sounded in his ear, and Joe looked at the receiver, bemused. Zane had hung up on him!

"Well, I'll be damned." He'd been half-kidding, but maybe he'd hit too close to the truth. Maybe Zane had taken the mighty fall, and was still fighting it. The idea was enough to scare any red-blooded bachelor into forgetting his manners, so Joe forgave him for not saying good-bye.

Grinning now, he replaced the phone in the cradle. Rubbing his hand over his bristly jaw, he mentally made a few plans.

Zane in love. Now that was something he definitely wanted to see.

Eleven

Tamara heard the shop door chime the next morning. She looked up and saw Zane sauntering in, wearing dark slacks and a gray button-down shirt. He looked tired. She wondered if he'd gotten enough sleep, then immediately berated herself for the concern she felt. She would not start fussing over him. "Good morning."

He kept coming, his long legs carrying him quickly past the reception area to the counter. Flattening both palms on the polished mahogany, he leaned forward and took her mouth in a warm, delicious kiss. Against her lips, he murmured, "Morning."

"Mmmm." Her head swam with the heady taste of him. Lazily lifting her eyelids, she said, "I like greeting the day this way."

"Me, too." Zane straightened, touched her cheek, and smiled. "Do you have the phone on you?"

Shaking her head at his persistence, Tamara patted her pocket. "Right here."

He glanced at her hip, where the phone rested in her deep skirt pocket, and satisfaction mingled with a much warmer emotion. She saw the brief flare of desire in his eyes, before he masked it.

When he looked at her, it was with concern. "How are you feeling today?"

It irritated her that he thought her so weak and insubstantial that a small scratch might cause lingering effects. She pulled up the loose sleeve of her lavender and silver peasant blouse, baring her arm. "It's fine, see? Hardly noticeable anymore."

Zane held her arm, gently stroking with his thumb, then bent to brush it with a kiss. "Looks painful as hell to me, but I'm glad it's not bothering you." He smiled. "I was actually talking about your upset over being chased yesterday."

"Oh." Once it had been over, Tamara wasn't sure what she'd felt. And she was no longer so certain she was chased. Yes, she'd seen a man, but once she'd started running, her fear had obliterated any other sensation. If the man had chased her, she hadn't seen him. It was just as likely he'd run the opposite direction.

Not knowing made her uneasy. She'd thought she was fine. But off and on throughout the night, she'd jerked awake, startled and tense, as if she were being chased again. She felt unsettled, edgy. The whole thing was disconcerting.

Especially since she wasn't positive she had been chased. The man in the ski mask might just have been another poor soul caught in the downpour. He'd looked at her, and there had been something unexpected in his gaze—not really sinister, but threatening in a subtle way.

But had he actually come after her? She couldn't stop thinking about it, running the different scenarios through her mind. She didn't explain any of her worries to Zane because it had *felt* like she'd been chased, and that would be impossible to put into words.

Zane's eyes, dark with concern, met hers. "Did you sleep okay?"

She hadn't—but it wasn't entirely because of the man in the ski mask. It was partly Zane's fault.

She hadn't been able to stop thinking about him and wishing his brothers hadn't interrupted them. Though she had planned to go strictly by the book, upping the odds of her first time with Zane being all she had envisioned, she now thought making love against the wall of his storage room would have been wonderful, too. And that definitely wasn't in the book. She knew. She'd read through it again last night, trying to put herself to sleep after he'd called.

It hadn't worked. She'd lain awake for hours, burning up with the remembrance of his touch.

"Of course," she lied. "I slept just fine."

"You'd have slept better," he promised, "if I could have stayed with you."

Oh, the way he said that. She leaned closer, staring at his mouth. "Yeah?"

"Yeah." His large hand slid around her neck, under the fall of the wig. "I'd have exhausted you."

Tamara almost melted on the spot. She wondered if he intended to exhaust her tonight. It sounded like a fine plan to her.

"I've been thinking," he said, and Tamara hoped the subject of his thoughts was sex. She'd know today if the offer on the building was too good to pass up. If it was, their time together would soon be over. She needed to make every available minute count.

His fingers stroked through the long strands of the wig. "I know your family encourages you to dress this way."

Tamara blinked at the change of subject. Of all the things he could have said, that was the least expected. "Yes, so?"

"I think they're wrong. I've seen you both ways now, and honey, you're fetching no matter what. But without all the props, the real you shines through. I think it'd be great for business if you showed yourself as you really are."

Tamara drew back. "Aunt Olga and Aunt Eva would have a fit."

"So? You're a grown woman and you can do as you please." He brushed her cheek. "Right?"

She wondered if he knew he was issuing a direct challenge. It was probable. Eyes narrowed, she nodded. "True. And it's always pleased me to please them."

Zane tilted up her chin and nibbled on her bottom lip. Her stomach tightened with a sweet ache. "What about pleasing me?"

Her thoughts got muddled whenever he touched her. "Yes."

"Then just give it a try. See what the customers think."

She supposed it couldn't hurt anything. And she did hate the wig. The clothes and the jewelry . . . well, she didn't mind them so much. But the rest of it was uncomfortable and a bother.

Tamara nodded. "I don't have time to change today, but . . . we'll see what happens tomorrow."

Before he grinned at her, she could have sworn she detected a brief flash of relief in his eyes.

"I wonder," he teased, "if your transformation will throw everyone else as hard as it did me."

She remembered his reaction very well, and teased right back. "I doubt anyone else will kiss me over it."

A different voice intruded, sultry and thick. "Oh, I don't know about that."

Zane's head lifted, his expression alert. Tamara watched him as Luna sauntered through the curtain separating the rooms. He was aware of her, but unlike most men, he didn't seem dumbstruck by her appearance—which today was more eye-catching than usual. Her mink brown hair hung straight and sleek from a center part, and her golden brown eyes were highlighted by loads of lush mascara.

Barely contained within a long-sleeve tube dress of pale gold, Luna's very full breasts looked ready to spill free at any moment. Black, high-heeled boots were laced all the way up to her knees, and a chunky black leather belt hung loosely on her rounded hips. She looked chic, sexy, and full-blown, like a movie star pinup.

"Zane, my assistant, Luna Clark. Luna, Zane Winston."

Zane's gaze never wavered from Luna's face; Tamara knew that because she was jealously watching. He nodded. "Luna."

Luna smiled, but didn't come any closer. She fiddled with a thin gold necklace around her throat and said, "If you talk her out of wearing the costume, you might be surprised by the reactions she gets."

Zane's brows lifted. "Meaning?"

"Meaning half the men who come here are already infatuated with her, and it wouldn't take much to make them fall in love."

Zane shifted, turning the slightest bit. He looked to be readying himself for battle, but he gave no verbal reply.

"With the costume," Luna continued, ignoring Tamara's frantic gestures to halt her, "she comes across as part of the props, a little loony, a little whimsical. I bet that's why you overlooked her for so long."

"Who says I overlooked her?"

Luna laughed at that. "This is the first time I've seen you playing kissy-face with her over the counter."

His shoulders tensed. Tamara had no idea what Luna was up to, but she wished she'd knock it off.

"Your point?"

"Most of her innate generosity of spirit is mistaken for part of a con, a way to reel in customers and give them what they're paying for. Without the costume, the whole world will see her for what she really is."

Tamara wanted to slink off in embarrassment. Or else grab some packing tape and use it to seal Luna's mouth.

Quickly, she rounded the counter to stand between Luna and Zane. She tried to laugh, but wasn't pleased with the sickly sound. "Luna is a big kidder."

Proving the point, Luna held her hands together and said in a theatrical voice, "Luna is all-knowing, all-seeing." Then she winked at Zane. "And Luna tells it like it is."

"Luna is becoming a pain in the butt!" Tamara glared at her.

Luna laughed and slipped around the counter to the appointment book. "I wonder, Zane, if you want her to lose the costume because it embarrasses you." Her gaze shifted to Tamara. "Did you happen to meet any of his family lately? Maybe in your Gypsy getup?"

Tamara frowned, but before she could say anything, Zane straightened. His eyes were narrow slits, his dark brows drawn down. "Embarrass me? I don't think so. It was her Gypsy outfit that first drew me in."

Tamara leaped onto that explanation. "True! The first time he came knocking at my door"—she didn't explain that she'd offered herself to him—"he hadn't seen me without the Gypsy costume."

"Is that right? Then I wonder what his motives really are."

Tamara wondered that, too, but she wasn't about to ask Zane now. "Leave it alone, Luna."

Luna grinned. "Don't worry, honey. I won't scare him off. I have the feeling Zane Winston is made of stern stuff. He's not a man to turn tail and run."

Zane, Tamara thought, looked like a man ready to ignite. Tamara took his arm and dragged him out of Luna's hearing. They stopped beside her round table with the hand-crocheted lace tablecloth and the ornamental crystal ball set on a lighted stand. People were often disappointed when they realized she used the crystal ball only for decoration, not to summon spirits.

"She's a little . . . eccentric," Tamara explained.

And though she'd spoken barely above a whisper, Luna said, "That's the pot calling the kettle black, honey."

Tamara growled at her, but Luna didn't look up from where she was checking over names in the appointment book. She did, however, have a small smile on her mouth. Tamara sighed.

"At least you're not working alone today," Zane said, bringing her attention back to him. "I'm glad."

That reminded her of why she'd asked Luna to come in. "I got a call from my Realtor."

As if he, too, realized the ramifications of that, Zane paused. "An offer?"

"Yes."

He surprised her by cursing. "Are you going to accept?"

"I don't know yet. I'm going to his office this afternoon to find out the details. If. . . ." She swallowed, hating to say the words. She loved the old building, and she loved the area. She'd so hoped her unsettled days were over. "If it's a good offer, I have to take it."

Zane paced away from her. He walked over to the door and stared out the window. Evidently not caring that Luna was listening, he said, "Will you do me a favor and wait before making any decisions?"

She wanted to say yes. She wanted to wait forever, or not sell at all. But she was a realist. "It won't make any difference. I need to sell."

At this point, Tamara figured it didn't matter if Zane knew everything. She wanted him to understand that she wouldn't leave him without good reason. "Every day my situation gets a little tighter. A good offer right now would be a blessing."

Still without facing her, Zane said, "I could make you a loan."

A heartbeat of silence went by before Tamara caught her breath. She shook her head, incredulous that he'd said such a thing. "No."

"You have options, damn it."

Her temples pounded, her heart ached. "Taking money from you," she said, forcing the words past her tight throat, "isn't one of them."

He put his hands on his hips and dropped his head forward, as if contemplating things. When he looked at her, determination was plain in his eyes. "If the offer is good, it won't go away just because you take a few days to consider it."

"I suppose not."

"Then promise me you'll talk to me before you sign anything."

Luna started laughing, and when they both glared at her, she held out her hands. "Sorry!"

Tamara fretted. She didn't like giving him so much control, because that made him partially responsible. But at the same time, she wanted every second with him that she could get. "I'll tell you what the Realtor has to say."

"You won't agree to anything today?"

"No."

His shoulders relaxed, and he smiled at her. "Tonight, what time will you close?"

With the appointment book open in front of her, Luna said helpfully, "Four o'clock."

"I'll be here at four-fifteen."

Tamara felt breathless again, now for an entirely different reason. "Okay."

Zane walked up to her and kissed her. She was aware of Luna watching, and also aware that Zane didn't care. He touched her chin. "Tonight."

"Yes."

Zane nodded at Luna, who winked, and turned to leave. He'd taken two steps toward the door when it opened and a man stepped inside.

Arkin Devane was early. And even more surprising, another man walked in, right on Arkin's heels.

Zane turned to look at Tamara with lifted brows, curious over this early morning rush.

Arkin smiled his wide, sincere smile and said, "Tamara! I hope you don't mind. I couldn't wait a minute more."

Zane's curiosity turned to a frown. Tamara could feel Luna grinning behind her.

The second man, tall with inky black hair, bulky with muscle, and dressed expensively, looked around the shop with interest. "I gather I'm in the right place."

Arkin moved straight to Tamara and clasped her hands. Tamara struggled not to look at Zane; she didn't want to see his reaction, not when she could already feel the heat of his watchfulness. He was alert, but for what, she didn't know.

"Arkin, you can wait in the first room. I'll be right with you."

Luna, being a proper assistant, stepped forward and introduced herself to the second man. "Did you want an appointment this morning?" she asked him.

The man looked her over, and before Tamara could reach Zane to send him on his way, he said, "Yes, but not with you."

He turned to Tamara. She automatically took a step back, unable to stop herself. The man was just so . . . intense. And the way he looked at her—with barely veiled surprise, now tinged with hunger. Did he have preconceived notions about her, based on her occupation?

She forgot her speculations when he gave a slow, very male smile and said, "I want *you*."

Zane had never had a sixth sense, except where women were concerned. And then it was razor-sharp. He'd watched Tamara retreat from the man, and everything male inside him went on red-hot alert. He took an aggressive step forward.

Luna touched the man's arm. "I'm sorry, but Ms. Tremayne is booked for the day. You'll need to make an appointment."

Without looking away from Tamara, the man intoned, "I'm Boris Sandor," as if that held some significance.

Tamara glanced at Luna, then at Zane, before turning her attention back to Boris. "It's nice to meet you, Mr. Sandor. My assistant, Luna Clark, can help you set an appointment if you'd like."

He shrugged off Luna's hand. "How much do you charge?"

Annoyed, Luna propped her hands on her hips and lost her ethereal tone. She named a price, which, going by Tamara's expression, was a bit high.

Boris said, "I'll pay twice that."

Arkin stuck his head around the curtain. "Tamara?"

"I'll be right there." She pressed a hand to her forehead. "Look, Mr. Sandor, it doesn't matter what you pay, I'm booked, and I can't leave scheduled clients waiting. If you'd like to see Luna, she's free. Otherwise, you need an appointment like everyone else."

Zane wanted to explode. Damn, it was starting already! He didn't have to see Luna's expression to know she was smirking at his discomfort. He'd had no idea Tamara was so popular, and he sure as hell hadn't envisioned her clientele as male. He'd assumed she dealt mostly with young, fanciful women wanting to know about their boyfriends, or older women hoping to receive a message from a deceased husband or great-great-aunt.

He realized that he really had no idea what Tamara did. She'd told him again and again that she wasn't psychic, though he still had his doubts about that, as well as doubting her ability to cast spells. She'd certainly done *something* to him.

Her front window advertised palm reading, futures told. Run-of-the-mill carnival acts, as far as he knew.

Yet two men, both of them appearing to be reasonable, intelligent sorts, were here first thing in the morning, demanding her attention.

He considered throwing the bulky Sandor out. After all, the man obviously made her uncomfortable with his constant leering, and he was verbally rude to boot. Only the knowledge that she would resent his interference kept him standing there quietly.

When he leaned against the wall beside the door, settling in for the duration of this little confrontation, Tamara sent him an apologetic, dismissive shrug. He ignored it.

He might have enough wit left to let her handle her

business herself, but no way in hell was he walking out when he could feel her uneasiness.

She glared at him for not budging, then turned all her annoyance on Sandor. "Luna will give you a card. Feel free to set an appointment for another time."

"Your aunt sent me." He made that announcement as if the queen herself had told him to come calling.

"I'm sure my aunt told you to set an appointment."

"Of course not. She wanted us to get . . . acquainted. As friends, not in a professional manner."

The way he said "professional manner" was very insulting. Zane watched Tamara's mouth thin. "Why?"

"We're from the same homeland."

Zane snorted. "And that would be?"

Sandor turned to him with a show of displeasure. "Excuse me, but the lady and I are having a private conversation."

"In the middle of the shop?" Luna asked, and this time Zane wanted to kiss her for her well-placed zinger. "Besides," she added, waving toward Zane, "he's her man. So of course he's going to listen in."

I'm her man. Zane liked the sound of that, as outdated as it might be.

Boris said, "But your aunt assured me you were unattached!"

"Her aunt was wrong," Zane replied lazily, and he noticed that Tamara wasn't looking at him now, her gaze intently focused on Boris. He didn't like that.

Arkin Devane stuck his head around the curtain again. This time he sounded uncertain when he said, "Tamara?"

Her concentration scattered. "Yes, I'm sorry, Arkin." She started toward the dark curtain. "Excuse me, Mr. Sandor, but as you can see, I'm rather busy. If you'd like to come back another time—"

"Tonight?"

She paused, glanced at Zane, and her face colored. "Ah, no. I already have plans for the evening."

"Then how about lunch?"

Appearing harassed, Tamara said, "I'm sorry, but that won't work either. Luna, will you see if you can fit him in for Monday?"

Zane wanted to laugh at the look on the pompous ass's face. He definitely did not like being dismissed, or put off for so long.

Tamara didn't wait around to see if he accepted or not. She ducked behind the curtain, and Zane heard a door close. At least the fellow she was with now seemed unassuming.

He caught Luna's eye, and she winked at him. "Arkin has an especially long appointment today. Hmmm. Wonder why?"

Her suggestive tone raked along his nerves, and he knew damn good and well she did it on purpose.

"Well, Mr. Sandor? Shall I fit you in on Monday?"

Face red, Boris nodded. "Around noon."

"Sorry." Luna propped both elbows on the counter, leaning forward with the appointment book in front of her. "That's her lunch break." Her breasts fell softly forward, displaying quite a bit of cleavage. Boris gave them an appropriately appreciative look.

Zane struggled with a grin. At first, he hadn't liked Luna much, but now she felt like an ally—when her barbs weren't aimed at him.

"Fine," Boris snapped, recalling himself. "When does she have available?"

"Let's see." Luna took her time looking at the book. Boris took his time ogling Luna's breasts. Pencil in hand, she glanced up finally and asked, "How about two?"

"I'll be here." Without another word, Boris stormed out.

"Oh my, oh my," Luna said. "Someone has a burr under his bottom."

Zane laughed. "You handled him well."

Shrugging, she stuck the pencil behind her ear and grinned. "Part of the job description—handle the crazies."

"Are there many of them?"

"Not usually."

"He said her aunt sent him."

"Her family does that a lot. They're always trying to fix her up." Luna sauntered around from behind the counter. "And just think, thanks to you, the next time Boris sees her, she'll look like herself. Makes you wonder how he'll react to that, huh?"

Zane almost swallowed his tongue. Damn it, she was right! He briefly considered discouraging her from the change, then shook his head. "No," he said aloud. "She's not happy wearing all that camouflage. She only does it because her family makes her feel like she needs it."

Luna's mouth fell open, then she pressed a hand to her heart. "Well, I'll be damned."

"Why?" Zane asked, put out by her exaggerated pose. "What'd you do now?"

"You're authentic, aren't you? You really do have her best interests at heart."

"You believed your own nonsense about her embarrassing me?"

"Yep."

He laughed at her honesty. "For about half a minute, you would have been right. Of course, when my brothers met her, she wasn't just a Gypsy but a soaking wet Gypsy with ruined makeup and a crooked wig."

"And they couldn't understand what the mighty Zane Winston was doing with her?"

Luna was the type of woman you wanted to hug one minute, and turn over your knee the next. With any luck, some guy would do the honors real soon.

"You underestimate my brothers," Zane told her, refusing to react to her sarcasm. "They would never be that rude to a woman, or that crass." And they had known exactly what he was doing, they just hadn't been certain why.

She still looked a little shell-shocked. "You know, Zane Winston, you may be exactly what Tamara needs right now. At least until she sells."

"*If* she sells," Zane insisted, because he was still determined to find a way to fix things for her. And thinking of that, he glanced at his watch and knew Joe would be waiting. "I have to run. Will you be here with her all day?"

"Yes, but Monday she's working alone again, and I have to tell you, you're not the only one worried."

"So we'll both try to keep an eye on her, and in the meantime, I'm working on figuring it out."

"I wish you luck." She sent him a level look and whispered, "As long as you don't hurt her. Because if you hurt her, you'll be the one who ends up sorry."

He realized Luna cared about Tamara, so he didn't take offense at the warning. Instead, he returned Luna's earlier wink and headed for the door. Hurt Tamara? Hell, all he wanted to do was keep her safe.

And make love to her for at least a year.

Twelve

Tamara held one of Arkin Devane's slim hands between her own. There were no dimmed lights, no special effects. Music drifted into the room; Luna had turned on the CD player. She assumed Boris Sandor was gone. Which likely meant Zane had left, too, since he'd only been hanging around as a guard dog. She should have been amused by his protectiveness today, but instead, she'd been oddly reassured by it.

She tried to concentrate, to say all the words she knew Arkin expected to hear, but the feeling of unease lingered.

She didn't like Boris Sandor. When he'd looked at her, she felt his concentration like oil, sliding over her skin, clogging her pores. It had filled her with uneasiness. His interest had first been calculated, but had quickly turned red-hot, even intimate. She'd felt his anticipation overtake the dread. Why? What had he been dreading, and why had his emotional state changed? She didn't want to deal with Boris, but he'd said her aunt had sent him.

The level of her awareness had startled her. Zane was the only other man she'd felt like that. Zane was the only man she *wanted* to feel like that.

"Are you all right?"

She met Arkin's concerned gaze and frowned at herself. He paid good money for his time with her, and here she was, daydreaming. "Yes. I'm sorry."

The worry in his pale blue eyes remained. "If it's about me taking up so much of your time. . . ."

"No, no, that's fine." She smiled, and squeezed his hand. "I gather we have a lot to talk about."

"But you had to turn that other man away."

Her smile slipped the tiniest bit. "That's okay. I'm sure Luna took care of him. Now, let me see here."

She stared at Arkin's palm, already knowing what she would see, and what he wanted to hear. At the last second though, before she started her discourse on heart lines and hand coloring and finger zones, she looked into his face. It took her only a moment to make up her mind.

Today, Arkin needed the genuine article, and she intended to give it to him.

Tamara squeezed his fingers, then laid his hand aside. "You're obviously in love."

Arkin's eyebrows lifted. He nodded, eager and wary and hopeful. "Very much so."

"The thing is," she told him with a grin, "she's very interested in you, too."

Drawing back, he asked, "How can you know that?"

"To be honest, Arkin, I'm not sure. But I feel it, and," she added gently, "I could feel it only from you." Tamara regarded him. "You realize the truth, you're just too afraid to do anything about it."

Covering his face with his hands, Arkin groaned. "It's true. I'm afraid of messing up, of doing or saying the wrong thing. She's not like me, Tamara. She's. . . ."

Her heart melting for this gentle man, Tamara suggested, "Exuberant? Alive and outgoing and free-spirited?"

With a sigh in his voice, he said, "She reminds me of you."

Tamara laughed at that. "You're an attractive man, Arkin. You're kind and responsible."

"And dull as dust."

"That's not true."

"I need help, Tamara." He looked beyond morose. "I always say the wrong thing at the wrong time."

"You've approached her?" She couldn't help being surprised by his initiative. Arkin Devane was not the aggressive sort. More often than not, he entertained himself with books, not women.

"I tried." He winced. "She smiles at me, and I go mute."

Tamara thought of the journal she had upstairs. The first few entries had been on approach, and based on the outcome with Zane, they were quite successful. Again, she took Arkin's hand. "I think I can help you."

His eyes gleamed. "You can?"

"Yes. I found an incredibly interesting journal that's filled with excellent advice. I'll gladly share it with you."

His expression went blank, then hopeful. "A journal?" He half-laughed, somewhat uncertain. "Well, you know how much I enjoy reading."

"Oh, I didn't mean you need to read the whole thing. There's a lot in there that doesn't apply to you, and besides, I'm still reading it myself. But we have plenty of time today, so I'll just go over the pertinent stuff."

Arkin shifted in his seat. "Go over the . . . pertinent stuff?"

Feeling enthusiastic now that she'd made up her mind, Tamara didn't hesitate. "The first thing we need to discuss is what type of woman you're approaching. That's vital to how we handle things."

"Wouldn't it be easier if I read it myself?"

Tamara dismissed his suggestion. "The journal is upstairs. Besides, I can tell you what it said."

Because he was shy, Tamara tried to be as matter-of-fact and blunt as she could, without embarrassing Arkin with unnecessary explicitness. The time flew by, and before she knew it, she needed to leave for her appointment with the Realtor.

Arkin seemed introspective when he finally said goodbye. Considering all the information she'd just shared, he likely had a lot on his mind. She smiled as she watched him leave, hands in his pockets, his head down, deep in thought.

Luna came up behind her. "Tamara, do you know where the astrology charts are?"

"What do you mean?" Distracted, Tamara turned to get her jacket and her purse so she'd make it to the Realtor's on time. "They're right where they always are."

"Nope." Luna followed on her heels. "I had a customer who had questions about her horoscope, but I couldn't find the charts."

Tamara walked to the shelving behind the counter. Running her finger along the numerous books neatly placed there, spines out, she searched for the binder that held the various charts. It wasn't where she'd left it.

Her storage room was disorganized; the rest of her shop was not. Once she sorted through things, she always put them in a specific place so she could grab them in a hurry, if need be.

Propping her hands on her hips, she said, "That's weird. They were here last time I looked."

"When was that?"

"Just a few days ago."

"If you took them out, maybe you accidentally put them away in the wrong spot."

Tamara gave her a look, and Luna said, "I know. Not likely."

Kneeling, Tamara quickly searched through the other books. She didn't have time for this right now. "Well, damn. The address book is in the wrong spot."

Luna knelt, too. "It's even on the wrong shelf." She sounded a little dazed by that discovery. And a little worried.

"Everything is mixed up." Tamara looked at Luna, and

saw the same conclusion on her assistant's face. "Someone has been going through our stuff."

Luna plopped down to sit on her bottom. She chewed her lip a moment, then asked, "Do you think one of your aunts was looking for something?"

"They haven't been in since I had the astrology charts out."

Luna's next question surprised Tamara. "Are you going to tell Zane?"

Tamara groaned at the thought. "God, I don't know. I can just imagine his reaction if I do."

"Funny, I was thinking of his reaction if you don't."

Tamara couldn't help smiling. "There is that."

They both stood. Luna dusted off her backside, then brushed Tamara off as well. "For what it's worth, I say tell him."

"I'll think about it. If the offer today is good enough, it may not even matter. None of this will be mine anymore."

"What if all this," Luna asked, indicating the shop, "isn't what they're after? What if someone is after *you*?"

Tamara snatched up the big bag she used as a purse, and headed for the door. She didn't want to even consider the possibility, yet Luna's words hung with her, and she felt on edge as she caught the bus that would take her to the Realtor's. But it wasn't just the misplaced items in her shop that had her apprehensive.

Again and again, she felt watchful eyes on her, yet no one on the bus seemed to be paying her any mind. Tamara even looked behind her, and saw no one who should make her feel so suspicious. Her heart tripped with the realization that she was being followed.

Her business with the Realtor didn't take long; the offer was good, but it wasn't quite what she'd hoped to get, what she knew the building was worth because of its location. She breathed a sigh of relief as she wrote out a counteroffer. She'd just gotten a small reprieve. She'd bought herself a few more days with Zane.

The second she stepped outside, she again felt the weight of someone's attention. She didn't detect any real menace, but the intensity of the focus bit into her, making her legs feel like Jell-O.

Trying to hide her nervousness, she made her way to the bus stop. There was a crowd of people there—an elderly couple talking quietly, and holding hands. Several college kids milling around, loaded down with books and using curse words for adjectives, loud enough to make the elderly man scowl at them. There was also a tall, dark man dressed in ragged jeans and a flannel shirt, chatting easily with two buttoned-down businesswomen. The man was big, a muscular, unshaven hulk, disheveled, disreputable, impossible to miss. Tamara shook her head at how the women fawned over him, and how he encouraged them with a sexy smile.

No one seemed aware that they were being watched, but Tamara knew. She still felt it.

During the bus ride, her tension eased. But the second she got off the bus, along with several other people, she sensed the renewed observation. Attempting to be discreet, she studied the people who'd gotten off the bus with her. The group separated, each person going his or her own way and Tamara found herself standing alone. Vulnerable.

Unlike the last time, today the sun was bright and warm, a beautiful spring day. Tamara drew a deep breath to calm herself, and headed down the sidewalk. The lunchtime traffic was heavy, and she was jostled several times. Each touch by a stranger pulled her nerves a little tighter. By the time she turned the corner and could see her shop, she was practically running.

The CLOSED FOR LUNCH sign was in the window. Tamara quickly extracted her key to unlock the door, then burst inside with unnecessary fanfare. From the other side of the counter, Luna looked up. The New Age music Tamara preferred had been replaced with Tom Petty, and the volume was turned up several notches. Luna had removed her boots as she idly danced. She had a half-eaten sandwich in one hand, a diet Coke in the other.

Tamara locked gazes with her, knowing what she had to do. She sucked in several calming breaths before she finally spoke. "I'll tell Zane tonight."

Luna had stopped dancing the second she spied Tamara's pale face. Now she gulped down the bite in her mouth, choked, and wheezed out, "What made you change your mind?"

"I've been followed again."

It was a few minutes before four o'clock when Zane entered her shop. He didn't see Tamara, but the second the door chimed, she popped up on the other side of the long, polished counter. She still wore her Gypsy costume, but he hadn't expected her to have changed.

Fifteen feet separated the door, where he stood, from the counter, and still he could see the dust on Tamara's nose and the look of alarm in her eyes. When she realized it was him, the wary look was replaced by a tentative smile. "You're early."

"I couldn't keep away." He pushed his hands into his pockets, forcing himself to remain still. Something else had happened, something that had upset her. He was sure of it, just as he was certain she didn't want to tell him about it.

Zane studied her as he considered ways of getting her to open up to him. Her glossy lipstick was gone, leaving her soft mouth naked and twice as appealing. The neckline of her blouse gaped a bit, giving him a peek of cleavage.

When she saw the direction of his gaze, she rearranged herself nervously, watching him the whole time as if she expected him to leap on her. "I've been a little anxious to see you, too."

Zane hid a smile.

She might have instigated their relationship, and she wanted to call the shots, but the last thing she needed was for him to rush her upstairs. He'd have to be patient, even if it killed him. "You're alone now?"

She watched him, wide-eyed and waiting. "Luna left only a few minutes ago."

After locking the door and pulling down the shade, Zane moseyed closer. She had a book in each hand, and a few were sitting on the floor. "What are you up to?"

"Just organizing some things." She hesitated, then said, "Somehow they got out of order."

She bent to push the remaining books into place, and Zane, unable to stop himself, smoothed his hand over her softly rounded ass. She jumped.

As she quickly turned to face him, he cupped his hand around her nape and smiled. She was warm, soft. He couldn't stop touching her. "You have the phone on you?"

"Yes." Exasperated, she frowned at him. "You don't have to keep asking that, you know."

"Just checking." She started to grouse again, and he kissed her. He meant it to be a light, teasing kiss, just enough to still her resistance. But she leaned into him and the kiss lingered.

She tasted so good. He wanted her naked, open, so he could taste her everywhere. His groin throbbed, his testicles pulling tight. He would feast on her, and still it might not be enough.

He closed his eyes for a moment, forcing himself to calm. "Have you had dinner?"

"I'm not hungry."

"That's not what I asked you."

Her hands crept up to his shoulders, then looped behind his neck. "I haven't eaten, but couldn't we eat . . . after?"

His breathing deepened. "If that's what you really want." Damn, how could he be patient if she wouldn't cooperate? More than anything, he wanted this to be good for Tamara, and with the state he was in now, it'd be over before it started.

Her smile was sweet, shy. She left him to wander around the shop, snuffing out incense and pinching out candles. Though she'd watched him lock it, she double-checked to make sure the door was secure.

Her long, wispy skirt flirted around her ankles, and her ankle bracelets rang musically. The late afternoon sunlight coming through the large front window glinted off her jewelry, and left a golden sheen along her skin.

Her movements were graceful and practiced, and Zane accepted that the shop was a part of her, just as his store was a part of him.

He knew how hard he'd worked to make his business a success. How hard had it been for Tamara? She was so young, and where he had his brothers backing him, helping any way they could, she had older relatives for whom she felt responsible. Her burden far exceeded his, emotionally and financially. "How did it go at the Realtor's?"

She turned off the CD player and a heavy silence settled into the shop, mingling with the scented smoke. "The offer wasn't enough. I made a counteroffer."

Some of the tension eased from his shoulders. "This may all work out yet." He made the suggestion uncertainly. He had no real idea of how dire her financial situation might be. She'd said she needed to sell, and knowing Tamara, knowing how headstrong she was, if there'd been another way to cope, she'd have found it already.

"Maybe." It was plain she didn't want to talk about it. She looked at him through her darkened lashes. "Are you ready to go upstairs?"

Inside, Zane smoldered, while outside he maintained an expression of indifference. If Tamara knew how savagely aroused he was, she would probably change her mind and throw him out.

"Yeah, I'm ready." Zane took her hand and allowed her to lead the way up the dim, narrow stairwell.

Tamara closed the door behind him, and turned the key that stayed in the lock. Zane was aware of her in every pore of his body, her nearness, the scent of her, the heat of her skin. Her uncertainty.

She wanted him, but casual sex was unusual for her. That pleased him.

"I need to change out of this stuff," she whispered in a shaky voice, "and shower off my makeup."

Zane fingered the wig. He wanted to feel her own soft curls, not the heavy coarseness of the wig. "I could shower with you."

As she stared up at him, her eyes glittered with sensual awareness. "I've never showered with a man before."

Zane paused. "No?"

"No."

He started to ask her exactly what she *had* done, but he held the words inside. Jealousy was a new emotion for him, and he wasn't ready to broadcast it. "Let's make tonight a first then."

"You don't mind?"

He cuddled her cheek in his palm, enthralled with the velvety, warm texture. He had a feeling she'd be that soft all over, even softer in the places where he badly wanted to touch her, taste her. "Of course not." He liked it that she would experience something new with him. It would forge a special link that she wouldn't be quick to forget.

"I know I gave the impression of having loads of experience. . . ."

"Shh. It doesn't matter." He touched her bottom lip. "By the morning, you'll have all the experience you need."

Her lips parted on an indrawn breath. Because he knew she was nervous and he didn't want her to be, not with him, Zane kissed her. Her lips parted, her tongue accepting his, twining with his. The tempting sweetness of incense clung to her skin, and beneath that, more subtle, was her own unique hot scent. His hands opened wide over her back and drew her into his chest until he could feel her plump breasts cushioned there.

He broke the kiss with some effort, while he still could. They both labored for breath.

In a near daze, Tamara turned and headed for her bedroom. She went straight to the window and opened the blinds, letting in the fading sunlight. It slanted across her desk, just missing the bed. Zane noticed the computer manuals spread out on the desk, but he didn't comment on them. Not right now.

Tamara flipped her head forward, eased the wig off, and ran her fingers through her blonde hair, leaving it seductively disheveled. She looked tousled, as if she'd already had sex.

Zane used the wall for support. Watching Tamara transform proved incredibly erotic.

She turned her back to him and removed the contacts. When she faced him again, she stole his breath away. Her hair was in disarray, her eyes now bright green with the kohl liner providing a striking contrast, giving her a more mystical aura than the dark contacts could ever have achieved.

One by one, she pulled off her rings, and it was a type of strip show he would never forget. She worked methodically, slowly. His heart quickened, his cock swelled. Tamara watched him, and as she removed each ring, her eyes grew heavier with arousal.

When her fingers were bare of jewelry, she sat on the edge of the bed and pulled her skirt up to her knees. As she bent to take off her sandals, Zane forced himself to move.

He went to one knee in front of her. "I'll do it."

The tiny bells on the ankle bracelets chimed as he circled her slim ankle with his hand. Her skin was warm and silky smooth, and he imagined her feet braced on his shoulders as he drove into her, holding her hips, refusing to let her retreat from his thrusts.

His hands shook when he lifted her left foot and slipped her sandal off. Carefully, calmly, he set it on the floor beside the bed. Teasing himself as much as her, he worked each ring off her small pink toes. He did the same with her right foot, and when he'd finished, rather than stand, he parted her legs and moved between them.

Her already raised skirt bunched a little higher, forced up by his body.

Tamara made a soft sound and stroked her hand through his hair. "I've wanted you ever since the first time I saw you," she murmured.

Zane laid her back on the bed. Sultry and sweet, she stared up at him. Her blonde curls formed a halo around her head.

He caught her hips and pulled her to the edge of the bed so that the notch of her thighs cradled him. He could feel the gentle heat of her mound against his abdomen, even through their clothes. "We're going to take it slow tonight," he promised.

Lazily, she nodded. He had his hands braced on either side of her hips, and her left hand circled his right wrist. "We're supposed to look at each other naked."

Hell yes. "I'll look, all right."

"I mean, according to the book. We're supposed to get used to each other naked."

Heat curled inside him, threatening his control. He didn't need a damn book to direct him now. "Just trust me, okay?"

She stared at his mouth. "In this, I do."

That wasn't the answer he would have chosen, but no way would he argue about it now. Her peasant blouse had a drawstring neckline. He pulled the neatly tied bow loose, allowing the neckline to expand. The blouse was tucked into a dark blue skirt of layered gauzy material, and Zane tugged it free from the waistband.

Without protest, Tamara watched him undressing her. "Are we going to make it to the shower?" she asked breathlessly.

"Yeah." He could barely talk. He was twenty-seven years old, and he couldn't remember ever wanting a woman this much. Her nipples had drawn into tight, small points he could see through her blouse and bra. He couldn't wait a second more and bent to put his mouth over her right breast.

Tamara reacted with a groan, arching her body and clenching her left hand in his hair. "Zane."

He sucked on her, her blouse and bra so thin as to be inconsequential.

"I can't take it," she said in a whimper when he switched to the other nipple. Her hips lifted into his and her legs wrapped around his waist.

Zane slid his hand beneath the small of her back, farther down over her bottom. He lifted her more firmly into him. "You can take this, and a whole lot more."

"No." Her head pressed against the bed, throat exposed, eyes squeezed shut.

"Yeah." He rubbed himself over her. "Let's get to the naked part, okay?"

She froze for a moment before nodding. "Okay."

"I've been thinking all day about getting your panties off you, feeling you wrap your legs around me."

Her lips parted.

"Raise your arms," he instructed in guttural tones. She did, slowly.

Thankful that it was loose-fitting, Zane worked the blouse up, exposing her midriff, her ribs, her lace-covered breasts. She was small and pale and so smooth he couldn't stop stroking her. She lifted herself a little so he could get the top free and toss it aside.

Her puckered nipples showed as dark shadows through the lace of her bra. Zane plumped both breasts together and rubbed her with his thumbs. The hiss of her breath pleased him. The sight of her pleased him.

Getting inside her would please him more, but he was determined to make it last, to devastate her with pleasure.

The bra had a front closure, and he snapped it open with one hand. The material parted, stopping just shy of completely freeing her breasts. Zane bent, nuzzled it away, and found one taut nipple waiting, ready for his mouth. He didn't hesitate. He sucked her deep and then held her close as she lifted into him.

Her fingers in his hair alternately squeezed him closer

and struggled to pull him away. She gasped and groaned, telling him one minute that she liked it, and the next that it was too acute, the pleasure too sharp. Relentless, determined, Zane controlled her movements and took his time leisurely tasting her.

A ragged moan escaped her. "Zane, please!"

He sat back to survey her. Her painted eyes were heavy, dilated with need. Her breasts rose and fell with shuddering, uneven breaths, her nipples glistening from his mouth.

A surge of raw, primitive possessiveness locked his muscles tight. Damn, she was his and he wouldn't let anyone hurt her. He wouldn't let her get away from him either.

Tonight, he'd do whatever was necessary to bind her to him.

It might not be what she expected, but Tamara Tremayne would be satisfied with the results. So satisfied she wouldn't be able to shut him out anymore.

He was counting on it.

Thirteen

Zane fought to subdue the raw emotions and turned Tamara onto her stomach. In the past few days, he'd thought about little else except this moment, having her naked and accepting, ready and anxious for him. Now the time was finally here, and he wouldn't let anything or anyone stop him from taking her.

Startled, Tamara pushed up onto her elbows to stare at him over her shoulder. "Zane, what—"

With one hand at the small of her back, he held her still. The skirt had an elastic waist, without an opening. Zane gave up, too impatient to work it down and off her hips, and instead flipped it up and over her bottom, exposing her.

"Zane!" She attempted to push the skirt down, but got it only as far as the small of her back. Zane bunched it in his fist and moved it completely out of his way.

"Let me look at you," he said in smoky tones, words nearly impossible.

Her panties were stretchy lace, like her bra. He could see the soft globes of her rounded bottom through the material. His lungs compressed, and he rasped, "You have a great ass, Tamara."

Her hands curled into the covers, but she held still.

Zane teased himself, cuddling each cheek in his large hands, squeezing, caressing. She was soft but firm, curvy without being voluptuous. He spread his hands wide, measuring her, letting his thumbs meet at the base of her spine. She wiggled at his touch, prompting him to slowly trace her spine, down, down, over the panties and lower, until he pushed his fingers between her legs and found the damp material there. Satisfaction filled him; she responded so quickly to his touch, even while showing her shyness.

Everything about her fascinated him, inflamed him.

The lace panties were like fancy icing on a delicious cake. But now they were too much distraction. He wanted her naked flesh under his hands, his mouth.

Hooking his fingers in the waistband, Zane stripped them down her thighs to her knees.

With a yelp, Tamara dropped her head forward and hid her face in the bedcovers. He heard her give a soft sigh of embarrassment and soothed her with murmured words, gentle strokes and squeezes.

"Damn." Even with the skirt tucked up around her waist, she was sexy as sin. His erection thrust against his slacks, bringing him to the point of near pain. He couldn't remember ever feeling so taut with need. His skin burned, his muscles ached, his stomach clenched.

Zane sat back on his heels and began unbuttoning his cuffs. "Do you have any idea," he growled, "what I want to do to you?"

She panted, nervous and excited and embarrassed. She didn't speak, but her head moved back and forth on the mattress.

Zane smiled hotly. "Everything. I want to do everything to you." Seeing her stretched out, her white backside his for the taking, was a powerful aphrodisiac. He wanted to slide into her from behind, to feel that soft bottom against his abdomen as he took her. He concentrated hard, knowing what he did and how he did it was important if he wanted her to give over to him completely. And he did.

He wanted Tamara to come to him, to need him for everything, not just sex. In the past, if a woman had asked for more than temporary companionship and mutual physical pleasure, he'd have broken things off to keep from building her expectations, knowing he was a bachelor and damn well intended to stay one.

With Tamara . . . all he knew for certain was that he wanted and needed more. Whether or not it'd last, he had no idea, but for now she was his, and he wanted her to admit it.

"We'll play by your rules, sweetheart, and get used to being naked together first."

That had her peeking, her head swiveling around to watch as he undid the last button on his shirt and shrugged it off his shoulders. He tossed it toward the floor while keeping his gaze glued to her face.

Heat suffused her delicate skin, and she licked her lips. "Go . . . go on," she urged.

Knowing he had her undivided attention, Zane unhooked his belt and slipped it free from the loops. He opened the button at the top of his slacks and carefully eased the zipper down past his throbbing hard-on. And even that touch, with his own hand, was almost too much.

"No," he said abruptly, not about to give up control so soon. "I have to leave my pants on for now, or we're done for."

"But. . . ."

"Shh. Trust me, sweetheart. Let me make you feel good."

Her slender, pale shoulders trembled as he touched her, as he dragged his fingers over the inward dip of her waistline, over to her graceful spine, and down to the twin dimples in her bottom. He leaned forward and lightly bit the plumpest curve of her right cheek.

Tamara wiggled and squirmed. Her thighs were clamped tight together.

"Open your legs, sweetheart."

Two heartbeats went by before she slowly edged her thighs just the tiniest bit wider. Again, Zane smiled. She amused him almost as much as she turned him on.

He wedged his fingers between her legs, enthralled with the darkness of his large, rough hand against the paleness of her tender inner thighs. Her body tensed as he moved her legs wide open, letting him see her, every inch of her.

"Beautiful," he murmured, desire twisting his guts and adding to his ache. He sat there like that, holding her steady, open, and looked his fill.

"Zane?"

Her voice was muffled, her face still hidden. Rather than reply, he spread his hands over her upper thighs, parting her more, and touched her glistening pink flesh with his thumbs. Her body shuddered, her legs shifted, and she gave a soft cry.

"So wet for me." He slicked his thumbs back and forth, spreading her moisture, readying her, feeling her.

"Oh God." Her bottom lifted into his hands, begging for more. Her hands tightened in the sheets, her arms tensed with the strain. But he continued, slowly sliding over her lips, opening her, petting her, wanting her as turned on as he'd been ever since her proposition.

And he looked at her, the ultrasoft pink flesh, swelling with excitement. His heartbeat increased with each small gasp she made, until he knew he wouldn't be able to take much more.

"Do you want to come for me, Tamara?"

"I don't know," she whispered brokenly, the words low and rough.

"Well, I do know." Zane stretched out next to her and turned her into his arms. She watched him with dark green, dazed eyes, her mouth open, her nostrils flaring with each deep breath. Fingers damp, he touched her mouth, then licked her.

Tamara moaned and launched herself against him. She was wild, and he loved it, holding her closer as she bit at his mouth, sucked at his tongue.

"Zane, oh God, I didn't expect this."

"I know." Everything with Tamara was harder, hotter, more intense. Hell, he felt ready to come himself, and she hadn't even touched him yet. But touching her was exciting enough to send him over the edge.

He tangled his hand in her hair and tipped her head back, making her back arch so he could reach her breasts. He drew on her nipples, sucking and tonguing and teasing. He pushed her to her back and kissed his way to her soft belly while his fingers combed through her tight damp curls. The hair on her sex was darker than that on her head, a rich, glossy, dark blonde.

Again, he parted her, and this time he pushed his finger deep. To his immense surprise, she cried out in mingled excitement and discomfort. Panting, Zane came up over her to stare at her face. He held still while her inner muscles clamped down on his intruding finger.

Her eyes were squeezed shut, her lashes spiked, leaving long shadows on her cheeks.

"Tamara?"

Her hips lifted, adjusted. Her only answer was a shuddering moan. She gripped his wrist with one hand, holding him, while she dug her nails into his shoulder with the other.

Zane could barely breathe. "Another first, baby?"

"Please don't stop."

Slowly, entranced, Zane leaned down and kissed each puckered nipple. He rested his head on her rib cage and inhaled her scent. It took his mind a little time to catch up with his emotions. His pulse rioted and now, above the lust, was a tenderness so deep, so overwhelming he felt on the point of no return.

Very, very carefully, he pulled his finger almost out. Just as carefully, he pushed it into her again, measuring her, testing her readiness. Her nails on his shoulder bit deep, bringing a stinging pain that he relished.

Chiding her, giving his mind time to clear, he said, "You should have told me, sweetheart."

Her hips rose with his next gentle thrust, a rosy blush expanding over her breasts.

"You never wanted me," she gasped, and Zane wondered if she even knew what she was saying. Her eyes were squeezed shut, every inch of her body trembling. He could feel the pulse beat of her heart against his jaw, and around his finger.

Already she was close. Very close.

"I want you more right now than I've ever wanted anything else in my life."

The words hung in the air like a thick storm cloud, and then Tamara sniffed. Big tears seeped from her eyes, ripping out his heart. "You mean that?"

"I mean it."

He kissed her ribs, her cleavage, each breast, and finally her mouth. Smiling down into her beautiful, tear-filled green eyes, he told her, "You are one special lady."

She looked at his mouth. "You know you're killing me?"

His smile nearly became a grin as he maintained the slow, rhythmic in-and-out motion of his finger. "You don't like it?"

"I like it too much." She drew a halting breath, a wave of pleasure nearly taking her, before she continued. "I didn't realize it'd be like this."

He was careful not to touch her clitoris, swollen and taut. "Let's try something else, okay?"

Her answer was a moan of acceptance.

"Easy now." Zane worked another finger inside her. "You are so tight."

She shook her head. "I've never done this."

"I know." He'd thought he understood about her responsibilities, but for a woman as sensual and naturally giving as Tamara to remain a virgin so long, she must have been more restricted than he'd figured.

Another small piece of his heart crumbled, and he decided she was ready now, she had to be ready now. This was something she *would* take from him, and he intended to give it all to her.

"You'll like this," he predicted, and shifting his hand just a little, he found her with his thumb.

Her body stiffened and she turned her face into his shoulder.

"Kiss me, Tamara."

She tried, but she was panting as the pleasure quickly escalated beyond her control.

"Zane!" She reached for him, pulling him to her, kissing his jaw, his neck, biting, squeezing him. Her hands clutched at his back and she moved against him, against his stroking fingers. She cried out, her moans raw and real.

He encouraged her with whispered words and careful touches until finally, all she could do was writhe and gasp.

When her body finally went limp, Zane held her to him, smoothing her soft hair from her face, caressing her bare back, her plump bottom. With her face tucked into his neck, he heard her sniffles. He smiled.

"Hey? You okay?"

She bumped his chin when she bobbed her head.

Feeling emotionally complete, and sexually explosive, Zane managed to say calmly, "You ready for that shower now?"

Again, she merely nodded, but her arms tightened around him.

"Is that a yes or a no, sweetheart?"

It took her a moment, and then she sighed. "Yes, I'm willing, but I don't think I can move."

"Easily remedied." Zane stood, kicked off his shoes, pulled off his socks, and then scooped her into his arms and against his bare chest. The skirt, which had been tangled around her waist, fell into place and something solid bumped his knee.

Tamara, preoccupied with running her hand over his

chest, gave an apologetic shrug. "The phone you told me to carry. It's in my pocket."

Her makeup was smudged again, this time by her tears, but it didn't detract from her smoldering sensuality. Her eyes were filled with lazy repletion after her climax, and curiosity at what she knew was yet to come. She was the most endearing, surprising, sensual woman he knew. "I'll take care of it."

Zane carried her into the tiny bathroom and stood her on her feet. He slipped his hand into her hair again, unable to stop touching her. "Towels?"

She looked shy and sweet, standing there on wobbly legs, wearing only a Gypsy skirt and a warm blush. Her breasts were lovely, small but perfectly shaped, her nipples flushed dark. He had no idea how much longer he could last.

She bent and pulled two towels from the cabinet beneath the sink. When she straightened, Zane dropped his slacks and stepped out of them.

The towels fell from her hands. Staring so hard he felt her gaze like a touch, Tamara said, "Oh my."

It hurt to smile. Hell, it hurt to breathe.

It seemed the Winston curse had a stranglehold on him, and he wasn't sure if he should fight it or embrace it. Tamara threatened him in every way he'd sworn a woman never would. Before she'd entered his store and whispered that she wanted him, he'd been doing an admirable job of staying on his given course. Most of his attention had been on growing his computer business. He'd balanced that with his responsibilities to his family. Family, in his book, always came first.

Between his business and his family he'd managed to fit in the occasional woman—like twice weekly—to keep his body sated. He was a very sexual man, and since there had always been willing women, he'd seen no reason to deprive himself.

But now other women didn't interest him at all, and more often than not, Tamara shattered his concentration on business and family. She lurked in his mind, crawled under his skin and into his dreams, and she was easily pushing her way into his heart.

He'd watched his brothers tumble into love, one right after the other. They hadn't fought it, as he'd always intended to. Hell, Cole had sought it out, and Mack had grinned his way to the altar. Even Chase, so quiet and deep, had accepted his fate.

Zane had thought he could keep Tamara in a neatly assigned slot, that he could accept her proposition, get her out of his system, and then get on with his bachelor ways.

It seemed she had the same intent: sexual pleasure, and nothing more. And being the perverse bastard he was, that drove him nuts.

He wouldn't allow it, damn it. Neither the Winston curse, nor any spell his little Gypsy might cast, was going to keep him from doing exactly as he pleased. And at the moment, it would please him to be inside her, to feel her climax while she was under him, moving with him and groaning out his name.

He could see the pulse thrumming in her throat as she stared at his groin. He could have sworn he got harder just from her interested gaze. "Have you come to any conclusions?"

Her focus lifted to his face, but not for long. "Yes."

Zane smiled. "Well, I hope you like what you see, because you're going to be seeing it a lot."

Tamara's heart pounded so hard, she felt faint. Zane was... more than she'd expected. She'd known he had a wonderful body; slim jeans and clinging T-shirts had revealed that even before she'd seen him without his shirt.

But now, standing in front of her in the raw, he was the most magnificent thing she'd ever seen. Her legs felt like butter, her skin was hot, her stomach dropped. She couldn't stop staring.

Surely no sane woman would look away from the sight

of him. His hips were lean and hard, his legs long and muscled, big feet planted firmly apart, as if prepared for a battle.

She nearly snorted. She had no intention of fighting him. She wanted him, and the pleasure he'd already given her hadn't diminished that desire one whit.

She licked her lips and perceived his slight movement. When she glanced up, his face had gone hard, his eyes dilated. "Can I touch you?"

Her fingertips pulsed with the need to feel him, all of him. His wide shoulders gleamed under the fluorescent light. Nearly hidden beneath dark chest hair, she saw his small brown nipples, and lower down on his abdomen, his navel was circled with the same dark hair. His stomach was flat, ridged with muscles, and she wondered how he stayed in such excellent shape with all the hours he worked. Genes, she decided, thinking of how gorgeous his brothers were, too.

"I want you to touch me," he told her, his voice dark and mesmerizing. One corner of his mouth kicked up. "Hell, I'm counting on it."

Tamara inched closer, but he stopped her, saying, "Let's get you out of that skirt first."

Her mouth went dry. It was silly, considering he'd already looked at her in great detail, but she blushed. "I hadn't pictured it going quite like this."

"Like this how?"

He stared at her breasts, which throbbed, her nipples pulling tight. She waved a hand at the bathroom. "Here, where the light is the brightest."

"I want to see you." His gaze snared and held hers. "And you want to see me, too, remember? Your book said we should get comfortable naked."

He looked plenty comfortable to her. And with good reason. A man couldn't look any better than Zane Winston. "You can be proud of your body."

His gaze heated, moving over her bared upper body. Stepping closer, he caught the waistband of the skirt and worked it over her hips. He brushed it down her thighs, and when he let it go, it dropped to rest around her feet. He stared, swallowed hard as he looked at every naked inch of her.

His voice gentled. "And you think that you can't?"

She wouldn't cower in front of him. "I didn't mean that. But I'm . . . average."

Sliding both hands into her hair, Zane tilted her face up so he could rub his mouth over hers. "No average woman could make me shake with lust, or keep me up at night, or wake me in the early dawn with a wet dream."

She blinked at him. "Wet dream?"

His thumbs brushed the corners of her mouth. He made a low rumbling sound. "Yeah. Not since I was a teen, damn it." His expression was wry, even faintly amused. "But I've been going to sleep wanting you, and I guess that carries over. I walk around with an erection all the damn time lately."

His solid, warm chest beckoned, and she opened her hands on him. "I think about you a lot, too."

He kissed her temple, her jaw, the sensitive skin beneath her ear. "Maybe we've been sharing our dreams. What do you think?"

"Are your dreams about . . . different ways for us to have sex?"

"Yes. And more often than not, they're too damn real for comfort."

She nodded, intrigued by the idea that they might in fact have shared a dream. "I wake up in the middle of the night, hot and tight and achy."

"Do you touch yourself, thinking about me?"

Tamara pressed her face into the curve of his shoulder. She didn't know people talked like this, that such things were discussed. Face burning hot, she admitted, "A little."

A slight shudder ran through him, and his tone was gruff when he asked, "But not to climax?"

Good God, did he need every detail?

"Tamara?" He reached for her breast, his palm rough-textured. His mouth opened on her neck, placing soft wet love bites here and there. Just that easily, he began fanning the fire all over again.

Feeling unsophisticated and clumsy, she whispered, "I don't know how."

Zane froze. The heavy slamming of his heart against her breasts told her how surprised he was. Then he hugged her so tight he lifted her off her feet. "Are you saying," he rumbled against her ear, "the climax I gave you is your first?"

Clinging to him, glad that the way he held her made it impossible for him to see her face, she nodded. "It's . . . it's kind of an elusive thing. At least, it always has been for me. And now, well, it's not at all what I expected."

The words had barely left her mouth and he was there, kissing her voraciously, his tongue in her mouth, his teeth nipping. He was like a wild man turned free. Tamara found herself hefted onto the sink counter, her back against the cold wall while Zane moved her legs apart and continued to kiss her silly.

His hand fondled her breasts, then down between her legs. He cupped her. *"You're mine."*

She tried to rear back, not at all certain what he'd said or how he'd meant it. Surely he hadn't just staked a claim, not when she'd had to fight for his initial agreement, not when he knew she'd be moving away soon. "Zane."

His long fingers probed, stroked, sank deep.

Overwhelmed with the suddenness of his touch, the air left her lungs in a *whoosh,* forcing her to pant. Her body arched, her thighs opened almost of their own volition, and with a groan Zane went to his knees. Through a haze of searing need, Tamara stared, nearly incoherent with shock as he parted her gently and leaned forward. Seeing his dark head between her thighs went beyond anything she'd considered, anything she'd even fantasized.

His tongue touched her. "Zane!"

"Be quiet, sweetheart."

He teased, came closer and closer, and then his mouth

opened on her most intimate flesh. Arms rigid, she braced herself with her palms flat on the sink counter so she wouldn't slide onto the floor, a puddle of scandalized excitement.

"Ohmigod." If his fingers had been wonderful, it was nothing compared to his mouth, the wet rasp of his hot tongue.

His face still against her, he said, "I want you to come for me again."

Even his hot moist breath made her shudder. Nowhere in the journal did it say this might happen. At least not this soon. There had been a vague reference in the eighth chapter . . . *ohmigod.*

Her thoughts scattered again when he found that ultra-sensitive spot and suckled. She nearly bucked away from him.

Zane lifted her legs over his shoulders and his strong hands gripped her hips. "Just relax, baby. I've got you," he murmured, and then he was drawing on her again, his tongue flicking, his teeth holding her gently, securely, and she couldn't stop the long, ragged groan of release, hitting her fast this time, like a tidal wave.

The way he pleasured her now was more intense, almost painful as her already ravaged senses exploded again.

"Mmm," he said with so much satisfaction, Tamara almost found the strength to smile. Almost. She felt drained and wrung out and for the first time in ages, totally devoid of tension.

After several lingering tastes, he whispered, "That was nice." Zane kissed her inner thigh, her hipbone, before lifting her legs from his shoulders and allowing them to dangle over the edge of the counter. He stood and touched her chin, his gaze direct. "You're incredible."

Slumped against the wall, more boneless than not, Tamara said, "Ah, it was nothing."

Zane laughed, and in his laugh she heard sexual excitement and male triumph, mirrored by the naked hunger in his eyes. He scooped her up and stepped with her into the shower.

The first blast of icy water revived her before he adjusted the temperature. Watching her, still fully aroused, he soaped his hands while she stood there, concentrating hard on keeping herself upright.

"The book," Tamara interjected, knowing she had to do something, "made it clear that both partners should give. I don't want to be selfish."

A devilish gleam entered his eyes as he worked the soap into a lather. "Believe me, honey, when a woman moans as nicely as you do, she's not selfish."

The water was deflected by his broad back, and only a misty spray reached her. She drew a deep breath and inched closer to him. It wasn't difficult because her tub was short, leaving them little room to maneuver. Tamara touched his shoulder, traced her hand through the water beaded there. "Tell me what to do."

His soapy hands settled on her breasts. "Touch me," he advised. "Any place, any way that you like."

Concentrating, which wasn't easy considering his soap-slippery fingers now rolled her sensitized nipples, she put her hands on his biceps. She loved how hard he was, how his muscles flexed and bunched as he moved.

He wasn't overly hairy, like Uncle Thanos, but a neat diamond of dark hair stretched over his chest, from pec muscle to pec muscle, then made a very distracting trail down his abdomen to his navel, and on again to his groin to frame his large sex.

Tamara chewed her lips, screwed up her courage, and gave in to her curiosity. She reached down and clasped his penis in her fist. He moved to lean against the tile wall. Water sprayed in her face and she wiped it away, intent on examining him. Everything about Zane fascinated her, but his body was of special interest.

She thought he probably had to be larger than average. Surely not all men were that big. She considered asking him, but he'd gone curiously still the second she'd touched him, and now he almost looked in pain. "Am I hurting you?"

"No."

She gentled her hold, stroking him carefully from base to tip, and heard his low curse.

His size intimidated her. Just having his fingers inside her had been vaguely uncomfortable, though pleasure had quickly followed the discomfort.

This though, this was entirely different. He was long and thick, solid, with a velvety soft covering, and her fingers could barely circle him. She squeezed experimentally and watched a drop of fluid appear on the broad head.

Zane's eyes closed as a raw sound of pleasure rumbled from deep inside him. The shower spray pulsated down around him, water streaming over his lean, powerful body. Watching his face, Tamara detected every emotion, every nuance of pleasure that he experienced. And more than that, she absorbed it. Zane was so open to her, sharing each and every sensation, it was almost frightening. He relished her touch, quickly spinning out of control, and she felt it all.

"You like that," she said with awe, amazed at how she affected him.

"Yeah." His voice was hoarse with strain. "I like it. Too damn much." He caught her upper arms and pulled her to his muscular frame. "Kiss me, Tamara."

Still holding him in her hand, she tipped her face up and gave him her mouth. The kiss was lush, slow, consuming. His erection pulsed in a rhythm that matched her racing heartbeat.

"What you did to me?"

"Which part, honey?" He labored for breath, and his legs were locked, braced apart to support them both.

Moving back a little, she brought her other hand up to close around his heavy erection, circling him with both hands now, tracing each vein, cuddling his testicles. She slipped her thumb over the head to test the slippery secretion there.

His expression burning, Zane watched her, so he understood when she said, "You kissed me."

A fine trembling passed through his limbs. "You want me to do it again?"

She looked up, and their gazes locked. "I think I want to do it to you."

"Damn," he groaned, "I can't take it. I've waited too long."

Experiencing her first surge of feminine power, Tamara said, "Yes you can."

Zane laughed and caught her wrists. "No, little Gypsy," he answered emphatically, "I can't."

He easily controlled her as she did her best to convince him. When she realized he intended to get them to the bed first, she quickly washed the makeup from her face and shampooed her hair. Zane scrubbed himself, but not without touching her every so often, slicking a soapy hand over her breasts, trailing his fingers down her spine on the pretense of helping her rinse. He wouldn't let her touch him, catching her hands each time she tried. But that didn't stop him from doing as he pleased to her body, and making her crazy in the process.

When they'd both finished washing, he turned the water off and pushed the shower curtain aside. "I hope you're satisfied that we've met the standards of the book, sweetheart," he said as he reached for the towels, "because I have to get into you. Right now."

The way he spoke so openly about his need for her, and how he wanted to touch her, only added to her growing desire.

In a near daze, Tamara found herself hustled out of the shower, a towel briskly rubbed over her body and her hair, and then Zane picked her up and carried her to her bedroom. He kissed her nose seconds before he tossed her onto the bed.

Tamara only had time to open her arms and Zane was

there, moving over her, his mouth covering hers, his damp body sliding against hers.

She still didn't think she'd done her fair share. And she wasn't at all certain he'd fit. But he gave her no more time to worry about it.

Fourteen

Zane forced himself to let her go long enough to crawl to the side of the bed and snag his slacks. It wasn't easy, considering what she'd been doing right before he'd ended the shower. Tamara in a curious mood was more exciting than consummation with other women.

He fumbled for his wallet, cursing and sweating, his body in a fever. He was good at donning a condom at the most frantic times; he never took unnecessary chances on parenthood and always wore protection. But now, he felt like an awkward schoolboy and he deeply resented the need to wear a rubber.

It didn't help that Tamara was busy kissing him, trying to pull him back to her. She kept up a rambling monologue that would probably make him laugh after he'd sated himself and could conjure rational thought again.

"You're so big, Zane," she said with breathless wonder, in between hot kisses to his shoulder, his spine. "And so hard."

Her soft hands reached around him, and she attempted to assist him with the condom.

"Baby, wait." Zane knew he was on the verge of exploding. One small touch was all it'd take. He felt her breasts on his back, her pointed nipples rasping him. He felt her breath in his ear, her damp hair tickling his jaw. Damn.

"I know I'm not supposed to like it this first time." She spoke into his ear, breathless and anxious. "I mean, I'm new at this and you're not and you're sort of on the enormous size, so it'll probably—"

In one movement, Zane turned to her, carrying her back down to the mattress and pinning her in place with his body. "It'll be fine, you'll see." The things she said, and how she said them, made him both wild with lust and tenderly amused. "I'm barely bigger than average," he lied. "Trust me."

"I thought"—she gasped as he kneed her legs apart—"I thought men always bragged on their size!"

Zane caught her face. "Shhh. Look at me, Tamara. There's no reason to be nervous. I'm not going to hurt you."

Solemn now, her eyes wary, yet still ablaze with excitement, she nodded. "I know you wouldn't on purpose. You're a very gentle, considerate man. But you're so— oh."

Zane pushed into her, not much, but enough to get her attention. It would be a tight fit, he realized with mind-numbing excitement, and struggled to keep control of himself. Her muscles squeezed at him, contracting at the intrusion. His heart thumped and his pulse surged, urging him on.

"No," he grated through his teeth, fighting the need to drive into her, "don't close your eyes. Look at me."

He wanted every connection to her, mind and body. He wanted her to feel what he felt.

Her hips moved, wiggling in an attempt to accommodate him, and he nearly lost it. The very head of his cock was bathed in her wet heat, her body milking him as small spasms ran through her. It was the most exquisite torture he'd ever endured. She was so tight, so silky and wet.

"Easy," he groaned, as much to himself as to her. "We'll go slow."

Her hands gripped his shoulders. "Will you kiss me again?" she asked shakily.

Zane lowered his head and took her mouth. He meant the kiss to be reassuring, but then Tamara locked her arms around his neck and her legs around his hips and he gave up. With a groan, he pressed forward, slowly sinking into her as her body gradually opened to him. The exquisite friction weakened his resolve.

Tamara didn't retreat, just squeezed him tighter.

He heard her small whimper and lifted his head. "Are you all right?" he asked, destroyed by the idea that he might be hurting her after all.

He did his best to remain motionless, to let her get used to him.

"This . . . this is incredible," she said, and pressed her face into his shoulder. "You're around me and inside me, and the smell of you, the taste of you. . . ." She licked his shoulder and groaned. "It's almost too much, but I don't ever want it to stop."

"It won't stop," he promised. "I *can't* stop." Carefully, he flexed his buttocks and went a little deeper, his way eased by how wet she'd gotten, how closely she held him. He withdrew, and pressed forward again. On the third stroke he entered her completely and they both moaned.

Her mouth opened on his chest and she bit him, not a harsh bite, but a hungry one. Her heels dug into the small of his back as she lifted into him, trying to get closer.

He fell into sexual oblivion.

His every thrust heavier than the one before, he pumped into her while a roaring sounded in his ears. His entire body sizzled like a live nerve, every small touch electrifying him, driving him higher until he didn't know if he could survive it, but he knew he couldn't pull back. His hands contracted on her hips, holding her to him.

Vaguely he heard Tamara cry out, but the wave of sen-

sation cresting upward through his body, flooding his
mind, obliterated everything else. And then he felt the
draining release, the burst of pressure that was both pleasure and pain, and he tensed over her as his body shuddered.

How long he rested on top of her, he wasn't certain.
He was horribly afraid he'd fallen asleep, because the sun
had set and long shadows crept into the room. The light
on her desk glowed, but other than that, the room was
dim.

The smell of sex lingered in the air, and the smell of
Tamara filled his nostrils as he drew in a deep breath.
Their bodies were practically melded together, his head
on her breast, her thighs still around him. The steady
drumming of her heartbeat sounded in his ear.

He became aware of her right hand on his nape, idly
stroking through his hair. Her head was turned, her mouth
nibbling on his right hand where it rested beside her on
the pillow. Her tongue licked delicately at his salty skin.

"Tamara?" He felt drugged, and struggled to push himself up to his elbows. He was far too heavy to have stayed
atop her, yet she hadn't complained, in fact had held him
the entire time.

Her eyes were liquid as she looked at him, filled with
tears and churning emotion. Her smile quivered over her
soft, swollen lips. "You are the most remarkable man,"
she whispered.

He stroked her hair back from her face, caught a tear
that trailed down her cheek. "Sweetheart, why are you
crying? Did I hurt you?"

"Oh no." She shook her head, and gave him another
beautiful smile. She held his hand to her cheek, rubbing
into his palm with sweet contentment. "You have a lover's
hand. Did you know that?"

Bending to kiss the corner of her mouth, Zane said,
"I'm glad you think so."

She laughed with the delight of a child. "No, I meant
that as a palm reader, I can see the defining elements in

your hand for a lover. I've been studying it while you dozed."

Damn, so he *had* slept. He was a pig, but God, he felt replete, with both sexual satisfaction and emotional fulfillment. No other experience, no other woman, had prepared him for this. Then he thought about her words.

Her shop window advertised palm reading, and Zane was curious. He smoothly disengaged their bodies, despite her protests. "Don't move. I'll be right back."

But once he stood, he paused to admire her lying there, warm and soft, nestled into the bedding. With a slight blush, she turned on her side, facing him, her soft, slender thighs closing, one arm covering her breasts. A lock of fine, blonde hair fell over her eyes and she brushed it away. Her smile was one of sharing, of intimacy.

Zane inhaled deeply. He accepted that he was in deep—and he intended to get a bit deeper.

It took him only a moment to get rid of the condom and splash water on his face. He brought a cool washcloth back with him and sat on the edge of the bed.

"What are you doing?" she asked, eyeing the washcloth with the same fascination she might give to a rattlesnake.

Humor rose in him, sharp and sweet. "Playing the servant."

"No." She started to sit up, and he wrestled her back down. Wrestling with Tamara was more fun than any man deserved. Especially since they were both naked.

When he had her flat on her back again, he said, "This will give me pleasure, Tamara."

Skepticism darkened her vivid green eyes. "You're sure?"

"Positive." She relented, but her shoulders remained stiff, her disposition wary while he bathed her face, her throat, her tender breasts.

A catch in her breath and the sight of her nipples puckering told him she liked the impromptu bath as much as he did.

"I want you to be comfortable." With a gentle, slow

touch, he brushed the damp cloth between her legs. Her thick lashes dropped to hide her eyes, and she made a small purr of surprise.

Damn, he loved how quickly she responded to him.

He threw the cloth aside and stretched out next to her, pulling her into his arms. He wanted to hold her all night.

He intended to make love to her again and again before they slept, but she was new to lovemaking and needed time to get used to him. In that, her book was correct.

The hand she'd been kissing was now filled with her breast. "Explain this palm reading business to me," he said as he fondled her. He didn't think he'd ever tire of listening to her, touching her.

Tamara lifted his hand, depriving him of her breast, and kissed the palm. "Here," she said, tracing a thin crease that ran the width of his hand. "This is your heart line. See how long and curvy it is? And it ends between your second and third finger. That means you have a tendency to freely release all emotion and passion that your head would normally block. You have a bigger capacity to experience sensation than many other people."

She twisted to see his face, her smile impish. "It also means you're good at pleasing yourself and your partner."

The twinkle in her eyes charmed him. "And you agree with that assessment?"

"Wholeheartedly." She brought his hand to her mouth again, and this time she bit his baby finger. "See how your little finger is long and straight and sort of leans out to the side? Now that reveals a freethinker, unconcerned with the restrictions of others."

"You're serious?"

"And often accurate."

"Huh. So the services you advertise aren't entirely bogus?"

"Of course not."

She didn't sound hurt by his skepticism, so much as resigned. That bothered him. He didn't want her to accept him as the typical doubting Thomas who didn't understand her. He was more than that, much more.

"I can tell by reading your palm that you're willing to try things."

Trying things held a definite appeal at the moment. Fascinated, Zane studied her breasts, how her nipples were now soft and smooth, her delicate skin a little abraded by his five o'clock shadow. Were her silky thighs scratched too? He cupped his hand protectively over her mound, promising himself he'd shave before pleasuring her that way again.

"What kind of things?" Thoughts of what he intended to do with her and to her made his voice huskier.

Her voice was deeper, too, as she said, "Sexual things."

At least they were on the same track.

"You're not content," she said, "to just make love in the missionary position, on a bed and in the dark."

Zane snorted. "Hell no."

Curiosity brought rosy color to her cheeks. "Where else would you like to make love?" Tamara continued to examine his hand, every so often kissing a fingertip or licking at his flesh.

The "love" word, even in the context of physical love, kicked his heart, making it miss a beat. Infatuation, possessiveness, pounding lust—they were all emotions he could deal with. But love? Jesus, he just didn't know.

As his thoughts progressed, she turned her face against his shoulder, and once again he wondered if she could read his mind. He was the one who'd originally insisted on calling their intimacy "lovemaking." She'd been more than happy to label it mere sex. And here he'd upset her. It seemed that every time he got agitated, *she* was the one to react.

He frowned, reluctant to let anyone into his head. And yet, how could he stop her? Especially when she denied any such thing. It was certainly something for them to discuss, once she stopped being so close-mouthed.

He nuzzled her temple, rubbed his bristly jaw into the

soft coolness of her hair. "Before I start sharing fantasies, we need to eat."

He felt her lips form a smile against his skin. "I suppose a man your size gets hungry often?"

"In more ways than one." She lifted her face, staring up at him with invitation. He kissed the end of her nose. "Let's eat, and then," he promised, "we'll trade fantasies."

"The book suggested we should do that. You share a lot of the same philosophies with the woman who wrote it."

Zane stood and pulled her to her feet. After everything they'd already done, she still looked shy, her thighs quickly pressing together, her shoulders hunching as if to hide her breasts.

Patience, he told himself, unwilling to shock her, refusing to let her feel used. But containing his marauding tendencies had never been so difficult. All he had to do was look at her, and his blood raged. Seeing her fresh from his lovemaking had the impact of a wrecking ball on his composure.

Distracting himself, he glanced around the room. "Where is this infamous book?"

Twisting and dipping at the waist, she reached beneath the mattress. Zane clenched his fists to keep his hands off her delightful bottom. It wasn't easy.

She straightened, holding a slim, worn, blue volume with a ribbon poking out from between the faded pages. A marker, he realized, and wondered how far she'd gotten.

Taking it from her, Zane flipped it open. Tamara went on tiptoe to look with him. She pointed. "Right here. Sharing fantasies. It says it's an excellent way to really get to know your lover."

He wasn't sure he'd live through hearing her sexual fantasies, but he was willing to try. "Why don't we check this out while we eat?" He could definitely use some nourishment right now. And filling his mouth with food, while not nearly as satisfying, would keep him from tasting her again.

Tamara held back as he tried to urge her toward the door. "I need to get my robe."

Laughing, Zane pulled the sheet from the bed, tossed it over her shoulders, and lifted her in his arms. "Honey, I like you this way, buck naked. And there's no one in your kitchen to see us, is there?"

"No."

"Then why deprive me of the sight?" Zane strode into the kitchen and plunked her onto the counter next to the refrigerator. He pulled a mock frown when she scrambled to get the sheet around her. "Spoilsport."

He didn't ask permission, just opened the refrigerator and found cheese, mustard, lettuce, milk. "Where's your bread?"

Arms crossed over her breasts to anchor the sheet in place, she nodded toward a pantry. "Over there."

"Stay put." Zane fetched the bread and went about making several sandwiches. "How many can you eat?"

"A half."

He eyed her slim body, practically swallowed by the voluminous sheet, and shrugged. "Okay, but that means we'll have to have dessert, too."

"There's strawberry ice cream in the freezer."

"Perfect." More than perfect, he thought with anticipation.

For the next hour, Zane showed her how to play while giving himself time to recover. He didn't want to admit it to Tamara, but his legs were still rubbery and his pulse still sluggish. She'd zapped him of his strength. He needed all his wits and dexterity to deal with her and the sensual plans he'd made for the night.

The sight of her perched so prettily on the counter did a lot toward helping him reach that goal.

He fed Tamara, occasionally licking one of her fingers, even trailing wet kisses up her wrist to her inner elbow. He found all the places that made her eyes go heavy with desire, and he showed her how and where to kiss him in return.

She enthusiastically complied with all his instructions— even referring back to the book a few times.

"Did you know," she asked, "that women have a bio-rhythm for when they're most easily excited?"

"Is that from the journal?" He'd read some of the elegant, sloping script, and found it to be amazingly precise and on target.

"Yes." She scooped up the book and thumbed carefully through the fragile pages. "An observant and caring man," she read, "will make note of when his lover is most receptive. A woman can be convinced to do anything if she's approached at the right moment."

"Anything, huh?"

"That's what it says."

"Well now. I think that's terrific information to have. When are you most receptive?"

She lowered her lashes, relaxed enough to flirt, and asked, "What is it you want to do?"

"Everything."

The fluttering of her pulse gave her away. "I . . . I think I'm susceptible to you anytime." She watched him without guile, open and honest. "I meant it when I said I've wanted you since the first moment I saw you. I think about you most at night, because that's when I'm least busy and I can concentrate more. But you—this—is always in my mind, even while I'm working."

"This?"

"Having you here." Like a lingering touch, her gaze moved over him. "Naked and willing and mine at least for right now."

His stomach dropped, his chest swelled. "What else do you want? I mean, in life." He was so curious about her, all of her. The more he knew, the better equipped he'd be to deal with the nearly smothering emotions.

She sighed and turned to stare at the floor. "I want to

keep my shop. I want whoever is bothering me to leave me alone. And I want to be normal."

Her words hurt him, an actual physical ache that was more powerful than lust could ever be, and more painful than anything he'd ever experienced. "Normal?"

Gesturing, she flapped a hand toward him. "Like you. Like people who go about every day with their regular jobs and their regular lives."

"Not a Gypsy?"

Her lips pressed together. "I'm sorry." When she looked at him, her gaze was clear, all remorse hidden. "I shouldn't be complaining. In so many ways my life has been extraordinary."

"And restrictive."

"Yes. But my aunts and uncle did what they could. And I'm grateful to them. They raised me and loved me, and that's more than a lot of people have."

And it was nothing compared to what he'd been given in his life. He felt spoiled and shallow; he'd pushed through life taking what he wanted, rejecting what he didn't need. He'd had a backup system of love and support and acceptance that he'd often taken for granted.

"I am sorry." Her laugh was self-conscious, frustrated, and it loosened his knees, made his eyes burn and his throat feel tight. "I can't believe I'm yakking on and on like this."

"What?" He bent to look into her face, to see her eyes, her expression. "We can't talk? Can't share?" He kept his tone soft, neutral, carefully hiding the surge of urgency he felt. He wanted, needed, her to tell him more. "Says who?"

Tamara gripped the cloth-covered book tightly. Her hair skimmed her shoulders as she shook her head. "According to the first chapter, I shouldn't be burdening you." She chewed her lip. "It's just that I've never been involved before, so it's hard to remember what I should and shouldn't talk about."

"And here I was thinking that the journal was written

by a smart lady." He made a deprecating sound that she immediately reacted to.

"Oh no, we should talk and share. But I don't want you confused over what I want from *you*. Those other things . . . they're not your concern. They're things I'm working out on my own."

How many times, he wondered, had she had to summon up that rigid streak of pride to protect herself, claiming it was what she wanted? How often had independence been her prop for loneliness?

He wouldn't dent her pride for the world, so he let it go. By morning, she'd know in no uncertain terms that she was his in every way, not just within the boundaries she dictated.

She was getting his help whether she wanted it or not, but she didn't need to know that just yet.

For a while they ate and talked about inconsequential things, foods they both liked, movies they had enjoyed. Zane located a few ticklish spots on her—the back of her knees, her hipbones—and he relished her laughter, her small smiles, and her teasing rebukes.

"What else can you do besides read palms?" he asked when they had just about finished all the food. They were both semi-aroused, freely touching and kissing in a lazy, savory way.

Tamara had become unmindful of her nudity. She'd even gone so far as to place the notorious journal aside, and let the sheet drop to her lap, giving him free access to her breasts, letting him do as he pleased. And it pleased him to touch her, kiss her. He couldn't keep from it.

He loved watching her move, the way she gestured with her hands or tilted her head or curled her toes. He'd been with a lot of beautiful women, stacked women, but she had the cutest body he'd ever seen, all soft and pink and petite, with an undeniable feminine strength. He was as enthralled with her as he'd been with his first naked woman. He remembered the fascination then, lying in the sunshine in a field with his junior high school sweetie being very accommodating, giggling as he'd explored with his fingers, moaning when he'd used his tongue to taste her. It had been like having the candy store opened, and everything was free.

He felt that way now, magnified about a thousand times, constantly needing to stroke her or nibble on her in some small way. The ice cream hadn't been dessert enough—he wanted to start at her toes and work his way up.

"I do astrological charts," she said, and even her voice, lyrical and soft, aroused him. "Tarot card readings, and things like that."

She swallowed another bite of strawberry ice cream, then licked her lips. "I do some fortune-telling and predictions of the future, too. Usually that can be based on something the client says." She grinned at him, a wicked, teasing grin. "In other words, a good guess."

"Where'd you learn all that stuff?" Zane finished off his ice cream, and reached past her to put his bowl in the sink. The sheet hung around her waist. He stepped up to her and brought her breasts against his chest. Her accelerated heartbeat kick-started his own. They'd been teasing one another for some time now; he wasn't sure how much longer he could wait.

"I've read books." She slid her hands over his back to his hips, tugging him closer. "I have a whole selection on each topic. When I first came here, I had to fight with the relatives to get rid of the more bogus stuff."

"Like?"

"Using the crystal ball—which is just decoration now. Special light effects, eerie music, incantations, all that. We compromised. I got to apply what I'd actually learned about the craft, and they got me to dress up in my silly costume."

Zane put his hands on her thighs. The thin sheet had absorbed her heat, and with her sitting on the countertop, she was just the right height to kiss. "Your silly costume makes me wild."

She laughed. "It does not."

"It didn't use to," he agreed, "but it does now. I keep thinking about all those rings on your little toes, and all that attitude you have when you're dressed up."

Her lips quivered with a suppressed laugh. "Rings on my toes, huh?"

Trailing a finger over her smooth shoulder, he made his way down the slope of her right breast, stopping just short of her nipple. He watched it pucker, draw tight, just from his teasing. "You're obviously popular with the men, so others must agree with me."

Her breath hitched. "I don't know. I do well enough, I suppose."

Removing all indications of jealousy, Zane tipped up her chin. "You were pretty busy this morning."

She stared at his mouth, and it was easy to know her thoughts now. "Arkin has become a regular only the past few weeks. He's a nice man. I like him."

Logic told him that plenty of women liked nice men. There was no reason for the spike of possessiveness. "And Boris?"

She made a face. "He's a little eerie, isn't he?"

"How so?" True, Zane hadn't liked him, not even a little. And he'd thought him an arrogant jerk, too pushy for his own good. But he hadn't really considered him frightening.

"I don't know. He just made me edgy." She rubbed her arms and looked thoughtful, as if considering her own reaction.

Zane didn't quite understand her uneasiness either. Of course, he wasn't a woman playing at being a Gypsy, determined to stand alone no matter what. Tamara, with her eclectic ways and stubborn disposition, was more vulnerable than most, and from what he could tell, more sensitive than most. If the bastard had frightened her somehow, Zane didn't want him around her again.

With a small sound, Tamara wiggled out of his arms,

scooting back on the counter and trying to escape his hold. Zane felt her withdrawal like a punch.

He gripped her arms and lightly shook her. "What is it?"

"Nothing." She pressed away from him.

"Bullshit." He turned her chin toward him. Her green eyes were cloudy with distress. "I can see it on your face, Tamara. Don't shut me out. Tell me what's wrong."

"I don't want you to get mad."

"At you?" She nodded, and Zane automatically pulled her into a hug. She relaxed against him. "Baby, I'm not going to get mad at you. I *want* you to tell me what you're thinking."

A deep breath and several seconds later, she said, "You still think I'm a charlatan."

"What?"

"I understand," she rushed to assure him, ignoring his surprise. "I mean, there's not a whole lot of legitimacy I can lay claim to. But Zane, I truly do want to help people, and a lot of times, I can. Just today, with Arkin Devane, I was able to tell him things he needed to know, important things."

Mired in confusion, Zane fought to make sense of her words. He didn't doubt her sincerity, and never had. "Honey, what makes you think I'm judging you that way?"

Her teeth sank into her soft bottom lip and her eyes were big, vulnerable. She swallowed. "Because I feel what you feel." Her hand touched his jaw, slid down to the pulse at the base of his throat, her fingertips lightly pressing. "When you're mad or annoyed."

"You feel what I feel?" He didn't mean to sound so incredulous.

"Yes." Hesitation was plain on her face, then she lifted her chin and forged ahead with a near belligerence. "When you're aroused, too. It's . . . a little shocking, how turned on you get."

Her admission should have stunned him, but instead, it

made sense. "You're . . . what do they call it? Empathic?"

"To very few people."

Heart racing, Zane asked, "Those people you care about?"

Her gaze never wavered, and she whispered, "Usually."

Cradling her head in his palms, he kissed her eyelids, her nose, her delicious mouth that tasted faintly of strawberries and woman and sexual hunger. "Then know this, little Gypsy. It pisses me off that you won't open yourself to me completely, that you won't trust me to do what I can for you. It makes me madder than hell that anyone would upset you, especially a man. I want you all to myself, and if you left it up to me, Boris Sandor and Arkin Devane and any other man who wants to use your talents would never get within shouting distance of you again."

Tamara blinked at him, her lips slightly parted.

He opened himself to her, sharing as he wanted her to share. "If you know me so well, Tamara, what am I feeling right now?"

Unerringly her hand moved down his side, inward over his hipbones to his groin, and closed hotly around his erection. "Desire. Possessiveness."

His breath hissed at the gentleness of her touch. "I told you before," he said through his teeth, "and I'm telling you again. You're mine. Now more than ever."

He took her mouth, his tongue pushing deep, demanding, and Tamara dropped the sheet to hold him close to her heart.

Zane decided now was a good time to confide a few fantasies to her. His emotions were suddenly so raw, so explosive, it was all he could do to contain them. He had to get inside her, and soon.

He wanted to take her every way known to man. From behind, so he could slip his hands beneath her and stroke her between her thighs, cuddle her breasts. He wanted her over him, so he could watch her pleasure as she came, with free access to her sensitive nipples. He wanted her on her knees in front of him, and he wanted to hear her beg so he'd know he wasn't the only one twisting with need.

He wanted a lot, everything, and he intended to get it.

He lifted Tamara in his arms and carried her into the bedroom. They were both breathing hard, and Tamara frantically touched him everywhere she could reach, her small hands hot and busy, her mouth damp, hungry.

Zane strode to the bed, and just as he laid her on the mattress and stripped away the sheet, the lights went out. He heard Tamara's catch of breath, felt her shock of fear. Then she whispered, "Oh God, he's back."

Fifteen

Through the open door, Zane could see how dark the house had gone, not a single light in evidence.

It was silent too, the hum of the refrigerator stopped, no buzz of electricity of any kind. It made his skin prickle and set his senses on alert. "Stay here."

He reached for his slacks and pulled them on, but didn't bother with the zipper or button. Tamara didn't reply, and he knew she was afraid, but he couldn't spare the time to reassure her.

He headed out of the room, enraged that anyone would come into her house when she might have been there alone. And he didn't doubt that someone had. She was empathic—that much he believed with a certainty that touched his soul. She'd know if someone had intruded— and not just any someone, but the same someone. There wasn't a power failure, there wasn't a blown fuse. Some- one was in her house.

This was a direct threat to her, and he wouldn't tolerate it. Tamara might not want to admit it, but they'd come to an understanding. She was his to protect, and he'd damn well start tonight.

* * *

From his car parked in a vacant lot across the street, Joe saw the house go black in the blink of an eye. He shook his head. Hell, Zane had been at it for hours. His respect for his cousin grew, though after having seen the woman, Joe had to wonder about his choice. She wasn't quite the type he'd always figured Zane would settle on.

Using his finger, Joe stirred the lukewarm coffee in his cup, trying to distribute a packet of sugar. Hell, he was hungry and tired and bored out of his mind. He should just head back to the motel, but some vague intuition nagged at him. That sixth sense had saved his ass more than once, so he wasn't about to start ignoring it now.

The coffee went down in two long gulps. Boredom was a bitch. For a while there he'd entertained himself with thoughts of what Zane might be doing with the black-haired woman who wasn't really black-haired at all but wore a wig. Weird. A little fascinating, but still weird. Zane had never struck him as the type to go after the strange ones.

But even pondering sexual acrobatics had grown old after a few hours. There sure as hell wasn't anything Zane could do that Joe hadn't already done himself. Several times. And likely with more skill.

He smiled. Hell, lately none of it interested him all that much.

Joe studied the building. He looked at the dark upstairs windows where he presumed Zane was going another round. What a stud. Personally, he'd have left the lights on. There wasn't anything prettier than a woman waiting naked for a man.

Unless, of course, they were finally settling down to sleep. It was a little early yet, but hey, sex could be an exhausting business when a man gave it his all.

Joe was smiling at his own sense of humor when it struck him that the faint lights from the downstairs had gone out as well. The entire house was pitch black.

Neat trick, he thought, cursing his slow perception while wondering who had just killed the electricity and why.

The car's interior remained dark and shadowed, the lights disengaged earlier, when he opened the driver's door and slid out. He moved silently, his gun already in his hand, his gaze constantly scanning the area, watching for even the slightest movement. At times like this, he forgot his damn knee and ignored the nagging discomfort. His movements were fluid, as practiced as any human could make them.

The front door of the shop was locked when he reached it, so he slipped around to the side of the building, keeping his back to the brick wall, inching along without so much as disturbing a piece of gravel or stirring up dust. He stuck his head around the corner, trying to locate the back door.

There wasn't one.

A faint scraping sound reached his ears, coming from the other side of the house. Joe moved, running flat-out and circling around the back. The security lights from Zane's computer business were bright enough to carry across the alley, but faded as they reached the metal stairs leading to the upper story of the building. Joe had great night vision, or he'd never have seen that the door at the top of the stairs was ajar.

"Fuck." Nothing made Joe madder than realizing he'd made a mistake. Here he'd been watching the front of the house—hell, Zane was upstairs for Christ's sake!—and someone had slipped up the side stairs.

He'd taken two somewhat hobbling, pain-filled steps toward the stairs when he heard the *whoosh* of movement behind him. Joe turned, his eyes zeroing in on a moving shadow. Too far away to chase and catch, a body dashed into the darkness. There was little for Joe to commit to memory. The person had dressed all in black, and even the face was covered.

Joe looked back at the upstairs door. More cautiously now, in case the runner hadn't worked alone, he climbed

the stairs. They were rickety, and some noise was un-
avoidable. He flattened himself against the outside wall,
peeked inside and detected nothing but darkness. He slid
his bad leg in, felt the way was clear, and ducked his
body inside.

With the help of the moonlight, his eyes were quickly
adjusting. He could make out a couch, a table. To his
right, an interior door stood open, probably the door that
led to her downstairs shop. He glanced at it, but kept his
eyes moving, searching, unwilling to let anything else get
past him. He'd learned through experience that staring too
hard, especially in the dark, shattered your awareness. A
little focus was good, too much could be deadly.

Through the open door he heard a noise, that of shuf-
fling feet, and a muffled curse.

Zane.

Joe took a hasty step in that direction, then ducked as
his instincts screamed a warning. A whistling filled his
ears and something *whooshed* past his head, coming far
too close for comfort. Another swing, but the aim was off
and the object—something flat and hard—smashed into
his shoulder.

Without so much as a grunt of pain, Joe turned for a
tackle, his gun held tight. He collided with a small, slim
body and they went down in a clatter of disrupted furniture and knocked-over knickknacks. His hands encoun-
tered bare skin—silky bare skin—but before he could get
a good grip, something toppled onto his head with a re-
sounding *thunk*. Stunned, he slackened his hold, and the
body slithered away and up.

"Tamara!"

Zane's roar would have scared a dead man out of his
grave, if the thunderous footsteps racing up the stairs
hadn't already accomplished just that.

Joe reached out and caught a piece of material as it
drifted over his arm. It snagged in his fist, then went loose
and empty.

"Goddammit." He struggled to his feet, his eyes searching—and a flashlight came on.

Joe found himself staring at a woman.

Small, blonde, wide-eyed and sweet.

Buck naked.

Well hell, talk about shattering a man's focus.

He couldn't hear over his madly drumming heartbeat. Was someone following, hands reaching out, ready to catch him even now, despite his rapid flight? Fear, disgust, was a bitter taste in his mouth, making his stomach churn. Puking was a very real possibility.

When he could run no more, his lungs burning, his heart straining, he slowed, labored for breath as his ears continued ringing. He ducked behind an old abandoned truck parked in an alley and waited. Silence. Nothing but dead silence, thank God. He shook all over.

She was supposed to be out! He'd heard her say so with his own two ears, so what was she doing at home?

It was a long minute before he accepted that he was truly safe yet again. His heart gradually slowed, but his thoughts churned. Holding his side, cramping, feeling the sweat on his face and back, he came out of his hiding place and began hobbling home, defeated, frustrated.

He was wrong, so wrong to do this to her. He knew it, accepted his guilt. But then, when in love, the heart and mind knew no conscience.

He would do what he had to do.

Tamara's teeth chattered, she was so afraid.

The flashlight's beam bounced wildly around the room when Zane shoved the tall, intimidating man staring at her. The man stumbled and went down on one knee, wincing in pain, but he still stared. Hard. Unrelenting. Of course she recognized him.

She didn't know what to do, how to help Zane. She clutched the journal, ready and more than willing to use it against the man's head if necessary. But then Zane stepped in front of her. She was in the shadows again.

"He's the man from the bus stop," she told Zane urgently, her breath catching in small gasps. She struggled to peek over his shoulder, to keep the man in her sights while Zane struggled to get the sheet around her and still hold the flashlight in one hand. She didn't want Zane to turn his back on the big bruiser. He was quiet now, but he had a gun, which he clutched in a large fist hanging loosely at his side. He looked more than capable of murder or any other number of misdeeds.

"Hold still, damn it."

Confusion closed in on her. Zane didn't act the least worried about the man—all his concentration was on covering her. Who cared if she was naked, if the man planned to shoot them anyway? And why did he just stand there, watching as Zane covered her?

When Zane was satisfied that she was decent, he turned and shone the light directly in the man's face.

He flinched away. "Hey, damn it, knock it off!"

At his gravelly tone, Tamara stepped forward to swing the book again, and to her surprise, though he was blinded by the light, the man caught the book in midair, wrapping the long fingers of his left hand around it and wrenching it away from her. She heard the aged fabric cover rip, saw a section of pages drop out.

She hastily backed up again, and scowled. "You're ruining my journal!"

"Lady, you're the one trying to bludgeon me with it!"

Zane smirked. "I see your reflexes are still good."

"Lucky for me, or she'd have knocked my damn brains out."

"Quit cursing." Zane now sounded more amused than annoyed.

"Go to hell. But first, tell me what's going on." His gaze, when it landed on Tamara, was flinty—but quickly softened. Speculation flared in his eyes, then interest. She squirmed.

Zane puffed up in renewed outrage. It was rather amazing to see, even in her state of confusion. "I swear to God, Joe, if you don't stop leering—"

The man shook his head. Tamara got a glimpse of a small gold hoop in his ear and longish, silky, blue-black hair that matched the beard shadow on his lean jaw.

"She was naked, Zane," he said in a dry voice. "Sorta took me by surprise, ya know?"

Zane took a threatening step forward, his arms rigid at his sides, and once again the flashlight beam scattered around the room.

Tamara jumped between the two men and jerked the light away from Zane. She wanted to know what was going on, not watch a display of testosterone one-upmanship. "I take it you know each other?"

Zane gestured vaguely. "He's my cousin, Joe Winston."

Suspicion rose in her, ugly and raw and mean. "Your cousin?"

Zane scowled. "Yeah."

"He followed me today," she informed him. "On the bus, when I went to the Realtor's."

A little surprised, Zane cocked a brow at Joe.

Joe shrugged. "She's good. I have no idea how she spotted me."

Every volatile emotion she'd just experienced—fear, panic, anger—coalesced into a fiery rage. She readied herself to blast Zane, to maybe get the journal back and use it on his head this time, when he whipped around to face her and growled, "Why didn't you tell me someone followed you?"

Indignation cut through her. She sputtered several seconds before spitting out, "Why didn't *you* tell *me*!"

He leaned into her fury, giving back his own. "I was trying to protect you! If you wouldn't keep shutting me out, maybe it wouldn't be necessary!"

She sputtered again. "I didn't ask you for protection!"

"I know. You won't ask me for anything except—"

Her hand slapped over his mouth. "Don't—you—dare."

Joe laughed as Zane caught her wrist and carried her hand to her side.

"You may not want my protection, but I'm giving it anyway. And God knows you need it." Using his hold on her wrist, he tugged her closer. "And didn't I tell you to stay in the bedroom?"

"Zane!" Did he have to outright announce their relationship that way?

Joe made a *tsk*ing sound. "Now, children. . . ."

Tamara reached for the battered journal, wanting to smack him a good one for scaring her so badly, and finding his unwanted audience a good enough reason.

Since Joe was so tall, about an inch above Zane, it was easy for him to hold it out of her reach. "Easy love. Before you start trying to scatter my brains again, do you think we could find some lights?"

Relenting went against the grain, but she saw no option. "I have candles."

"I don't think that's necessary." Zane flipped the flashlight around the room. "The downstairs is still locked."

"I know." Joe, too, looked around. "The fuse box?"

"That's what I assume. How else could he have gotten the whole house to go dark at one time?"

They both looked at Tamara, brows raised, expressions identical though their features were polar opposites.

She almost laughed. Zane stood there, tall, lean, beautifully masculine, a man who oozed charm and sex appeal through every pore, every breath. A man who made her want him just by being.

And next to him, Joe, who looked darker, meaner. She doubted his cousin even knew how to spell charm, much less employ it. He didn't ooze sex appeal—he shouted it. It fell off him in chunks.

"You two are pretty intimidating, you know that?" Then she poked Joe in the chest. "Only I don't intimidate that easily."

Zane slung an arm around her shoulder and hauled her close. "Now Tamara, don't abuse my cousin. As annoying as he is, he's trying to help."

"*Trying* to help?" Joe asked with mock offense. "I got here in time to scare off your intruder. I'd say that's a little more than trying, considering you don't look like either of you were prepared to do battle."

Zane, hair rumpled and eyes heavy, had on unbuttoned and unzipped slacks, riding low on his muscular hips. He was barefoot, bare-chested . . . her heart punched into her ribs. He looked *so* good. She squirmed beneath the sheet as her heart turned over and her toes curled.

Zane's muscled arm around her shoulders went taut. "You saw someone?"

"Ran off past your store, down the street. I could have given chase, but I didn't know if you'd need me in here."

"Damn, I understand and I appreciate the concern, but I wish you'd run the bastard to the ground."

"I'll get him next time."

Tamara slipped away from Zane—and was promptly hauled back. She nearly lost her sheet, which got Joe's attention and had Zane snarling again.

"Where's the damn fuse box?" he demanded.

"That's where I was going," she informed him with just as much heat, and again tried to move away.

"You'll go with me. We can't be sure that whoever did this is entirely gone."

"Your cousin said he saw him run away."

Joe cleared his throat. "Yeah, well, that doesn't mean there was only one guy."

Tamara felt no sense of intrusion, no sense of threat. Whoever had been there had left. But she merely shrugged. If it'd make Zane feel better to keep her close, she had no quarrel with that.

Using the flashlight and trailing her sheet, she led the way to the metal stairs. On the outside wall, to the left of the entry door, the fuse box stood open. The main breaker had been flipped.

Tamara clicked it over and the house buzzed to life. A glow poured from her bedroom window, adding shadows that hadn't been there before.

Joe and Zane stared at her, Joe in open-mouthed wonder, Zane in vexation. They presented a united front—against her.

Clutching the sheet a little more closely, she squared off with them. "What?"

"That's a damn stupid place for your fuse box."

Joe grinned. "I'd have put it more delicately than that, but he's right. At the very least, you should have a lock on it. Hell, anyone could come in here and—*omph!*"

Tamara didn't hang around to see if the big buffoon liked getting hit with the flashlight more than the journal. She doubted she'd hurt him, though. His abdomen was as hard as Zane's.

Marching in the door, she briefly considered slamming it behind her, and contented herself with stomping to her bedroom instead. "Insufferable, insulting. . . ."

Zane said into her ear, "Do you have to entertain every damn male relative I have?"

She yelped. She hadn't known he was following on her heels. Rounding on him, she thumped his bare chest with a fist. "Damn it, don't sneak up on me!"

"Quit stalking off, and I won't have to."

Tamara stopped at the bedroom door, gestured for him to precede her, then went in and slammed the door. She couldn't remember ever slamming a door before, but then, she'd never dealt with a hardheaded, autocratic male before either.

Jumping right into her grievances, she said, "I don't appreciate having a watchdog that I know nothing about. And I most definitely don't want you poking fun at me or insulting me in front of other people. And while we're on it, don't you ever run off in a dangerous situation and expect me to just cower behind."

Zane pulled her to her tiptoes and kissed her hard. "Joe stays until we figure out what's going on. If you don't like it, tough. I refuse to apologize for worrying about you." He kissed her again, this time sliding his tongue deep until she softened in his hold. He said against her lips, "I didn't mean to insult you, and for that I apologize. But if we're ever in another dangerous situation, you can damn well believe I'll tie your sweet little ass to the bed if that's what it takes to keep you safe."

His words were so low and seductive and filled with tenderness, it took Tamara a moment to absorb their meaning. When she did, she jerked away. She started to let loose on him—but the look on his face did her in. Damn, he looked so . . . affectionate. Perhaps people in a relationship always carried on that way. She just didn't know.

She swallowed hard, suddenly overcome by all that had happened. Her stomach pulled into a knot. "Someone," she whispered, "was trying to get in my house."

He nodded slowly. "With you home." His big hands smoothed up and down her back, comforting, protecting.

"I don't know what to do."

"Pack. You'll stay with me until we figure out what the hell is going on. With Joe on the case, it shouldn't be long. He's good at this kind of crap."

"I can't." Tamara knew what Zane's expression would be without looking at him. She stepped over to her dresser, dropped the sheet and found a pair of jeans. Forgoing underwear, she stepped into the soft denim and zipped up. A T-shirt was next, followed by a red pullover. She had no idea what she'd done with her shoes, but from beneath her bed, her slippers peeked out. She went to her knees to retrieve them.

When she straightened, her feet now resembling white bunnies, Zane crowded against her.

"You're coming home with me, Tamara."

Hoping to placate him, she put one hand on his naked chest. Warmth and security rose from his hard flesh—it'd be so easy to give in to him, to let him take care of her problems. But there were some facts she couldn't overlook. "Everything I own is here, Zane. Everything. I'm not leaving it. What if he comes back?"

"Exactly."

"No." She shook her head, not quite meeting his eyes. He wouldn't understand; his life was full in so many ways. Compared to him, her most valued possessions were few. "This is my life. I can't just abandon it to be ransacked."

His brows pinched together, warning of a full-blown rage. Tamara hugged herself to him.

"I've had a fire, Zane, a flood, snoops. Today, I realized someone had been going through my shelves. I have no idea why, what he was looking for, but a lot of things had been displaced. Someone got in here and rifled through my things." She shuddered. Saying it out loud made it somehow worse, more real. "I don't like this, Zane."

He hesitated, his body thrumming with near violence that she knew wasn't directed at her. "Why the hell didn't you tell me?"

"I was going to, but you distracted me with sex."

Something dangerous flashed in his eyes—possession, protectiveness—then his strong arms came around her and held her tight. "All right. If you won't come home with me, I'll stay here with you."

"You don't have to do that."

"I'm staying."

Iron laced his words, and she swallowed her sigh of relief. "Thank you."

Zane tipped up her chin. "Honey, no matter what your journal says, there's nothing wrong with leaning on me a little."

She worried her bottom lip between her teeth. "There's . . . there's a chapter on intimacy leading to more. I didn't want to do that. I didn't want to start something that you don't want to finish, and I *can't* finish."

"And why can't you?" He smoothed her hair, brushed her temple with his thumb, snugged her hips up to his, and wrapped her in his heat and scent and comfort.

She felt like a limp noodle, weak in body and mind. "I'm selling, remember?"

"And where will you go?"

A question she couldn't answer. God, would this night never end? "I don't know. We've worked the circus before, small fairs, places like that."

"The circus?"

He sounded appalled, forcing her to dredge up a smile of reassurance. "Every kid's dream, right?"

"Was it? Don't lie to me, sweetheart. Tell me the truth."

"The truth, huh?" The truth, in her opinion, was ugly. It wasn't something to be hashed over, but she could pick and choose her words. She shrugged, willing to share a little of the past life she'd never been suited to. "I hated constantly changing friends, forever attempting to build new relationships."

"So finally, you just gave up?"

"My aunts and uncle became my friends."

"It's not the same as kids around your own age."

"No. But you know what bothered me even more? In the circus, it's never quiet, and you're never alone, where you can just think. My parents loved that chaos, the continual excitement, and so did my aunts and uncle. But I used to dream of just being all alone, maybe sitting in a rowboat in the middle of a lake, or out in a field with only the bees buzzing."

He caressed her, his rough palms moving up and down her back. "Which is why you like living alone now?"

"Yes." Zane looked far too grim to suit her, and she attempted to lighten the mood. "Maybe I'll just relocate, start a smaller shop somewhere else."

His dark eyes were so intent, so probing, she felt more naked than she had before getting dressed. He touched her face, his fingertips gliding over her chin, her nose, smoothing out her puckered brow.

"If Joe finds out who's doing this, you wouldn't have to sell, would you?"

Confiding in anyone, leaning on anyone, was as uncomfortable as a toothache. Because of the way she'd grown up, she'd never done it, didn't know how, and could already tell she wasn't going to like it. But Zane was a mix of tumultuous emotions, cresting against her reserve like a continual wave, wearing her down, smoothing away her worries. He was aroused—but he was always aroused whenever they were alone together. She was getting used to that—or, rather, accepting it. He was also tenderly concerned, openly caring. He wanted her, not just for sex, she realized, but for more.

She shook her head, unwilling to start an internal debate on that subject. What he wanted, how much he wanted, would remain a mystery until he told her outright. It was too important for her to play guessing games. She could sense his feelings, but she wasn't a mind reader who could dissect his every thought with accuracy.

"I lost a lot of money," she said wearily. "The shop does fine, but not when there are a lot of unexpected expenses. It . . . put me behind. Recovering enough financially to stay here would be difficult."

"Do you have some upkeep for your relatives?"

"Not a whole lot." She felt protective of them. They never asked for much, and after all they'd given her, she didn't mind helping them now that they were older. "Because their house is already paid for, their expenses are minimal."

Turning away, Zane picked up one of the software manuals on her desk. He flipped through a stack of notes there, picked up and examined a disk. "And what is all this?"

She flushed. What she did outside of being a Gypsy was just so . . . personal. Stiffening her spine, ready to accept any jokes he might feel compelled to make, she said, "Strange as it may seem, I'm a technical writer."

He glanced at her over his shoulder, his gaze full of censure. "Not strange, honey, so don't put words in my mouth." Laying the manual aside, he crossed his arms and rested against the edge of the desk. "I just want to know more about you, about your situation."

"You don't think it's funny, the contrast in the two professions?"

"You're a jumble of contrasts, so it makes sense that you'd seek other outlets." His voice gentled. "You're a complex woman, Tamara Tremayne, and I find I like discovering all the different angles."

She sucked in some necessary oxygen for her laboring lungs and deprived brain. The emotions he felt now were layered and varied and too entwined for her to even begin to sort them out. They mixed with her own emotions, until she felt light-headed.

"Is it hard work?"

Her heart raced at the sincerity of his question. She loved her computer work, but it wasn't something she'd ever been able to share with anyone.

A burst of light, like a ray of sunshine, cut through everything else, warming her, filling her up. She smiled, this time a natural smile. "It seems I have a knack for making the complicated sound simple." It was a boastful statement, but with Zane, she felt free to lose her modesty. She knew he wouldn't mind and that, in fact, he'd expect no less.

"I work with a software company on getting instructions down in a user-friendly way. Our work mode varies, but generally I sit with the programmer and get trained how to use the software. I document the smallest details, then organize everything and write a manual on how to use it."

"This is added income?"

"Yes." She could tell he'd misread the particulars, and her smile widened. "I'm not working in the coal mines, Zane."

"No, but I've seen your light on late into the night, and now I know why. The job you have is already full-time. You haven't left yourself much time for you."

The irony of his statement amused her. "Gee, how is it

you've seen my light on, unless you were just leaving your job, too?"

"One job, Tamara. Not two."

"The technical writing is something I enjoy." How to explain it, she wondered. And how much should she explain? "It's . . . serendipitous."

His gaze softened, his shoulders softened. A small, understanding smile turned up the corners of his sensuous mouth. "Part of that 'normal lifestyle' you were talking about earlier?"

"Yes."

Zane watched her a moment more, then started to close his slacks. "We've got a lot to discuss. And if I know Joe, he's probably out there snooping around right now."

Startled, Tamara's brows shot up. "Snooping? In my house?"

"Yeah." Zane shrugged. "It's sort of what he does now."

She barely heard him, having already turned away. Long, anxious strides carried her out the bedroom door and down the hallway. But Joe Winston wasn't snooping. Nope. His big body was lounged out on her sofa, long legs in disreputable tattered jeans stretched out in front of him. He was engrossed in the journal.

A pair of black-framed reading glasses perched on the end of his slightly crooked nose, looking horribly out of place against his rugged and whiskery face. His golden earring glinted under the soft light of the end table lamp. His chiseled mouth was pursed in contemplation.

On the seat next to him, the pages that had gotten torn from the book when she'd hit him with it, had been smoothed out flat.

Without looking up to acknowledge her presence, he muttered, "I never figured Zane for the type to need instructions," then he turned another page.

Heat rushed into her cheeks. Behind her, Zane threatened Joe in the most lurid way imaginable.

Joe glanced up, unconcerned with Zane's ire. "A lot of

it is hogwash, but you know, some of it is right on target."

Zane took two long steps forward and snatched the book from his cousin's hand. "I sure as hell don't need you to clarify for me."

"Well, not after reading that book, anyway." Joe calmly folded his glasses and slipped them into his jacket pocket.

Tamara hid a smile. Zane's cousin epitomized outrageousness, possibly even more so than Zane. No woman could take him seriously.

"We weren't using the book as a guide," she said.

"No?" Joe stood, his gaze piercing Tamara, holding her to the spot. "Well, if it's just an experiment, count me in, love."

Zane grabbed him by the front of his shirt and twisted. "I'll count you out if you don't leave her the hell alone."

"Zane!" Alarmed, Tamara stepped between them. "What's the matter with you?"

With a shove, Zane released Joe. "He's coming on to you, right in front of me."

Even during Zane's attack, Joe hadn't looked away from Tamara, and now humor lit his dark blue, heavily fringed eyes. "He's jealous, sweetheart, anyone can see that. Seems Zane has a possessive streak, at least where you're concerned. I don't remember him getting his shorts in a bunch over any other woman."

Heart racing, Tamara dared a quick look at Zane. She expected immediate denials, a resurgence of his anger, something volatile.

He surprised her. No longer rigid, a mocking cynicism lit his eyes and a smirk made his sexy mouth go crooked. "Let me guess. This your way of helping out, Joe?"

Joe shrugged. "Just call me your guardian angel. Left to your own devices, I was afraid she'd throw your sorry ass out."

"He's staying here tonight," Tamara announced. She was uncertain what the two of them were prattling on about, but she felt it necessary to defend Zane just the same.

"Not smart," Joe said immediately.

"She refuses to come home with me." Zane caught her hand and pulled her to his side. "She doesn't want to leave the house unprotected. I can understand that."

"Ah." Joe tipped his head at Tamara and said with a shrug of acceptance, "Then I suppose it makes sense after all. Zane definitely shouldn't leave you here alone. But," he added, "we'll have to set up a few safeguards first."

"Tonight, and more tomorrow."

"That's what I was thinking."

Tamara leveled a look on both men. "You're thinking without my input, and I won't have it."

Joe laughed, and she had the suspicion it was at her expense. "I should get out of here and let you both get to sleep." His gaze warmed. "You have to be exhausted."

"Joe . . ."

"I gather there's no point calling the police."

Zane again looked ready to brawl, but he subsided. "I'm calling them. I just don't think they'll do anything."

"Any idea who might be behind this?"

"An idea, yeah. It'd have to be someone with access to a key, someone with a motive."

"Someone you already don't like?"

"That's right. But my not liking him is incidental to the facts."

Joe pondered the possibility. "The bad guys don't always look bad or act bad, you know. Don't get it set in your head or you're liable to miss other more likely possibilities."

Zane nodded. Standing beside him, Tamara bristled. "You have about two seconds, Zane Winston, to tell me who you think tried to break in here."

His grin wasn't at all nice this time. It was predatory. "He wanted to see you, and you turned him down. He knows your relatives—"

Tamara picked up on his train of thought. "And my

family has keys for emergency use. He could have gotten one from them without them knowing."

Their gazes locked, and they said together, "Boris Sandor."

Sixteen

Zane held the tattered journal against his bent knee. Next to him, Tamara stirred just a little. He soothed her with a hand on her hip, stroking slow and easy. He loved the feel of her, both under his hand and beside him in bed. Warm and sleep-heavy, she sighed.

The chapters on sexual satisfaction had been incredible. They'd gone through most of them last night when Zane realized Tamara was too upset to sleep. Joe had promised to hang around outside until sunup, even though they were both relatively certain their visitor wouldn't be back that night. Tamara had seemed stunned by such an offer, but Joe assured her that surveillance was nothing new to him.

The police, as Zane had suspected, could do no more than make out a report and promise to drive by occasionally. Since Joe was already there, the offer was unnecessary.

Zane smiled now, reluctantly admitting to himself that Joe had been the hero of the night. If it hadn't been for him, the intruder might have been the one to stumble onto Tamara naked. The thought made Zane shudder. Deep down, he trusted Joe implicitly, or he'd never have asked him for help. If it had been a stranger ogling her, he'd have been tempted to kill the man.

He supposed he'd have to thank his cousin. Zane grinned as he imagined Joe's reaction to sincere gratitude. Coming from Zane, it was liable to give Joe a heart attack.

Zane chuckled softly, looking over at Tamara's tousled hair and slightly parted lips. In a very short time, she'd become so special to him, so precious.

As per the damn book's instruction, she would accept sexual satisfaction from him. Accept, demand, revel in. In all his mature years, he'd never met a woman who more equally balanced his sexual drive, taking and giving. During the night, he'd suggested things in a heated whisper, and she'd accepted openly, hungrily, drowning in anything and everything he wanted to do.

His body reacted now to the memory, and that was nothing short of a miracle. He'd let her drift off to sleep only a few hours ago. He should have been dead to the world, carnal activity beyond him, for at least a day. Possibly two. But just feeling the heat of her next to him, hearing her soft breathing, made his sex stir in anticipation.

He wanted her again.

He wanted her always.

Zane turned another page and skimmed the text. This was the part of the book Tamara hadn't bothered to share with him. It detailed ways to make your lover fall in love. But she didn't want love from him. She'd asked him for sex, and like the most noble of negotiators, she refused to try to take more.

Tough.

Zane had never needed much sleep, usually five hours tops, but now he was nearing exhaustion. Still, he didn't want to sleep, didn't want to waste a single second of this opportunity. Getting Tamara to lean on him, to trust him and accept him in every way, wasn't going to be easy. Because, he realized, she didn't know how.

She knew how to stand on her own, how to take care

of others and get through life any way she could, but she didn't know how to ask for help, or how to accept it, because she'd never been given the opportunity to learn.

He discounted what her relatives had done for her as a child. Of course they'd taken her in; she was family and that's what family did. He'd bend over backward and walk on his hands for his brothers if that's what they needed from him. And now, by association, his brother's wives and children had the same loyalty. *That* was life, that was the course you took when you had family. There wasn't a single doubt in his mind that any of his brothers would do the same for him.

Which reminded him. Joe now had an inkling of what Tamara meant to him, but he should clear it up with Cole, Chase, and Mack, too. Just on the off chance something happened to him, he wanted her taken care of. He didn't want her to have to sell and start over. He didn't want her to be on her own, ever again.

Share your fears, your dreams, your hopes for the future.

The journal held a lot of insight, not only on sexual satisfaction, but also on falling in love. After reading it, Zane felt he knew the woman who'd written it. Her loneliness and her determination were there on the page, seeping through the words, sharing personal things if only someone cared to see them. Things Tamara could relate to because she was alone and lonely as well.

His heart ached.

He'd never said those three incredible little words that could change a man's life. Now they burned in his throat, wanting out. But Tamara wasn't ready for that. He needed to woo her, he decided with a smile. He needed to follow the instructions of the manual and share his heart bit by bit, before making it an offering.

All his ruminations had brought his mind and body into agreement. He did indeed need Tamara again. Was she sore? She sure as hell hadn't complained last night, and he knew she could use the sleep now. But the combination

of love burning behind his eyes and in his heart, joined
with the slower, hotter pulse of desire, had his hands shaking.

He'd never been in love and he wanted, needed, some
form of confirmation from her, even if only physical.

With infinite care, he eased the sheet off her body.

Being accommodating, she turned to her back, put one
arm over her head, and snuggled her sweet bottom into
the mattress. Looking at her brought all the swirling emotions and sensations together into a razor-sharp point.

His hand on her pale, slender thigh, urging her legs
wide, looked dark and rough. The contrast maddened him,
made it hard to breathe.

Her scent clung to the sheets, to him, to the cool morning air around them. Drifting his long fingers through her
crisp pubic curls, he watched her body shift, awaken. Her
belly sucked in a little, and he had to kiss her there, had
to dip his tongue into her cute little navel.

Her hand settled in his hair, and in a sleep-foggy voice
she said, "Zane."

There was satisfaction in her tone and he chose to think
affection as well.

"I missed you," he whispered, kissing his way up her
torso, nibbling on her hips, each rib, until she squirmed
and he could hear the growing excitement in her sigh.

She twisted to see the bedside clock. "It's been only a
few hours since you . . ."

Her voice trailed off, delighting him with her continued
reserve when she opened her body so completely to him.
"Since I loved you silly?" he asked, and kissed the small
vertical worry lines between her slim brows. "I love loving you."

Her frown deepened. Zane hid his grin, knowing he'd
confused her, that she was unsure how to take him or the
words he'd slipped in. *Sate yourself*, the journal said, *on
the pleasure you give your lover*. Wise words from an
obviously wise, caring woman. He intended to follow the
instructions to the letter, and all the while he'd talk to her,

tell her things that she'd be unable to respond to.

Light as a breeze, his fingers continued to tease over her, dipping every so often through her curls to touch warm, moist flesh. Teasing. Tempting her into that whirlwind of carnality.

"You are so soft."

"You're not," she said, and reached down to circle her hand around his throbbing cock where it pressed into her thigh.

Zane let her hold him, squeeze him; God, he loved her touch. He loved her frowns and her independence and her vulnerability. He loved everything about her.

Her breath caught, then her gaze skittered to the journal, open on the bedside table. "You've been . . . reading?"

Uncertainty warred with her growing pleasure. He could see it in her beautiful green eyes. "You read it," he explained, "and I wanted to know what you'd found there."

Balanced on his side, he put his right leg over hers and pinned her down, keeping her legs open. She was wet now, her tender vulva swelling, readying for him. Slowly, with infinite care because he knew he'd been excessive through the night, he pushed his middle finger into her.

Her back arched and a small catch in her breath thrilled him. "Does that feel good, sweetheart?"

"Yes."

"You're not too raw?" He worked his finger in and out, pressing deep so that his knuckles rubbed against her distended clitoris, then withdrawing to tease the soft swollen lips, before pressing in again.

She tangled her fingers in his hair. "Kiss me."

He withdrew again, readjusted his hand, and caught her small clitoris with his fingertips. He tugged very lightly. "Here?"

"Zane!" Her thighs opened more, struggled against the restraint of his.

"Or here?" He leaned down and licked one begging

nipple. His tongue swirled around and around until he heard her long, broken moan. "Like this?" He sucked her deep.

Her body twisted, writhed against the sheets. The pleasure would be sharp, he knew, after all the loving they'd done. She was ultrasensitive, and her body quaked, trembled. "I can't," she cried, pressing her hips into the mattress, trying to pull away.

"Shhh," he said against her breast. "My tongue is softer. It'll be easier for you."

"No. . . ."

He wasn't sure what she protested, the pleasure he'd give her, the use of his mouth, or her own wavering uncertainty.

Zane sat up and threw the sheets completely from the bed. Tamara's body, flushed and taut, stretched out like a sacrifice before him. He wanted to devour her until she screamed his name and said those three words he felt bound to hold inside.

Kneeling between her thighs, he caught her breasts in his hands and roughly caressed them. "You have the most delectable body I've ever seen, Tamara."

Neck arched, eyes closed, she whispered, "Yes."

She wasn't even aware of what she said, he realized, pleased with the results he'd gained. He thumbed her nipples and watched her strain for more. Her breasts flushed, swelled in his hands.

"So sweet," he whispered, and bent to take her into his mouth again. She lifted, the open juncture of her thighs pressing into his abdomen, warm, silky wet, making him insane. He drew on her nipple while he caught her thighs and held them. It would be so easy to slide into her now. It wouldn't take more than six hard, fast pumps to put him into nirvana.

He wanted more.

Blindly groping across the head of the bed, Zane found his pillow and snagged it with a fist. He lifted away from her delicious breasts, leaving her nipples darkened, glistening wet. He caught her slim hips and lifted, pressing the pillow beneath her, making an offering of her lush heated sex. Moisture gathered in his mouth as he looked at her, hungry for the taste of her, for her pleasure.

He traced the delicate pink flesh with one fingertip, his chest working like a bellows, never able to get enough air. "Open your legs wider for me, sweetheart."

She moaned softly, squirmed, fisted her hands in the sheet next to her hips.

"Do it, Tamara."

"It's too much."

"And not enough. I know. Do it."

Tentatively, in small degrees, her legs spread open. Zane stared at her lovely face, eyes squeezed shut, teeth sunk into her bottom lip. The hair at her temples was damp with sweat.

God, he loved waking her like this.

"Wider," he ordered and saw her mouth open on a groan. Her thighs quivered, stretched wide.

"Yes." He lowered his head and took one long, leisurely lick, swirling around her clitoris so that her hips left the cushioning pillow and she cried out.

He did it again, and again, teasing her, giving her just a little, but not enough. Anchoring her in place, he kept her legs spread with his hands tight on her upper thighs. On the sixth lick he lingered, suckled, and she screamed out her climax, making him shudder with the pleasure of it.

She felt boneless, her limbs limp, her body dewy. He rested his head on her thigh and continued to toy with her—light, gentle touches that kept her aroused but didn't cause discomfort to her sensitized nerve endings.

After a while her long, deep breaths began to quicken once more. Satisfied, Zane turned his head, seeking her again with his mouth. This time he was gentler, slower, nuzzling into her, nibbling, until her long ragged groan, hoarse with nearly painful pleasure, split the quiet morning.

He blew on her, cooling her, teasing again. Moving up her body, he kissed her lax mouth, smiling against her lips. "You're incredible."

No response. But that didn't bother him. He rolled to his back and pulled her atop him, letting her body drape over his chest and hips like a blanket. He spread her thighs in one smooth movement and pushed his erection into her wet heat. She was so wet, she accepted him easily, and he was content to simply hold her like that for a time, connected physically in all ways.

The journal had emphasized the importance of holding. He'd never had a predilection for difficult women, but he wanted this difficult woman to love him. He wanted her to feel everything he felt, and hoped she understood it when she did.

Sexual tension vibrated in his every pore, but a lot of the urgency he'd felt earlier, prompted by a need to claim her, had diminished. She was his; he'd made up his mind and now he just wanted to enjoy her in every way he could think of.

She mumbled into his chest, her heated breath a taunt on his skin, "You're not wearing a condom."

Zane kissed the top of her head. Because he loved her, he wanted to give her choices. Now wasn't really fair because she was literally spent, limp as a drugged fish, but fairness seldom came into play when you were in love. His reasoning sounded weak even to his own mind, but he didn't give a damn.

"I want to feel you, and just you," he explained. Still, he asked, "Do you care?"

She hesitated, and he held his breath. Her soft hair tickled his chin, her heartbeat thumped in time to his own. Her body welcomed him, holding him snug in slippery wetness and sizzling heat.

"No."

That one simple word broke his control. It said and meant so much, more than he'd dared to hope for so soon.

He cupped her bottom, held her steady while he began to thrust.

Tamara struggled to sit up, inadvertently deepening his penetration. They both groaned. He felt her womb, felt all of her. She braced her small hands on his chest and like a siren, whispered, "Let me."

Keeping still was about the hardest thing he'd ever done. Her every movement enflamed him, the way she shook her fair hair over her shoulders, arched her neck, pushed her breasts forward.

With concentrated deliberation, Zane forced his fingers to unclench on her hips and raised them to her breasts. He cuddled them, stroked her nipples as she lifted, fell, lifted, fell. Her movements were unpracticed, but enthusiastic.

"Roll your hips," he told her in a rasp, knowing it would increase her pleasure.

"Like this?"

It was his turn to arch, and they both moaned at how deeply he entered her.

Her thighs strained, the sleek muscles pulled taut. She clasped him, her sex pulling at him like a voracious mouth. He fought hard not to come yet, to hold off until she'd taken her own orgasm one more time.

"I don't believe this," she whispered a few minutes later when he felt her tightening around him, milking him.

He clenched his teeth to keep words of love unsaid. Watching her, seeing her beautiful face twisted and real with the savage pleasure of their lovemaking, was a gift he'd never forget.

She cried when the last spasms had left her, and Zane turned her beneath him, licking at her tears and driving into her hard and deep and rough, once, twice . . . He threw his head back and shouted as he came.

Tamara managed to get one arm around him when he fell heavily atop her. They were both sweaty, heat pouring off their bodies, adhering them together. She made a sound, like wonder or disbelief or . . . *love*.

God, let it be the start of love.

Puckering required more dexterity than he could summon, but he moved his lips against her neck, the only reply he could muster.

He was just thinking life couldn't get any better when a fist rattled the bedroom door and Thanos's voice rang out, imperative and angry.

"Tamara! Are you all right? Answer me, damn it."

"No," Zane mumbled, unable to reconcile his sluggish brain and depleted body to the fact of intrusive relatives right now, at this precise moment. Relatives he hadn't heard enter the house. Relatives who were loony, and apparently angry to boot. "No, no."

The small, warm body cushioning his stiffened alarmingly.

"They not only have a key," Zane managed to mumble, "but they use it?"

Taking him and his debilitated body by surprise, Tamara became a small whirlwind and threw him off. He almost slid over the side of the wrecked mattress to the floor. He was just stabilizing himself when a naked thigh came over his head and Tamara scrambled to her feet.

"Just a minute, Uncle!"

Zane reached for her wrist and missed. Seconds later his slacks hit him in the face. "Get dressed," she hissed, then scurried around the room grabbing for clothes. Her movements were awkward and jerky, but then, she'd just come several times. He was shaky, and he hadn't lost his senses nearly as often as she had.

Feeling very put upon, Zane dragged himself to a sitting position on the side of the bed. His knees were rickety, damn it. "What are they doing here?"

Tamara's face was pale, her eyes filled with mortification. "They come every Sunday."

"And you forgot to tell me this?"

She fried him with an evil glare. "You distracted me."

From the other side of the door, Thanos said, "I can hear every word."

"Go away!" Tamara wailed, her face bright red.

Incredulous, Zane stood, waited to see if he'd fall flat on his face, and when his legs didn't give out, he pulled on his slacks.

Thanos's booming laugh reached them. "I'll be in the kitchen with the others. I gather you could use some coffee. Don't dally or I'll be back."

Yanking a shirt over her head, Tamara ordered, "Hurry. Finish dressing."

"Tamara." Zane caught her and held her still when she struggled. "Honey, I know this is a little embarrassing—"

"Ha!"

"—but you're a grown woman and this is your house. You don't have to explain anything to anyone."

A look of absolute incredulity crossed her face. "Explain? I think they understand already!" She paused, looked at his chest, and touched a small bite mark over his pectoral muscle. She remarked in distressed tones, "A shirt. You definitely have to put on your shirt. And shoes, too. I don't want my aunts eyeing your naked feet."

"Who gives a damn about my naked feet?"

"I do!" She tugged on the same jeans she'd worn the night before, glanced in the mirror, and hastily finger-combed her hair. "This is just awful."

"Well." Zane sat on the edge of the mattress to don socks and shoes. God forbid he should flaunt his damn feet. "That's a great way to lacerate a guy's ego."

She looked harassed. "I don't mean *you*. I mean *this*— getting caught, facing nosy relatives." She paused to say with heartfelt sincerity, "You were . . . indescribable."

Still without his shirt, Zane stood and folded her close. "Shh. They'll hear you." But he was grinning and couldn't seem to stop.

She covered her face and dropped into his embrace. "I can't believe I forgot about them. I can't believe we didn't *hear* them. They always knock first. Who knows what they thought when I didn't answer."

"We know what they're thinking now, that's for sure."

He slid his hand beneath her tangled hair and clasped her nape. "But don't worry about it. We have plenty to distract them with this morning."

She groaned as a new reality intruded. "Last night is almost a blur. Do you realize whoever broke in could have come back today and we wouldn't have noticed?"

"Which is why," Zane told her, seeing the perfect opening, "you're not going to argue with me when I have an alarm system installed to cover the doors and windows."

"No, I don't—"

"I know. You don't need or want my help." He pressed his thumb over her lips, and when that didn't appease him, he replaced his thumb with his mouth. This kiss was filled with the love he not only accepted, but relished.

She inspected his face, and Zane wondered how much of what he felt was apparent to her. How much of it could she perceive? When her gaze softened, he assumed she was aware of at least some of the emotional depth she'd taken him to.

"You make me feel like a high schooler on prom night, Tamara, waiting to see if I'll be asked to dance. I don't like it."

"Oh Zane." Her tone was apologetic, concerned, as it always was when she feared she might have hurt him somehow. "I don't want to make you feel bad."

"That's a start, sweetheart." He kissed her again and then set her away from him. "I want you protected, so I'm taking care of an alarm. It doesn't ingratiate you to me in any way. It doesn't tax me financially and you don't owe me anything in return."

"Zane. . . ."

"And it means nothing more than that I care. Because you sense my emotions, you surely already know that, right?"

It was an admission, plain and simple, but not one that would threaten her independent nature.

Green eyes dark and intense, she nodded slowly.

Relief flooded through him in near painful pleasure.

"Excellent." He touched her cheek. "I want to do what I can to see that you're safe when I'm not with you. Okay?"

Every line of her petite body bespoke exasperation and uncertainty. "How am I supposed to respond to that?"

Zane caught her face in his hands and said with as much seriousness as he could muster when his body was so sated and his heart so full, "I know you don't have much practice at this, but you could just say 'thank you.'"

She worried her bottom lip between her teeth. "But. . . ."

"No buts, sweetheart. No doubts. You either trust me or you don't." He added, unable to stop himself, "Trust me, Tamara."

She sighed. "You keep saying that, though what it has to do with trust, I don't know."

"It has everything to do with trust."

As if pondering world peace, she considered what he said. Zane thought she took far more time than the situation, or the proposition, warranted. It was her uncle bellowing down the hallway that the coffee was ready that helped her make up her mind.

In a rush, she said, "Okay," and almost as an afterthought, "Thank you."

She started out of the bedroom in a rush. Zane caught her, pulled her back, and stuck the cell phone in her pocket. "You're to carry it on you at all times, remember?"

Tamara rolled her eyes and took off again—the phone with her.

Loving an independent, headstrong Gypsy with meddlesome, wacky relatives wasn't going to be easy.

But not loving her was the impossible alternative, so like each of his brothers before him, Zane smiled as he accepted his fate.

The Winston curse had struck again.

Seventeen

Tamara prepared herself as best she could to face her aunts and uncle. It wasn't easy, being so distracted. Zane cared. Not just about the wonderful physical relationship they'd started, but about her, as a person. His affection washed over her like a soothing hand, giving immeasurable comfort, unqualified support. She'd never experienced anything like it before.

It was both pleasurable and frightening.

She hated being vulnerable, like a small child once more, unsure where she would go or what she would do after her parents' death. The thought of moving again was bad enough, but at least that was her decision, a way of maintaining financial security rather than sitting around and waiting to lose her shop.

Above all, she needed to be in charge, even in failure.

Zane's attention kept her utterly out of control, with her mind, her body, her emotions.

Her heart.

She knew how to handle most situations—by pushing forward with sheer strength of will and stubborn determination. She'd learned to do that as a means of survival, even before her parents had passed away. Her relatives were on the money when they called her a white sheep. Compared to them, she was so sedate, she bordered on dull. To them, she *was* dull.

What they found exciting and carefree, she found intimidating and unstable. She wasn't meant to be a Gypsy, at least not the mobile kind. She wanted to keep her stationary life. She wanted to keep her shop.

She wanted to keep Zane. *Damn.*

Ignoring the aching in her heart, she plastered a serene smile on her face and stiffened her backbone, primed to face her aunts and uncle and all their speculation.

No way was she prepared for the guest they'd brought along.

She stopped dead in her tracks when she saw the man sitting at her small kitchen table, sipping coffee with elegant grace.

Zane, following close on her heels, ran into her. He grabbed her shoulders to steady them both. Tamara accepted his heat, his strength at her back.

They were both frozen for a mere heartbeat before her temper detonated and she lurched forward.

"You!" Ready to commit murder, to gain retribution for the night's fright and the other deeds that had cost her so much, Tamara reached for Boris. Her fingers caught air and she drew up short when Zane snagged the back of her jeans.

Sublime confusion on his aristocratic face, Boris Sandor observed her with one raised, sardonic brow. "Excuse me?"

"What the hell are you doing in my house?" she roared. Her vibrating anger was slightly diffused by the fact Zane had her up on her tiptoes, his hold on her waistband unrelenting.

"Calm down, Tamara," he told her in a nearly bored voice that only she realized was laced with real menace. Oh, he was furious all right, but he was also more collected. That only annoyed her further.

"Let me go," she said to him.

"Will you control your volatile tendencies?"

It was there in his voice; he wouldn't let her go unless she could restrain herself. Though she knew he was right, it galled her. "For now."

He acknowledged her concession with a smile. "Just keep in mind, sweetheart, that I'd hate to have to kill him with your relatives looking on."

The relatives gaped at each other in fascinated awe. She was used to Zane now, but they certainly weren't.

He continued, saying, "Better not to provoke him until we've had a chance to talk."

That made sense, damn him. They did need to understand the motives behind the break-ins. And she didn't want Zane killing anyone, especially not for her.

Her aunts kept giving her horrified looks, and her uncle had risen from the table, alerted by her fury.

Thanos's bushy beard quivered as he demanded, "What is it, little one?"

Glaring at the intruder, Tamara asked, "Why is he here?"

Boris Sandor slowly came to his feet. He was immaculately dressed in gray trousers, a dark blue sweater over a silk shirt, and polished shoes.

The contrast to the rest of them was striking. Her aunts wore loose, colorful dresses layered by either a shawl or a home-knit sweater, and Thanos was in brown jeans and a flannel with rainbow striped suspenders. Behind her, Zane's hastily buttoned shirt hung loose from his waistband and had wrinkles from a night on the floor. Her own clothes were rumpled and slightly askew.

Boris Sandor's annoyance slapped against her. Once again, she was surprised by the depth to which she experienced him. It made her feel queasy.

"Ms. Tremayne?" Vague distaste threaded through his icy politeness. His gaze encompassed her from ears to toes and back again. "My God, is that truly you?"

Both her aunts jumped in to explain, anxious for a new

tack to take, other than her embarrassing outrage.

"She's forgotten her wig."

"She seldom looks so . . . rumpled."

"Apparently we've interrupted"—Olga shrugged help-lessly—"something."

The scattered statements ended with more wide-eyed conjecture. Their confusion was apparent, as was their cu-riosity.

The emotions in the room were high; Boris's ugly con-templation, her aunts' and uncle's confusion, speculation. And Zane's barely leashed anger. Her head throbbed. She wasn't used to feeling so many people at one time. She felt overloaded, weighed down.

The only way she could think to get through this was to take charge.

She cleared her throat, thrust up her chin, and avoided her aunts' gazes by staring at Boris. "Yes, you've inter-rupted. But that doesn't tell me why the hell you're here."

"Tamara," her uncle growled. "I'd like you to explain your behavior."

She felt heat flare in her cheeks, and the touch of Zane's body on her back. Her chin went up another inch. "You knew I wanted him."

Mouths dropped open, eyes widened. Boris made a sound of derision.

On a choked laugh, Zane said, "I think he means your temper, sweetheart, and your reaction to your . . . guest."

Embarrassment was lost beneath invective. Oh, she could tell them why she objected to Boris!

Aunt Olga beat her to the punch.

"My word," she exclaimed, "she's been debauched."

Eva clasped her hands to her generous bosom. Even with the start of cataracts, her black eyes were piercing and bright. "You think?" Then to Olga, "She's showing signs of the Tremayne passion."

Olga, who also looked dumbstruck, yet thrilled, cried, "But it's for the wrong man! It was supposed to be Boris."

"What?" Tamara couldn't quite believe her aunts' au-

dacity. It was obvious to one and all what they had blundered into that morning, and they persisted in the delusion she might be interested in Boris? Forget that they didn't know he was a criminal of the meanest sort, ruining her business for heaven only knew what reason. Forget that she barely knew the man.

Zane, tall and proud and gorgeous beyond compare, stood directly behind her. His large hands were on her shoulders in a proprietary display, a display she in no way objected to. She leaned into him.

They could *see* him.

Surely they didn't for a single moment think she'd trade down for Boris? The mere thought had her curling her lip.

Boris cleared his throat. "Perhaps this isn't the most auspicious time for me to call."

Zane's fingers tightened. "For what you have in mind, Sandor, there won't be a better time."

Olga stepped forward. "Don't be so hasty, young man. It's good for a woman to have suitors scrap over her. And Boris is better suited for what we have in mind."

Tamara gasped. "For what *you* have in mind?"

Thanos tugged at his ear. "He's wealthy, little one, and influential. There's a lot he could do to help us, and he understands our people."

"I'm from the homeland," Boris reminded them.

Tamara felt the throbbing waves of Zane's anger, but could think of no way to reassure him. She said with dripping disdain, "Since when do we need anyone's help or influence? I can handle my problems on my own."

Zane's hands moved from her shoulders to lightly encircle her throat, as a gentle reminder that *he* would help.

She absently patted his hand to let him know she accepted him, then continued. "And you say he understands our people? Then he's one up on me, because I sure as hell don't."

Horrified, Olga turned to Boris and patted his shoulder.

"She's a white sheep, never quite getting into the swing of things, if you know what I mean."

Eva added, as if it were a sin, "She's . . . steadfast."

With courtly condescension, Boris murmured, "I do understand." His gaze was hungry as he scrutinized Tamara.

Tamara wanted to distance herself from the physical interest she sensed in Boris, which conflicted with his emotional disdain. He didn't like her, but he wanted her.

She stepped back, and found herself encompassed by Zane. There was no reason for her to cower, no reason for her to let Boris frighten her. She was here, as Zane had said, in her own home. She wouldn't tolerate Boris's haughty imposition.

"I was born and raised in America," she said. "Only my most distant relatives were foreigners. Your claims don't mean a thing to me, Boris."

Dismay had her aunts fretting and Thanos shaking his head. Tamara decided to get it all on the table. "Besides," she sneered, "I don't associate with disreputable scoundrels."

A collective gasp stirred the air.

Zane's gaze first met with Tamara's, then swept the room to include each of her relatives in his disclosure. "He's the one who's been harassing Tamara, breaking into her shop, setting fires and causing the plumbing to flood. He's the one forcing you all to move."

Boris slammed both hands down on her table. His face turned a mottled red and his eyes bulged. "How dare you! I've done no such thing and I refuse to stand here and be besmirched by the likes of you."

Zane merely grinned at Boris's contempt. "Can you prove it wasn't you?"

Thanos crossed his massive arms over his chest. "I can see you care for her, Zane, but wild accusations won't win her over."

"This isn't a contest, damn it, and she isn't a prize."

Tamara's nerve endings tingled with Zane's outpouring of annoyance. *On her behalf.* She had to think of a way to defuse the situation. It would break her heart if her beloved uncle and Zane got into a fight.

Thanos said, "No? Then what is this all about?"

"He wouldn't understand," Boris sneered. "Loyalty to family is obviously beyond him."

Tamara sucked in a startled breath. Oh no. She knew, even if Boris didn't, that he'd just crossed the line.

With eerie calm, Zane set Tamara to the side of him and took two measured steps toward Boris. "I don't know what you're up to, but you can forget it right now. She's not alone anymore."

Olga took exception to that. "She's never been alone. She's been with us."

Anger swirled around Zane as he turned to her aunt. He was polite, even gentle when he spoke, but Tamara knew the turmoil he contained.

"No? What has she gotten from you? Complete acceptance for the woman she is? Or a lot of pressure to be what she isn't?"

Olga and Eva glanced warily at one another.

"Have you given her unwavering support?" Zane demanded. "Have you tried to understand her and her needs? Or have you forced her into a mold that best served you?"

"Zane," Tamara whispered uncertainly.

"She's a Tremayne." Eva made that statement as if it explained everything.

"She's a woman first." Zane didn't back down.

"That's enough," Thanos remarked quietly, moving to stand beside the two older women.

"Damn right it is. Enough of costumes and veiled insults—"

"Zane, they've never meant to insult me."

"Yet they do," he answered, looking at each of them in turn, "every time they suggest that you don't measure up."

Olga looked aghast, her wrinkled face going pale. "Dear God, we love her."

"Then let her be her own woman."

Tamara shook off her shock. Never in her life had she stood idly by while her relatives were badgered, not by spectators, not by law officials. She wouldn't stand by now, not even for Zane.

His defense galled her, even as his understanding melted her heart.

"I can deal with my relatives on my own, Zane Winston."

He turned, not the least put off by her imperious tone, her bristling attitude. His smile was intimate, private, and he said, "But you no longer have to."

He meant it. His earnestness was a live thing, drumming in time to her heart. But he didn't understand her aunts and uncle, didn't know how difficult it had been for them to take on a little girl.

She cleared her throat. "Maybe . . . maybe you should go."

"Me?" Incredulous, he pointed at Boris. "What about him?"

"I can deal with him."

"Like hell." Zane crossed his arms much in the same fashion as Thanos. Standing near one another, they looked like mismatched bookends. "I'm not taking one step out of here, babe, so forget it."

Boris pushed himself past the table to face off with Zane. He was nearly as tall, older by a decade, heavily muscled. Yet, there was no comparison. Zane was competent and strong and self-assured, while Boris appeared bloated with bluster.

"How dare you speak to her with such a lack of respect!"

Zane looked down his nose at the older man. Ignoring the question, he took a step forward and forced Boris to retreat. "You tried to break in here last night, didn't you?"

"No!"

"You're trying to run her off, and I'm curious why."

"That's absurd!" Boris was quickly wheeling backward now, and he bumped into Thanos.

"You get your jollies by terrorizing women alone, is that it? Only she wasn't alone last night, was she?" Zane caught him by his shirt collar. "She won't be alone ever again."

Tamara went light-headed at his words. *Ever again.* Her heart thundered, her stomach dipped. What was he saying? Surely not what she . . . no, that was ridiculous. Numb in the brain, she muttered, "I was not terrorized, Zane."

Boris pushed his hand away. "And I did not attempt to come into her home uninvited."

"I don't believe you."

Thanos asked, "I think you need to back off, Zane."

Blank disbelief filled Zane. "You still champion him? After what I've just told you?"

Thanos shrugged. "I don't know about that. I need to give this all some thought. But Boris wasn't here last night, that I do know."

Tamara moved to Zane's side, giving him her silent, unquestioning support. He accepted it by taking her hand. "How?"

With another shrug, this one of apology, Thanos admitted, "Because he was with me till very late."

"With you?" Then with more suspicion, "Doing what?"

"Having drinks, sharing conversation." Glancing at the aunts, back at Tamara, Thanos winced. "Planning your future."

A red haze clouded his vision. Through set teeth, Zane growled very softly, "Planning her future?"

With his own show of bluster, Thanos said, "It's an uncle's duty to see that—"

Zane interrupted him. "Did I plan into this future?"

Thanos cut a quick look at Boris, and that more than answered his question. "I don't fucking believe this."

"Zane!"

The two aunts looked ready to swoon. Thanos scowled

darkly. "You'll watch your mouth, young man."

"Yeah, right. I'll watch my mouth while you try to push her off to this joker?"

Boris sputtered. "I've had just about enough of you. I agree with Ms. Tremayne. You should go."

Zane's eyes glittered. "Why don't you put me out?" His hands curled into fists, the need for physical violence boiling up inside him.

Boris, looking uncertain, turned to Thanos.

And then Tamara was there, standing in front of him, a small smile on her beautiful face. She touched his chest, his face.

"Zane, I really would like it if you'd calm down."

His jaw felt too tight to speak. Through set teeth, he repeated, "I'm not leaving here."

"Of course you're not."

Boris cleared his throat. "I thought perhaps we could spend the day together, Ms. Tremayne. Your uncle tells me your Sundays are free."

Her gaze still locked on Zane's, she said, "My uncle is wrong. My Sunday is very taken."

"Well," Eva mused briskly as she patted her streaked black and gray hair back into a tidy bun. "It's apparent she's made up her mind."

"But she works so hard."

Zane drew a calming breath and turned to Olga. "What did you say?"

"She works so hard to make ends meet. And Boris is rich, so. . . ."

Zane shook his head. "You're worried about her?"

"Yes of course."

Eva nodded in agreement, and Thanos looked grim.

"You're all so concerned, yet you'd leave her alone with him?" He nodded toward Boris with the same regard he'd give a worm.

"This is outrageous." Looking to Thanos to back him up, Boris said, "He's spewing outright slander. You know I didn't come here last night."

Every muscle on Zane's body bunched. He wanted, quite simply, to drag Boris outside and beat the hell of him. Not just because he'd been troubling Tamara, but because her family had chosen him.

Too bad.

Thoughtful, Thanos scratched his beard. "But someone apparently was here."

Tamara patted Zane's chest and turned, then she leaned into him until her bottom was snuggled up against his groin. Damn. Zane knew she only wanted to offer support, to share some of her own calm, but if she kept that up, he'd be embarrassing them both.

She said to Thanos, "Someone shut off my electric and tried to waltz right in." Here she glared at Boris. "He had a key."

Olga and Eva looked at each other, then at Thanos. Thanos said, "We didn't give him a key."

"Of course you didn't," Boris agreed. "Why, Ms. Tremayne and I haven't even gotten properly acquainted." He unwisely added, "Yet."

Surging with intense fury—partially based on jealousy and possessiveness—Zane reached past Tamara and caught Boris by this shirtfront. He rattled him like a paper bag. *"You're not getting anywhere near her."*

"Zane!"

He was damn sick and tired of her remonstrating with him. With Boris gasping for air at the end of his arm, Zane said, *"What?"*

"You told me to control my volatile tendencies."

"Yeah. So?" Boris made a strangling sound and Zane shook him again. Olga and Eva watched, like captivated viewers of a train wreck, while Thanos appeared pensive over the whole thing, unmoved by Boris's reddening complexion.

"So," Tamara said in exasperation, "you have to get a grip. This isn't going to solve anything."

"It'll make me feel a helluva lot better."

She actually laughed. In the middle of everything happening, with her family trying to hoist her off on a criminal and the criminal leering at her with lascivious intent, she managed to laugh. Damn, she was something else.

And she was his.

Zane let Boris drop, gagging and gasping and cursing, back to his feet. "All right," he said, addressing Thanos, "if it wasn't Boris who broke in here last night, then who the hell do you think it was?"

"All I know for certain is that he didn't get the key from me." Apparently affronted by the very idea, Thanos added, "I would never be so careless with my niece."

They all ignored Boris as they considered the possibilities. As Joe had said, it wasn't always as obvious as it seemed, though no way was Zane ruling out Boris as a probable.

Olga clutched at her throat and Eva pressed her hands together. Almost in unison, they cried, "Uncle Hubert!"

Boris, having regained a modicum of his aplomb, rasped, "Who the hell is Uncle Hubert?"

Zane smirked at him. "The family apparition, of course."

Boris cast on him a look of scorn. "Hogwash."

Just that easily, he alienated Eva and Olga.

Zane, seeing his opportunity, turned to the quailing women. He slipped his arm around Olga's frail shoulders and patted Eva's delicately veined hands. "Not a ghost this time, ladies. We saw him running off. He's flesh and blood." Zane deliberately didn't mention Joe; the fewer people who knew about him, the more effective he could be.

"Someone really did force his way in here?" In a quick turnaround, Eva and Olga rushed to Tamara. "Our poor baby! Are you okay?"

While the women were occupied smothering Tamara with concern, Zane narrowed his eyes on Boris. "Get lost."

"I'm ready to leave," he announced in cultured tones. "But I'll be back."

Zane opened his mouth, and before his rejoinder could reach any ears, Tamara said, "Not without an appointment."

And Boris agreed, "Whatever it takes."

Eighteen

Luckily for Zane, the customer's conversation was sufficiently
mundane that he didn't need to pay close attention. Truth
was, he could barely think at all and the condition got
worse every day.

For two weeks now, Tamara's business had been booming. Not only was Boris the bore still hanging around,
doggedly it seemed, but Arkin Devane showed up more
often than ever, as did a dozen other men. Though a scattering of women also called, her clientele consisted largely
of the male persuasion. It made him nuts.

Tamara had done no more than present her own naturally sensual, seductive self to the world, and the male
populace had fallen to its knees.

As the customer's monologue drew to a close, Zane
handed him a receipt, bade him farewell, and went to peer
out the window. Two women and a man loitered on the
walk in front of the old house.

The upside to all the attention Tamara had garnered was
that her financial situation was more stable than ever. She
might even recover her losses. The Realtor had presented
her with another offer for the house, but it still wasn't

quite as much as she had countered. Because of all her
good fortune of late, she'd been comfortable in negotiat-
ing for a higher price. Zane didn't even want to consider
the day when the offer might be good enough. There was
no way he was letting her go, even if he had to take out
a loan and buy her damn building himself.

But he wasn't stupid, so he hadn't told her that.

The downside to all her added business was that she
worked more hours. Which meant she had less time to
spend with him. He'd actually cut back on his hours, not
that it had done him much good. Her days were busy.

But her nights . . . well, her nights belonged to him.

Smiling, Zane pictured her in his mind as she'd looked
that morning, with her green eyes bright, only lightly
made up, her blonde hair bouncing with natural curl, and
her boundless energy.

God, he loved her energy. The way she made love with
him each evening, and most mornings, boggled his mind.
Other than his one overly emotional slipup, he'd used protection every time. Because he cared so much about her,
he forced himself into fair play.

Tamara had made even that especially tantalizing, by
learning how to put the condom on him—slowly. So
slowly that he wondered if he was a little masochistic for
enjoying the torture.

She was creative and, in the tradition of her heritage,
free-spirited. They'd made a rather sexy game of the journal, trying everything the author suggested, and em-
bellishing on a few.

More and more Zane wondered about the woman
who'd patiently organized so many erotic details—if
she'd died happy, if her life had been all it could be. Did
she write out of a need to share her happiness, or to try
to help others find what she couldn't?

One night, after he'd loved Tamara into near exhaustion, she'd voiced the same concerns. Though they'd
never met the woman, her journal had given them great
insight into her personality. Her caring and loving nature

had come through on paper, and had endeared her to them. Whoever she might have been, Zane felt sure she'd been a very special woman with a very large heart and a zest for life and love.

Now that he held Tamara every night, he couldn't imagine sleeping without her. He hadn't mentioned leaving her home, and neither had she. He'd simply picked up more items from his place as he needed them, and now all his shower and shaving supplies were in Tamara's bathroom, and her closet held a good portion of his clothes.

Sometimes, in the early evening, he'd sit in bed, pretending to read, and watch her work on the computer. She was intense then, her slim brows narrowed in thought and her face, in the blue light of the computer, endearingly studious. When she'd finally shut off the computer, he'd put aside his book and open his arms.

A new alarm system had been installed, and a floodlight mounted on the side of his building was aimed at her lot. There had been no more run-ins with masked men in the middle of night, no more dead rats or small fires. Zane had no reason to remain with her except that he needed her; he hoped she understood that.

It still enraged him off that Boris had an alibi. It didn't matter in the long run, because Zane wasn't convinced that Boris was innocent. Perhaps he hadn't been there that particular night, but it was possible, even likely, that he'd paid someone to do his dirty work. Until Joe actually caught someone, Zane wouldn't be able to let down his guard.

"Brooding again, I see."

Zane wanted to groan. He'd "hired" Joe as an assistant to give him a reason to be close to Tamara, to snoop around and check into things. But having him in the store all the time was trying. The women who usually flirted with Zane now divided their time with Joe. Zane didn't mind on a personal level because Tamara was the only woman who interested him. It just nettled that Joe might think he was stealing the women's attention.

"I see you forgot your name badge again."

Joe grinned, unrepentant, then rubbed at the left side of his chest. "Hell, I nearly pierced my nipple with the damn thing. Get a stick-on name tag and I'll wear it, but no more pins, thank you. Besides, I don't need it. Everyone knows me already."

True enough. The women whispered his name in hushed excitement and the men grumbled about Joe's policy of "ladies first." It didn't matter how long a male customer had been waiting, if a woman walked in, Joe moved to assist her. He was the worst sort of employee, but Zane wasn't about to fire him.

"So what has you mooning this time?" Joe asked.

Zane moved away from him. "Just anticipating closing time." Which was still several hours away, damn it.

Seeing through Zane's lie, Joe said, "She's a sweetie, I'll give you that. It'd be hard not to think about her."

Zane wondered if Joe had his own mind-reading abilities. "I can do without your experienced opinion on the matter."

Joe laughed. "You wanna hear what I've found out about your buddy Boris, while the crowd is gone?"

Zane jerked around to face Joe. "You've found out something?"

"Of course. What, you thought I was a totally ineffectual snoop?" He snorted. "That doesn't say much for you, since you hired me."

"You've been here all morning and it's damn near lunchtime now! Why the hell didn't you say something sooner?"

Joe shrugged. Along with not wearing a name tag, he refused to dress up for his bogus job, preferring to stick with jeans and T-shirts and boots so scuffed they had to be ten years old. His hair was too long, his earring too damn noticeable, more often than not he forgot or refused to shave—and the female customers adored him. It was a good thing Joe didn't know anything about computers, or he'd likely have accepted some of the inquiries on home service.

"Your place is busier than I expected." He clapped Zane on the shoulder. "You run a helluva business, cousin. I'm impressed."

Zane sliced his hand through the air, dismissing the compliment in favor of hearing more important news. "What did you find out?"

Propping his hip on the counter next to the cash register, Joe retrieved a knife from his pocket. He flicked it open, then closed—an annoying habit he had. "Boris is married."

Of all the things Zane had expected, that wasn't anywhere on the list. "No shit? The bastard has a wife?"

"A wealthy wife. Not that Boris comes from a poor background. His family was well-to-do, but lost a lot in the last ten years or so. I gather he married as a way to restore the family financial standing."

Pacing, Zane muttered, "This is incredible."

"And he's not from Romania, as he supposedly told Tamara's uncle, but his wife is. Very Old World. Her family dates back to some impressive and influential names."

I'll kill him, was Zane's immediate thought. But first he had to find out what Boris wanted with Tamara. Then he could work him over. He flexed his hands, imagining them around Boris's thick neck. "What do you think he's up to?"

"Can't tell you that, but I can tell you that his wife's family is not the type who'd take kindly to news of his activities." Joe flipped the knife open again, polished the blade along the denim on his left thigh, and held it up to the fluorescent lights to admire the shine. "If they knew he'd been sniffing after another woman, the proverbial crapola would hit the fan."

"You're sure he and his wife aren't separated?"

"Nope. I could find no mention of it, and this isn't the type of family who puts up with separation." He closed the knife and slid it back into his pocket. Hopping off the counter, he crossed his arms and said, "You marry, you stay married. Finito."

"I've got a really bad feeling about this."

"Rightfully so. It proves without a doubt that you're dead-on, that Boris is unprincipled to say the least, and up to something sinister at the most."

"He's going to be seeing her again today." And Zane intended to be there. Damn, at least now he had something solid to use against Boris. Surely this would make her relatives detest him as much as Zane did.

"Yeah, well, I'd put an end to that real quick."

Zane flashed Joe an irritated glance. "I tried reasoning with her. She's convinced that as long as Boris is minding his manners and paying for her time, she should indulge her relatives by pretending to give him an opportunity to woo her."

Joe shook his head in a pitying way.

Because his attitude mirrored Zane's own, there wasn't much he could say.

Of course, that didn't stop Joe. "You should know better than to attempt to reason with the female brain, Zane. Take the guy aside, break his nose, make him understand that he's to get lost and stay lost." Joe cracked his knuckles. "And if you're not up to it, I'm game."

It was no less than what Zane wanted to do, but he found himself laughing. "You've become a bloodthirsty cynic, you know that? Besides, this isn't the Stone Age. Women are allowed their own thoughts and choices."

"More's the pity." Joe shook his head. "If I was ever gullible enough to fall in love—which is doubtful—it'd damn sure be with a woman who knew how to listen."

Before Zane could react to that by knocking Joe on his ass, a laugh sounded behind them. They both turned, and found Cole and Chase standing there. Chase pointed at Joe. "You're going to eat those words one day."

Cole nodded. "I just hope I'm around to see it."

"Not me." Zane hefted a box of keyboards and carried

it to an empty shelf. "I don't want to be anywhere around. It's a bitch to get blood out of clothes, and it's for certain, the woman in question would flay him alive."

Totally unconcerned, Joe laughed. "What are you two rogues doing wandering loose today? Where are your little ladies?"

Zane knew Joe had spent quite a bit of time visiting with Cole and Chase at the bar. Mack and Jessica had gone there several nights to join in. They all got along well, and Mack had laughed, explaining how the women at the bar had doted on Joe. Zane didn't care how many women chased him, as long as he didn't go after Tamara.

"Actually," Cole said—and Zane felt his brother's gaze boring into him—"our wives are visiting Tamara, along with Mack."

Zane dropped the box as he spun around. "What?"

"Yep. Sophie was pretty annoyed that you hadn't brought her around to meet the family yet, and she got Jessica and Allison all riled, and like a female militant group, they headed off. We decided to follow along just for the hell of it."

Zane marched to the window and looked out. It was quiet in front of the Gypsy shop now, no more customers standing around. Were they all inside already? What would his darling sisters-in-law say about him?

Since marrying into the family, they'd taunted him end-lessly for his bachelor ways, his overindulgence in female attention. And Zane had encouraged them by being more outrageous than ever. He enjoyed his sisters-in-law and loved bantering with them.

Would they blather on to Tamara about his disreputable ways?

Damn, he didn't want the fragile bond he'd forged with Tamara disrupted. She'd forgiven him for his outburst with her relatives, especially considering they'd paid heed to him and had quit pressuring her about the damn wig and dark contacts. If anything, they were doubly pleased that she could attract so much attention without artificial devices.

She'd also quit pushing him away at every turn. He wouldn't go so far as to say she'd accepted his help graciously. But she'd only frowned a little when he installed the spotlight and aimed it her way. She'd complained that it'd shine in her bedroom window at night.

Zane remembered her slow smile when he'd told her that he liked being able to see her clearly when they were in bed together. She trusted him with her body; she was beginning to trust him with her pride. Soon, she'd trust him with her heart.

He said abruptly, uncaring who paid heed, "Watch the place for me," and headed for the door. He had to get over there to make certain no one got her thinking too hard on his less sterling qualities.

Cole laughed and met him at the door. "Not me! If you're running over there, so am I."

"Why?"

"To watch, of course."

"Me too," Chase added, hot on their heels.

Zane stopped, frustrated, wondering what his customers would think if he simply locked his door for a few hours.

Leaning against a wall, Joe stretched and put his arms behind his head. "Go on, Zane. You can leave everything to me."

Appalled by the idea, Zane said, "You've got to be kidding."

Cole and Chase caught his arms and started out, dragging Zane backward. "Joe will do fine."

"Ha!"

"Do you want to visit Tamara or not?"

Joe stood there, utterly confident as usual. He even went so far as to grin. "No need to thank me, Zane. You know I'm always glad to help out. But send over some lunch, will ya? I'm starved."

"We'll see to it," Cole assured him. "It's the least Zane can do."

Zane considered knocking his brothers' heads together, but then he thought of Tamara getting her ears filled, and he relented. "At least let me walk in under my own steam."

They released him, but not without a few more good-natured jibes. Considering how he'd riled them when they were falling in love, Zane figured he had it coming.

They marched next door, and Cole's long stride suited Zane's impatience just fine.

In an offhand voice, Chase asked, "Ready to give in to the Winston curse yet?"

Zane reached Tamara's door with the gaudy painted sign and flashing light. He turned the knob. "I gave in two weeks ago, if you want the gory details. Now I just need her to succumb." He walked into the foyer with the sound of Chase's and Cole's boisterous laughter behind him. Damn fools. Didn't they understand that this was serious stuff?

His female relatives were clustered around the counter when he entered. Mack stood close by, holding his wife in front of him, and they had Tamara encircled. The music from the CD player had been turned low to allow for easy conversation.

Smiling, flushed with pleasure and unrestrained laughter, Tamara was a sight to steal his breath. Today she had her hair pulled back on one side with an enamel comb. Dangling earrings brushed her shoulders. She still wore the enticing, flirty jewelry and sexy, flowing skirts. But her makeup was different, subtle, her lips a glossy peach instead of bright red, her long lashes dusty brown rather than inky black.

He liked seeing her like this, a part of his family, a part of his life.

Chase and Cole shoved past him, nearly knocking him over.

Jessica noticed them first, and she turned her big chocolate brown eyes on Zane.

Oh hell, he thought, and braced himself for a raucous

joke of some kind that would undermine all the progress he'd made with Tamara. Instead, Jessica winked, then looked over her shoulder at Mack. His doting brother kissed her temple.

Allison, still laughing, turned and held out a hand to Chase. He went to her without missing a step. Those two, it often seemed, spoke on some private plane that no one else could hear. Zane had always thought it a little strange, but now he envied them their rapport.

Cole didn't wait for an invite. He strode forward and looped his arms around Sophie's waist, settling his big hands on her still-flat belly with paternal affection. Sophie positively glowed.

Zane swallowed a lump. Damn, he wanted what they all had. He hadn't at first, only because he hadn't fully understood the completeness of it, the depth of emotion. He knew they were happy, knew marriage suited them, but he'd thought himself different, thought he needed more time to enjoy life and his freedom. He was a real dumb ass on occasion.

Tamara looked up and her beautiful green eyes lit at the sight of him. "Zane! I thought you were working."

She separated herself from the group and came to him. Her smile was warm, and the bells on her ankles tinkled. She made his heart race, his pulse quicken. Aware of their amused audience, Zane restrained himself and indulged only in a light kiss.

Tamara stared up at him. "What's wrong?" she asked in a soft whisper. "You're fretting or something."

Her ability to understand him no longer seemed threatening. In fact, he counted on it, so she'd know he was sincere in his declarations—when he got around to declaring himself.

"I missed you," he murmured.

He heard Chase snort. "More like he felt compelled to come here and defend his honor."

Bemused, Tamara asked, "Defend your honor from what?"

"Not what," Cole said, ignoring his wife's attempts to hush him, "but who. Our wives do like to give him a hard time."

Sophie elbowed Cole hard enough to make him grunt. "That's not true! We *adore* Zane."

Mack, ignoring his sister-in-law, added, "Blissfully content married women refuse to believe that any man can be happy without a wife to keep him that way."

Looking like an imp, Jessica said, "But Zane's so sexy and sweet. He can't help but attract scores of women." Mack promptly growled, attacking her neck in a tender assault that had her laughing. She amended her statement, "But not as sexy as Mack! No way!"

Allison peered over the top of her glasses and addressed the assembled group. "Chase is by far the sexiest, but that's beside the point. We all adore Zane and want nothing more than to see him . . . happy."

Wondering if he should strangle the lot of them, Zane snarled, "Then you should be deliriously satisfied, because I *am* happy." At least he would be if they didn't scare her off.

To his surprise, Tamara sighed. "It must be wonderful to have such a large family."

Damn, there she went again, ripping his guts out.

Cole asked, "Was it lonely growing up alone?"

Just then a door opened and the black curtain moved. Luna and Aunt Olga stepped out, two clients behind them.

Tamara smiled at her aunt. "I had my aunts and uncle to keep me company."

Olga grinned at her, then sent an "I-told-you-we-loved-her" look toward Zane.

He ground his teeth together, but no one noticed with the buzz of the two clients setting future appointments and saying their good-byes.

Zane had a few moments to consider Olga's continued aloofness toward him. She was still a little ticked, but she had obviously listened. All three of Tamara's relatives now appeared to support her more, encouraging her in her uniqueness. They even claimed to like Zane well enough, yet they forever sang their litany of praises for Boris.

He forced himself to smile at Olga now. "It's nice to see you again, Olga."

"I'm working today," she informed him loftily. "We decided Tamara needed more help, especially with all the added business." Her pointy chin went into the air, her black eyes challenging. "And I wanted to give her some time off. She deserves it."

Zane looked down at Tamara in time to see her grin. "It's true," she said. "They've been wonderful."

Luna, looking as outrageously delicious as ever with her golden brown eyes alight and her mink-colored hair loose, said, "She even has time for lunch." Then she winked. "Of course, your relatives have already claimed her, and invited the others to join them."

Zane was curious as to what others, when the door chimed and Thanos and Eva walked in. He'd wanted a few minutes alone with Tamara to talk to her about Boris. Once she knew the scoundrel was married, she'd surely tell her relatives and they'd quickly toss him off the prospective beau list. But now it looked as though he wouldn't have a chance, not with his brothers and sisters-in-law organizing a damn tea party.

Introductions were made. Olga and Luna volunteered to stay behind and watch the shop in case anyone dropped in, and the rest prepared to go up to Tamara's home to dine. Zane remembered Joe and his request for food. He whispered to Tamara that he had to feed him, and Luna overheard.

Zane wondered if Luna had super powers, because it seemed the softer he spoke, the more clearly she understood him.

"A new assistant, Zane?" she asked.

Though he'd told Tamara to keep Joe's identity secret, he had half-expected her to confide in Luna anyway. He was pleased that she hadn't. "Yes, just hired in the last few weeks."

Luna's lips curled with feminine curiosity. "I'm going to run out to the deli. Want me to stop over there and see what he wants?"

Zane already knew what Joe would want from Luna, but if ever there was a woman who could hold her own, it was Luna Clark. He smiled, very pleased at the prospect, and said, "That'd be great. Thanks."

She gave him a suspicious look, but smiled. "No problem."

Zane expected to order pizza for their lunch, but he wasn't overly surprised to see his sisters-in-law had taken care of it. The feast they supplied was more like dinner than lunch, with carry-out fried chicken, potato salad, biscuits and honey, and a chocolate cake for dessert. They refused to let Tamara do a thing—other than her job. They wanted to know their horoscopes, have their palms read, and Sophie even asked if Tamara could tell her the sex of her baby.

Sitting close beside Zane, Tamara laughed. "I can't predict the future. All I can tell you is that you don't really care if it's a boy or a girl, you just want a healthy baby."

Astonished, Sophie stared at Tamara and said with awe, "How did you know?"

"You're the type of woman who loves with all her heart. That doesn't leave room for conditions. Besides, you now have a son, and Allison has a daughter, and you're content with that mix."

There were murmured agreements among Zane's relatives as to Tamara's accuracy, and prideful boasts by Tamara's relatives for the same reason.

Excited, Sophie stuck out her hand. "And my palm? What does that tell you?"

Tamara studied her hand. She glanced at Zane, then around the room, before tilting her head at Sophie again. "This won't embarrass you?"

Nonplussed by the question, Sophie drew back. "Am I going to be found lacking?"

"Of course not." Tamara inhaled, then lightly traced a fingertip over the very base of each of Sophie's fingers, where they met with her palm. "This is the E zone. You see how this area is plumper and softer than the other areas of your fingers? Well, that means you're a person who loves to touch, and especially loves the pleasures of the body."

Cole choked on his raspberry tea. Sophie gave a twittering, pleased, but self-conscious laugh.

In typical brotherly fashion, Mack and Chase saluted Cole.

"You work in a boutique, right?"

Sophie nodded, wide-eyed.

"That's a little unusual. Generally speaking, a woman with hands like yours would be more likely to be a massage therapist or have some other type of physical contact work."

Cole said, "Well, she does like to—*omphf.*"

Sophie glared at him, and in a stage whisper said, "That is *private*, Cole Winston."

He laughed, set down his glass, and scooped her into his lap. "All right, sweetheart."

Since they were all used to Cole cuddling Sophie, most especially when she was pregnant, the brothers and their wives ignored them. Thanos and Eva, however, along with Tamara, couldn't help but smile at their affectionate display.

Jessica stuck her hand out. "I'm next."

And so it went, each of them taking turns having Tamara read their palms. Thanos and Eva added their own colorful and mystic predictions to Tamara's study-based readings, and they all acted like old friends.

Zane took pleasure in watching Tamara charm his family. It put him that much closer to winning her over.

He supposed he owed his sisters-in-law gratitude rather than suspicion for their impromptu visit. When Allison gave him an inconspicuous thumbs-up, he knew he was right. Damn, he was a lucky cuss to have such a wonderful family.

Soon, they'd be Tamara's family, too.

Nineteen

Tamara breathed a sigh of relief after everyone had gone. As enjoyable as it had been, she was impatient to spend some time alone with Zane. She'd made a decision that she hoped to discuss with him.

They walked Zane's relatives back downstairs to the door. Luna had returned, but her lunch was left uneaten on the counter while she fumed, pacing around the shop. Tamara and Zane shared a look of concern.

"What's the matter?" Tamara asked, never having seen her assistant in such a state.

Luna's smile was gloating, wicked. "Nothing. *Now.*"

Zane winced. "Uh-oh. Does this little upset of yours have anything to do with Joe?"

She snorted loudly. "I wouldn't allow that moron to upset me." Then she stormed into the backroom and slammed the door. Hard.

Tamara cleared her throat. *Oh dear.* She certainly hoped Joe had survived whatever had passed between them.

Cole put his arm around Sophie and broke the uncomfortable silence. "We need to get going. I have some new guys working for me, but they haven't entirely got the hang of it yet. Leaving them alone at lunchtime was iffy."

Mack grinned. "We had a teacher's in-service day, so I was able to go out for lunch. But I have conferences starting soon, so I have to go, too."

"And I have a woman showing up in half an hour for her portrait." Jessica embraced Tamara, and whispered in her ear, "He comes from good stock. Hang on to him."

Not knowing what to say to that, Tamara laughed. But Jessica's hug galvanized the others and she got passed around from person to person as they explained the jobs and people they needed to get back to. Being a business-woman herself, she understood. It was apparent they'd taken time from their busy lives to meet her.

Did that mean anything? A glance at Zane, who wore a vacuous smile, didn't tell her a thing.

Luna returned to the counter. She went about business as usual, but she still looked a little rattled when Arkin Devane came in a few minutes early. Tamara promised him she'd be right there, and because he was a regular and knew the routine, she sent him ahead to the room to wait for her.

"Will you be okay out here?" she asked Luna. "Or would you rather I have Aunt Olga take over?"

Olga, who was busy dusting all the knickknacks scat-tered about, looked hopeful.

Luna scoffed at the concern. "I'm perfectly fine. Per-fectly. Fine." She added, miffed, "I don't know why you'd think I'm not."

"Well," Tamara admitted with some humor, "you have little bits of what looks like egg salad in your hair, and you keep cursing under your breath."

Luna snatched a hand through her hair. "Well damn! I thought it all went on him." She looked at her fingers, now holding bits of boiled egg, and made a sound of disgust. "Must have splattered on me, too."

"Him?" Zane asked, full of interest.

"Your new hire." She made a face, and her eyes

flashed. "I threw his sandwich at him, but only because he deserved it."

Grinning, Zane said, "I'm sure he did."

Tamara had the suspicion that Zane was thoroughly enjoying the mental picture of Luna attacking Joe. She bit back a laugh.

Luna sent Zane her haughtiest look. "If he's worth whatever you're paying him, he's cleaning the floor right now." So saying, Luna again stalked off to the tiny bathroom in the backroom.

"Good heavens," Tamara muttered, but she could barely hear herself above Zane's laughter. "What in the world do you think happened?"

Still chuckling, Zane wiped his eyes. "Joe happened, and God, I'd give a hundred bucks to have been there."

"Zane Winston, you're terrible. He's your cousin."

"And he's entirely too cocksure of himself where women are concerned. You know, if I had to venture a guess, I'd say Joe likely acted like himself and Luna rightfully took exception."

"He can't be that bad."

Zane hugged her. "Sweetheart, I swear, he's a good deal worse."

The door chimed again, and this time Tamara groaned. "Darn it, why is everyone coming early? I wanted a chance to talk to you."

Zane smiled down at her. Those warm, intimate feelings of his drifted over her with the coziness of a posh blanket.

"They're early," he whispered, "because, like me, they're eager to see you."

"Oh Zane." Words of affection, of . . . *love*, were just about to escape her when another, colder voice broke in.

"I see I'm interrupting yet again."

Teeth bared in a parody of a smile, Zane turned. "Boris."

Boris looked past Zane to Tamara. With his normal

pompous disregard for propriety, he said, "I trust you're ready for me?"

Tamara's smile wasn't much better than Zane's. "You're early, so you'll have to wait for a bit."

That brought him down a peg. He scowled in disbelief and disappointment. "But I had hoped. . . ."

Zane rumbled with anger. "Why don't you just leave, if you don't have time to wait till your damn appointment?"

Tamara wished he *would* leave. She needed to talk to Zane, and with Boris's entrance, the need became nearly desperate. She wasn't sure what was wrong, or what Boris wanted, but she thought talking to Zane about it might help clear things up.

She trusted him, she realized with some consternation. In the past, she never would have entrusted someone else, relied on someone else to help her understand a situation and deal with it. But Zane had worked his way into her life, into her confidence.

Into her heart.

Now, she couldn't imagine not sharing with him. The sudden insight was both disturbing and oddly liberating.

She was anxious to share her new insights with Zane, to tell him her astounding revelations, but of course Boris didn't go away. Beyond her own emotional upheaval, she picked up on Boris's determination, his hard insistence, the darkness of his thoughts that seeped into her mind like thunderclouds.

He pretended an indifference she knew to be the direct opposite of what he really felt. His smile was a barely veiled sneer. "I'll wait, of course."

A wave of sickness made her suck in her breath.

Zane quickly put his arm around her. "Are you okay?"

"Yes. I . . . I'm fine." She fashioned a smile, as much to reassure Zane as to fool Boris. She didn't want him to know what she felt. God, she'd figured a few things out only that morning, and now Boris was back and everything was coming to a head. She had to talk to Zane.

Bringing her attention back to him, Zane asked, "Do you need to sit down?"

"No." She couldn't take the chance of alerting Boris by acting like a fainting dolt now, so she searched her brain for some innocuous bit of conversation, something everyday and mundane. She came upon the perfect tidbit. "I wanted to talk to you about the journal."

The reflection of sensual, satisfying memories plain in his dark eyes, Zane murmured, "Is that so? One of my favorite topics." His smile gentle, he added, "Planning something new? What page are you up to?"

A wave of heat flooded her cheeks. Boris had taken a seat on the sofa in the foyer, but he made no pretense of ignoring them. His attention was openly, fixedly, set on their conversation.

That was fine. At least he wouldn't suspect anything when she led Zane upstairs.

Tamara cleared her throat. "Actually, I was thinking of giving the book away."

She'd shocked him. Zane frowned as he said, "Give it away? Why?"

Since Boris knew nothing of the book or what it contained, she felt safe saying, "To another client. I've been sharing parts of the book with him, and I think that may be the main reason he's coming around so much. If I give him the book. . . ."

Zane caught on. He took her arm and steered her out of hearing distance of Boris. He moved her over by the stairs that led to her rooms. "Arkin Devane?"

"Yes." With complete honesty, she admitted, "I feel horrible taking his money and his time when all I do is relay parts of the journal to him. It's not fair to charge him for that, because it's not my advice or insight, it's straight from someone else."

"He gets the information from you, though."

"Yes. But. . . ." Tamara hesitated. Zane gave her so much, it was time she became more honest with him. He deserved at least that much. It took a fortifying breath for her to be able to say, "He's in love."

"With you?"

She laughed at his bristling annoyance. "No, not with me. With someone else." She put her hand on his neck and smiled up at him. "Now that I'm so . . . happy, I want everyone else to be that happy, too."

A heartbeat passed while Zane searched her face, then he gathered her close. "So you're happy, huh?"

"Remarkably so."

She felt his smile against her temple. "With me?"

Leaning back to see his face, she nodded. "I didn't know it was possible to be this happy."

His expression softened, grew intent. "Damn, I wish I was alone with you right now."

"Me too." Impishly, she reminded him, "There's tonight, of course."

He became arrested, then groaned. "Don't."

"Don't what?"

Laughing under his breath, he said, "Don't look at me like that, don't talk like that. God, you'll make it impossible for me to walk."

Delighted with his open response to her, she said, "You affect me the same way."

"Damn it." He closed his eyes and said, "That's it. One more word and you'll miss the next three appointments."

Tamara laughed. "You're so easy." Then, to get them back on subject, she pointed out, "You see? We don't need the journal anymore. Don't you think we should share it? That the author would have wanted us to share it?"

"Maybe. But I've grown partial to it, you know. I feel . . . protective. I don't want to give it to just anyone."

She smiled at this further proof of how sensitive Zane could be. "Yes, I know. But it'll be in good hands. Arkin's a wonderful man, and I'm sure he'll feel the same as we do."

Zane looked at her mouth. "You're sure it's some other woman he's fixated on?"

"Yes. I keep telling you and Luna that he's not really here for me. It's because I understand him and his shyness and I have the book to help him."

"Well, God knows I'm all for weeding out your gentlemen callers."

Tamara couldn't help but laugh again. She found it hysterically funny whenever Zane pretended to be jealous.

Her laugh died in midbreath. "Oh no."

"What is it?" Zane caught her arms. Alarm darkened his eyes. "Tamara?"

"You don't sense it?"

"Sense what, damn it?"

Urgently, feeling like a fool for not realizing the truth sooner, she said, "We need to go upstairs for a minute."

Zane's bafflement was plain, but he didn't argue with her. He turned to Luna. "We'll be right back. Can you hold down the fort?"

After one long, searching glance at Tamara's face, she gave Zane a salute. "Not a problem."

They were barely up the stairs and through the door before Tamara said, "Boris is the one."

"What one? The guy who's been trying to ruin you?"

"Yes."

Grabbing her shoulders, Zane barked, "Did he say something to you? Did he touch you?"

"Shh. Calm down, Zane." Tamara bit her lip in slight uncertainty, but then she shook her head. This was Zane. She trusted him, and he'd never laughed at her. Not once. "He hasn't done or said anything. I just . . . I *feel* it."

Zane didn't allow himself to relax. Tension vibrated off Tamara, as did her hesitancy. But she'd trusted him, confided in him. "How long have you known?"

"Almost from the beginning. I couldn't be certain, but I knew something about him didn't seem right. Whenever he was around, I felt his . . . evil. He was so easy to read—"

A new anger washed through him, one constructed of jealousy. "I thought other than family, I was the only man you could read." He'd assumed, based on what Tamara had told him, that she cared about him whether she admitted it or not, and that was what facilitated her ability to know his feelings. "I know damn good and well you don't care about Sandor."

"Of course not. He makes me nauseous, the emotions in him are so black and ugly and thick. But that's precisely why I can read him. Strong emotions, of any kind, are sometimes apparent to me. It's just that most people don't feel that strongly."

"You're losing me, Tamara."

She rubbed her forehead as she considered how best to explain. "It's like with your relatives. Sophie is easy to know because her feelings for Cole are so powerful. And the same is true of Cole. Love sort of pours off him when he looks at his wife, when he looks at you or your brothers."

"That's how you knew Sophie didn't have a preference for the baby?"

"Yes. And it's how I know Arkin Devane is in love, and how I know your cousin Joe is basically a very good, honorable man, and how I know . . ." she drew a steadying breath ". . . that Boris is a very bad man."

Zane propped his hands on his hips and dropped his head forward to think. "If you knew this, if you could feel what kind of man he was, why the hell did you let him hang around?"

"I wasn't certain if he was the one who'd done all those things to my shop. Sometimes I felt him, but sometimes, like the night of the break-in, and the night I was followed, it was different somehow. Fractured. Not as strong or as negative." She shook her head. "Not Boris."

"Maybe he hired someone to do those things for him,

but it still doesn't explain why the hell you didn't say something to me sooner."

"I knew if I did, you'd get all macho and protective and you'd try to put a stop to his visits. Then I'd never be able to find out what he was after."

Zane fought the urge to shake her. "You still don't know, do you?"

Tamara was shaking her head when a voice from behind her said calmly, "Perhaps I'll enlighten you."

In one swift movement, Zane had Tamara at his back. And then he saw the gun, a polished thirty-eight, in Boris's meaty hand. Fear tightened his throat. If Tamara got hurt. . . . He felt her pressed against him, felt her quickened breath on his shoulder.

She wouldn't be hurt. No matter what, he'd make sure of that.

Boris must have come up the outside stairs, Zane realized. It was the only other entrance. But the alarm should have gone off. . . .

Tamara went on tiptoe to whisper in his ear, "I didn't set the alarm. We were here, and there were visitors, and I, well, I only use it at night or when I'm away."

Zane wanted to groan. Instead he asked, "What the hell do you want, Sandor?"

"Why, to set the record straight, of course." Waving the gun, he motioned them away from the stairway leading to the shop and quietly stepped past them to close the door. Zane's heartbeat stuttered and nearly died each and every time the barrel pointed at Tamara. He would not let this maniac hurt her.

She said, her voice laced with nervousness as she peered around him, "Don't you dare be a hero, Zane Winston." Her hands knotted in the back of his shirt and she shook him. "I mean it."

Boris laughed. "A hero? My dear, he can hardly do battle with a bullet."

"I asked you what you wanted." Zane spoke in order to keep Boris's attention away from Tamara.

"Well, first, I wasn't the one who broke into your home. And no, Mr. Sherlock, I didn't hire anyone to break in either. That would have been too risky."

Zane could barely move with Tamara clinging to him like a vine, but that didn't stop his mind from churning. Boris was older, heavier. Zane was quick, his reactions razor-sharp. Adrenaline pumped through him. He could take Boris. He might get a bullet in the bargain, but that was a chance he was willing to take. "You think I'm going to believe you?" he asked, buying himself more time.

"Why would I lie?" Boris acted almost cavalier about the situation. "You see, I did start the fire and cause the flood. It was easy enough to pay a disreputable sort of fellow to pry open the old storeroom window and toss in a burning cigarette butt." His expression hardened. "Unfortunately, she came home too soon, and the fire was extinguished before it could do the job."

"What job is that?"

Boris ignored him. "And the rat in the toilet was a brainstorm. A slightly more difficult feat, requiring a child who could fit through the window, but luckily, I'd hired a family man. He had a son who was just the right size."

"You used a child?" Tamara demanded, not bothering to hide her loathing.

Boris shrugged. "The boy thought it was a lark. I believe he enjoyed himself. And it stood to reason that if the place flooded, everything on the floor would be destroyed. Again, misfortune smiled on me." He glowered at Tamara, his jaw tightening, his lip curled. "She'd already removed it from the boxes in the storeroom. I know because I paid good money for a man to go through her garbage."

Tamara went on tiptoe to see over Zane's shoulder. "I'd already moved what? What are you talking about?"

Just that easily, Boris's composure slipped. *"That goddamned journal!"*

Both Tamara and Zane froze. Zane backed up a tiny step, crowding into Tamara, forcing her to back up, too.

The farther from Boris she got, the easier it'd be for her to escape while he distracted Boris with an attack.

"Hold still! Neither one of you is going anywhere."

"What do you want with the journal?" Tamara asked, edging out from behind Zane, thwarting his efforts. He tried to stop her, but she moved too quickly for him.

Boris shrugged, collecting himself as if he hadn't just shouted, as if he didn't have a gun pointed at them. "It's rightfully mine." He grinned, an evil baring of teeth. "My aunt Felicia wrote it."

Zane casually strolled across the room until he was once again standing in front of Tamara. "I don't buy it."

He appeared taken aback at Zane's doubt. "It's true."

"The woman who wrote that journal was generous, open, and warm." Zane shook his head. "A coldhearted bastard like you couldn't possibly have the same blood."

Boris snarled. "She was a whore, fucking anything that got close enough and then having the audacity to actually write about it."

"That's not true!" Tamara again left the dubious safety of Zane's back. "She wasn't detailing conquests! She wanted to share emotional connections and physical pleasure. She was a sensual woman who enjoyed male companionship. That's only natural."

"She was a vulgar bitch behaving below her station. What she did was plebeian, and if society found out, they'd crucify not only her, but every man she named as well."

"Which would cause some mighty repercussions, wouldn't it? I have the feeling some of her partners were influential men, men who wouldn't take kindly to being named. Why didn't you recover the journal sooner?" Zane asked.

Boris shook his head. "When the bitch died, I was glad to be rid of her, and I had all her belongings sold. But I didn't know about the ridiculous journal until I cleaned out her safety-deposit box and found a letter about it. She actually wanted me to give it to a friend of hers. Can you imagine?" He shuddered. "Luckily the company who handled the estate sale kept a record of transactions. It was easy enough to track it here, but more difficult to recover it. Now, though, I'll finally be able to destroy the goddamn thing."

Tamara was nearly beside herself. "But *why?*"

Again moving to block Tamara from Boris, Zane whispered, "Because his wife's family is traditional in the extreme, and they move with the upper crust. If they found out about the journal and knew it had the ability to damage their reputations, they wouldn't be content with just destroying it. They'd want any and all links to it gone."

Boris, looking surprised by Zane's information, didn't argue the point. "They'd disown me, damn them and their insistence on supercilious deportment."

"You said that with a straight face, Boris," Zane taunted, "but you know better. From what I understand, they abhor scandals and leave nothing to chance, especially if it concerns their good name and their standing in the community." He looked Boris in the eyes and said, "They wouldn't risk letting you walk free with all that information in your head. They'd get rid of you, permanently, and you know it."

Boris trembled with rage. Zane wanted him to tremble, he wanted him to quake with fury. The more out of control the man got, the more mistakes he might make.

"Once the two of you are dead and the journal is destroyed," Boris spat, "they'll never know, will they?"

Zane snorted. "If you shoot that gun, everyone will hear. The downstairs is crowded with customers and relatives and employees. The police will be here and you'll be taken away. But then, prison might be better than what your wife's family will have planned."

Very slowly, Boris raised his gun hand and aimed at Zane. Madness gleamed in his dark eyes. "Maybe I won't shoot you, then. I'd planned to burn the journal. Hell, I'll just burn the whole shop. It's a blight on an otherwise modern area anyway. The police will assume the fire was caused by whoever broke in here. God knows, Ms. Tremayne, you've lodged enough complaints lately."

"Thanks to you."

"I'm sorry, but I can't take all the credit. It seems you're racking up enemies left and right."

Why would he still lie? A sickening suspicion curled in Zane's gut, making him cramp. "She saw you outside her building one night, Sandor, wearing a ski mask."

"No."

"Then it was someone you hired."

"Not I."

"Damn you, you shut off the electric and tried to break in."

He shook his head with mock regret. "As I said, I can't take credit for that."

Tamara literally heaved with anger. "You went through my belongings, rearranged my books."

He sniffed. "I haven't been in your shop except for the appointments, and the one time Thanos brought me over. Ah, he had such grand hopes of us getting together, you know." He slid his lecherous gaze over Tamara, lingering on her breasts, her hips. "I must admit, the thought of taking you wasn't completely displeasing. You've a certain . . . raw appeal with your vampish clothes and rough manners. Quite took me by surprise."

It was all Zane could do to keep from lunging at him. He wanted to tear Boris apart for leering at her that way, but he had to ensure that Tamara wouldn't be hurt by his actions.

Then Boris shook his head. "I had hoped to get close enough to you to simply steal the book. Otherwise, I assure you, I'd have no use for a Gypsy fraud with cheap tricks." He sighed with regret. "Now I'm afraid this little conversation is over. Both of you, into the bedroom. It'll be a fitting place for you to die."

Zane planted his feet apart, let his arms hang loosely at his sides. "I don't think so, Sandor."

"You refuse to cooperate?"

Zane shrugged. "Why should I make it easy on you?" Damn it, he needed more time to think.

The gun aimed past him. "Fine." Boris grinned again. "I'll shoot her first, and then you. Everyone will think it a murder/suicide, that you acted out of jealousy, perhaps even jealousy of me. Her relatives are in my favor, so that would seem logical to them."

"Luna will know you came up here."

Zane was proud of how brave Tamara sounded. He could hear the quivering in her voice, but she wasn't going hysterical on him.

"Your fine assistant, my dear, bid me adieu and watched me leave in a fit of annoyance over your delay. She thinks I'm at home by now, brooding over being scorned."

Zane's last hope vanished. There was nothing left for him to do but take Boris by surprise—and hope for the best.

Twenty

Bare-chested and short on temper, Joe sat stewing behind the register. Two female customers, the only ones in the store, continually favored him with funny looks—admiring looks—but it did nothing to lighten his mood. He still couldn't believe what had happened. What he'd allowed her to do. Why, if he ever got within three feet of her again, he'd. . . .

"Joe!"

He looked up when the same crazy broad came barreling in. He quickly stood, a demonic grin spreading over his face as he prepared for battle.

"Back so soon?" he drawled, gaining the attention of the other two women who watched in frozen fascination. "You should know I let you get away with flinging food at me once, but I'll turn you over my knee if you try anything like that again. Don't think I won't."

She kept coming, moving at a fast clip. There was a harried, nearly panicked look in her big golden brown eyes that took him by surprise.

Joe backed up. Not sure what the hell to make of her,

he muttered, "That was one of my favorite shirts, you know."

Luna grabbed him by the chest hair, and he howled. Using her secure hold, she brought his face down to hers over the counter and hissed, "I don't know what the hell is going on, but Boris Sandor just snuck up the outside stairs to Tamara's, and she and Zane are both up there."

"Ah, shit." Joe leaped over the counter in one smooth move. Thank God Luna let go of his chest hair when he did, otherwise his chest would have sported an impressive bald spot. He didn't have his gun on him, but before he even realized it, his knife was in his hand and open, the razor-sharp blade gleaming under the fluorescent lights. "Go call the police."

"Already done. They're on their way, but I was afraid to wait."

"Good girl." He was aware of her clipping along behind him, out the door and across the lot.

"Tamara and Zane went upstairs," she whispered, very close on his heels. "When they didn't come back down, Boris said he'd reschedule his appointment. He'd never done that before, so I peeked out the window when he left and I saw him go around the side of the building. I got there just in time to see him pry the door open and waltz in."

"The alarm didn't go off?"

"She only sets it at night."

"Shit." Joe stopped to push her flat into the brick facing of Tamara's building. "Stay back."

"No."

A string of near-silent curses tripped off his tongue. "Damn it, woman, do as I say."

"Go," she urged him, and gave him a shove to get him moving again.

Not seeing any hope for it, Joe muttered, "You make one single sound and so help me God, I'll throttle you."

He didn't wait to see if she heeded his warning. On light feet, ignoring the stiffness of his busted knee, he dashed up the metal stairs. The door there was closed, but not locked. It let out a tiny squeak when he opened it. Luna was so silent, if it hadn't been for her breath on the back of his right ear, he wouldn't have known she was still there.

Voices carried to him, and he crept forward, his knife at the ready. He peeked around the kitchen door to the hallway, and he saw Boris standing there with a gun. A simple thirty-eight, but hell, they were deadly if you had a decent aim. And at that close range, how could he possibly miss?

Fingers spread, Joe reached behind him and flattened his free hand on Luna. As attentive to the current situation as a man could be, he still realized that his hand was on her belly, and that she felt very nice. *Damned irritant.*

Luna immediately stilled, not out of intimidation, he was certain, because a herd of wild buffalo wouldn't intimidate that one, but out of common sense. She knew he was about to act, and didn't want to get in his way. Joe gave her points for intelligence, if not for discretion or moderation.

"Once I have the journal," Boris said, disgustingly smug, "my aunt Felicia's disgrace will be forever dead, buried with her where it belongs."

Joe drew back, his body perfectly balanced. A balisong knife wasn't really meant for throwing, but the distance was short and he was good, very good. He'd locked the knife open and had not a single doubt that he'd hit the mark.

In that final moment before the blade would have sliced through the air, another voice intruded, screaming, "Bastard!"

Joe paused, senses heightened, and stared, incredulous, as a slim man threw himself at Boris. Both bodies tumbled. The next few seconds were chaos.

Boris cursed, Zane yelled, and the gun went off with a deafening roar.

"Stay here." Joe pushed Luna back just to make sure

she knew he meant business, and a second later he entered the fray. If he hadn't been so worried for Zane and Tamara, for innocent bystanders, *for Luna*, he'd have actually been having fun.

Zane couldn't credit his eyes when Arkin Devane opened the stairwell door and crept forward. *Jesus,* he thought, *were they working together?*

Then Boris made his threat, and the meek and mild Arkin went into a red-hot frenzy. His screech of fury nearly drowned out the blast of the gunshot. Zane bore Tamara down to the carpet and covered her with his body, his arms over her head, protecting her as best he could.

She made a muffled sound that might have been a protest. Zane tightened his hold while Arkin and Boris wrestled for control of the gun, but since Boris was insane and much heavier than Arkin, Zane knew where he'd put his money.

"Stay down," he instructed Tamara, and started to rise so he could ensure Arkin's success.

Tamara rolled to her back and clutched at him, her voice desperate and high. "Zane, no!"

"Shh. It's all right, baby." He pried her fingers loose and bounded to his feet. To his right, he saw Joe lunge forward. The gun went off again, and Zane caught his breath. Arkin slumped back with a painful groan.

Boris lumbered to his feet. "Miserable little . . ." He aimed at Arkin, who writhed on the floor while a sluggish flow of blood pulsed from the top of his right arm.

Grinning evilly, Joe kicked out and the gun went flying. Zane grabbed Boris by the shoulder, flung him around, and did what he'd wanted to do since he'd first met the man. He drove his fist into his face.

Cartilage gave way with a satisfying crunch.

Boris yowled, grabbing at his nose and staggering drunkenly under the impact of the blow. Tamara, disregarding orders as usual, scurried on her knees to the gun and picked it up. She aimed it at Boris.

"You broke his nose," Joe remarked to Zane in a barely winded voice. He sounded impressed.

Ignoring his cousin, Zane motioned to Boris. "C'mon, Sandor. I'm not done."

Boris shook his head. "No, no." Blood poured from between his fingers, made his words choked and garbled, and already his eyes were turning black.

Flabbergasted, Joe said, "You're quitting because of a bloody nose?" Then with utter disdain, "You big baby, that's pathetic."

Slowly, Zane shook his head. "Oh, no, he's not quitting." He grabbed Boris, hauled him forward. "You held a gun on her," he said, and punctuated his words with a hard punch to Boris's midsection. Boris doubled over, spewing more blood.

"*Eeuw.*" Luna made a face as she sauntered into the room. "That's disgusting. What a mess."

Joe, after giving Luna a sidelong glance, laughed and bent down to Arkin. "You okay, buddy?"

"I'm shot!" Arkin clutched at his upper arm and rolled back and forth, his knees pulled up in the fetal position.

"Yeah, well, I can see that." Joe held him still with one hand, and lifted away the bloody edge of his sweater to peer at the wound. "Doesn't look too bad to me. Luckily he hit your arm and not your chest."

"*Luckily?*" Arkin quit wailing long enough to fry Joe with a look. "It hurts like hell!"

Unconcerned, Joe shrugged. "Gunshot wounds are a bitch."

Luna edged closer, looking over Joe's naked shoulder at the fallen man. "You've been shot before?"

Joe glared at her. "None of your damn business."

She lightly touched a mark on his shoulder. "Here?"

Shuddering, Joe rasped, "Yeah," and then he shook his head, cursed, and scooted out of her reach.

Zane wrapped a fist in the front of Boris's shirt and

hauled him close yet again. His anger was a live thing, needing release. He'd get that release with Boris.

But, proving what a coward he was, Boris held both hands up to cover his face and began pleading. He wasn't much sport, Zane thought in disgust, and flung him away. Boris dropped to his knees, moaning.

"Zane?" Tamara trembled, causing the bells on her ankles to chime musically, and the gun in her hand to jerk. But she managed to keep it pointed at Boris.

Gently, Zane covered her hand with his own. "Let me have the gun, honey."

"Oh no." She shook her head hard, making her blonde hair fly. "You're going to shoot him."

Joe cocked a brow at that, interest lighting his eyes. He looked almost . . . hopeful.

"No I'm not." Zane kept his tone as even and calm as possible, especially since he knew Tamara was likely experiencing her own feelings, and his as well. It was a lot for one small woman to deal with.

She turned to look him straight in the eye. "Yes, you are. You can't lie to me."

Zane smiled. "I'd like to," he specified. "But that's not the same as I would." And he added, "You can trust me, honey."

Her big green eyes stared up at him, and she blinked. "Oh, Zane. I know that." The gun went limp in her hand, and Zane took it. He held Tamara close with one arm and handed the gun to Joe. "Here, you can shoot him."

Tamara stiffened, but Joe only laughed. "Very funny." He palmed the gun and squatted down by Boris. "You hear that, old man? I get to shoot you."

"No!"

Tamara curled into Zane. "He won't really . . . ?"

"Nah." But Zane added as an afterthought, "At least, I don't think he will."

Joe agreed. "I won't. Shooting him would only add more mess to Tamara's place, and he's caused her enough trouble."

Tamara relaxed, leaning into Zane and turning her face to his shoulder.

"That is," Joe went on, "I won't shoot him as long as he just lies there and stays quiet. Give me a reason, any reason, and I'd be glad to give him a little taste of what he gave your buddy there."

"Arkin Devane is not my buddy." Zane reached for Luna, dragged her next to Tamara, and told them both, "It's okay now. I can hear the sirens. The cops will be here in just a few minutes."

Luna patted Tamara. "Being females, and thus weak, we're supposed to comfort each other, right?" She smiled. "Well, don't worry. We're fine."

"Tamara?" Zane wanted to hear her speak to him before he put even three inches between them.

"Yes." She smiled. "I'm okay. Just a little . . . shook-up."

"Adrenaline," Joe remarked. "Comes in real handy when you need it, but it's tough to shake off afterward."

Zane squatted down next to Arkin. "What the hell are you doing here, Arkin?"

Arkin moaned, putting his head back and letting it loll on the carpet. "Tamara didn't show up, so I came to see why. I saw Luna follow Boris, and I followed her." He swallowed hard. "I figured something was up when she ran up the stairs with that other fellow, and he had a knife."

"How are you involved in this, Arkin?"

He moaned again. "Please."

"Jesus," Joe said with loathing. "They don't make 'em very tough in Thomasville, do they? All this pleading and whining is about to make me puke."

"He saved us," Tamara protested, ready to defend her number-one client.

"No." Zane narrowed his eyes. "I have the feeling Arkin was saving the journal."

"It's true." Arkin opened his eyes long enough to look at Tamara. "I'm so sorry. So very, very sorry."

Pulling away from Luna, Tamara went to him. She knelt down next to Zane and slipped her hand in his. He clasped her fingers warmly.

"Sorry for what, exactly?" she asked.

"I. . . ." He choked, swallowed hard, then continued. "I'm the one you saw that night in the ski mask." In a rush, he added, "I wasn't chasing you, I swear. I was just looking for the journal. But then you came back early and. . . ." He managed a shrug and a self-conscious smile. "We both had quite a shock."

"And the other night?" Zane asked. "You're the one who cut the electricity?"

"Yes." He turned his head away, hiding his shame and shutting out Zane's contempt. "I heard her tell Boris she was going out. I didn't think anyone would be at home. I'd already checked everywhere downstairs and couldn't find the journal."

"So," Tamara said, "you realized I'd taken it upstairs and you were going to steal it from me?"

"Yes. You told me you had it upstairs, when we talked about. . . ."

"The lady you're in love with," Tamara said as the truth dawned.

"How the hell did you get in?" Zane wasn't over the edge enough to batter a man already shot, a man with tears in his eyes, a man curled up like a damn baby. But— he wanted to.

"The Realtor selling her place. I stole the key from him, had a copy made, and then returned it."

"You wanna tell me how you managed that?" Zane tried to keep his tone even for Tamara's sake. She looked more shocked than ever.

"I know him. The Realtor, I mean. We went to college together."

Somewhere behind Zane, Joe laughed. "Tidy."

"Do you mind?" Zane wondered how the hell Joe could be enjoying himself now, but it was plain to see he was having a ball. He always had been a man who thrived on trouble.

"My rearranged books." Tamara whispered the words more as a statement than a question.

"That was me." Arkin added in a heartfelt rush, "The journal should have been *mine*. Felicia was such a dear friend, such a lovely woman. I taught her piano, you know."

Zane and Joe shared a look, but Tamara had all her attention on Arkin. "You were friends?"

"Yes. She told me about her journal, and promised to share it with me. Like you, she understood me."

Zane turned. "You said there was a note in her safety-deposit box, Sandor. Is that who she left it to? Arkin Devane?"

"I don't remember, damn it."

Joe said, "My trigger finger is twitching. Look at that! Damn, I can barely keep from—"

Discolored eyes opening wide, Boris said, "Yes! Yes, it was Arkin Devane."

Arkin's pain-filled expression softened, his body relaxing for the first time since he'd been shot. "She knew I was falling in love," he whispered to no one in particular, "but that I needed some . . . help. She promised to give me the journal. Then she died and Boris"—Arkin managed to raise his head enough to glare at the other man —"had all her things sold, everything, even her most prized possessions. Suddenly everything she valued had been handed off to strangers."

"The estate sale," Tamara said.

"Yes. I tried to buy the journal, but it had been packed away with the rest of her library, and you bought it all."

"Like Sandor, you got that information from the estate sale company?"

"Yes."

"And that's why you sought me out, why you started coming to me."

He nodded, looking more miserable by the second.

"Why didn't you just ask me for it outright, Arkin?" And then, with some hurt, "I thought we had become friends."

"We *are* friends!" He gulped, and more tears gathered in his eyes. "You're one of the kindest women I know. But Felicia had kept the book private. If I started asking about it, if I mentioned it to *anyone*, others might have discovered it. The scandal she'd so hoped to avoid might still have come about. She didn't deserve that. She'd already been so badly mistreated by her family."

"Boris and his relatives?" Zane asked.

"Yes. They never understood her. She'd shamed them merely by being her own woman, and they'd disowned her. I almost had a heart attack when you had that flood"— Boris got another glare, this one even darker—"and you threw away all those boxes of things. I was so afraid it was gone forever, and then you mentioned it to me and you were sharing it with me. I knew it was upstairs, and I tried one last time to get it. But then we talked more, and I . . . well, I realized that I didn't need to steal it, not from you. I didn't use the key again after that."

He squeezed his eyes shut. "You understood. You read Felicia's journal with the same emotion and acceptance as I'd have given it."

Zane dropped back on his behind with a curse. "I don't believe it. All this over a journal."

Boris groaned. "She was a blight on the family. I had to recover and destroy that damn book before my in-laws found out, before good men got ruined, before—"

Joe nudged him with the toe of his boot. "I hear the police coming up the stairs. Looks like you won't have to worry about any of that after all."

But it wasn't the police who came barreling through the door. Cole and Mack stumbled into the room, their gazes searching, frantic. When they spotted Zane, Tamara at his side, both of them healthy and whole, they slumped against each other, wheezing and gasping for air.

Zane caught Tamara's arm and helped her to stand. "What are you two doing here?"

Cole, his hands on his knees while he bent forward, trying to catch his breath, nodded toward Luna. "She called us. She saw Boris sneaking in and told us she had a bad feeling."

Mack did his own huffing and gulping, and now flopped limply against the wall. "Her bad feeling gave *me* a bad feeling," he said, "and we got here as fast as we could. Of course, we ran into the damn police, sirens blaring, on the way."

"Which only worried us more."

Smiling, Tamara went to each brother and hugged him. "Thank you."

"Chase came, too," Cole told them, finally able to straighten on his shaky legs enough to put his arm around Tamara. Mack crowded in on her other side. "But there was a group of customers milling around your parking lot looking confused, so he went to check things out there."

"Oh hell." Joe jerked upright. "I left your place empty when Luna told me what was going on."

Zane hesitated only a moment, and then he reached for Joe. Taking him completely by surprise, he pulled his cousin into a tight bear hug. "I'm glad you did, Joe. Thanks."

At that moment the police charged into the room, weapons at the ready. Joe turned to them and said, "Here, you better take this gun." He grinned stupidly, wavered, then clutched his bare chest. "I think I'm going to have a heart attack."

The bar was crowded when Tamara wended her way through the door. She heard a laugh and lifted her head, seeing Zane on a bar stool, sipping from a steaming mug. Cole, holding his baby niece, Sammy, against his shoulder, chatted with Zane while Chase alternately served drinks to the customers and joined in. It took her only a moment to locate Mack, situated at a nearby table with Trista, his teenage daughter. Joe was seated there, too, cuddling baby Nate, with the wives positioned around him. Her heart gave a funny little catch at seeing them all together.

Poignant regret. Pain, smothering and stark. And a silly flare of hope.

She stopped, attempting to gather her thoughts, to shore up her weak female emotions so she wouldn't embarrass herself. In that instant, Zane looked up and his smile lit up the room.

He smiled at something Cole said and started her way. Tamara watched the women watching him. Two called out to him, making him pause. Another grabbed his arm; he leaned down to listen, then laughed.

Within thirty seconds, he stood before her. His welcome, his warmth and his scent wrapped around her in comforting familiarity.

It had been two weeks since the awful debacle at her home. In that time the bloodstained carpet in the living room had been replaced, the bullet hole in the ceiling from the first gunshot had been repaired. And Zane had all but moved in with her.

Just that morning he'd sat on the edge of the tub and watched her put on her makeup. He'd made them coffee and she'd fixed toast. He'd kissed her good-bye at her front door, then sauntered across the lot to his store. It had all seemed so domestic, so . . . lasting.

Tamara reached up and touched his face. "Hi."

He tilted his head. "You're a little late," he said softly. "My brothers have been razzing me about getting stood up."

Tamara dropped her gaze to his throat. "No woman in her right mind would ever stand you up, and you know it."

With one finger beneath her chin, he lifted her face again. "What's wrong, sweetheart?"

She drew a deep breath, prepared to tell him. And suddenly Joe was there, hooking an arm through hers and dragging her to the bar where the others waited. He balanced year-old Nate in his other arm. The baby had dark hair, vivid blue eyes, and looked like he could have been Joe's son instead of Cole's. Nate chuckled happily as Joe made him bounce.

Trista, Mack's daughter, leaned into his side while Chase refilled all their mugs of hot chocolate. The women had left the table and were now in various positions with their husbands. Zane trailed indulgently behind her as Joe stole her away.

Pretending to be gallant, Joe brushed away imaginary dust on a stool right in the middle of the family clan, then, despite Nate's sturdy little body, he bowed. "Take a seat."

Zane slid into place beside her, not saying a word but giving Joe a look that plainly told him to seat himself elsewhere.

Joe just grinned. "Pretend all you want, Zane. But I'm on to you now. You're crazy nuts about me. Hell, I may even be your favorite cousin."

Zane rolled his eyes. It amused Tamara how Joe now needled him endlessly, ever since that ill-advised hug, and Zane complained every single time.

"I'm sorry I'm late," Tamara told them all, still a little bemused by the attention they bestowed on her.

Sophie crowded closer. "So what did you decide to do with the journal? Zane said you'd made a decision, but wouldn't even give us a clue."

Tamara glanced at him behind her, then cleared her throat. "That's probably because he disagrees with me. But I gave it to Arkin. It was rightfully his all along, and he never did any damage to my place."

Zane, clearly disgusted by her choice, said, "She even forgives him. Can you believe that? It was bad enough that she didn't want to press charges, but—"

"He did save your asses," Mack pointed out.

Jessica objected. "I think Joe had as much to do with that as Arkin."

"Yeah," Cole said, "all Arkin did was get shot."

"And that saved Zane from getting shot," Tamara pointed out, "because he was just about ready to jump Boris himself." Tamara nodded when they all stared at her. "It's true."

Joe shifted the baby against his chest. His dark blue eyes warmed on her face. "How do you know what Zane was going to do?"

She faltered. No way would she tell them she was empathic. She merely shook her head.

Allison sniffed. "Everyone knows a woman in love is attuned to her man."

Chase reached over the bar and stroked her cheek with one finger. "And husbands are attuned to their wives, too."

Allison grinned shamelessly while Mack and Cole said, "Hear, hear."

Joe shook his head. "Any man worth his salt knows what a woman wants and how she thinks. Especially at select times—like in bed."

Zane groaned. "For a man bent on staying a bachelor, you sure seem to enjoy holding the babies."

"*Other* people's babies," Joe said, putting emphasis on the first word. "They're great to hold and cuddle—and then hand back to their papas." To demonstrate, he started to hand Nate over to Cole. But Nate had other ideas, and knotted his chubby fists in Joe's hair, just over his temples. Joe yelped, then gave up with a laugh.

"You should get a haircut," Zane suggested, but Joe pretended not to hear him while he went about growling into Nate's neck.

Propping his arms on the bar, Chase brought the conversation back around. "Olga and Eva are pretty downcast that it was Boris, not a ghost."

A genuine smile found its way past Tamara's sadness. "I know. Aunt Olga feels guilty that she blamed poor Uncle Hubert for Boris's misdeeds. Now she's certain he'll come haunt her for discrediting him."

They all laughed, but Chase said, "Hmm. I wonder."

Zane bent to her ear. "So where were you? I was starting to get worried."

Knowing she couldn't put it off any longer, Tamara turned to face Zane. It was cowardly of her, but she preferred to share her news right here, among his family, where she knew she couldn't break down and cry and embarrass them both.

Forcing a smile that hurt, she said, "My Realtor called."

Zane hesitated in the act of picking up his hot chocolate. After just a second, he took a healthy swallow and set the mug back down. "Is that right? What did he have to say?"

Hoping she looked happy rather than despondent, Tamara said, "I was offered my full asking price."

Though noise continued in the bar, everyone around Tamara had gone silent. The brothers exchanged worried glances and Joe ducked his head, whistling low. The wives were all staring at Zane, waiting to see what he'd do.

He narrowed his eyes on Tamara. "I assume you turned it down."

"I . . . no." Holding a smile was nearly impossible. Her eyes burned. "I told him I'd have to get back to him."

"There's no reason for you to sell, you know."

Nervously pushing her hair behind her ears, she stammered, "My finances are. . . ."

Zane cupped her cheek and repeated, "There's no reason for you to sell. Not now."

His meaning dawned on her. "We've been over that, Zane. I won't take a loan from you."

"You won't have to. Now that I've moved in, I can pay my share. That'll cut your expenses in half, right?"

Tamara glanced around her. Not a single one of his family made any pretense about listening in. They were engrossed.

Her throat felt tight, and she cleared it. "You intend to . . . keep living with me?"

"Damn right."

"But. . . ." She wasn't sure what to say. Everything was up in the air, nothing was settled.

"You could be pregnant."

His statement caused a stir of whispers and inhalations among his family. Tamara scowled at him. "I'm not."

Zane shifted. He looked down at the floor, at the ceiling. He propped his hands on his hips and made a sound of disgust.

Joe bit back a laugh, which seemed to galvanize Zane. He pierced Tamara with a look and said, "You *could* love me."

She caught her breath. It hit her—everything he was feeling, everything he thought, the depth of his emotion. She couldn't seem to drag in enough air for her starved lungs. Tears stung her eyes, overflowed, and she smiled. "I do."

This time Joe went ahead and laughed, a big whooping laugh. Chase snatched Nate out of his arms and Mack shoved him right off his bar stool.

Zane never even bothered to glance his way. "I love you, too," he said to Tamara.

And she whispered back, "I know. Now."

As Zane pulled Tamara close for a heated kiss, Mack looked on and rubbed his hands. "Well, then, there you go. It's all settled."

Epilogue

"She's beautiful."

"Yes. She'd have looked even prettier if she'd worn the red dress."

"Perhaps. And a tad more makeup."

Thanos hushed Olga and Eva. "She couldn't wear red to a wedding, even if it was the dress you both wore."

"Antique lace and hand stitching. It'd have to be taken in some for her."

"Especially in the bust," Olga agreed, "because we are more endowed than our little Gypsy, but still—"

"But it wouldn't have been appropriate," Thanos insisted, "not for Tamara."

Eva sniffed. "A Tremayne can do as she pleases."

He agreed, and said with a grin, "She did that."

Tamara heard her relatives whispering, but she didn't mind. They'd taken her marriage to Zane rather well. According to Eva, Zane was just outrageous enough to please their free spirits.

Thanos had given her away, looking extremely dapper in his tux, his beard trimmed and his smile bright and proud. The aunts stood together as mothers of the bride, alternately crying and whispering since the music started.

Tamara felt wrapped in a cocoon of love, the emotions emanating from her relatives, her soon-to-be in-laws, and the incredibly handsome groom.

To her side, Luna stood as maid of honor, with Sophie, Allison, and Jessica lined up as bridesmaids. Next to Zane, Cole was best man, with Mack and Chase and Joe in line behind him. The minister kept things blessedly short, which was good since her heart was so full, she had a hard time concentrating.

Zane touched her chin. "I do."

She stared at him, sighed, and said, "I know you do."

Cole choked, which prompted a round of masculine coughs. Tamara's aunts twittered in delight, and Thanos let out a booming chuckle.

Zane grinned at her. "Almost your turn, sweetheart."

"Oh!" She knew her face was red, but fortunately the veil hid it.

When asked if she took Zane as her husband, she managed to say quite properly, "I do."

Stifling his own smile, the minister said, "I now pronounce you man and wife. Zane, you may kiss your lovely bride."

Zane carefully lifted her veil.

Tamara looked at him, at his beautiful smile and the naked love in his eyes. She trembled, shook, struggled for breath, and in the next instant she hurled herself into his arms. "I love you so much!"

Laughing, Zane caught her to him and twirled her around.

Olga whispered loudly, "Oh, that girl does me proud," and Eva agreed.

Being a good friend as well as an assistant, Luna cheered, and everyone else followed suit.

An hour later, they were cutting the cake when suddenly the lights went out. Tamara froze, Zane cursed. A low rumble of confusion drifted through their guests. Then Aunt Eva wailed, "It's Uncle Hubert!"

The lights came back on as quickly as they'd gone out. "Sorry," came a low masculine voice from the other side of the room, "I, ah, leaned on the main switch." Joe, a look of apology on his face, stood next to Luna, her hair disheveled, the bodice of her gown askew. They were in front of a narrow corridor, and they both looked guilty.

Chase rubbed his hands together. "And the curse continues," he said with relish. All the Winstons—all but Joe—gave a mighty cheer.

Tamara laughed. And to think she'd wanted a *normal* life. How silly.

USA Today bestselling author
Lori Foster

The Winston Brothers

The sinfully sexy stories of the Winston
brothers collected in one volume.

**"LORI FOSTER WRITES ABOUT REAL
PEOPLE YOU'LL FALL IN LOVE WITH."
—STELLA CAMERON**

0-515-13173-3

**Available wherever books are sold or
to order call 1-800-788-6262**

NICOLE BYRD

Widow in Scarlet
0-425-19209-1

When Lucy Contrain discovers that
aristocrat Nicholas Ramsey believes her
dead husband stole a legendary jewel, she
insists on joining his search.
Little does she know they will be drawn
into deadly danger—and into a passion
that neither can resist.

Also Available:
Beauty in Black
0-425-19683-6

Praise for the romances of Nicole Byrd:

**"Madcap fun with a touch of romantic
intrigue...satisfying to the last word."**
—Cathy Maxwell

**"Irresistible...deliciously witty,
delightfully clever." —*Booklist***

Available wherever books are sold or
to order call 1-800-788-6262.